Praise for *If This G...*

"*If This Gets Out* is an absolute sl...
and adorable, this bright, joyfu...
for in a queer YA romance—...~~...~~ Cale
Dietrich tell this story in perfect harmony."

—Phil Stamper, bestselling author of
The Gravity of Us and *As Far as You'll Take Me*

"*If This Gets Out* is the perfect book. . . . It deftly explores
the dark side of fame [and] the giddy thrill of first—and
forbidden—love."

—Mackenzi Lee, *New York Times* bestselling author

"[A] sweet and swoon-worthy romance. Zach and Ruben are
a pitch-perfect duet!"

—Caleb Roehrig, author of *Last Seen Leaving*

"Dazzle[s] . . . with a narrative of queer boy-bandmates who
wrestle with newfound fame, and newfound feelings for
each other. Readers will fall in love."

—Adam Sass, author of *Surrender Your Sons*

"*If This Gets Out* blends the ache and the beauty of coming
out under the lights of celebrity with the ways in which queer
love is told to stay hidden, even when it's the only thing
keeping the music going."

—L.C. Rosen, author of *Camp* and *Jack of
Hearts (and Other Parts)*

"*If This Gets Out* will suck you in from page 1 . . . [and] stick
with you beyond the finale." —Associated Press

"Fun, heartwarming, and a vital purchase for all collections
serving teens." —*School Library Journal* (starred review)

"This unexpectedly poignant love story . . . subverts expectations in refreshing ways. . . . A lively novel with as much appeal as the band itself." —*Kirkus Reviews*

"Dietrich and Gonzales keep the tension high and Ruben and Zach's voices distinct in this friends-to-lovers romance that shines with passion and verve." —*Booklist*

"Riveting . . . *If This Gets Out* is the perfect read for anyone who loves music, friends-to-lovers romances, or ever secretly shipped members of a band!" —*Nerd Daily*

IF
THIS
GETS
OUT

IF THIS GETS OUT

SOPHIE GONZALES & CALE DIETRICH

WEDNESDAY BOOKS
NEW YORK

Published in the United States by Wednesday Books, an imprint of St. Martin's Publishing Group

IF THIS GETS OUT. Copyright © 2021 by Sophie Gonzales and Cale Dietrich. All rights reserved. Printed in the United States of America. For information, address St. Martin's Publishing Group, 120 Broadway, New York, NY 10271.

www.wednesdaybooks.com

The Library of Congress has cataloged the hardcover edition as follows:

Names: Gonzales, S., 1992–author. | Dietrich, Cale, author.
Title: If this gets out / Sophie Gonzales & Cale Dietrich.
Description: First edition. | New York : Wednesday Books, 2021.
Identifiers: LCCN 2021026661 | ISBN 9781250805805 (hardcover) |
    ISBN 9781250805812 (ebook)
Subjects: CYAC: Boy bands—Fiction. | Fame—Fiction. |
    Friendship—Fiction. | Gays—Fiction.
Classification: LCC PZ7.1.G6532 If 2021 | DDC [Fic]—dc23
LC record available at https://lccn.loc.gov/2021026661

ISBN 978-1-250-86181-8

Our books may be purchased in bulk for promotional, educational, or business use. Please contact your local bookseller or the Macmillan Corporate and Premium Sales Department at 1-800-221-7945, extension 5442, or by email at MacmillanSpecialMarkets@macmillan.com.

First Wednesday Books Trade Paperback Edition: 2022

10 9 8 7 6 5 4 3 2 1

TO CAMERON STEINERT AND SHAYE DIETRICH

IF
THIS
GETS
OUT

ONE

RUBEN

Almost plummeting to my death before a stadium full of screaming people is a warning sign, in an endless parade of warning signs lately, that I need more sleep.

We're performing the last concert for the American leg of our Months by Years tour when it happens. I'm about fifteen feet above the stage, on a raised platform illuminated to look like a city skyline. It's time to gracefully lower ourselves to sit on the edge to croon the start of our last song, "His, Yours, Ours," but instead of gracefully lowering myself, I overshoot my step, overcorrect, then start lurching over the edge.

Before I can lean too far into thin air, a hand clasps my shoulder and steadies me. Zach Knight, one of the other three members of Saturday. His hazel eyes widen the tiniest bit, but otherwise he acts unruffled. *Nothing to see here.*

I don't have the luxury of pausing to acknowledge or thank him, because stage smoke—intended to represent either clouds or city pollution, I never did figure it out—is engulfing us, and the opening chords of the song have started. Zach keeps his hand on my shoulder while he sings, as though it was all part of the choreography, and I lean into my off-balance pose, totally collected. At least, outwardly.

After twenty-seven and a half consecutive shows this year alone, this isn't exactly the first time one of us has had to smoothly cover up a trip or choreo mistake. It *is* the first time one of those mistakes almost caused me to plunge fifteen feet onto solid ground, though, and my heart's probably never pounded *quite* this hard, but we're a show.

To be clear: we aren't *giving* a show: we *are* the show. And the show doesn't take two minutes to compose itself after almost breaking its neck.

The show is suave, and in control, and it meant to do that.

When Zach's lines are over, he gives my shoulder a quick squeeze—the only acknowledgment the whole ordeal is likely to get for now—then drops his hand while Jon Braxton chimes in for his verse. Jon always has the most solo parts. I guess that's what you get when your dad also happens to be the manager of your band. We don't really have a leader, but if we did, it would be Jon. When we have eyes on us, anyway.

By the time Jon's finished and it's my turn to sing the song's bridge, my breathing's more or less steady again. Not that it matters—every song, without fail, I get given the simplest solos without a high note in sight. Frankly, I could pull them off with a sock stuffed in my mouth. They don't care that I have the highest range out of all four of us. For reasons they'll never care to explain to me, they prefer me bland. "They" being our management team and, to a lesser extent, our record label—Chorus Management and Galactic Records.

And god forbid I push against those cramped boundaries with a vocal run or tempo change. We're meant to sound just like we do on the master recording. Planned, packaged, and neatly presented.

Still, inhibited vocals or not, the crowd seems to explode with energy when I sing—the blinding camera flashes that dot the vast blanket of the crowd become frenzied, the technicolor glowsticks are waved with more abandon, and the hundreds of MARRY ME, RUBEN MONTEZ posters are raised up higher. It's only my perception, I'm sure, but when I'm singing solo, everything locks into place. It's just me and the crowd, vibrating at exactly the same frequency.

Right now, I could stand here forever, singing the same, safe line on repeat, hearing the same screams, seeing the same signs, and forever would feel like a moment.

Then Angel Phan takes the song's pre-chorus line in his husky, breathy tone, the backing music drops to a whisper, and the stage is plunged into darkness. Like we've done dozens of times before, we get up in unison and stand on our assigned glow-in-the-dark X's as the skyline platform is lowered back down to the stage. As soon as I step off and my feet are back on level ground, I relax.

It's short-lived. Suddenly, laser lights rip through the darkness as the chorus instrumental, with its upbeat tempo change, booms. They illuminate us and the audience in crisscrossing lines of fluorescent green and blue, and we launch into the chorus half-dazzled. In a cruel joke to us, this final song has the most demanding hip-hop-inspired choreo of the night, which we're expected to nail while also holding a four-part harmony. I was in shape to begin with, pre-tour, and it still took me two weeks of singing on the treadmill last year to get my lung capacity up enough to pull this one off.

We make it look easy, though. We know each other to our bones. Even though I'm not looking at them, I know what they're all doing.

Zach's got his serious-face on—even after all these years he gets nervous during the more intense choreo—and shifts straight into concentration mode.

Jon's closing his eyes for half the chorus—his dad's always

lecturing him for that, but Jon can't help getting lost in the emotion of everything.

As for Angel, I'd bet anything I own he's eye-fucking the audience, adding in little pelvic-pop movements and half-kicks at the end of his steps, even though he's not allowed to. Our choreographer, Valeria, is constantly calling him out in our post-show notes meetings for that. "You're standing out too much," she says. But we all know the real problem is that our management team has spent two years branding him as the virginal, innocent guy girls would want to take home to their parents, when really he's anything but.

After the chorus, we move into our next positions, and I catch a glimpse of Zach. His chestnut-brown hair is plastered to his forehead with sweat. They have me and Zach both in jackets, a bomber for me and leather for him. Let me tell you, with the lights bearing down on us and the smoke clogging the air and the body heat from the audience packed into the enclosed stadium, it's over a hundred degrees up here at the best of times. It's a miracle our onstage mishaps haven't included heatstroke yet.

Zach catches my gaze and shoots me a brief smile before turning back to the audience. I realize I'm staring, and I quickly tear my eyes away. In my defense, our hair and makeup artist, Penny, a curvy woman in her mid-twenties, has him growing his hair out for this tour, and it's the kind of length that's *made* to scream sex when it's slick with sweat. I'm only noticing what most of the audience has already noticed. In fact, the only one who *doesn't* seem to notice how good Zach looks is Zach.

I let my mind go blank and allow the music to sweep me into autopilot, spinning and stepping and jumping in a dance my body knows by heart. The song finishes, the lights sign off in a blaze of orange and yellow, and we freeze, panting, as the crowd leaps to their feet. Zach takes the chance to push his damp hair off his forehead, tipping his head back as he does so to expose his throat.

Shit. I'm staring again.

I force myself to focus on Jon making his way center stage, where he directs the crowd to thank the musicians, and the security team, and the sound and lighting team. Then it's *Thank you so much, Orlando, we've been Saturday, good night!* and we're waving, and the cheering is so loud it drowns itself out into near silence, and we're jogging backstage.

And that's it. The American leg of the Months by Years tour is done, just like that.

Erin, a tall woman in her forties with a rounded figure and long auburn hair, meets us as we step off the stage onto the gray concrete of the backstage area. "Congratulations, guys!" she says in her booming voice, holding a hand up to high-five us all in turn. "I am so proud of you! It's a *wrap!*"

As our tour manager, Erin's kind of the stand-in for our absent parents when we're on the road. She's responsible for our schedule, our rules, disciplining us, congratulating us, remembering our birthdays and allergies, and making sure we're where we're supposed to be all day, every day.

I like Erin enough as a person, but, as with all Chorus Management employees, I never let my guard down around her completely. Chorus Management might be the team that markets, promotes, and organizes us, but they're also the team that molded us into the shape we take today. The team that strictly enforces who we speak to, and what we say, and what freedoms we have.

As far as freedom goes, there isn't a whole lot of it. So, I try not to give them reasons to limit it further.

We all do.

Zach falls into step beside me as we pass various stage

crew. His hair's fought its way free again, hanging in unruly waves over his still-damp forehead. "Are you okay?" he asks beneath his breath.

My cheeks warm. I'd forgotten about slipping. "Yeah, fine, I don't think anyone noticed," I whisper.

"Who cares if people noticed, I just wanna know you're okay."

"*Yes*, forget about it."

"Why wouldn't he be okay?" Angel asks, forcing his way between us and throwing his arms around each of our shoulders. Given Angel's half a head shorter than me, while Zach clears six feet, this isn't an easy task for him. "We're done. We're going *home tomorrow!*"

"For four days," Jon says wryly as he falls into step with us.

"Uh-huh, thank you, Captain Obvious, I can count," Angel says, side-eyeing Jon. "A, I'll take the four days of downtime if I can get them, and B, within those four days will be the biggest event of your lives."

"Oh, is your birthday party bigger than the Grammys, now?" I ask.

"And the Billboard Music Awards?" Zach adds, throwing me a smirk.

"Both," Angel says. "There's gonna be peacocks."

Jon snorts, and wipes the grin off his face when Angel shoots daggers at him. "I can still withdraw your invitation," Angel says.

"No, please, I can't miss the *peacocks*." Jon flips around so he's walking backward, clasping his hands together toward Angel.

"Thin. Ice. Braxton."

We reach the dressing rooms, where our team is waiting to undress us. Surrounding us are four portable clothes racks, and as we're systematically stripped, the clothes get tagged and placed in the right order on the hangers to be dry-cleaned. It's on them to keep meticulous track of the dozens and dozens of outfits, which of the four of us wears what outfit, and when. They make their jobs look as easy and seamless as we do ours, but I don't envy them the headache.

As someone who grew up performing in musical theater, I'm used to stripping off costumes after a show. The difference here is that while we're on tour, it's out of one costume and into another: we don't get to dress ourselves anytime a camera can see us. Chorus Management chose our roles years ago. When our stylists aren't juggling the conveyer belt of ensembles for the shows, they're compiling and purchasing casual outfits for us to keep us on-brand whenever we're on duty. And we're always on duty.

Essentially, our clothes—our costumes—tell the story of our personalities. Just not our real ones.

Zach's something of a bad boy: leather and boots and ripped jeans and as much black as they can cover him in. Angel's the fun, innocent goof, which means lots of color and prints, and nothing too tight-fitting or remotely sexy—much to his chagrin. Jon's the charismatic womanizer, so the golden rule of dressing him is *show off those muscles on pain of death*.

As for me, I'm the inoffensive one with the pretty face, approachable, safe, and unremarkable. Most of my wardrobe is filled with crew-neck sweaters and cashmere in warm neutrals designed to make me seem soft and huggable. And, of course, there's no point looking safe and unremarkable if you don't act it, so my guidelines are clear. No mention of my sexuality in interviews, no showing off onstage, no strong opinions, and *definitely* no public boyfriends. I'm the blank canvas that fans can paint their dream personality onto. The wild card option for those whose tastes weren't satisfied by the other three.

The opposite of everything I was raised to be.

As curated as we are, though, the interesting thing is our most devoted fans often see straight through it. The ones who watch and consume everything involving the four of us. I've seen them describe our personalities online in a way that's much closer to the truth—referring to a sensitive, sweet Zach, or a type-A, cautious Jon. A wild, hilarious Angel, or a perfectionist, darkly sarcastic me. I've seen them get into arguments with other fans online, as both sides insist they know the *real* us. None of them know the real us, of course, because they don't *know* us at all, no matter how much they wish they did. But some see us more clearly. They see us, and they stay. They *see* us, and yet they seem to like us more than anyone does.

Go figure.

Erin's scrolling through her iPad as we're undressed, a steady anchor in the middle of organized chaos. "Once everyone's ready, I want to meet with you all about next week," she says. We groan in unison, and Zach initiates a competition with me over who can groan the loudest. The winner is unclear, because Erin shushes us before either of us reaches our max volume. "I *know*, I know," she says. "You're all tired—"

"We're zombies," Angel corrects, before taking the lid off a water bottle with his teeth.

"Yeah, Ruben almost *fainted*," Zach pipes up, and I kick his shin as Erin looks at me sharply.

"I didn't faint, I just . . . got clumsy."

"It'll only be a few minutes," Erin says. "Ten, tops."

Jon hands his button-down gray shirt to our stylist, Viktor, revealing a broad, hairless chest that, like the other two's, is almost as familiar to me as my own by now. While Jon's standing topless, Angel shakes his water bottle to spray icy cold water on him. Jon gasps and yelps, jumping on the spot while Zach cackles. "Angel! You *suck, why*?"

"Bored."

"Are you *kidding me*?"

Zach, still laughing, tosses Jon a hand towel, which he rubs over his brown skin to mop up some of the water, muttering to himself. Even though Jon's undeniably handsome, and is standing only feet away from me, half-naked and dripping, I'm not especially distracted by it. Stripping around each other is a daily routine for the four of us, so it takes more than a good-looking guy with a six-pack and no shirt on to catch me off guard these days.

Of course, when Zach moves to take off his T-shirt, I make sure I'm looking anywhere *but* at him, just like I've done every concert for the last few months now. Because whatever indefinable "more" it takes to spark my attention, Zach's got it in spades, and as hard as I try to kill this feeling, I can't quite shut it off. In other words, until I manage to squash whatever practical joke my brain's playing on me lately, I have to treat a shirtless Zach like Medusa. No looking, on pain of death.

Angel has his back to me, so I snatch up the nearest water bottle and splash it over his head, soaking his black hair and sagging it into limp tendrils. He gasps and whips around. "Betrayal," he declares. I run to crouch behind Zach, who's got his shirt on now, and is therefore safe to acknowledge again.

"Guys, guys," Penny says, darting in front of the table housing her vast makeup kit like a desperate mother throwing her body in front of her only child. "No water fights around the makeup. Enough. Ruben, you need a makeup wipe, come on."

Angel lowers his water bottle and holds up his hands in submission, then uses one to push his dripping hair out of his face. I emerge from behind Zach, and, with a flick of his wrist, Angel splashes water my way. It doesn't quite make it.

I dodge past him to take a handful of wipes and start on my eyes first. Over the last couple years, our eye makeup has gotten less and less subtle, to the point where neutral-but-obvious eye makeup has become part of our brand. These days, Penny goes through about one brown eyeliner per week. She has a way of smoking out the liner with soft shadows and a light touch to make our eyes pop. I tried to replicate it once and I ended up looking like I was auditioning for a Pirates of the Caribbean movie. Since then, I've left the liner to her.

Finally, fresh-faced and clean-clothed, we traipse into the green room after Erin. I throw myself onto the couch, lay my head on the armrest, and close my eyes, while Zach, who sits in the armchair next to me, amuses himself by rhythmically poking my head. I hide my smile behind the armrest and wave a hand in his general direction to halfheartedly buzz him off as Angel and Jon cram in beside me.

Angel kicks at my feet until I lower them to give him more space, forcing me to sit up straight where Zach can't reach me anymore. I stop myself from giving Angel a petty nudge back in revenge, but only barely. Mostly because I don't have the energy for it.

Angel wasn't kidding when he said we're zombies. We haven't had a break in weeks. Every single day has been the same. An early start, followed by publicity events—interviews, TV show appearances, waving to crowds from building windows like we're the freaking royal family or something—followed by dinner, then warm-ups and getting ready, a concert, getting un-ready, then either going to our hotel rooms or straight to a private jet to get flown to the next state to do it all again.

But not tomorrow. Tomorrow, we get to go home.

Personally, I'm not exactly overflowing with anticipation— my mom's passive-aggressive on her best days and garden-variety aggressive on her worst, and Dad might as well live at work. I'm looking forward to the chance to sleep past sunrise, though.

"Okay," Erin says, and I open my eyes, but don't lift my head. "I wanted to gather you here to make sure we're all on the same page for next week, and to give you the chance to ask last-minute questions while we're together."

Next week. Next week we're getting on a plane and kissing the home of the brave goodbye for months while we go on the international leg of the tour. First stop, London.

I've never left the country before. Over the past couple years, I've gotten used to leaving my parents for weeks—and sometimes months—at a time, but it's never felt as serious as this. Until now, I've always been in the same country as them. Even though I've technically been *farther* from them before in terms of flight times, somehow, flying to Europe feels bigger. Honestly, it's all kind of overwhelming to think about, and I haven't given myself the chance to dwell on it yet. It's been easier to think of it as something that future-me would face.

Problem is, future-me is about to become present-me.

I knew there was a flaw in the plan.

I raise a sleepy hand as I remember there is *one* question I have. Well, two. "Can I triple-clarify you're not surprising me with tickets to a West End show?" I ask.

"Wouldn't be a very good surprise if she told you," Jon points out.

"No, it wouldn't," Erin says. "But just so you don't get your hopes up, I can confirm we definitely don't have time for a West End show. Sorry, Ruben."

I can't muster up the energy to be disappointed. "I figured. But you said we might be able to check out the Burgtheater in Vienna . . . ?"

Erin smiles. "I did, and we will. I promise, I've made

a point of getting it on our itinerary. We should be able to spare an hour."

I perk up at this. My family is made up of theater geeks. I was raised on Andrew Lloyd Webber and bred on Sondheim. My mom threw me into private singing lessons to perfect my vibrato and belt in kindergarten, and I started touring with professional theater companies in elementary school. I've seen everything America has to offer in terms of musical theater history, but I can't go to Europe without at least doing *something* touristy, and I've always been in love with the vibe and history of the Burgtheater. That, and we don't have time to visit the Globe, to my disgust.

Jon, who's the only one of us not slumping in his seat, speaks up now. "We're still visiting the Vatican, right?"

"Yes, absolutely."

Because of course, we couldn't put aside four hours for a West End show, but we're spending a whole morning at the Vatican for Jon. It's not surprising, I guess: Jon's super Catholic, like his mom, and even though his dad, Geoff Braxton, isn't, Geoff's obviously going to make sure we have time to do whatever's important to Jon. It's how things have always been.

Erin nods at Angel. "Anything you need to clarify, hon?"

Angel pretends to think about it. "Um, is the drinking age in London still eighteen?"

She sighs. "Yes."

Angel grins. "No further questions, Your Honor."

I lift my head to look at Zach, who's resting his chin on his palm. "You're quiet," I say.

"Hmm?" He blinks. "Oh, no, I'm good. No questions. Theaters and drinking and, um . . . Jesus . . . all sound good."

"Bedtime, huh?" I ask, and he nods, his eyes heavy-lidded.

Erin takes the hint. "Okay. The minibus's out front. Email

me or text if you have any questions, otherwise I'll see you bright and early on Sunday."

We all scramble to get out of there before Erin remembers any more items on the agenda. "I know all of you follow the law and don't drink underage!" she calls to our backs. "But just remember hangovers and transatlantic flights don't mix, all right?"

Zach and I take the back seat in the minibus, while Angel and Jon sit in front of us, in separate seats. Usually we're chatty on the way back to our hotel, but today I'm a special kind of tired. Like I've just finished running a marathon: the final reserve of energy used to propel me over the finish line finally exhausted. We haven't had four whole days off in . . . a really fucking long time.

Even though our hotel's barely five minutes away in night traffic, Angel curls up and naps on his seat, and Jon puts his headphones on to wind down with some music.

Essentially alone, I glance at Zach. "I can't believe it's over," I say.

Zach raises an eyebrow. "We've still got all of Europe left."

When Zach whispers, his voice barely changes. That's how soft-spoken he is. His voice is a fawn's pelt. A soft bed of moss. You could fall asleep to its lull.

"True. It feels different, though."

"It'll be the new normal in no time."

"I guess. Like how all this"—I wave a hand around vaguely—"feels normal now."

"Right."

"That's kind of a depressing thought."

He tips his head back, exposing his neck. "What?"

"That it doesn't matter how big or exciting something is, it just becomes average after a while."

The minibus goes over a bump, and Angel snuffles as he's jolted. How is it possible he's already asleep?

Zach considers this, pensive, then gives a surprised "hmm" of agreement. It's never failed to amuse me that Chorus Management *insists* on branding Zach as the dark, brooding type with a bit of an edge to him, when his real personality couldn't be further from it. Zach isn't quiet because he's brooding or tortured. He's just thoughtful, and careful—the type to evaluate what you say for a beat too long while he decides what answer you most want to hear. He might not be the type to dominate a conversation or enthusiastically work the room, but he's dark in approximately the same way a puppy is dark. Whatever the media may claim to the contrary at our publicity manager David's behest.

He puts his feet up on the back of Jon's seat, his knees against his face. Somewhere in the back of my mind, a voice tells me that if the minibus crashed, his legs would drive right through his head. The concern is going to keep niggling at me if I try to ignore it, so I place my hand on his shins and gently press his legs back down. He gives me a crooked half-smile, and grudgingly obeys. "The canals in Amsterdam," he says out of nowhere.

"The Alps in Switzerland. I love Mad Libs!"

"No." He elbows me in the side. "That's what I want to see. You guys all have your things, and I didn't want to say it in front of everyone, but if I get to do anything over there, I hope it's that. Just . . . sit by the canals for a while."

"Why didn't you want to say it in front of everyone? It's not exactly scandalous. If you'd said the red-light district, maybe . . ."

"Oh, I wanna do that, too," he jokes.

"Naturally."

His grin fades, and he presses the toe of his shoe against

the seat in front of him again. "It's stupid. Just, that's where my dad proposed to my mom. I want to see what it was like. I know it won't magically bring them back together or anything, I just . . . I dunno."

"It's not stupid," I say. "We'll make sure we do it."

The smile returns. "Yeah?"

"Yeah. I mean, we're letting Angel loose in Europe, so I'm sure Erin's scheduled in some blocks to go to the police station at least twice. If we're making time for that, we can make time for the canals."

"I can *hear you*," Angel grumbles in a muffled voice.

I kick his seat in response, and he yelps in protest.

Angel's the kind of person who has no business being called Angel. In fact, his legal name is actually Reece, but no one's called him that since we formed the band. In our initial publicity meeting David got all paranoid about the media confusing "Ruben" and "Reece," and Angel happened to come with a long-established nickname already. He got it from his dad as a toddler, because Mrs. Phan took offense to the original, more accurate nickname of "devil child," and Mr. Phan had a well-developed sense of ironic humor.

Beside me, Zach slumps back to close his eyes, and his arm presses against mine with the shift in posture.

I don't think I breathe again for the rest of the drive.

TWO

ZACH

I'm pretty sure my driver is a fan of Saturday.

He keeps glancing up at me through the rearview mirror, making eye contact and smiling before looking away.

He does it again, making the hair on the back of my neck rise. He's supposed to be taking me to Mom's place, but I'm all too aware he could take me anywhere he wants to, and my gut is telling me he might have a basement covered in Saturday posters.

I run a hand through my hair and focus on the streets outside. I should think about this logically. Erin organized this driver for me, so he has to be trustworthy, if only because I know her career would take a pretty major nosedive if I got kidnapped and murdered on her watch. Deep down, I know nothing suspicious is happening.

So why is he smiling at me like he's up to something?

I hear a familiar guitar riff. Oh, no.

He lifts his eyebrows and grins at me like *Oh, yes*.

The driver turns the volume up just as my voice comes through the car's speakers. I almost wish he were a murderer now. It's not that I don't like "Guilty"; it's fun, one of my favorite Saturday songs, actually, mostly because of that sugary-as-hell guitar riff and Ruben's career-best vocals. Seriously, he sounds so freaking good on this song.

I rest my head against the glass as the chorus starts. It's one of our earlier songs, before I'd fully shaken off my punk style of singing, the one Geoff kindly described as whiny and uncommercial, so my tone is shaky and the auto-tune is unmissable. I'd do it differently if I got a do-over, but when you're famous, everything you do follows you forever.

I check the mirror and yep, the driver is still watching me. It's fucking creepy.

I bob my head along to the beat, pretending I'm having a good time. Like, *"Guilty," yes, love it.*

"My daughter is obsessed with you, Zach," he says, making eye contact through the mirror. "All of you, but especially you. She says she's a 'stan.'"

I wince and force a smile. "Oh wow, thanks, that's really nice of you to say."

He chuckles. "You're welcome. You know, I'm more of a rock guy, but some of your songs are pretty catchy. Just don't tell anyone I said that, okay?"

I'm pretty much used to this now. Basically, no guy will compliment Saturday without an asterisk of some sort. *You kind of suck, but . . .*

"I won't." I pause, then decide to go for it. "I'm more of a rock guy, too." It's the first honest thing I've said to him.

I pick at my leather bracelet, which my stylist makes me wear.

For the record, I do love our songs. It's just they aren't my favorite thing to listen to during my downtime, nor is it what I'd choose to sing if I had control over that sort of thing.

Which I don't. So it doesn't matter.

Approximately half our discography later, in which I find out just how much one boy can cringe, I'm finally home. I slide open the door, step out into the midmorning sunshine, and crack my back as a cover to look down the street. There's nobody around, though, and more importantly no paparazzi, at least that I can see. One of the weirdest things about being famous is seeing photos of yourself in magazines when you don't even remember paparazzi being there. It doesn't help that they're getting sneakier, with cameras that can take pictures from miles away. I'm in magazines all the time now, so I always feel like someone, somewhere, is staring at me. For all I know, they are.

I check my reflection and start preening, because Chorus Management would lose their shit if a photo of me gets out where I look like trash. My hair is messier than it should be, with a few strands sticking out. Under Geoff's direction, I've grown it long instead of my usual zero-maintenance short spikes, and I'm still not used to it. It keeps getting in my eyes or tickling my neck. It's a major pain in the ass, and I'm not sure it even looks good enough to warrant the effort.

The driver retrieves my suitcase, catching me in the act.

"Thanks," I say, as I tip him a fifty-dollar bill.

"No worries." He keeps watching me. "Would you mind if I got a photo? My daughter would kill me if I didn't."

I make sure my smile is extra cheery. "Go ahead!"

He takes out his phone, and leans in close to take a few selfies with me. Part of me wants to wrap it up so I can just get out of here and see Mom, but I stop myself. *Don't be one of* those *celebrities,* a voice lectures me in the back of my head. It's just a small favor. It's fine.

Once he's taken enough photos to fill an album, I go inside, and enter the elevator using my key card, and then go up to the top level. I knock on the door, and a few seconds later, it opens.

Mom rushes out and grabs me in a tight hug. I think she's

dressed up for this, since she's in a striped button-down tucked into jeans. When we break apart, there are tears in her eyes. She wipes them like it's something to be ashamed of and not the sweetest thing ever. Then she reaches out and grabs me again, hugging me hard enough it kinda hurts. She's wearing perfume, so yep, she definitely dressed up just for this. My dad might be an absent piece of shit, but I lucked out with her.

"I've missed you so much," she says.

"Why?"

She laughs and shakes her head, then takes a moment to look me up and down. "When did this happen?"

I tuck a hand into my front pocket. "Erin makes us work out twice a day now."

Mom frowns. I know she has strong opinions on the, in her words, "batshit" hoops Erin and the rest of Chorus Management make us jump through, and the constant workouts are a part of that. But I'm not being overworked. It's fine. When I used to go to regular school, I was a forward on the soccer team, and that was a huge commitment, but I loved it anyway. When I'm a part of a team, or working toward a goal, following orders doesn't feel anything like work. Being in Saturday is similar. Plus, I'm eighteen now, so I get it. There's only so much mileage you can get out of *cute*, and I really need to transition to *hot* if I want to have a career. Which I do. Maybe not as badly as, like, Ruben, but I still do.

"What?" I ask.

"Nothing, you just look so much like your dad."

I wonder how that must be for her. I mean, I see the resemblance, especially now that I've put on some mass. But that means I look like the guy that peaced out on her to start a new family with a coworker ten years younger than him. The same guy who only started regularly calling when Saturday started hitting the news. The guy who told me pursuing music was a horrible idea and he wouldn't support me if I went down that path, and then expected to reap every single one of the rewards once the band took off.

But I just nod.

Mom's apartment is sprawling and well-decorated, with an incredible view of Portland through the glass doors that lead to the balcony. I didn't grow up here; Mom had to move because there was no way to make our old place secure. Which it became clear was necessary when a fan found out where she lived and camped out, hoping to see me. I bought Mom this place a few weeks later.

"How's the album going?" she asks.

"Good, I think. I submitted a couple songs I wrote to Geoff, so fingers crossed Galactic likes them."

"I'm sure they will. I've always loved your songs."

"Yeah, but you're my mom, you have to say that."

"Would you rather I said I think they're terrible?" She's smiling, so I know she's joking. I shake my head.

"Then watch your mouth." She grins. "Seriously, how do you feel about it? This is a pretty huge deal."

"I know. I just don't want to get my hopes up, I guess. But it'd be cool to have a song out there that's mine."

"Then you'll be a true artiste."

I pretend to dry heave.

I finally find Cleo, our cat, hiding in Mom's bedroom. She's definitely gotten bigger since I last saw her, and is kind of a brick now.

"Hello," I say as I scoop her up, comically overexaggerating how heavy she is, to make Mom smile.

Still clutching Cleo to my chest, I go back through to the kitchen. Mom's made a towering chocolate cake with the words *Welcome Home Zach!!!* written in wobbly icing on the top. I'm not sure when she had the time, because she still works full time at a nursing home, even though I make more than enough for both of us.

"It's okay if it's too much," she says, her expression uneasy. "I just wanted to make you something."

"No, I love it, thank you. I need a shower, though, so can we wait like, five minutes?"

"Okay," says Mom. "What are your plans for the rest of the day?"

"Why don't we binge trashy TV, maybe order some only slightly healthy food?"

"I'm so in."

I go to my room and put Cleo down on my bed. My old room had punk band posters all over the walls, but this one is totally barren. It's more adult, but also worse. I grab a faded T-shirt and a pair of sweats, and go to the shower. I'd never be allowed to wear this somewhere I could be seen, and I think that's kind of the point. Right now, Zach Knight from Saturday is checked out. I'm just Zach again. Finally.

When I come back out, I see that Mom has also changed into her PJs. There are two plates of cake on the coffee table, and *American Ninja Warrior* is paused on the TV. A wave of nostalgia washes over me, and I'm fifteen years old again, watching TV with Mom like we used to every night. Before seeing Mom turned into a biannual thing.

I sit down, and pick up my plate as Mom hits play.

"So," she says. "Have any girls made it past the meet and greet?"

I check my smart watch. "I've been home twenty minutes. *That's* how long it takes for you to start prying into my personal life?"

"I'm not prying, I'm curious. Come on, who is she?"

I keep my stare steady. "I haven't really been dating, I'm focusing on my writing at the moment."

"Well, okay then, Mr. Mysterious."

"Are there any guys in your life?" I ask.

"I'm not telling if you're not."

I roll my eyes.

A text from Ruben arrives, and I smile as I read it.

I miss you already!

"What's that smile for?" asks Mom. "Is it a girl?"

I tilt my phone away. "It's just Ruben."

"Already? Didn't you just say goodbye to him?"

"Yeah but he's my—Ruben."

Mom musses my hair. I leave it; I like it better this way anyway.

I type back: I miss you too man.

Ruben responds with a thumbs-up, which I *know* is just to annoy me. I've ranted to him before about how I think they're passive-aggressive.

TAKE THAT BACK.

He gives me another thumbs-up.

Bastard.

I smile, then I turn my phone off, with no plans to turn it back on for at least forty-eight hours.

Whatever happens, happens. It can wait.

Zach Knight of Saturday is officially checked out until I get to Angel's party.

Angel's party is, in a word: ridiculous.

He wasn't even kidding about the peacocks. I can see a few of them now, strutting their stuff on the lawn. They're on leashes, held by handlers in green jumpsuits. So yeah. Ridiculous is the only appropriate word. This venue is enormous, built in front of a large lake, and a lot of the free space has been done up like a fair, with stalls and entertainers. There are two carnival rides: a pirate ship and a spinning one with a rotating arm. There's even an enormous bounce house.

For who? Who knows?

As utterly over the top as this whole setup is, I can't help but smile. It's so very Angel. Plus, there aren't any paparazzi or fans here, and while there's a big crowd, it's only people in the game. Security guards prowl the perimeter, which means I don't have to have my guard up as much as I normally do. In terms of safety, anyway.

I'm standing beside Jon in the parking lot, looking out at the whole spectacle. His shirt is tight and I'm wearing all-black, so we're on-brand, even here. He pulls out his phone and scrolls. I get it, he's been around stuff like this his whole life, whereas when I was a kid the most exciting party I ever had was at McDonald's, and as a younger teenager I usually skipped having a party in exchange for more presents. The others would never get that, especially Ruben and Jon—they were always rich and got richer—but I never would've gone to anything even close to this if it weren't for Saturday.

It's probably my emotions talking, but I kind of wish Mom could see this.

Earlier today, I had to say goodbye to her. I chew my lip, trying to keep the building ache in my chest down. I want to enjoy myself tonight, so I should stop going down this mental rabbit hole. There's no getting out of it if I really let it sink in. It's just, I only *just* got back—

"Are those fire dancers?" asks Jon, and he points toward two buff, oiled-up shirtless dudes holding fire sticks.

The younger of the two has a tattoo going down his side, but I can't get a proper look without staring, and then I'll be staring at a half-naked guy. Like the rest of Saturday, I've had countless gay rumors spread about me, and people are *always* looking for evidence to confirm the theory that I'm secretly gay. I hate how invasive and presumptive the rumors are, and how they've turned me looking at a guy's tattoo into something I need to be cautious of.

I raise an eyebrow and cock my head. "That, or terrible strippers."

Jon's gaze is fixed on the dancers so we go and watch, joining a crowd of partygoers who have circled around the pair. I recognize a few soon-to-be A-list actors and millionaire Instagrammers, and oh my god, there's Randy Kehoe, lead singer of Falling for Alice. He's stroking his chin with leather-gloved hands, and his skull T-shirt has a red stain splashed down the front of it, turning the once-white skull an eerie bloodred. His hair is bubblegum pink now, to match their latest album, the one I practically have a crush on. I'm dying to say hey and become a gushy mess for a few minutes, but we're all off duty at the moment. Nobody wants to be fawned over.

I also want to pick Randy's brain about his writing process, but just the thought makes me blush. He's an amazing lyricist, and I'm over here singing candy-corn factory-produced lyrics about girls that don't exist. Why should he give me the time of day?

The fire dancers start a new dance, spinning their flaming batons around impossibly fast. I feel the heat on my face as they move, both totally in sync. Tattooed guy is really handsome, with dark hair and solid cheekbones. Then they both raise their batons to their mouths and spit, making it look like they're breathing fire.

A cheer breaks out for them.

Oh, screw it. I chance a look down. His tattoo is of a dragon, its tail ending on his hip.

Huh. It actually looks awesome. I file the idea away for a future version of me that can finally get the tattoos I've been longing to get for years now. A version of me who doesn't have to run anything I do to my own skin past my management team for approval first.

By the entrance to the main building, I see Geoff Braxton, holding a glass of champagne. He's alone, too, which doesn't happen often. People are demanding of us, but it's nothing compared to him. I get it, if he decides you're worth it he can make you a global superstar, richer and more famous than you can ever imagine. If you want to be famous, he's a god.

"Go say hi," says Jon. "Ask him if he's heard back from Galactic about your tracks."

"Really? I . . ."

"Just go!"

Jon pushes me on the back, and I swallow hard, then go up to Geoff. Unlike Jon, he's white, and I'm pretty sure he's started dyeing his thinning hair to cover up his grays. I don't even want to know how much his sleek suit cost, but I'd guess it's an obscene amount.

I offer my hand, and he grips it tight, giving me his perfect, professional smile. I think it means I have maybe a minute of his time. If a long talk is coming, he will generally act like I'm his long-lost best friend.

"Having fun?" I ask.

"I am." He looks down. "But I can see on your face you didn't come over here to make small talk. Want to talk shop?"

"I do."

"Good, I like your priorities." We move over to a quieter spot, down the side of the building.

My heart swells. I don't want to get my hopes up, but if he liked even one of my songs, that would be enormous.

"So, what did you think?" I ask.

"I liked them. But you should know, Galactic Records decided to pass. Not because they're bad, it's just not the direction they're hoping to go in with Saturday."

I bow my head, and can't bring myself to look into his eyes. "Oh. All right."

"I want you to stick with it, because you've obviously got the chops, and I'd *love* to swing you a songwriter credit on the LP."

"Right. So what should I do?"

"Just keep in mind what kind of band Saturday is. Play to what Galactic wants, not what you would want. We're a pop act. If you're stuck, try thinking of a song that would play on the radio, or in a mall."

I wrap my arms around myself, and try to keep tears from welling up. This is just business. Even if it feels like it because of the amount of myself I put into those songs, it's not personal. But seriously, a mall? I can't imagine anything I've written making sense there.

"Cool, okay. I'll take another swing at it."

"Great. Good to see you. Have fun at the party."

"Thanks for your time." My voice cracks, damn it. "I'll try again, and be more pop this time."

"I'm looking forward to it."

I break away, my shoulders sagging. Geoff would never come out and say to my face that he thinks my songs sucked, but in reality that's what he just said. I try to push that away, though. It's fine. Who cares if Saturday never sings about the stuff I actually care about? It's a job, that's all. In what world does anyone with a job get to do whatever they want?

I wander inside the main building. It's lit like a nightclub, with blue lights cutting through the darkness, and music so loud I can feel the thud of the bass. There's a DJ and a bar, and to the side, I kid you not, is an enormous ice sculpture of a roaring lion. There's even a tattoo station set up, where a girl is getting a tattoo on her arm. I peer closer, and see she's getting the word *GUILTY* in cursive.

At the far end of the room, leaning against the wall, is Ruben, looking unfairly cool in a sweater and wool coat. Fans are constantly saying Ruben could be a model, and I can see it, what with his perfectly tousled black hair and angular jawline. I might need to work out to transition from cute to hot, but Ruben is already there, and I'm pretty sure he knows.

He's talking to a modern-day Adonis. This other boy laughs, then rests his hand on Ruben's shoulder for just a moment. I feel a weird stab in the pit of my stomach. The media and general public don't know about Ruben yet, and even at a private party I want to tell him to not be so obvious. For such a smart guy, he can be kind of thick sometimes, especially around hot guys. I get it, girls make me stupid, too, but my stupidity has a much slimmer chance of causing a worldwide headline.

Jon appears, clearly having been looking for me. "Hey," he shouts, over the music. "Have you seen Angel?"

I shake my head. "Not yet."

"Shoot," he says, his brow furrowing. "Nobody can find him."

"Oh, crap. Okay, I'll text him." Panic starts to set in. Angel has always been the biggest partier of all of us, but lately he's moved on to things heavier than alcohol. He has a whole new group of friends, who can supply him with anything he wants, and . . . yeah. I get why Jon looks how he does right now.

"I already tried, but, go on."

> Hey, just got here, where are you?

The typing bubble appears, then vanishes.

"He's conscious," I say.

"Well, that's something, I guess."

He scans the crowd. I recognize a few more people, their famous faces only momentarily lit up by flashing lights. A lot of them are already staggering all over the place or grinding on each other in pairings that would make magazine editors salivate.

"Where's Ruben?" Jon shouts.

"He's talking to a guy over . . ." I stop, because he's not there anymore. I try not to think about *what* he's doing now.

Jon looks at me curiously.

"Er, I saw them when I came in. They seemed close."

Jon presses his fist to his forehead. "Can you find him and ask if he's seen Angel? I'll keep looking. Text me if Ruben knows anything."

"Okay."

I leave the dance floor, and go back out into the fair, searching for Ruben. I bet he's here with that Adonis guy. I can only hope they aren't being too obvious.

I shake my head. What Ruben does is his business.

I just wish he'd be careful about it. Anyone could've seen him. If I noticed, I'm sure other people did.

Except I spot Ruben by the pirate ship, and he's no longer with the Greek god. He's alone, and he seems to be in a hurry, his hands tucked into his coat pockets. A girl shouts

his name, but he waves, and keeps walking, leaving her looking crestfallen.

I follow after him.

He stops a ways from the party, by the shore of the lake, and
picks up a rock. He skips it, and it goes so far I lose sight of it.

I keep my head down all the way until I reach him. There's
nobody else anywhere nearby. Just us, and the lake, with the
neon lights and sounds of the party distant behind us.

I notice his eyes are glassy. All thoughts of Angel fall away.

"Are you okay?" I ask.

He shrugs. "I'm . . . whatever. Nice shirt."

"Nice sweater," I say haltingly.

He picks up another rock, and throws it. I shove my hands
into my pockets and step closer to him. Usually, I'd let him
get away with changing the subject to small talk. But something happened to him, something to do with that guy, I can
feel it. If I'm going to fix it, we need to cut to the chase.

"Does this have anything to do with a guy?" I ask. "Want
to talk about it?"

"Um. Nope. Not really."

I pick up a rock, and try skimming it. It only skips once
before sinking. Back at Camp Hollow Rock, the performing
arts camp where Saturday started, I got really good at this,
but I've clearly lost my touch.

"Okay, so," he says. I smile, because Ruben has never
been the silent and stoic type; I'm not shocked it only took
him two seconds to crack. "I was talking to this guy, and it
was going well. Like, *really* well, you know?"

"I do."

"But then he asked me if I could listen to his demo, and
show it to Galactic Records if I liked it."

"Oh fuck."

He gives me a tight smile. "Yeah."

"I'm sorry."

"Yeah. Well. It's not like it's your fault." He skips another rock. "Sorry, I'm being moody. I just thought he might've liked me for me, you know?"

As I scan his face, I get a pang in my chest.

Ruben's the sweetest, best guy. But he seems to be a magnet for guys who just want to use him. I don't even know why; objectively, Ruben is hot, and funny, *and* cool—the trifecta, essentially. Yet he's always treated like he's disposable. Someday someone is going to figure out that he's a dream guy. It's just a matter of time.

I hope it happens soon, though. Because seeing Ruben like this guts me.

"I'll be over this in ten minutes," he says, gesturing to himself. "I just need a second. You don't have to stick around for it."

"I'm fine."

"You sure? You're missing the 'biggest event of our lives.'"

I smile.

Because, honestly? I know I'm exactly where I want to be.

THREE

RUBEN

Zach sits with me while I simmer down. I didn't mean to throw a tantrum in the middle of Angel's party, and I'm annoyed at myself for dragging Zach away, but mostly I'm grateful to have him here.

My mood is twofold. I'm pissed about being used for my connections—by a guy I'd started to suspect was actually straight by the end of our chat, to add in an extra helping of humiliation. This would be bad enough for most people, but after my experience with Christopher Madden (Oscar-winning actor for a reason, apparently, because he did a *world*-class performance at convincing me he was into me before abruptly insisting he was straight when the lines got too blurry last year), I'm especially impatient with being treated as a new experience rather than a human being.

Usually, I'd be able to take this in my stride and push past it, but tonight, I'm essentially a toddler that didn't get his naptime. This four-day break was meant to be my opportunity to slow down and recharge, but after all that quality time with my parents I feel more wound-up than ever. I guess I'd forgotten what being at home was really like. It's funny how time and space cast a rosy glow over memories, making them seem less painful than they were in reality.

There's no such thing as recharging, or downtime, in my family. They think it's time wasted. And, hey, I did end up here, a member of one of the biggest acts in the world right now. So, maybe they're on to something. Maybe I wouldn't have achieved this without them. Maybe I need their little reminders, their jagged pep-talks, their acidic constructive criticism.

I shove my hands in my coat pockets to ward off the evening chill and rock back on my heels. "We should head before Angel sends a search party."

"Actually, we can't find Angel."

"What?" A gust of wind blows through, and I tuck my arms in for warmth against the early March chill.

"You haven't seen him, have you? I figured you noticed."

"Um, I couldn't find him when I got here but I thought he was probably on a ride or something. Then that guy distracted me. Why didn't you tell me he was missing?"

"He's not *missing*," Zach says. "He's probably around somewhere. I was gonna tell you but you were upset about the guy."

I groan. "Fuck that straight, social-climbing asshole." I spit out the words. "We need to go find Angel. Come on."

"Yeah, fuck straight people," Zach deadpans as we walk, and I'm reminded why it's imperative for me to squash these recent crush-like feelings for him, stat.

"No offense."

"Some taken. Ruben, it's okay. Angel will be around somewhere. Jon's probably with him by now."

The concern that's niggling at me must be obvious on my face. He's right. He's totally right, I'm just being overly anxious. But the thing is, Angel's had a few particularly wild nights lately, especially during the second half of our tour. Mix exhaustion with unlimited money, low supervision, and connections with dozens of celebrities who use all sorts of cocktails to treat their own exhaustion and boredom, and things are bound to happen, I guess. Only tonight's a gigantic night for Angel, and he's surrounded by those very connections, many of whom will be giving him *birthday presents*. Is it paranoid for me to want to make sure someone in this ridiculous event has spotted him over the last hour? If he's not unconscious in a bathroom somewhere, *someone* will have seen him. He's unmissable on his most casual days.

The party's gotten even busier in the past half hour, with the last of the fashionably late arrivals trickling in. I step around a peacock and scan the crowds of people. "See Jon anywhere?"

Zach spots Jon in a group of people congregating in the direction of the pirate ship ride, so we head over. Jon's busy talking to Teresa Narvaez, the original cast lead of my favorite musical, *In This House*. When he sees us, he excuses himself and charges over. If I wasn't so concerned about the look on his face, I'd be disappointed to miss the opportunity to meet Teresa, and I make a mental note to ask Jon to introduce me to her before the night's out.

"It's been over an hour, and *no one's* seen Angel," Jon says, his tone urgent. "Not even his parents. And I can't tell them I'm freaking out without explaining to them *why* it would be concerning that he's disappeared."

"Okay, let's be rational," I say. "He's probably on the property. I don't think he'd miss his own party no matter what someone else offered. So, if he's here, he's probably inside somewhere, or someone would've run into him by now."

Jon makes a show of turning around. "I can't see many buildings here, can you?"

"I see porta-potties," Zach says.

I turn to him slowly. "You don't think . . ."

"Probably not," he says, but he looks unconvinced.

"Great," Jon says. "That's just how I wanted to spend my night. Breaking into occupied porta-potties to search for our unconscious best friend. This bodes *well* for the tour."

"Let's keep those as a last resort," I say. "I vote we try inside one more time."

Inside, the party's really started kicking off, with crowds of people eating, drinking, and filling the dance floor. I scan the room hopefully, but if Angel's here, he's buried by the crowd.

I start to head deeper into the room, when the DJ's booming voice replaces the music.

"All right, everyone, if you'll head on inside the main building, the guest of honor is about to arrive. Find a place and grab a drink, because I've just been informed the party's about to *really* get started."

I stop in place and turn to the other two.

"Well," Zach says, blinking. "Sounds like we're in the right place, at least?"

"Tell me he did not hide out somewhere for the first two hours of his own party so he could make a dramatic entrance," Jon says.

I shake my head. "I need a drink."

There's a bar without much of a line to the left, so I head over to it, with Zach and Jon tailing me. "Erin said not to drink," Jon says over the resumed music.

"Erin's not here," I say with a too-bright smile.

"You're spending too much time around Angel," Jon says.

"Honestly, I'm spending too much time around all three of you. Though you'd think your influence would balance me out, Jon."

He scowls at me as we reach the bar.

The nearest bartender is a skinny guy with acne and blond hair. He barely looks any older than us. I flash a dazzling smile, and he wilts. "Hey," I say, "Can I please get a whiskey and Coke and . . . Zach, what would you like?"

"Oh, um, the same, I guess."

"Two Jack and Cokes, please?"

The bartender shifts his weight. "Do you, um . . . have your ID?" he asks, presumably stalling for time, because there's no way he doesn't know I'm underage.

Joy. Trust me to zero in on the newbie who hasn't been given a proper induction. It's generally an unspoken agreement that drinking laws don't apply to us—*especially* at private parties. I smile even bigger. "You know? I left it in my suitcase. I'll tell you what, we'll get out of your hair for a minute, and you can leave our drinks on the edge there. We'll grab them when we're ready." I slide a generous tip his way—not because I think we need to bribe him, but because the poor guy looks so terrified—and steer Jon and Zach by their elbows a few feet away to give him some plausible deniability. He greets the next customer, tells them he'll be a second, and grabs a bottle of Jack Daniel's, glancing sideways to see if his coworkers are watching. Like they give a shit.

Zach laughs and Jon rolls his eyes in a long-suffering way.

Drinks in hand, the three of us find a spot to stand in just as smoke starts to billow out from the ground at the far end of the room.

Nearby a girl asks in alarm if the place is on fire. No one answers her.

Then a row of cold spark machines lights up like a fountain, shooting blinding white flames into the air. The music surges into a regal chorus of trumpets and strings, before breaking into a hip-hop beat. I can't quite see what's happening up front at first, then I realize: Angel's emerged from a trapdoor in the floor, standing atop a rising platform that's also bordered by spark-effect fireworks. His arms are held to the sides and his head is tipped back, legs planted apart. Like a phoenix rising from the goddamn flames or something.

"What was that you were saying about a dramatic entrance, Jon?" I say mildly as the crowd breaks into applause.

"Bigger than Billboard," Zach muses, before taking a sip.

"I hope he isn't flammable," Jon adds.

"Probably not, but he's definitely high," I say, taking in his manic smile and the rapid rise and fall of his chest.

"Again?" Zach asks with a sigh.

"Why am I not surprised?" Jon mutters. "I just hope he doesn't fall."

"Thank you for coming here tonight!" Angel's voice booms over the loudspeakers. I spot the telltale bulge of a mic-pack. "Is everyone having a good time?"

The partiers roar. Angel, probably a few drinks in by now at a minimum, sways a little, and Jon looks like he might faint. "*Please,* don't fall," he says, like Angel can hear him.

"Tonight is my last night in the U S of A before we pack up and head off to *Europe, baby!*" More cheering. "I'm so psyched to be hitting up Europe with my fucking family. Zach, Ruben, Jon. You're my fucking family. I love you so fucking much. Everyone, I met those guys at *music camp,* did you know that? Fucking *camp.* I wasn't gonna go that year! I had a new girlfriend and I didn't wanna leave her. Can you imagine if I'd skipped?"

The crowd buzzes with laughter.

"And Zach and I met Ruben, and he dragged us to hang with Jon—who *none of us* knew was Geoff Braxton's son because he was *lying about his name,* which is supposed to be a sin, but whatever—"

Jon cups a hand over his forehead in disbelief.

"—and if that's not fucking destiny, I don't know what is."

Hah. Destiny, it wasn't. At first, I think Jon's unhappy moan is because he knows as well as I do that my becoming friends with him was anything but fated. Then I realize, no, he's just panicking, still.

He's like a parent with a toddler. If the toddler was high off its face and standing on a ledge.

"He's not gonna fall," Zach reassures Jon. "Look, he's not even rocking anymore."

The speech goes on for another few minutes, in which Angel remembers to thank his *actual* family, goes on a rant about staplers, and tells everyone they can pick one peacock each to bring home before his party planner reminds him that the peacocks are rented and not legal pets. Then, finally, the platform starts lowering him back down to land. Only when I'm sure he's safe do I make eye contact with the bartender and hold up two fingers, shooting him a smile. He nods and gets to making our second round.

Angel makes a beeline for us, swaying more now than he was on the platform. "Where's mine?" he asks as I grab the drinks.

"Sorry, figured you'd have one," I say. It's less judgy than "I thought you'd had enough," and therefore less likely to result in Angel downing a bottle of vodka to prove a point.

"Come with me," Angel says, walking off suddenly. The three of us follow him into the night, our way lit up by bushes and trees covered in glittering string lights, along with the flashing carnival rides.

"Where are we going?" Jon asks warily.

"Bouncy castle."

"Why?" I grin, and Angel flips around to point at me and Zach in turn. "Chug. Chug. Bouncy castle time."

I knock back my glass and take my coat off, and Zach tips the rest of his into the grass. Then we all kick our shoes off and follow Angel to climb into the unused inflatable castle.

Angel throws himself onto his back, laughing like a little kid, and Jon, by now the only sober one of us, sits primly down beside him. "You could've texted us back." he says. "I was worried."

Angel laughs again. "I didn't want to spoil the surprise. Also, I wasn't checking my phone." He pulls out said phone and starts filming Jon. "You're live. Jon, tell everyone what you just told me. I want it on record that you were worried about me."

Jon rolls his eyes. "I just wanted to make sure you were having a good time at your party."

Angel climbs onto his knees, going full shaky-camera mode. Bet his viewers *love* that. "Isn't that *sweet*, everyone?"

"Why don't you show everyone your party? They're more interested in that."

"No, they want to see you. Admit it. You love me, and you were all worried about me because you couldn't find me at my birthday party."

Now I know for *sure* he's high. Jon's right—there's nothing that irritates a sober Angel quicker than being fussed over. Apparently, whatever he's taken tonight has made him unusually affectionate. Molly, I'd guess.

"Angel."

"Say it!" Angel puts on a babyish voice and cups Jon's cheek with one hand so the camera can see. "Say you love me and you were worried about me."

"Of course I love you, and I'm glad we found you so we can have some *fun*!" Jon says, swatting Angel's hand away and turning his attention to the camera. "Everyone, be sure to wish Angel a happy birthday so he can read all of your messages on our flight to *Europe tomorrow*! *Here we come, baby!*"

A lifetime of media training definitely wasn't wasted on Jon.

Out of view of the camera, Zach stands coltishly in the middle of the castle, unsure of himself. Angel and Jon start to wrestle for control of Angel's phone, Angel screaming about freedom of the press and workplace assault at the top of his lungs. Their scuffle disrupts the castle and Zach stumbles, but manages to keep himself upright.

Not for long.

I take a running start and throw myself to land a few feet away from him, propelling him into the air with the force. He lands hard and bounces, gasping. "Ruben!"

He lunges at me and wrestles me into the floor while I cackle, pinning me down as best as he can with his legs. I squirm to get out of his grip, laughing so hard I'm out of breath. It strikes me that, as much as we take every opportunity to have fun when touring, we've had very few nights where we could just have fun together as a group. I've missed them.

My phone buzzes in my pocket and I pull it out to find a message from Mom. Found this. Worth being aware of, she's written, along with the link to a YouTube video. I don't click on it, but I don't have to—the title's visible in the message preview. *Ten times Ruben Montez moves his mouth weird in that spot during "Guilty"!*

"What are you doing?" Zach asks, panting and propping himself up on his elbows.

"Mom sent me a helpful video," I say lightly, showing him the screen.

"Oh my god, absolutely not." All traces of mirth vanish as he wrenches the phone from my hands. I try to retrieve it, and he shoves it in his back pocket, pressing a hand on my chest to ward me away. *He's straight,* I remind the butterflies that flutter to life in my stomach. "No. Stop. You're perfect, and you're the best singer I've ever heard in, just, my whole fucking life, and screw your mom. Sorry, I didn't mean that. But also, kind of?"

"She didn't make the video. She just wants to make sure I—"

"Shh. No." Zach presses his palm across my mouth, cutting me off. I lick him, and he recoils in disgust. "I'm throwing your phone away," he announces, climbing to his feet. "No more phone for the rest of the night. Your mom will get over it."

I grab Zach's upper arm and pull him backward and we tumble down together, landing in a tangle of limbs and giggling breathlessly. Someone's amped the music volume outside, and the thudding bass combined with the smell of beer and spirits has it feeling like an inflatable nightclub. "Oh shit," I gasp, a little breathless. "I think I'm drunk already. How much whiskey was in those drinks?"

Jon bounces over and lands next to us on his knees. "You two are gonna need some serious water if you wanna survive tomorrow."

"Water's for rookies," Angel says. His white suit is marred by dirt and grime already.

"Water's not gonna help *you* at this point anyway, man," Jon says. "Good luck."

"Luck? I don't need luck. I am eighteen, I am a man of the world, and I will be transported to England through a rainbow portal." Angel drops heavily, causing the floor beneath us to lurch up.

"I've got motion sickness," Zach moans, and I help him upright.

"You think it's bad *now*," Jon says, smirking.

"Let's get you onto solid ground," I say to Zach, scooping him up under his arms. "Come on."

We tumble out of the castle and onto the grass. Zach sags, resting his back against the inflatable wall. I join him there, but it's jolting so violently I shuffle forward and sit up straight. Zach lets his head fall heavily onto my shoulder. Wise move.

"Are you happier now?" he asks, closing his eyes.

The warmth of his cheek seeps through my thin sweater. I smile down at him, then rest my own head on top of his, and pretend for a moment that this is something it's not. "Yeah. Much."

Jon and Angel have left the castle now, and Angel waves to catch my attention. "I'm going to get some more drinks for us," he calls, "because apparently I have to do everything for myself around here."

"Thank you, Angel," I say sweetly.

I would offer him a hand with the drinks, but for now, Zach needs a second to regain his balance. And as long as he's leaning on me like this, soft and warm, with the sweet, heady scent of his cologne drifting around us, I'm in no rush at all.

FOUR

ZACH

I'm the only one trying to work on this flight.

I think the other members of Saturday, save for a very smug Jon, have accepted that they're massively hungover and they aren't going to be productive. The four of us are sprawled on white leather seats, spaced out across the private jet. It's over-the-top luxurious; each little thing, from the huge screens each of us have, to the fully stocked minibar at the back, feels almost unnecessarily decadent. We just had a dinner of rigatoni all'arrabbiata, which is basically just pasta in tomato sauce with sausage, only *expensive,* and ciabatta bread with truffles and garlic oil. Dessert was supposed to be foglie di fico, but we all declined. For our abs, I'm guessing.

Jon and Angel are dozing, and Ruben has his headphones on, presumably listening to music. Actually, there's a good chance he's working as well—he often puts on career advice podcasts that his mom makes him listen to. It's either that, or some old musical he's listened to a million times already. Erin is sitting on a three-seat lounge, reading something on her iPad. Our security team leaders and principal body-guards are both asleep at the back of the plane, but we're the only passengers.

I have my notebook open in front of me, and I'm trying to write a song, even though I'm queasy and it feels like my brain is being stepped on.

I bring my pen to the page, and write: *You're like a hangover.*

That's hardly fun, though. Plus I could get in trouble for referencing alcohol, given our target audience.

What Galactic Records wants is a pop smash. It needs to be sweet and easy to listen to, but can't be too much of anything. The lyrics need to be good, but vague enough that masses of people can apply the story to their own lives. People are always so dismissive of pop, but actually writing a hit pop song? It's way easier said than done.

I'm stuck because, as much as I want to be a renowned songwriter, I'm not really a pop smash kind of person. I never was, and even though I'm in a world-famous pop band now, I have my doubts that I ever will be. While Ruben was raised on musicals, I was raised on alt-rock. I like songs that are emotive and personal and honestly, a little weird. There's a reason loner kids like I once was gravitate toward that kind of music. I want to be that for someone, one day. To give them the lifeline music gave me.

Someone nudges my shoulder. It's Ruben, across the aisle from me. His headphones are now hanging around his neck.

"Writer's block?" he asks. The plane rattles as we go over a spot of turbulence. Even when he isn't singing, Ruben has a nice voice. It's deep and has this kind of wry spark to it, like he's always messing with you.

"Yeah. Got any advice?"

He holds out his hand. "Give it."

I feel my cheeks start to warm, but I ignore that, and show him my notebook, which only has one line on it, the one about the hangover.

He laughs. "I wonder what inspired this."

"My mind works in mysterious ways."

"Clearly."

I put my notebook down, and write down *mysterious ways*.

"Tell me you did *not* just write down 'mysterious ways.'"

"No, something else came to me."

His lifted eyebrow tells me there's no fooling him. Not that I ever thought I could. He's turned in his plush seat now, to face me more.

"Okay, fine," I say. "It's got a nice ring to it, don't you think?"

"Listen, you're a great writer, but no. You just think it does because you're hungover as fuck on an international flight. You *can* take a second to just chill, you know."

If *Ruben* is telling me to relax, I really should listen. He never stops, and is constantly trying to improve, even though he's already one of the most technically perfect singers in the game. He even transitioned from his theater upbringing to pop much more easily than I did, seemingly through sheer force of will. Because that's the thing about Ruben; he's maybe the one person I don't *ever* doubt being able to accomplish everything he wants. I still remember back when we were kids at camp, and we sat by the shore of the lake one night, and he told me he wanted to be a superstar one day. Right then, I knew it would happen with everything I have.

"Fine." I snap my notebook closed. "What are you listening to?"

He pointedly looks away.

"Seriously?"

"Is there a limit to how many times someone can listen to an album, now? Have you even listened to it *once*, yet, Zachary?"

I have the cast recording of *In This House* downloaded to

my phone, but I haven't listened to it yet, despite Ruben's constant gentle badgering. It's become a bit of a joke between us that I keep putting it off, but I don't have much else to do right now. I should bite the bullet, because it'll make his day. Or, night. I'm not sure what time it technically is right now.

"I will now," I say. "But only so you stop asking me."

"Do what you want, Zach."

I put my headphones on and find the album. It runs for two hours and five minutes. What the hell have I gotten myself into? There's no going back now, though, because Ruben has asked me to listen multiple times, and I don't want to disappoint him. That'd be like ignoring a puppy that wants to be petted. I'm not strong enough. And it's not like Ruben asks much of me.

I hit play, then lean my head back and close my eyes.

I'm exhausted, but the flight is over.

Up ahead are the frosted glass doors of the exit. I know what's coming, and I try to brace myself, even though I know from experience there's no way to prepare for this.

The doors open, and a deafening scream greets us.

Outside is a sea of mostly teenage girls, along with news crews and paparazzi. This happens more often than not now. Police have shown up, too, and have formed a line alongside airport security to try to shield us. I want to look around, to see if anything is different here, like different taxis or something, but the crowd is pulling all my attention.

They all rush forward, and our guards close ranks, pressing us into a tight huddle. One of them offers their hand. I grip their wrist and they pull me forward, into the crowd. A few of the girls are wearing shirts with my smiling face on them, which will never be anything other than super bizarre, especially because I look awkward in the photo they used. Clearly, Chorus Management wasn't expecting this crowd, otherwise we would've gone out a different way.

Actually, no. They must know. They want this, they want it to be all over the news here, and for fans to post this to their social media. They want buzz.

"Sign this for me, Zach!"

"Jon, I love you!"

"Oh my god, I'm touching Ruben!"

I glance up for a second to see a phone in selfie-mode inches from my face. I smile, and try my best to make it seem genuine, even though I hate this with every fiber of my being. I try to get it. Chorus may be using them, but they're innocent, and probably camped out for hours to see us. The least I can do is smile for a picture. They take a few photos, and two other phones are waved in front of me, both of them in hard plastic Saturday phone cases. I smile for those as well.

I hate thinking it, but I wish they'd just come and see us at our show.

With Keegan, a six-and-a-half-foot-tall hulk of a man, leading the way, we go toward the exit as fast as we can, shoving through the mass of people. Someone reaches out and touches me on the shoulder, then runs their hand across my bare neck. A chill goes down my spine as they shriek with joy and a bodyguard steps across, protecting my back. Paparazzi swarm around us, and I hear the familiar rapid clicking of their cameras, accompanied by blinding flashes, and their shouts to get us to look at them.

Just smile. Look here, Zach!

I squeeze the wrist I'm holding tighter.

I should've expected this.

It'll be over soon. It always is.

We make it outside, where a minibus is waiting for us, surrounded by security guards. The crowd is so thick now that taking even a single step is difficult. In this two-minute walk I must've posed for at least thirty photos, and my ears are ringing from the sheer volume of the screaming.

"Zach, this way!"

"I'm going to cry."

"I love him."

I glance up, and see Ruben through the swarm of people. He's seemingly unruffled, his handsome face basically expressionless. He notices me watching, and mouths *You good?*, concern etched across his features.

I give him a thumbs-up, finally smiling. Ruben normally only asks me something like that when my mask slips. I'm grateful; who knows what sort of stories will pop up if someone catches a photo of me looking anything other than freaking giddy at how I'm being treated.

Zach Knight isn't allowed normal human emotions when people are watching. No one in Saturday is.

I climb into the minibus, following after Jon. Luckily none of the fans try to get into the vehicle. That's as terrifying as it sounds, and I'd know: a girl jumped onto my lap once trying to get to Jon and she had to be pulled off by Pauline. She's our other head guard alongside Keegan—the long blond hair she always wears in braids makes her easy to pick out in a crowd, which is useful, given she's way shorter than any of us. She's probably the buffest of all of us, with a stocky build that served her well in her previous life as a competitive shot-putter.

I raise a hand and wave at the crowd, thanking the fans for giving me this space at least, and then the door slides across and slams shut, quieting them to a dull roar. Erin gets into the passenger seat casually, like nothing is happening outside.

I stare out the opposite window, before starting the deep-breathing exercises my child psychologist taught me.

"You okay, boys?" Angel asks from the back seat.

I shudder at the memory of a clammy palm touching my neck. Who were they? And who does that?

I take out my phone and type a message to Mom.

Hey, I just landed. :)

I hit send, then slide down my seat and rest my head against the rain-speckled glass. I can't get the crowd out of my head, and there's still a piercing, high-pitched hum in my ears. I wish I could shake this off quicker, because I'm in freaking London. The shine of airports may have worn off, but visiting a new country is still incredible. I want to see the bridge and the tower and hear someone say "cheerio!" or something else to reinforce the fact that I'm thousands of miles from home.

If I told myself when I was an angsty fourteen-year-old that in a few years I'd be in London for a show, I would've lost my shit. Before Saturday, I'd barely even left Portland. Mom tried her best, and she gave me a great childhood, but we didn't exactly have international-vacation money. I think it was harder on her than it was on me, because I didn't know any different. But she and Dad used to travel overseas a lot before he was laid off and had to take a much lower-paying job, which he always says was the start of the end of things between them. Mom let slip once that she thinks it has more to do with what he was really doing every time he said he was hanging out with his work friends.

The sounds of Erin going over the trip details fade to

background noise as I look out the windows at the passing city. It's weird how ancient the buildings can appear, only to be housing a Starbucks or a Pret A Manger—whatever that is. Apparently it's popular, because I count around a dozen of them. As we near the hotel I catch a glimpse of Big Ben and the London Eye, both standing out against the cloudy gray sky. For just a moment I really wish I could visit as a tourist. I want to explore the city, going wherever catches my eye, without having to think about anyone else or if I'm safe.

I don't even need to ask to know that's not in the cards. We've all been messaged our schedule, and it's packed full of photo shoots, press junkets, and rehearsals.

There's no time to see anything.

Before I know it I'm onstage, in the middle of an almost empty, weirdly silent O2 arena.

For the first time in a while, it's hitting me just how massive this is. I'm exhausted, but this is undeniably cool, and I muster up enough energy to feel real excitement. We've played at bigger stadiums back home, but the fact that this many people want to see us even overseas is totally surreal. Soon, all those empty seats, even the ones so far away they're barely visible, will be filled by people who paid to see us.

And we're going to give them the best show of their lives. Or, we're going to try.

Workers have built a long, glossy walkway that goes out into the audience. Every single time, it shocks me how quickly an entire custom stage can be assembled. It only takes them a day or two to create a huge spectacle. Behind us, our band name is already set up in towering letters. There's also a be-dazzled white piano on a crane that we'll climb onto to lift us out over the crowd for a slower, remixed version of "Last

Summer" and our cover of "Can't Help Falling in Love." Ruben will play while the rest of us stand or sit on it, our legs dangling in the air. The first time, it was terrifying, but I got used to it. Fans love it, too, which is the main thing.

I spin around, taking it all in. We're here to check out the stage and approve it, before our official rehearsal tomorrow afternoon before the show. That means tomorrow, I'll be here, singing in front of twenty thousand people. I can picture it now. The crowd. The flashing lights, stretching on and on.

We've been told by an employee of the stadium that the screens that have been set up are cutting-edge, and the same goes for the rest of the tech involved. Our voices should be crystal clear even to people in the very back rows. Plus, unlike on our US tour, everyone in attendance will be given a bracelet that automatically changes color for each song. It's going to go neon blue for "Repeat," to match the music video, gold for "Unrequitedly Yours," and then red for "Guilty." I appreciate the attention to detail. Even with crowds this big, or maybe even especially so, their energy really impacts my performance. I just feel as if I sing better if I'm sure they're having a good time, and every little thing that makes a show fun for them helps.

"All right, boys," says Erin. "What do you think?"

"I love it," says Angel. "Can we go now?"

"Almost. I just want all of you to be on your best behavior until after the show. That means no drinking, and yes, I'm looking at you, Angel."

I wonder if she even knows how far past drinking he's gone.

Angel puts his hand on his chest. "I'll behave. I wouldn't want Sherlock Holmes to arrest me."

"That's not what he does," says Jon.

"You'd know, nerd."

"Enough! I know it's exciting that you can drink legally here, but it's one of the worst things you can do for your voices. I beg you, please, *please* remember why you're here, and be on your best behavior."

Angel nods, but I doubt he is actually going to. I don't even think I am. Who would?

"Another thing," she says. "The paparazzi here are probably even worse than they are at home. So, if you have something you don't want the entire world knowing, I encourage you to be discreet."

Everyone goes really still as she looks at Ruben.

That sure as hell sounded like she just told him to not do anything gay while we're here. Which is bullshit, because I know Angel already has "networking" time set up with a bunch of models in almost every city. I doubt Chorus would want everyone to know about that, and yet he's not being dressed down.

"That all?" asks Angel. "No drinking, and no flamboyant homosexuality?"

"You're a riot. But yes, that's all. Thanks, boys."

Angel turns and leaves, and Jon and Erin follow after him, chatting about something. Ruben walks forward, and then sits on the edge of the stage. I sit down beside him. This stadium really is enormous, and it's hard to wrap my head around how big it is. I should be used to it by now, but I'm just . . . not.

"So, that sucked," I say, fiddling with my leather bracelet.

"What did?"

"What Erin said."

His shoulders slump. "Oh. Yeah."

"I'm sorry."

He nods. "Sometimes I'm tempted to come out onstage one day, if only to see the look on her face."

He's smiling at the thought, but it terrifies me. Geoff has made it *very* clear that we're not allowed to say anything on-stage, or ever, really, that hasn't been approved by him and his team at Chorus Management. He created this band, not us, and he has all the power. His advice hasn't steered us in the wrong direction so far, but he has made it *very* clear how important it is for us to control our narrative. Losing that ends careers.

Ruben stands up, grinning. The others have left the stage now, so it's just us here, in this huge space. I can't even see any security guards nearby.

"What are you doing?" I ask.

He brings his hands to his mouth, and shouts: "Thank you so much, London."

His voice echoes around the empty stadium.

I stand up, and go up to him. He's still grinning like he's up to something, even though I have no idea what it is.

"You've been a great audience, our best so far, right, boys?"

I glance around. I can't see anyone else nearby, but that doesn't mean there isn't someone just backstage who can hear us.

Or who might be recording.

"But hey, while I've got everyone here, I've got something I want to get off my chest. I'm sure you've all noticed that I've never had a girlfriend. Well, *in fact*, the thing *is* . . ."

"Shh!" I say, and I press my hand over his mouth. I did it instinctively, and now I'm right beside him, with my hand on his lips. And they're really soft.

I'm staring him down, and he's not flinching—actually, his dark eyes are level with mine, like he's in total control. Like it's not even a question that he's in charge, even with my hand over his mouth. Like me trying to tell him what to do is simply amusing.

I drop my hand. "Sorry. But didn't you hear what Erin *just* said?"

"Calm down, Zachary. I wouldn't actually do it. I'm not stupid."

I don't believe him, though.

That sounded way too rehearsed.

Our bus pulls to a stop in front of the Corinthia hotel, and we all follow Erin out of the light drizzle into a beautiful golden lobby. Erin goes up to the desk and the rest of us hang back. A table in the middle of the room holds several glass vases. I absentmindedly touch the closest one, running my fingertips across the petals.

I'm trying to figure out what Ruben means by what he said. He's clearly thought about coming out onstage, and he knows exactly what he'd say if he were to do it. In the past, Ruben has said he's okay staying closeted in public, as he was waiting for the right time. But there was something sort of annoyed in his voice earlier, like he wants to, but can't.

Ruben catches me looking at him, and his eyebrow arches. My attention is drawn to his lips. It's clearly been way too long since I've kissed someone, since now all I'm thinking about is the feeling of them against my palm. They were so soft. I should figure out which lip balm he uses. I want mine to feel like that when I finally *do* meet a girl again.

"What?" he asks.

"Nothing."

We follow Erin to an elevator, and we ride it up almost

to the top. Once the doors stop, we go outside, into a long, golden hallway.

"Zach, this is you," says Erin, as she unlocks a door with a key card.

"Why is he first?" asks Angel.

I think everyone is too tired to respond. Even his jab sounded half-hearted.

"Night," I say, waving to everyone.

They wave at me as I go into my room, and I close the door behind me, then latch it closed. The room is stunning, with a huge window showing a panoramic view of the London skyline. Even though I'm exhausted, I go over to the window and look out. It really is so pretty. I can see the bridge, the river, and the London Eye, all lit up. This is all I'm going to see of this city, so I need to make it count.

I touch my lips, and wonder if they're as soft as his, then I push the thought away.

My suitcase is already in my room, so I retrieve a change of clothes. Even though I'm the kind of tired you only feel after missing a whole night's sleep, it's only seven p.m., so I should try to stay up for a few hours, so my body can adjust.

I undress and go into the bathroom. I turn the shower on almost as hot as it goes. It pelts down. I step in, and tilt my head back, to let it run over my face. What a day. Most of the time, a shower wakes me up, but right now . . . nothing. I guess there's only so much hot water can do.

Is there a song in that . . . you're hot like water?

No, that's nothing. I'm delirious.

It must be why I'm so fixated on Ruben's lips. I'm delirious, that's all.

I turn off the water, and grab a towel, only to find out it's been warmed up by a heated towel rack. Heaven.

Finally feeling clean, I go out, put on some boxers, and jump into the bed and get under the covers, enjoying the silky feeling of the sheets against my skin. I turn the TV on, and the first channel I come to is playing a rerun of *Saturday Night Live*. Perfect. On the bedside table is a soft gold folder with the room service menu. I flip through it. It's weird; I'm hungry, but the thought of eating something substantial makes me feel a little sick.

I grab the phone and order a chicken soup and a black forest hot chocolate, because I can't not try something like that if it's an option.

I hang up and feel my eyes starting to close.

No.

Come on, Zach, you can do this. Think of the hot chocolate.

Maybe I can just close my eyes for a few minutes, though. That won't hurt. When the food gets here, the sound of knocking on the door will wake me up, and I'll have recovered enough energy to make it to a more reasonable time to sleep.

It's fine.

This is a smart plan.

I tilt my head to the side, and close my eyes.

The next thing I know, I'm wide awake, and it's three a.m. The lights and TV are still on, my blinds are still wide open, and my mouth tastes vile.

I must've been so out of it they gave up on delivering the food. I get out of bed, and go over to the window. This place must have some seriously amazing heating, since the city outside looks rainy and miserable, but I feel toasty. I watch a droplet streak down the window, then pull the blinds shut, then turn the TV and lights off. I'm not that tired, but I can at least try to sleep. I'll pay for it later if I don't.

My phone lights up from where I left it on my bedside table. I flop down onto my bed and check it.

It's a Snapchat message from Ruben.

RUBEN
Can you sleep?

I turn on my front camera, and take a selfie. I know I'm shirtless, but Ruben doesn't see me like *that*. After his experiences, he's the last person who'd let himself go and get feelings for a guy he already knows is straight.

My heart starts thudding at the idea of him seeing me differently, though. Like as just a guy, not his friend. What would he think of me if he didn't know me, and know I'm straight? Would he think I'm hot, then? And why am I even thinking this?

After editing the photo, I caption it: haha nope. I just woke up.

I send it.

Ruben sees it, and starts typing. Then the bubble disappears. I've noticed Ruben does this a lot. It's like he never trusts his first thought.

A picture comes in. It's of Ruben in bed, with his eyes crossed and his nose scrunched up.

Another chime.

RUBEN
OH HI YOU'RE UP.

ME
I am!

RUBEN
That means now is a perfect time . . .

I find myself grinning.

ME
A perfect time for what?

RUBEN
For you to tell me what you thought of In
This House. IN DETAIL, Zach.

I laugh. So maybe he isn't blown away by seeing me shirt-less, but this? I like this.

ME
I already told you I loved it?

I hit send, then let my head fall back against my pillow while I wait for a response. I open Instagram and scroll for a second, then I navigate back to Ruben's messages. There's no typing bubble yet.

I bring his photo back up. He's shirtless, but I can only see the top of his bare shoulders, and they're making my stomach twist. A face flashes into my mind. Lee, from mid-dle school, with the dimple. I used to pull up his profile picture, a photo of him staring intensely at the camera, and study it, searching for the spot where the dimple would be if he smiled. I'd mostly forgotten this feeling, but now, it's so familiar. Like, scarily familiar.

I exit Ruben's photo.

My heart's thudding just a little too fast.

Lee and his dimple didn't mean anything. Neither does Ruben, at least not like that. Looking at a photo doesn't *mean* anything. It's okay to like looking at a photo of someone you care about. Why do I always have to overthink stuff? Plus, I'm tired, it makes sense that my emotions are off-kilter.

I get a notification, which gives me a jolt, so I go back to my messages.

RUBEN

In what world is 'loved it' detailed? What did the songs make you feel? Which were your favorites? What did you think?? GIVE ME SOMETHING.

I smile to myself and start composing my reply. I know I'm supposed to be sleeping, but sleep can wait.

If I'm a little tired tomorrow, is it the end of the world?

FIVE

RUBEN

I'm in Paris, the most beautiful city I've ever seen in my life, and all I can focus on is how hungry I am.

We left London at the crack of dawn this morning after shoveling down some toast from the continental buffet, and hopped across to Paris. By the time the signage switched from English to French, I was already dreaming of coffee, and baguettes, and delicate pastries.

Unfortunately, it wasn't meant to be. There was no nipping into a café, and not one sightseeing stop to soak in the fact that we're in Paris. *Paris!* The only taste we've had of the city on foot was when we were unloaded into an admittedly pretty one-way street full of neutral, balcony-covered buildings. There, we were ushered into one—distinguishable from the others only by the sleek black revolving doors at its entrance—where we participated in an interview, followed by a front-page photo shoot.

It's already past lunchtime, and we haven't had a thing to eat since this morning's toast. We're in the minibus—separate from the tour buses and more conducive to inner-city travel—with Erin, Penny (who has to fix our hair every time a camera is in the same room as us), and our guards for the day. The company Chorus contracts, Tungsten Security, has multiple international branches. Keegan and Pauline, our primary bodyguards, traveled with us from the US, so one could be with us at all times, directing whichever guards Tungsten assigns to us in any given country. It gives us the consistency of continually working with guards who know us, while also letting us reap the benefits of security personnel who know the city, its dangers, and its escape routes, inside and out. Today, we're riding with Keegan and three French Tungsten guards, as Pauline is taking the night shift all week.

We're heading to the Eiffel Tower. Not for our personal enjoyment, but so we can pose for a promotional photo to post on the band's Instagram. I'm pressed against the window at the back of the bus, staring out at what will be our few snatches of Parisian sightseeing on this stop.

Angel unbuckles and peeks back at us over the head of his seat. "So," he whispers, "I'm gonna have a few people around my room later tonight."

"A few people?" Zach and I echo in unison.

"Mm-hmm. Kellin's in town, and he wants to bring Ella and Ted to hang."

He means Kellin White, Ella Plummet, and Ted Mason, three of the biggest singers in the UK. Ella and Ted are also notoriously messy, and both have been the center of more than one scandal in the last year. The British tabloids love them, because they're such good fodder. *Ella in royal-wedding brawl with Nadia Ayoub. Ted Mason arrested for cocaine possession. Ella and Ted: are the dating rumors true?*

"The tabloids would *love* that," I say dryly.

"I can be friends with whoever I want," Angel says. "That's not proof *I'm* doing anything wrong."

"Then why are you whispering?" I ask, and Zach smirks, his knee bumping against mine as we go over a pothole.

"Ruben, just . . ." Angel circles a hand in midair. "Just be cool, okay?"

Suddenly, Zach climbs onto his knees with his phone brandished. "Hold on, let me get a picture of this," he says. He places a firm hand on my thigh to steady himself as he takes a picture of the scenery, because he wants me to spontaneously combust, apparently. I do my best to think about anything except for the pressure and weight of him. In the end, all I can do is stare out the window and try to distract myself.

We're driving through a residential area that consists of dozens and dozens of creamy apartment buildings. It's the windows that grab my attention first, stretching tall with ancient panes and wrought-iron balconies, all adorned with rows and rows of flowers. There are flowerbeds in every window, and even more flowers hanging under every streetlamp in sight. I focus on counting the flowerbeds because Zach's still on me, and the warmth of his skin is seeping through my jeans, and—*five, six, seven, eight, nine*—

"Boys, I have a piece of good news!" Erin stands and shakily makes her way down the aisle to us.

Zach climbs off of me to sit back down in his own seat, and I don't know whether to feel relief or despair. "First, though, here. The wonderful ladies at the magazine gave us a welcome to Paris treat," she says, grabbing handfuls of plastic-wrapped candies from a black cardboard box. "These are salted butter caramels from Maison Le Roux. Hopefully these'll tide you over till lunch."

Thank god, *food*. We each shove a caramel square into our mouths, and I have to force myself to slow down and savor it instead of swallowing it whole. It's not like any caramel I've had in my life, a perfect balance of sweet with a hint of salt and a thick, gooey texture that coats my mouth in a melted layer that feels almost like cream.

"Okay, yep," Jon says thickly, unwrapping another one. "I like Paris."

Zach tips his head against his seat and closes his eyes, a tiny, funny smile on his face. Seeing him look like that makes my chest tighten.

I have just enough time to wonder if Erin's buttering us up with sweets when she makes her announcement. "The results from *Opulent Condition*'s Top Fifty Sexiest Men are in, and Ruben and Jon, you're both on the list!"

My first reaction is, honestly, to be sort of pleased. I can't help it. Positive feedback is my bread and butter, and you can't beat being told you're crowd-voted beautiful for positive feedback. It takes me longer than I'd like to admit to realize that if only Jon and I are on it, Zach and Angel aren't.

"How did *he* get on it and I didn't?" Angel asks in a huff, gesturing to Jon.

"That's not nice," Zach says. "Jon's sexy."

"Jon's repressed," Angel snaps. "Pretty isn't the same as sexy. Jon blushes anytime a girl looks at him."

Jon blinks rapidly, eyebrows sky-high. "Tell me how you really feel next time."

"You can't tell me this shit isn't rigged," Angel scowls.

"Of course it's rigged," Jon snaps, before turning to Erin. "They don't come up with this on their own. Dad submitted us, right?"

Erin doesn't deny it, and I suddenly realize I was stupid to think I'd been voted in by adoring fans. Of course Chorus picked who went on the list. I've understood the importance of maintaining our roles as romantic fantasies at all costs since the very beginning; Geoff made it very clear when I first told him that my hope was to come out publicly at sixteen. *Think of this like one of your musicals, Ruben. You're playing a part in a show. Those who want the part need to prove they're the best person for the role.* His point was that there would always be understudies. He didn't spell it out, but he didn't have to.

"You *got* on the list, Jon. Why aren't you happy?" Erin asks.

Jon scrunches the caramel wrapper in his fist, but won't look Erin in the eye. "Wouldn't you be weirded out if your dad submitted shirtless photos of you to a magazine?"

"I'm yet to take shirtless photos," Erin says. I think she means it as a weak joke, but no one laughs. She sighs. "That's what you get when your dad's your manager, I guess. Try to see the bright side. It's positive publicity."

"At least you're in it," Angel says. There's an edge to his voice.

Zach, who hates confrontation more than anything in the world, wilts beside me.

"It's not your brand, Angel," Erin says in exasperation. "But I get that you're disappointed."

"I'm not disappointed," he snaps. "I'm pissed off."

"Come on. Don't shoot the messenger."

"I'm fucking ripped, and I'm ten times the dancer Ruben is, and I've hooked up with more girls than Jon's mustered the courage to say hi to, but Chorus just happened to coincidentally decide that *I'm* the sweet virgin."

"Okay," Erin says, her smile looking strained now. "Noted. I thought the group of you might be happy about this exceptional promotional opportunity that will elevate the band as a whole. As always, I'm more than happy to pass on your feedback to Geoff."

Jon's suddenly interested in looking at the ground, and even Angel shakes his head noncommittally. The only thing complaining to Geoff does is get you stripped down. Nothing changes. Not even if it's his own son complaining.

"If it helps," Keegan calls from the front of the bus. "I didn't get on the list, either."

Zach clears his throat. "Congratulations," he says weakly, smiling at me, then Jon.

"See, that's the team-player attitude I was looking for," Erin chirps.

Jon glowers at her, then seems to give up. "So, who's excited to climb the Eiffel Tower?" he asks in a strained voice.

"Oh, we won't have time to go to the top," Erin says. "Just a photo, then we have to get you all to another interview at M6 Music."

From the looks on everyone's faces, no one's particularly surprised to hear it.

When Erin makes her way back to the front, Angel folds his arms. "You *know* they didn't submit me because they think an Asian guy can't be sexy," he mutters. "Fucking unbelievable."

Jon's smile is acidic. "Dad thinks he can't be racist because he married a Black woman. He's never gotten it, man. Doubt he ever will."

Angel gives a snort of disgust and turns his attention to his phone. Jon watches him, looking lost in thought, then, finally, slumps back in his seat and squeezes his eyes shut.

Zach glances at me, and his expression is as dark as I'm sure mine is.

Zach's shirtless in my hotel room, which is both amazing and a travesty on multiple levels.

Essentially, I'm doing my very best not to stare. And it's, uh, hard.

He knocked on my hotel room about five minutes ago, asking to borrow something of mine to wear to Angel's because he's already sick of his own, Chorus-curated, shirt selection. And now I have to look anywhere but at him to avoid making shit weird—shockingly, it's much easier to ignore a half-naked guy in a bustling room than in a one-on-one situation.

I settle for staring down at my phone with my back to him. I silently count to ten to give him enough time to get my shirt on, but when I look up he's still freaking shirtless, standing in front of the mirror and picking at his hair. A small strip of his briefs is visible above the snug waistband of his skinny jeans, and his skin is smooth and pale from lack of sun.

The thing about Zach is, he's quite beautiful. I've always thought that, even when it was a purely platonic opinion. He's slight but tall, not quite lanky, with the sort of thick brown hair that makes you ache to run your fingers through it, just to find out if it's as soft as it looks. Deep dimples, long lashes framing serious hazel eyes, a fine-boned oval face, arms that dip and curve with well-defined muscles. If today's list had been based on looks instead of propaganda, he would've been on it, hands down. Higher than me, too.

A shuffling noise tells me he's finally putting the shirt on. "Have you looked outside?" he asks. "There's so many of them."

I haven't, actually. There was already a pretty decent group of fans congregating outside the hotel when we arrived back from tonight's concert, though. I open the window and stick my head out, and a roar rises like a tidal wave as they spot me. It's a swarm. A writhing crowd of heads and hands, dozens of people deep, mostly teen girls. They scream at me. For me.

I'm the only thing that exists to them right now, even if sometimes my mouth looks weird, or my vibrato wavers, or I forget to smile for the press. It doesn't matter to them. It's unconditional.

I never knew "unconditional" before Saturday.

I wave down at them, and Zach squeezes in beside me, and the screams somehow get even louder. Deafening. *At least it'll drown out any noise that comes from Angel's room,* I think idly.

I throw my arm around Zach's shoulders, and he grabs my dangling hand to hold me there. *"Bonne fin de soirée!"* I shout, although I doubt anyone can hear me. Zach pulls me inside with a bear hug, laughing, and the crowd is muted again as he closes the window.

When we get to Angel's room, there are already about fifteen people inside. Jon's nowhere to be seen yet, even though we texted him when Zach got to my room.

The main lights are off, with only the lamps and the bathroom still lit. The music's at a reasonable volume—for now—and most people are chilling on the bed, chairs, or simply on the floor, their faces cast in shadows. There's a few people I recognize: Ella, Kellin, and Ted, of course, along with Daniel Crafers and Brianna Smith, both actors in their early twenties. I've interacted with both of them on Instagram a few times.

"Hey, you two," Ella says as we approach her on the floor, rolling forward to pour some vodka into plastic cups. "Welcome to *République française.*"

"Oh, do you live here, now?" I accept a cup.

"No, my love, we're here for the four of you."

I raise my drink in cheers. "Maybe we should be welcoming *you* to France, then?"

Angel appears from thin air, swaying on his feet. "Ruben, are you being sassy to the guests?"

"Yes, he is." Ella pouts, twirling a strand of dark brown hair around her finger.

Angel points at Zach and me. "Chug. It'll make you nicer."

"Speaking of the four of us," Zach says, instead of drinking. "Where's Jon?"

Angel pulls a face. "Hopefully staying away in protest."

"All the wonderful flavors out there, and you choose salty," Ella laughs. Someone turns the music up, and the vibe of the room changes. It's less chill catch-up, more nightclub. The bass vibrates through the floor and up through my fingertips, pulsing in my blood.

"I'm not salty," Angel says, plopping hard onto the floor between Brianna and me. He has to half-shout to be heard. "If I were, it'd involve Ruben, and I don't have a thing against my little Ruby, bless his heart."

"You'll always be the sexiest man on earth to me," Ella says to Angel, and Angel looks not-so-subtly pleased. She pours an extra few shots in his glass, as a "congratulations for being sexy" prize, I guess.

"I mean, we're right here," Zach jokes to me, but I have a feeling there's truth hovering beneath his lighthearted tone.

"Yeah, you're breaking our hearts, Ella," I join in.

Ella laughs, tinkling and light. "From what I hear, I'm the last person who'd have a shot at breaking your heart, Ruben," she says. "You might have more luck with Levi over there." She nods over to an unfamiliar blond guy standing by the bathroom door with Ted. "Shall I introduce you?"

I can't say I'm surprised she knows. Once someone's out to their team, their sexuality tends to be a bit of an open secret in the music industry, but the unspoken agreement is that what insiders know stays on the inside. The amount of money that gets spent per year on bribes and lawsuits shutting down front-page outings is eye-watering. It keeps the media in line, more or less. At least, as far as photographic proof goes. And any other celebrity will swear up and down that you're straight if they're asked about you—not least because they generally have plenty of dirty secrets of their own. But it's more than that. It's a community thing. A morality thing. An us-versus-them thing.

Too bad I don't actually *want* it to be a secret.

"Let's see where the night goes," I say, and she scrunches her nose at me cheekily.

Zach shoots a sharp, sideways look my way. He's historically been funny about me seeing guys. Zach's kind of a less-wired version of Jon when it comes to following the rules; he doesn't want drama, and he worries that I'll get with the wrong person and they'll go to the media or something and cause a scandal. Essentially, he doesn't trust me to be discreet. I prefer to think of it as flattering that he's protective over me, rather than irritating that he doesn't trust my judgement.

That, and it's hard to be annoyed at him when I've never told him that I even *want* to be out, not in so many words. As far as he's concerned, he's on my side, protecting *my* secret, not Chorus's.

"Who's going to break Zach's heart, then?" Angel asks, tapping on the bottom of Zach's cup. *Drink*. Zach obeys.

"Honestly?" Ella says. "Pick of the bunch. Who would you like to break your heart, Zach? I'm sure no one here would turn down the challenge."

The colors in the room seem to lose their vibrancy, all of a sudden. I hop up. "I'm gonna go check on Jon," I say.

"I'll come with you." Zach half rises, but Ella pulls him back down, giggling again. "I'm sure he can make the trip alone," she says.

I weave in and out of the people crowding the room—a few more have poured in since we got here—and almost run into a group coming through the door. Many more and they won't be able to squeeze in.

Just as I'm about to leave, the door opens and Jon enters. "The hotel's gonna say something to Erin," he says as he sees me. "It's *way* too loud in here."

"Probably. But what did you expect?"

Jon sighs and makes a beeline for Angel, and I tail him. Zach's by the window, talking to a girl with flowing black curls. Her legs are crossed at the ankles, and her head's tipped so far to one side her neck must be aching. She seems captivated by him. And so she should be. It'd be wonderful if she'd go get captivated by someone else, though. Literally, anyone else.

Ella waves to get my attention. She's with the blond guy she mentioned earlier, Levi. I hold a hand up to tell her to hang on, and someone places a drink into it as they pass me.

Sure, why not? I knock it back, then tune into Jon and Angel's conversation.

"We don't want to get a rep, Angel."

"Oh, no, not a rep for being too fun; girls hate that," Angel says, bouncing on the spot. He's obviously taken something. His energy is a touch too frenetic.

"Just a little quieter? Please?"

"You," Angel says, "are not our manager. How about you just have some fun and leave the sorries to me, yeah?" He grabs Jon's hands and moves them back and forth, trying to get Jon to dance. Jon rolls his eyes again, but he's smiling reluctantly.

Just as I finish my drink, someone taps me on the shoulder. It's the blond guy. Levi. "Refill?" he asks me.

I accept it, a smile spreading across my face.

Levi, it turns out, is an Irish model, which explains his ethereally beautiful face. He's also a lot better at handling his alcohol than I am, which I find out when I try to keep pace with him and quickly lose the ability to stand steady. He steers me to a free spot on the bed, and we sit while he tells me about a time he almost got arrested with Ella and Kellin. As we talk, we lean against each other more and more, and he starts brushing the side of my thigh with his thumb. Everything feels warm, and slow, and soft. Like those caramels.

The party's steadily growing louder as people knock back more shots and, I assume, whatever stash Angel took from is passed around. One group is loudly filming a video for Instagram while they play a drinking game that apparently involves banging on an end table and screaming every time someone speaks. Not far from them, a couple of guys and a girl have lost their shirts and are running around trying to procure an extra shirt for the girl. Someone else is playing trap music through their phone speaker, and it's clashing with the music on Angel's speakers so badly I can barely hear myself think.

I check on Zach a couple of times, and he hasn't left the girl with the curls. I guess he's chosen her to break his heart tonight.

And I guess I've chosen Levi.

"So, how long are you in Paris for?" Levi asks.

"Today and tomorrow. We leave the next morning."

"Ah." He pouts. "And you're staying here?"

"Yeah, my room's just down the hall."

"Oh, you all have your own rooms. Cool." He pretends to say it casually, but his hand presses more firmly against my leg, and something flutters in my stomach. My throat feels thick, leaving me a little breathless.

Someone grabs my arm, and I glance up to find a very concerned-looking Zach. "Can I get your help for a minute?" he asks.

I excuse myself from Levi, and Zach brings me to his heartbreak girl. Except she's sitting slumped against the wall, her head now so far to one side it's resting on her shoulder.

"Jesus, what'd you do to her?"

"Nothing! I think she's just drunk."

An unfamiliar girl appears with a bottle of water to hand to the girl. She takes it and clasps it between both hands. Zach crouches down. "Is she okay?" he asks.

"Yes, this happens sometimes," the new girl says in a French accent. "I'll call an Uber."

"How far is the drive?"

"Maybe thirty minutes?"

"That's a long trip. She doesn't look so good."

"We don't have anywhere else to stay."

"I feel sick," Heartbreak Girl moans. "Let me sleep on the floor, Manon. Please?"

Zach hesitates, then looks at me hopefully. It takes me a moment to realize what he wants through the haze of alcohol.

"If you wanna give her your bed . . ." I say with a shrug.

"You wouldn't mind? If I crashed with you?"

Well, Levi might mind. But Levi will just have to get over it.

Working in tandem, the three of us help the heartbreak girl to her feet and steer her into Zach's room. He hurriedly shoves his stuff into his suitcase, and I work with the girl's friend, Manon, to get her safely into Zach's bed. Manon thanks us on repeat, between composing typo-ridden tweets about how Zach Knight needs to be stanned until the end times. Then Zach and I drag his bags into my room, and I collapse onto my bed, officially too dizzy to stand anymore.

"Sorry to interrupt your, um, thing," Zach says in a weird voice. He hovers by his suitcases and hugs his arms to his chest.

I groan and throw an arm over my eyes to block out the ceiling light. "It's fine. What are friends for but to cock-block?"

"Crap. I'm sorry."

"I'm *kidding*. Kind of." I peek at him and grin. "I can't be mad at you when you're just being, like, the most decent guy. That'd make me shitty, wouldn't it?"

"You could never be shitty."

"I could, if I put my mind to it."

The mattress bounces. He must have sat on the bed. "You wanna head back over?"

"Mm-hmm. We could. But the bed is *really* nice, and the room's moving *way* too much suddenly."

"Tell me about it. Those kids can *drink*."

"Right? Levi had about half a bottle of vodka and he wasn't even slurring."

I send Jon a text to let him know we've ditched. No point texting Angel, he wouldn't see it until morning.

"Levi," Zach repeats. His voice is all weird again.

"Yeah, the guy I—"

"Yeah, no, I got that.'

I haul myself upright and yank my jeans off. "He's a model," I say.

Zach, who's started undressing, too, pauses with his shirt half over his head. "Of *course* he is. Wonder if he got on that list."

Oh, the list. I'd forgotten about it. "Fuck the stupid list, Zach," I say, crawling under the covers.

Zach flicks the ceiling light off, and a rustling of fabric tells me he's taking his jeans off. I fiercely regret him turning the light off. "Do I . . . can I just . . . ?" his disembodied voice asks in the darkness.

"Yeah, get in," I say. I want to add, "Where did you think you were gonna sleep?" but I somehow rein the sass in.

He gingerly crawls under the covers beside me. He's radiating heat.

"Screw Erin, too, and screw Chorus," I add.

Zach groans. "I don't care. I don't even . . . care."

"Good. Because they don't know anything, and they're stupid."

A shuffling on the bed tells me he's rolled onto his side, closer to me. "They didn't get it wrong. You're all better looking than me."

I roll over so fast my head lurches. Too fast for a drunk guy, apparently. "That," I say, "is the stupidest shit you've ever said. You're hot."

"Naaahhhhh."

"Yeeeaaahhh, you are. You"—I reach out to poke him, feeling around in the darkness until my fingers collide a little too hard with his chest—"should be on the top of that list."

"No."

"Number one!"

He swats my hand away, and our fingers entangle for a second. "Stop lying."

"I'm not."

He shuffles in place to get comfortable, and it brings him closer to me. "I've seen the guys you think are hot," he says "They don't look anything like me."

My breath catches in my throat. Why, exactly, does he give a shit about which guys I do and don't think are hot? "What?"

"They're all, like, buff or whatever. That's how I know you're lying to make me feel better."

Oh. That makes more sense. For the wildest moment I thought he meant . . . something else.

"Zach," I say, as clearly as I can. "You're beautiful. Like, actually beautiful."

We sit in a long silence, too long to be comfortable, and my skin starts prickling with anxiety. I can't see the expression on his face, but I'm suddenly worried I pushed it too far.

"Get some sleep," I say when he doesn't reply. "We have to be up in five hours." My head's spinning, and I'm already dreading the alarm. Tomorrow's going to *suck*. But it was worth it, I guess, for a night of letting loose for once.

"Right," he says, and he sounds weird, and I'm pretty sure I've made it uncomfortable, but my brain's too foggy to form a plan to return the vibe to normal. My brain's just starting to adjust to my eyes being closed when I get the feeling I'm being watched. "Zach?" I whisper.

"Yeah?" his breath falls on me when he speaks. That didn't happen the last time he spoke. He's moved in even closer. I'm sure of it.

Suddenly it's hard to breathe, because it's clicked. Something's happening right now, and I'd missed it, because I wasn't looking for it. Like an idiot. But something's happening.

He's so close to me that if I shifted just an inch, I'd be touching him. Legs, stomach, chest, lips.

I freeze, because I can't be reading this right. I just can't. And if I move, I'll destroy everything.

Why isn't he backing away? We're too close.

He lets out a heavy breath, and it's shaky. He's shaking. It feels like my whole body clenches at once.

He's *shaking*.

So, I shift in place. As though it's casual, an accident. But of course it can't be, and it's a stupid farce, because the "accident" brings our knees hard together, and our noses almost touching, and I leave it like that.

And he leaves it like that.

My shift was a question, and his unwillingness to pull back is the answer. And I'm still trying to talk myself into believing I'm seeing something that's not there when he breathes out again and presses his lips against mine, and his hands to my chest.

It's a barely there kiss, closed lips and gentle. Like air.

And I don't kiss him back. I let him kiss me, and I let him pull away. I let him sit in a beat of silence, and regret it. I don't pull him into a deeper kiss he doesn't want, can't want.

"I'm sorry," he breathes. There it is. There's the realization. A part of me dies, but another part of me is so, so grateful I didn't let him think I wanted it. "I thought . . ."

"It's fine. You're drunk."

"I'm sorry. I misread that. I'm sorry."

Now I'm confused, scrambling to keep up. "Wait, did you . . . want to?"

It takes so long for him to answer, I wonder if he means to at all. Then, his voice achingly soft, he breathes, "Yeah."

My brain, which is admittedly lagging far behind, tries to put the pieces together, because this is all entirely out of nowhere, and there was no sign, not a single sign, but there must have been a sign. It's all a bit much to process, though, and he's still so close to me, and I can still taste him when I run my tongue over my lips, and he sounds hopeful. *Hopeful,* for god's sake.

So, I cup the back of his neck. His chest is against mine, and I think I can feel his heart pounding. Or maybe it's mine.

When I kiss him, a small sound catches in his throat, and I think I might pass out. I open my mouth and kiss him harder, and I'm breathing in his exhale like it's my oxygen.

Kissing him is a key change colliding with a crescendo.

His leg goes between mine as he props himself up to hover over me, and the heat of it all, the softness of his bare skin, his tongue sliding gently against mine, is too much. I'm disintegrating, melting into the mattress beneath me, and the weight of him on top of me is the only thing anchoring me to the earth. He's pressing his hips down, and he's rock hard, and that makes no sense, because it's Zach, and he's straight, and he can't want me like this, but it's happening anyway, sense or no sense.

"Fuck, Zach," I manage to get out, and he kisses the words from me. My hands are on either side of my head and his are over them, interlacing our fingers, pressing down to hold himself up. I'm pinned into place by it. I want to rise up, to wrap myself around him, but I also want to lie flat beneath him until I die.

I've always wanted Zach to kiss me, I think. But I never thought he would. So, I kept it locked in a chest in the back of my mind. The place I hid things I knew would only hurt me.

I never meant to unlock it.

Hopefully, a voice pipes up in my mind, and I shut it down, suddenly certain the voice has nothing good to say.

Hopefully, the voice insists, louder this time, *he's not just kissing you for his self-esteem. Because you told him he's beautiful, after the world made him feel ugly.*

Something pulls in my gut, and I feel like I might be sick. I slow down the kissing, my head spinning with the new, horrible thought. Zach picks up on the change, and pulls away, panting. "Are you okay?"

No. I genuinely think I'm going to throw up. I try to breathe steadily, to bring the room, and reality, back into focus. The nausea settles, but the terror in the pit of my stomach doesn't.

I want to beg for reassurance, but he's drunk, and confused, and now isn't the time. He probably wouldn't tell me the truth even if he understood the driving force behind his kiss. And that's a big "if." For him, the clarity will come tomorrow, when he's reflecting and regretting.

And we'll be destroyed. And we might never come back from it.

All for a kiss.

Zach rolls off of me, and sits beside me. "Ruben?"

"I think maybe we should just go to sleep."

"I don't . . . I'm sorry," he says.

He sounds hurt. God, he sounds so hurt. But he'll thank me tomorrow, for stopping it before it went further. He's drunk. I'm drunk. When he's sober, he'll understand.

"Don't be sorry. It's fine. Just don't . . . worry."

I roll onto my side so he can't see me, and press a hand against my mouth to keep myself quiet. My lip's trembling, and my jaw is clenched tight against a wave of disappointment and panic.

Fuck.

Fuck.

Fuck.

What have I done?

SIX

ZACH

What have I done?

I'm still in bed with Ruben, as close to the edge of the bed as I can be without falling off. Every second since has stretched on and *on,* even as the sky got light. I haven't slept at all, but I'm forcing myself to stay still, so I don't make things weird.

Weirder than they already are, anyway. Because holy fuck.

I kissed him. Or he kissed me. We kissed each other, I guess.

And I liked it. I was drunk, but not so drunk I can't remember that. It was one of the best kisses of my life. It practically blew my mind, how good it was. But that makes no sense, because he's a guy. I want a *girl*friend. Like, when I think of my future I think of myself with a wife, a house, and a dog. The only thing that's changed about that picture since childhood is how expensive the house would be. That doesn't line up with the kind of guy who kisses another guy and loves every second of it. It just doesn't.

Ruben stirs next to me and I nearly jump out of my skin. I get the impression he's faking being asleep, though, his movements seem a little too deliberate. He settles back down with a soft moan, burying his head in the pillow.

His back is well muscled, and his hair is short and messy. He's so clearly a *dude*. Still, the kiss was hot and sweet and all-consuming, everything I want a kiss to be. I don't think I've wanted anything as much as I wanted to keep kissing him, to never stop kissing him.

It's not the first time I've ever thought of kissing a guy, of course. But those thoughts have only lasted a few seconds. They're anomalies, things I think when I'm tired or drunk or—

Or are they?

I've had fleeting feelings for guys that are something like *tiny* crushes. The sort where you start to notice someone *like that*, and then they force their way into your mind at random moments, and you can't stop your eyes from wandering to them whenever they're near. When they start to become really important, more than a regular friend. Normally it happened with a soccer teammate, and I'll admit my brain did go to mush one time when I was talking to our captain, Eirik, and he pulled up his shirt to wipe his brow mid-conversation.

After times like that I wondered if I could be gay. But I'm not. I'm *not*. I've fallen for girls before, hard. Gay guys have to pretend when they're with a girl, and I've never had to; kissing and sex has always been great. Hannah completely took over my world when I first fell for her. I don't think it's normal for a gay guy to have romantic feelings for a girl, nor for them to get their heart broken by one.

Obviously I know there are more options than gay or straight, too, but none of the other things have ever felt like they matched me, either. My crushes on girls have been a steady, recurring presence throughout my life, and the idea that it would happen again once I got over Hannah was extremely comforting. Like, I could tell myself it's fine, because I knew I would like someone again eventually, when I was ready. The crushes I got on guys were weird blips, things that would catch me by surprise and cause me confusion, and maybe a little panic, until I forced them out of my mind. Then I'd get a crush on a girl and she'd be all I could think about, and I'd get all swoony and happy and mostly forget about ever micro-crushing on a dude. That I even *could* crush on a guy, even if it was a small crush. I'm sure it's common to get such minuscule crushes on other people. It doesn't mean I'm queer. If I felt the way about guys that I felt about girls I'd know it.

But then, last night had felt a lot like kissing girls.

If he was a girl, I'd have known I'd found the next person I'm into. But it's Ruben. My very male best friend and bandmate.

So, essentially, what the fuck?

I sit up in bed, hoping he'll stop faking being asleep. He doesn't react, so I clear my throat.

Ruben opens his eyes, and smiles automatically when he sees me. But then his face shifts, his smile fading. I'm hit with a pulse of ice. The familiar old panic of *what does this mean* plays through my mind. I feel like I'm naked onstage.

"Hi," he whispers. His voice is uncertain.

"Hi." I can barely force the words out.

We fall into silence. I study Ruben. He's gorgeous, sure. But is it gorgeous in an "I want to consensually pin you down" sort of way, or an "I want to *be* you" sort of way? Every other time I noticed how handsome Ruben is, I thought that was just appreciation, or aspiration. Now there's no missing that there's at least some desire there. Probably because I know what it's like to kiss him.

Something flickers across his face, and he sits up a little. There's an uncomfortable-as-hell conversation coming up and there's nothing I can do to avoid it. Other than, like, sprinting out of the room, which does sound pretty appealing.

"How's your head?" I ask.

He hesitates, scanning my face. "Not as bad as on the flight over here."

"Yeah. Same. Although, mine's pretty bad today. I was *wasted* last night."

I want to be a million miles away so I don't need to navigate this fucking conversation. So I don't have to see him looking at me like he's gotten his hopes up and now I'm hurting him. Like I've led him on.

Holy fuck, I have. After all that shit with Christopher last year, using Ruben to figure himself out. And, what, it's been a *week* since that straight guy at Angel's party hit on him? Not to mention countless other encounters that have caused Ruben to shut down against the world, bit by bit. All the crappy dudes using and undervaluing him that pissed me off so much.

Now I'm one of them.

What the fuck is wrong with me? Even if I did want him last night, why did I *act on it*?

"I assume you remember last night?" Ruben asks, and there's maybe a sliver of hope left. "Not *that* wasted, I hope?"

"Yeah, I remember," I say. My face is flaming hot, and I know he can see it. "That was, um . . ." I clear my throat. "Kinda shitty."

"Kinda shitty?" he repeats flatly.

"Yeah. I mean, like, I shouldn't have kissed you. I was so drunk I wasn't thinking straight." *A+ choice of words there.*

Ruben opens his mouth, then shuts it. I think he has no idea how this is happening. And like, same.

Help. How the fuck do I save this without digging myself a bigger hole? Like *that's* even possible now.

"Okay," I say. I go to put my hand on his leg, because normally I would, but instead I close my fist and tap it against the mattress. "I just, I'm really in my head right now, and I'm panicking, because you're my best friend and I know you've been hurt by guys using you before, I *know* that, and the last thing I want is to be that. So if there's anything I can do to fix this, please let me know, I am *all* ears. Please."

"There's nothing to fix," he says finally. "I mean. It happens."

"I've never done anything like this before."

"Well, okay. Maybe making out with your straight friend while drunk doesn't happen all the time. But it did happen. So, maybe we just . . . pretend it didn't?"

That sounds like a bad idea, but will also buy me some time. Whatever came over me last night might never happen again. This way, we can put it in the past, at least until it's not so fresh. Categorize it under "dumb shit we did on tour." Move on. It's like a mini-crush. I probably won't think of this once I like a girl.

My eyes meet his, and I'm about to agree, when I notice something. The morning sun has changed the color of his eyes to a sort of amber. Suddenly, all I want to do is kiss him again. I want to wrap my arms around him and to have him smile at me and to just lose myself with him.

Which means . . .

What exactly?

It means I need a fucking second. I don't want to shut this down, but I don't want to open it up. I want to breathe, and have some space, and try to sort through my thoughts without Ruben *staring at me* like the world will end if I don't say the exact right thing. I need to figure this the fuck out, and then talk to him.

"Actually," I say carefully. "Don't freak out. But can we talk about this later? I don't want to pretend it never happened, but I don't think I'm ready to talk about it."

He blinks slowly. "Like . . . when?"

"I just need a few days?"

"A few days to . . . what?"

Great question, Ruben. *Excellent* question. "I don't know, okay. I really don't. I just could use some space. Please don't freak out, I just need some time."

"I'm not freaking out."

His voice is too sharp, so yep, he is.

This is bad. The way he's looking at me right now is full of hurt. A part of me wants to say I'm into him, just so he'll feel better.

I can't lie, though, and saying anything before I've figured this out risks lying.

I feel sick.

I'm going to throw up, I'm going to—

I'm going to hurt him.

I can't hurt him. I also can't lead him on. I can't say what I know he wants me to say, just to make him feel better. That's not fair on me, and it's not fair on him. It's better to just take some time, figure my shit out, and then talk to him once I know for sure what is going on, and what I want.

"I'm sorry," I say. "But I really need some space to process this."

"Don't be sorry, I get it."

"No, but I am. You know I really care about you, right? And the last thing I want to do is hurt you."

Ruben's eyes flare. "You know, we've got to go to breakfast

soon." His voice is hard, and I *know* he's hurt. But I will hurt him even more if I tell him I like guys and that turns out to be untrue.

"Totally." I shoot out of bed and search for my shirt. How the fuck did it get over by the *window*? "I want to have a shower first. I'll let you get ready, and I'll see you down there."

"Won't those girls still be in your room?" he asks, as he pulls his blankets around himself.

Crap. The girls. That's a wrinkle, sure, but my mind is screaming at me to get out of here before I say another thing wrong and make this even more of a mess.

"I'll use Jon's shower," I say.

"You can use the one here."

"No, no, I'm okay. Thanks."

"Zach."

"I'll see you at breakfast."

I all but launch myself out of the door. I close it, and rest my forehead against it for a moment, taking in a heavy breath.

What.

The. Fuck.

Have I gotten myself into?

I was hoping once I was out of the room I'd feel some sort of relief. No such luck, though, out here I still feel like complete and utter crap. The hurt in Ruben's eyes is killing me. I know Ruben, and if I saw he was hurt, it's only because I blindsided him. Normally he doesn't show pain. He brushes it off or says something snarky. Almost nothing gets to him.

But this did.

I walk back to my room, and rap my knuckles on the door.

The door opens, revealing one of the girls from last night. I think her name was Manon? Her hair's a mess, her mascara is smudged, and she's still in her purple cocktail dress. She has pale skin, and truly is extraordinarily pretty. I imagine kissing her, and I don't hate the idea. What the fuck, brain?

"Zach," she says. "Do you want your room back? Lily is still asleep, but I should be able to get her up, if you need?"

I wave a hand. "It's fine, I'll go for a walk, I was just checking if you're still using it. Take all the time you need."

"If you're sure?"

"Totally."

"Thanks, Zach, you're a lifesaver."

I go down the hall, and into the elevator.

My phone is sitting heavy in my pants pocket, so I pull it out and check it. Ruben is the last person I messaged, and seeing his name makes my heart rate spike. All I can picture now is his wounded expression. It fills my vision, taking over everything, making my stomach sink.

I'm a bad person.

I focus on my phone. I have an email, an itinerary for the day from Erin. Almost every minute of our day before the show is accounted for. In four hours I have an online chat room with fans, then another photo shoot, and then we're meeting the winners of a radio contest. So I have a full day ahead. All with Ruben.

I'm not sure how I can see him again.

But I guess I'm going to find out.

In the lobby, I see Pauline, playing on her Switch. I bet it's Animal Crossing; she's obsessed.

"Hey, Zach," she says. "What's up?"

"Oh, nothing, I was just wondering if I could go for a walk? I'm craving a croissant. Like, a real one."

She pauses her game. "Mind if I tag along? We'll have to go out the back exit to avoid the fans, but as long as we're quick it should be okay."

This is why I love Pauline: obviously I'd never be allowed to walk out into the streets without security. But Pauline never tells me what to do, and she always asks.

"Sounds good."

"Great, let's go. Just don't tell Chorus, okay?"

I zip my lips closed.

"Who does the best British accent?" asks Angel, reading one of the messages on the side of the screen.

We're on video in a chat room with five hundred fans, the ones who got in based on a random lottery. Their questions are all sent via text, and are screened before we see them. This chat room was Angel's idea, and Chorus loved it. I actually really like it; it's one of the most pure, unfiltered moments we get to have with fans all over the world.

Now, I'm just waiting for it to end.

Earlier, I had to talk to Ruben to get my stuff from his room, after last night. I was really careful, texting him that I wanted to pick up my stuff rather than just knocking on his door—I thought it would be really unfair of me to show up unannounced, after I asked for a few days of space. I timed it well, so I couldn't really stick around, because we both had to get ready for this. Now I can't stop dwelling on the fact that I had to do all this work just to interact with Ruben, my best friend, for five seconds. It was a little awkward, but he mostly seemed like his usual self, and didn't press me or anything.

"Not me," says Jon, trying his best at an English accent and horrifically failing.

"What is that?" asks Angel. "I think you're going more for 'fancy a tea, poppet?'"

I can't bring myself to join in. I mean, I'm never usually

the loudest in these anyway (Angel obviously is), but right now I'm only speaking when directly asked to.

"I think I can do one," says Ruben, before clearing his throat. "'The rain in Spain stays mainly in the plains.'"

It's actually pretty perfect. Figures. Of course he'd have a musical reference perfected and ready to go. I try to keep my eyes away from him. He's acting like he's already recovered from what happened last night, as he doesn't seem any different than normal. Right now he's smiling and looking directly into the camera, same as always.

Or maybe he has fully recovered. Maybe I think this is a bigger deal than it is. That does sound like me. It's my first guy kiss, but it's not his. Maybe this truly is a non-event to him. Maybe the hurt I thought I saw was all in my head. I do overthink things.

"So, clearly, it's Ruben," says Angel. "Unless you want to give it a go, Zach?"

"Nope."

"Fair enough." Angel reads the screen. "Oh, this one is juicy: how do you all feel about the sexiest men list?"

The question has been put in bold, which means the Chorus assistant who runs these has flagged it as a question we have to answer. I'm not sure Angel would've read it otherwise. I wish this list could die in a fire. It has whipped our fans up into a frenzy, with each of our fandoms fighting each other over it, which is exactly what Chorus wanted.

"Sexiness is subjective," says Jon. "Beauty really is in the eye of the beholder."

"Says someone who made the list," says Angel. "It's rigged! Clearly rigged. Any fair list would *objectively* put me at the very top because I'm, *objectively*, perfect, don't you agree, boys? Come on, Jon, you know you think I'm hot."

"Oh, naturally," says Ruben. "In fact, why put others on

the list at all? They should keep the title the same, put in a full-page photo of you, and call it a day."

"Exactly. Although, nah, I'll let the three of you on my list, too. You're sexy, too, Ruben. In a subjective sort of way."

I scratch my arm and fidget in my seat.

"Thoughts on the list, Zach?" asks Angel.

"Oh, um, yeah. It's probably rigged."

"Hold up," says Angel, clearly enjoying himself. "So you're saying you don't think Ruben and Jon are sexier than us? I thought we'd just established Ruben's subjectively sexy!"

"I mean, I can't really see it, but sure."

Angel lifts his eyebrows up.

"Yikes. Okay, sore spot, clearly. Anyway, let's go to the next question."

Ruben is watching me like he doesn't even know me. But cameras are on us and we're live.

I look away.

SEVEN

RUBEN

The thing about your dreams coming true is that, for a gold-spun moment, you catch a glimpse of what life could be like. Then when you lose it, and you crash back to reality, it's from such a great height, all you can do is lie there, winded and bruised, while you come to terms with the idea that a happiness like that isn't meant for you.

It never was.

I don't know how to adjust to this new world. Last week, Zach was my best friend. The one I locked eyes with whenever I laughed. The one whose side I gravitated to wherever we went. The one who always sought me out to check on me whenever I felt unbalanced.

In this new reality, Zach can barely even look at me. He puts as much space between us as he can, and he barely seems to notice that I'm dying with every century-long second.

I feel frozen in place. Equal parts of me scream that I need to back off and give Zach the space to process and move past it before we cause irreversible damage, but also that I need to beg Zach to notice me, and talk this through with me, and *see* what this is doing to me. I can't do both, but it feels as though if I pick the wrong approach, I could lose him forever.

A desperate, terrified twisting in the pit of my stomach warns that maybe I already have.

Right now, we're rolling through the darkened streets of Madrid post-concert, on our way to try some authentic tapas. It wasn't on our schedule, but Pauline, along with the Spanish guards, convinced Erin it was a low risk—and much needed—downtime detour. We're in *Spain*, the place my parents were born. I should be ecstatic to be here, surrounded by the culture that formed such a big part of my upbringing, and standing on the same ground my ancestors once trod. Instead, I can barely process the sights and sounds over my racing, fearful thoughts and the aching misery clamping down on my chest.

I'm wasting my chance to appreciate the country I've been tied to by blood, and I can't seem to snap myself out of it.

Zach's two rows ahead of me, chatting with Angel like it's the most normal thing in the world. Like he does that all the time. Like he hasn't sat in the back with me every trip we've ever taken, from Saturday's conception through to that night in Paris.

Jon's my seat buddy instead, and he's not trying to make conversation. My face is probably so cloudy it's scared him off. But I do appreciate that he climbed in beside me. I'm sure he knows something's up, but he doesn't press. Just gives his company.

The bus pulls to a stop and Erin lets us pile out. I'm surprised by how cool it is here in March. When I listened to the stories my abuela used to tell me when she was still alive about her life in Spain, I always pictured heat and humidity, an oppressive blanket of warmth. Not temperatures dipping to the low forties, woolen coats, and boots. But here we are.

I've heard people do things a little later in Spain, but if I'm honest I didn't expect it to be this busy at eleven p.m. It's practically bedtime for us, but the city's sprung to life here like six in the evening does back home. The paved, narrow streets are filled with people heading out to eat or drink, and the restaurants and bars we pass are buzzing with people and warm light. Instead of heavy drinking like I'd expect to see this late, though, it's much more casual. More groups of friends sitting at outdoor tables, sipping red wine and picking at tapas, fewer stumbling drunks knocking back beer after beer. The sound from inside the buildings isn't thudding music or raucous laughter and shouts, but the hum of social chatter. In a weird way, it feels familiar. Like, down-to-my-bones familiar. Is it possible to inherit memories through your genes, or am I just overtired? Probably the latter. We've been awake for eighteen hours now.

The smells of garlic, oil, and tomatoes waft through the air as we enter a dimly lit restaurant. It's crowded, and usually an extra group filing in past tables wouldn't attract attention. But Pauline standing by the table with one of the Spanish Tungsten guards while the other guards station themselves closer to the entrance apparently gives us away. If that doesn't, the growing crowd of fans gathering outside to gawk and scream at us through the windows sure does. It feels like every eye in the restaurant is fixed in our direction right now.

I move to slide into the seat at the back at the same moment as Zach. We both halt, and I give him an awkward smile. "You go," I say.

He nods, and I realize too late it places me right next to him at the table. Despite myself, my stomach flips. Pathetic, to be exhilarated by the thought of my elbow bumping against his right now, but here I am.

He grabs his menu to study it the second I sit down. *I'm*

way too engrossed to talk to you is the obvious message. But I try anyway. Despite his weirdness over the past few days, a hopeful part of me is still kidding myself that he'll soften if I keep trying. "I'll make sure no one orders any fish," I try. Zach's never been able to stand the stuff. The first night I met him at camp we had fish fingers for dinner and he dry retched so hard I gave him my fries out of pity so he wouldn't go hungry.

His eyes flicker up. "Thanks," he says. For a breathless moment I think he's going to smile, or say something else. But he just goes back to his menu. When I look at mine, I'm struck to see familiar dish after familiar dish. The kind of food that I ate all the time growing up but have never seen on a restaurant menu before. There's a sense of belonging in this. A shared experience with a country of strangers, whom I could've lived among in another life. An alternate timeline, when my grandparents never immigrated to the United States.

I look back up from the menu. "I can't make any promises about shrimp, though. It's in about every third—" I trail off as Zach gives me a tight smile. "Yup, okay, cool," I murmur.

"Ruben, what should we order?" Jon asks as he sits on my other side.

"No idea. I don't know what you feel like eating."

"That's okay. If it comes with a Spaniard's recommendation, I trust it."

From the way his eyes are sparkling, I can tell it's a joke. Chorus Management jumped on the fact that my parents are from Spain as soon as they found out, convincing our songwriters to include a Spanish bridge for me to sing in our first single, "Guilty." The problem being that I barely speak a word of Spanish. Mom and Dad spent *weeks* teaching me to pronounce the words correctly, and I still picture Mom's look of despair at my pronunciation every time I perform it live. Tonight was particularly embarrassing, performing it in, you know, *literal fucking Spain*. The crowd loved it, though. Even if I do have a feeling they loved it the way people love watching dogs trying to walk on their hind legs.

I shake my head. "I probably haven't ever eaten, like, ninety percent of the menu. Home cooking isn't the same as restaurants." I glance at the menu, then, grudgingly, add, "But if you want some suggestions, I'd go for the croquetas, the patatas bravas, and the gambas al ajillo."

"You're sexy when you speak Spanish," Angel says, and I know what's coming. "Don't you think so, *Zach*?"

Angel thinks Zach's jagged comment about my appearance the other day is the height of comedy. In fairness, he doesn't know the full context—as far as he's concerned, Zach's comment was just a straight guy being insecure in his straightness, a concept that Angel obviously can't personally relate to. So, because he's Angel, the only reasonable response is to take every possible opportunity to make Zach squirm like that again.

From the pained look on Zach's face, it's obviously still working.

It's made matters worse that the clip of Zach essentially calling me hideous has been making its rounds on the Internet under the hashtag #ICantReallySeeIt. *Everyone* has a hot take—Zach's right, and I *am* hideous, and he should say it; Zach's obviously better looking than me and he should've been on the list in my place; I'm obviously way better looking than Zach, and Zach's got a jealousy issue; the whole band is full of eyeliner-wearing pretty boys and anyone who thinks *any* of us belong on a sexiest men list needs their vision checked, stat. And on and on and on.

I could kill Angel right now.

I try to catch Zach's eye to silently . . . apologize? Laugh about Angel's brashness? I don't even know. It doesn't matter, anyway, because he acts like he doesn't notice.

Erin orders on our behalf instead of me, much to Angel's disappointment, then takes a photo for social media—the real reason we're here, whether Erin admits it or not. While she sends it to David so he and the rest of the publicity team can upload it with *just* the right caption, Angel turns to his phone and raises his eyebrows.

"Apparently, we all hate each other," he announces, waving around his phone like it's irrefutable proof.

"Could've fooled me," Pauline says, clearly eavesdropping from her nearby post. Erin beams at her.

"Now what?" I ask. Zach's eyes flicker toward me, but he doesn't say anything. He looks miserable. As much as his words hurt, and I want him to regret them, I still get the urge to grasp his hand under the table and assure him it's fine, and this will blow over in a day or two.

"Apparently the 'sexiest men' article tore us apart from the inside." Angel passes the phone to me, and I scroll through the story, published three hours ago in a popular celebrity gossip blog.

. . . A source close to the band confirms. "The Months by Years tour has placed a strain on the boys' relationships. The mood has definitely gotten colder, especially since the *Opulent Condition*'s Sexiest Men list was released. Some of the boys have started to resent the attention given to certain members." While our source declined to confirm which band members are feuding, an argument during a recent livestream might shed some light. On

Thursday afternoon, in a private livestream session for select fans, Zach Knight took pointed digs at fellow band member, Ruben Montez. Following a comment by Angel Phan on Ruben's placement on *Opulent Condition*'s list being well-deserved, Knight responded, "I can't really see it." Fans were quick to notice tension between the two. Another source, who declined to be named, doesn't seem surprised. "There's always been issues between Zach and Ruben," they said. "In front of the cameras they're on their best behavior, but behind the scenes it's a clash of personalities. Constant fighting, vicious words—it's even gotten physical a few times. They've also been assigned different dressing rooms so they can be separated and the rest of the staff can catch a break." Trouble in paradise? Who would've thought this group of "close friends" secretly disliked each other so much? Their fans must be devastated by this news.

I roll my eyes and pass the phone to Jon. Zach reads over his shoulder.

"'Constant fighting,'" I say. "Who might this 'source' be, exactly?"

"Fakeperson McDoesn't Exist," Angel supplies.

"It's incredible how much stock people think we put in the opinions of *Opulent Condition* readers," Jon says. "Like we're all hanging around with bated breath waiting for their validation."

"Easy for you to say, Number Twenty-Two," Angel shoots back.

"It's just an article," Erin says. "It's better to avoid that stuff. It's just gonna get you down. You know the media."

"True," Zach says. "They'll make something out of nothing if they can."

Nothing, huh? So attacking my appearance publicly was just no big deal? Whatever, move on? I flare up with a sudden anger, all thoughts of comforting him vanishing.

"They're really taking the 'I can't see it' thing and running with it," Jon says, ignoring her. "Must be a slow news week."

"Yeah," I say, pouring myself a glass of water. "It's a total shock that Zach wasn't able to make a shitty comment about me on a public platform without repercussions."

Zach reels back. I can't tell if he's guilty or offended. Like *he* has a right to be offended. "I already said I was sorry," he says.

"Did you?" I snap. "I must have missed it."

"Boys, boys," Angel says, laying his palms on the table. "You're both pretty."

That just pisses me off more. "It's not about that. It's about being respectful."

"I'm sure Zach's sorry he didn't show your sexiness the level of respect it so deserves." Angel laughs.

It's impossible. There's no point. Without the full context, I'm only gonna look like I'm overreacting to a bruised ego. And it's not like I can explain that those words would've been nothing if they'd come out of *anyone* else's lips, but from Zach's, they were a slap in the face. A reminder to not read into the other night, because he could *never* find me attractive.

He's straight. He was just drunk.

My glare must be harder than usual, because Angel's laughter actually fades. "Come on, Ruby," he says. "You know Zach puts his foot in it sometimes. It's why we love him. He didn't mean it to come out like that, did you, Zachy?"

Zach shakes his head vigorously. "Not really."

Not *really.*

Well, excuse me if I'm not instantly appeased by this convincing display of remorse.

What in the *fuck* is his problem? What right does he have to be angry at *me*? If anyone should be pissed off right now, shouldn't it be me? I'm the one who got my heart broken. I'm the one who got humiliated by him in public. I'm the one who's been iced out for days now.

And why *is* he icing me out? Have I somehow offended him? Did I say something? Do something? Could he tell the kiss meant more to me than it did to him, and is annoyed I turned a drunken experiment into something that needed an explanation?

Or am I somehow a bad enough kisser to destroy an entire friendship?

It's become more and more obvious we need to sit down and hash this out properly, whether Zach wants to or not.

The problem is, if I can't even get him to make small talk, how am I going to convince him to discuss *that night*?

And what will happen to us if I can't?

A local radio station in Rome ran a backstage pass competition a while back, so tonight we're all hanging back to meet some fans, sign stuff, and take photos. Usually this is one of my favorite parts of the job—we get whisked aside by Penny for a quick refresh and liner reapplication, then it's basically an hour of being gushed over, and meeting the people whose lives you've touched, and being able to drop your walls just a little because no one's recording what you're saying—the dozens of contract guards make sure of that.

Tonight, it's dampened early when a girl of about fourteen, with thick black hair and large brown eyes, asks me in accented but fluent English, "Is it true you and Zach don't like each other, Ruben?"

I pause midway through signing her tour poster and look up, alarm flashing across my face before I can arrange my features into calm reassurance. Zach's only a couple of feet away, talking to another fan, and both of them have stopped to listen in.

"Absolutely not," I say with as much firmness as I can muster. "These guys are my best friends. We were friends before we even formed the band. I love all of them."

Relief breaks across her features. "Oh, we're so glad to hear that," she says, turning to Zach's fan. Apparently, they're friends, too. "We love all of you, so much. The media makes up lies, eh?"

"Yup," I say, but she's not looking at me. She's looking at Zach, like she's waiting for him to jump in and validate what I'm saying. Instead, he gives an awkward smile, and goes back to signing his own poster, under the pretense of not overhearing. For god's sake, he's *got* to know how obvious that looked. The girls exchange a concerned glance, and I go into damage-control mode.

"Why don't the four of us take a selfie?" I suggest, and the girls nod enthusiastically.

Zach's face is unreadable as I go over to him. "I could take the photo of the three of you?" he asks, and I could strangle him.

"Your hair's *fine*," I tease, as though the reason he doesn't want a photo is vanity based. He stiffens as I stand beside him—I'm not even *touching* him—and shuffles to put an obvious gap between us while he smiles, his head tilted away from me. It makes the gap look even bigger in the picture.

"I have a question," Zach's fan asks before they leave. "About . . . Anjon? Is it . . . yes?"

"Huh?" I ask. I've understood their accents fine up until this point, but I have no idea what she just said.

"Anjon?" she repeats.

I blink. "What's the question?"

"That was the question. Anjon? Yes?"

I glance at Zach, who's distracted by something across the room. Of course. "Uh, sure?" I say, to be polite. "I guess?"

The girls break into shrieks and head over to get in the line to meet Jon and Angel, and I whisper to Zach while keeping a smile on my face. "I think we need to talk."

"Okay, if you want." He's not doing a very good job of acting pleasant.

"Meet me in my room when we're back? To talk," I clarify quickly as Zach stiffens again.

"Sounds good."

"Okay. Can we call a truce until then? You're acting really obvious."

"*I'm* acting obvious? You're the one who's forcing me to take photos with you so you can prove a point."

"I'm not trying to *prove a point,* I'm trying to prove we're *okay,*" I whisper, even though maybe it's a bit of both.

"Not all of us spent years in theater, Ruben. I'm not a good liar. Plus, if you actually wanted it to look less obvious, you'd keep your distance so we don't have to pretend."

"I'm sorry, I didn't realize it was so difficult for you to act like you liked me."

"Can you stop reading into *everything* I say? I don't mean it like that, I just mean it's weird, and you know it." He sighs. "I'm *trying,* Ruben, okay? If I'd known it was going to mess things up this badly I would've never—"

He stops, apparently remembering we're in a public place. And I bleed, and I bleed, and I bleed.

It's Christopher all over again. But infinitely worse.

My voice is venomous. "Yeah, well, it's weird for me, too, but forgive me if my heart isn't breaking for you the *one time* you have to act one way in public when you feel another way, because that's every day for me. If I can do it, you can. So *please*—"

People are staring at us. I shove my smile back on.

"Just be cool for the next thirty minutes."

"I'll be fine if you just leave me alone."

Oh my *god*. "Whatever, Zach."

We split up and head to opposite sides of the room. I can feel eyes on me, and I scan the room quickly, to find Erin watching me with her lips pressed together in a hard line.

If I don't get this under control *now*, we're going to be in a world of trouble with Geoff any minute now.

And who knows what'll happen then.

I, personally, don't want to find out.

Even though Zach still doesn't sit with me on the bus back to the hotel, I'm feeling hopeful for the first time in days. Just the fact that he's open to talking means our friendship isn't a write-off, right? I spend the trip in the back row with my legs drawn up to my chest, running through different scenarios in my head.

Zach says he hates me now, but is open to working together to keep the peace (not my favorite).

Zach says he could never hate me, and he's *so* sorry for his hurtful words, he just felt embarrassed and awkward about what we did. (This one seems most likely of the bunch, and I've decided I'll accept it and apologize in return if this happens. I just need to hear an acknowledgment that the comment about my looks was unwarranted. That's all.)

Zach says he's madly in love with me, and has been weird because he didn't know how to confess it (not going to happen, but still nice to envision).

Zach says he has no feelings for me, but proposes a friends-with-benefits agreement. (I mean, he *was* super into the kiss at the time. My reactions to this fantasy range from "hell no" to "oh, well, maybe" at random.)

Jon sticks his head over the back of his seat to smile down at me. "You okay?" he asks, his voice low.

"Yeah. Just tired."

"I know what you mean. It feels like we're working way harder here even though we have the same routine as we did at home, right?"

"Jet lag?" I suggest.

"Maybe. Or maybe we just need a break."

"We just *had* a break," I remind him.

"Hmm." He raises his eyebrows. "True. But, also, most people have breaks as often as *weekly*, you know."

"I don't believe it."

"I swear on my life. I knew someone once who got a break *every Saturday and Sunday*."

"Not possible. How did they stay productive?"

"They said their worth as a person wasn't tied to their professional output."

"Weird."

"*So* weird."

I try to catch Zach's eye as we pile off the bus and into the hotel, but he's definitely avoiding me. Still, I stay hopeful, even with my stomach plummeting, all the way to my room. As soon as I close the door, I whip out my phone and text Zach.

Ready when you are.

My heart starts pounding like I just sprinted up a flight of stairs, and I grip the sheets beneath my fist as three dots appear.

I'm so sorry, but I'm actually really
beat. Can we raincheck? Sorry.
Almost asleep already.

I stare at the message, crestfallen.

Almost asleep already. Twenty seconds after he went into his room.

Uh-huh.

I let my hand fall into my lap limply and I stare at the stark cream wall with blurring eyes.

It's not okay. As much as I desperately hoped it would be, it's not. And I don't know how to fix it.

Maybe I can't fix it.

I slowly roll onto my side and curl into a ball, hugging my knees into my chest and touching my forehead to them. I feel like this is the sort of moment where I should cry. But I've never been allowed to cry. My whole life, I was taught that crying is a waste of time. *Don't cry. Fix it. Sort it out. Stop feeling sorry for yourself.*

But I can't. And it feels like something inside of me is being sliced in half, and it wants to pour out, but it has nowhere to go. Instead, it presses against the inside of my chest, choking me, until I feel like I can't get enough air in. So, I bury my head in even tighter, trying to hide in the darkness. Like if I block everything out for long enough, it'll reset itself.

To think that only days ago I'd held Zach between my hands, and breathed in his scent, and tasted him, and for a moment I'd let myself believe that maybe miracles happened.

EIGHT

ZACH

I'm guilty of loving you.

That's the first line of the "Guilty" chorus, and it's stuck in my head now, so wherever I go, I hear that. It makes me think of Ruben, and the day we recorded it. We had the most fun ever in the studio that day, back when it felt like we shouldn't be there, and someone had surely made a mistake letting us in. Ruben had given me some really good pointers, teaching me vocal warm-ups and breathing exercises. There's no way I'd sound as good as I do on that song if he hadn't. Plus, I can hear how much fun I was having that day in my voice, which, again, is thanks to him. It was our first single, and it hit number one, so who knows where we'd be now if he hadn't helped me.

He's always been the best guy. Focused, sure, but also so kind and gracious and fun to be around. He wants to be a superstar, but he's never pushed anyone else down to get there, not in the way a lot of others do. He does the opposite, actually. Mom has always said that's why Saturday is so successful, because we're an actual team, and we're all genuinely close friends.

Right now, I'm being a bad friend. Not just bad. The *worst*.

I wanted to talk to him when he messaged, I really did, but as I was getting ready my anxiety skyrocketed, and I just knew I couldn't go, because I don't have an answer yet, and he'd expect one.

I'm not sure it's all my fault, though. I asked for space to think, and I haven't been given any. Instead, every second of every day, I've felt Ruben staring at me, like I'm supposed to tell him the split-second I figure my shit out, and our entire friendship hinges on my answer. The guilt is suffocating, the pressure enormous. I know he's hurt and I made it worse, but he hasn't exactly given me what I asked for, and the end result is I still don't know what I want.

Every time I start leaning toward the thought that *maybe* I kind of like him, that *maybe* the kiss was real, it gets confusing, because what if I only *want* to think I like him because it means I can say what he wants to hear? So I can be someone other than a shit guy who mistreated him? So I don't have to risk losing him forever?

And then I swing the other way and decide to tell him I used him to experiment, figured out it meant nothing, and genuinely apologize, but *that* doesn't feel right, either. Because even if my thoughts are a mess, I know that there's no way *that* kiss meant nothing.

And that would mean I'm what? Bi?

The word makes me feel queasy. Like, it's too close for comfort, breathing down my neck.

I bump into Angel, pulling me back to reality.

"Watch where you're going, Zach Attack."

I groan. I made the mistake of telling Angel one time that every single soccer coach I've ever had has called me that, which I despised, and now he loves to use it. I do what I did with my soccer coaches: try to ignore it.

Luckily, there are a lot of distractions. At the moment the four of us are on a guided tour of the Vatican, with Erin, Keegan, and some Tungsten guards. We got here at four a.m., to be a part of an early-bird tour, to make sure it's quiet enough that we don't get swarmed by fans. They've still found out we're here and are crowding outside, hoping to see us. Without the guards, they would've stormed the place. It'd be just like the airport. They'd fight their way to me, screaming and pushing until they get to touch me. I shiver.

Up ahead, walking slowly, is Ruben. I wonder what he's thinking about. I doubt it's me. There's no way his thoughts are as consumed by me as mine are by him.

I know we should talk to try to close this rift. But the thought of doing that makes my head spin. In a lot of ways, as much as avoiding him has been torture, it's also felt safe, because thinking about this stuff is one thing. Having to say it? That's terrifying.

Jon is walking next to me. His arms are crossed and he has an uncharacteristic slouch going on. Without any makeup, I can see the darkness under his eyes. Angel is on his phone, and even Keegan and Pauline barely seem to care about where we are. We're walking down the gallery of maps, and even though I have a lot of opinions on the impact that religion has had on the world, I have to admit, this place is impressive. Every inch of it is covered in art. It has to be one of the most incredible places I've ever seen.

It's all so pretty, but it doesn't matter. Not compared to Ruben. Maybe now is a good time to tell him what I'm working through. Maybe it shouldn't be planned. Maybe I should just tell him my thoughts are messy and I'm confused and that's just where I'm at right now. It'll be better than nothing.

He's in front of me, staring up at a map. I can't make any more excuses. It's time. Now or never.

I stop beside him. I feel frozen, and my throat clenches up. "Hey."

"Hello."

There's a dry sound in his voice, and an eyebrow twitches. I probably deserve that.

I'm worried he can see right through me, that he knows I'm here to talk about the kiss, and he's not happy about it, so I swerve away from my plan.

"This is cool, right?" I say, pointing at the map.

"Oh, yeah. Very cool."

Make it normal. Make it normal. "I like art."

Oh for fuck's sake. I glance around, looking for a window I can hurl myself headfirst out of.

"O . . . kay?"

"I just mean I like *this* art. It's like, cool art, you know? I don't like some paintings. Like Picasso or whatever."

"You don't like Picasso?"

"I mean, no, they're all squiggly and weird. But this art . . . it's good art. I like it." I seriously want to die.

"Do you?" His voice is light and airy. A little too innocent. "Some of these are *very* phallic. Didn't think you were into that."

My cheeks *burn* like I've been thrust inside an oven. "Um, yeah, phallic art isn't really my thing. But anyway. Um."

"You okay, Zach?"

"I don't even know anymore."

Ruben smooths down the front of his coat, then turns away, picking up his pace to catch up with Jon.

I stand back, and watch him go, unable to move. He used to be the guy I was closest to, and now he can't stand me. It's my fault, too. If I just knew what I wanted, then I could fix this.

We go inside the Sistine Chapel, and it's amazing, sure.

But I can't even really appreciate it, because everything with Ruben is wrong. I wish I could take the kiss back. Why did I have to go and mess everything up like this? Why couldn't I have just shut it down? I've done it before. It would've been as easy as deleting his picture, as crushing a thought I don't like.

I slow my step, as a spark of realization pricks in the back of my mind.

Shut it down. Crush the thought.

Is the truth that I don't get strong crushes on guys the way I get on girls? Or is the truth that whenever those crushes start to poke their heads up I squash them, and ignore them?

I think of Lee. I think of Eirik. I think of Ruben, and his photo.

Delete. Delete. Delete.

I put miles between myself and Lee and Eirik after I started noticing them in that way. It seemed like the smartest thing to do. I'd avoid them and brush them off until the feelings passed.

I feel a familiar sense of overwhelming terror. There's an explanation here, and maybe . . . *no, it can't be that. You'd know. You'd* know.

But what if I *do* know?

What if it just scares the crap out of me?

Could I have been repressing myself all this time? What if my whole life I've been avoiding *this,* because if I think about it too much, then I'll have to accept that it's a thing. And it will make everything harder.

Seriously, could I be . . .

"Hey, Zach," says Angel, pointing up at *The Creation of Adam.* I'm so grateful for the distraction I could hug him. I look to where he's pointing. It's sort of surreal to be staring at one of the most famous paintings in the world. Like, I've known about this thing for almost my whole life and now it's here, above me. It's how I felt when I used to see my favorite bands live, before that became almost impossible because of Saturday.

"What?"

"That dude is thicc," whispers Angel.

He's pointing at Adam. I laugh my first genuine laugh in days.

There's more to it than that, though. He only ever makes jokes as dumb as that when he can tell I'm down. We'll never talk about it, but I know he's there for me. Something like this is as close as Angel will ever get to asking if I'm okay.

"What's funny?" asks Ruben, glancing between us. The split-second of attention gives me chills. He's maybe the first guy ever who has properly seen me. The real me, complete with the side that maybe thinks about guys sometimes. And all I want is to not be around him right now. I want to do what I did with Lee and Eirik: pull away until it passes. I've never been this aware, though. So it's different.

Everyone is staring at us now, even the tour guide.

"It's nothing," I say. "Just a dumb joke."

In the past, he would've asked me what the joke was. For all his sophistication Ruben actually has a very crass sense of humor sometimes, and making him laugh at something stupid always made me happier than like, anything.

"Oh," he says. "Right. Whatever."

My heart sinks to new depths as a terrifying thought occurs to me. I've been so focused on trying to find space and figure out what the hell is going on with me, in the face of Ruben trying to push me to talk, that it hadn't occurred to me that he might not be open to talking anymore. He's not acting like he is. Before, he was eager to figure this out, stat.

But what if I've left it too long?

What if I've pushed him too far?

You'd think by now I'd be used to photo shoots.

But nope.

I never know how to pose, and they make me feel super awkward. Plus, given how I've been questioning my whole life lately, and things with Ruben are such a mess, the last thing I want is a camera on me, capturing this forever. I want to be in bed, alone, with a sad playlist and all the chocolate in existence, so I can figure this out. Yet I'm here, having to fake a smile over and over again, all while Ruben is treating me like I'm just a coworker, someone he simply has to be nice to because it's the professional thing to do.

He's getting the finishing touches on his makeup by Penny. I don't have to be queer to notice he looks incredible. He's wearing a deep purple suit jacket that's tailored perfectly to his frame. He looks every part the superstar I've known he'd be since camp. He makes a joke, and Penny laughs. He might never try to make me laugh like that ever again.

I don't want him to look at me, but it's also all I want. It feels like I'll die if he doesn't do something the old Ruben would've done like, right now.

I get the urge to go up to him, to say something, anything. Just so he'll stop acting like he doesn't know so much about me. But I can't. We're working right now, and he'll be even more upset with me if I do anything that messes with that. Or maybe I'm being a coward, so I don't have to say the words that almost give me a panic attack every time I even think them.

I could be bi.

"Zach?"

I snap back to reality. An assistant is in front of me, holding out a jacket.

"Sorry, thanks."

I take it and pull it on. It's made of black leather but is cut like an oversized suit jacket, which makes it kinda punk and cool. My hair has been slicked straight back, and Penny has already done my face, including the trademark Saturday eye makeup. It's a little more subtle for this upcoming album cycle promo, but it's still there.

I glance at Ruben. I was hoping he'd maybe be looking at me; I thought I saw him looking out of the corner of my eye when I was talking to the assistant, but no such luck. He's looking past me, at the set that's been assembled.

Please, look at me, Ruben. Smile at me. Convince me this will work out okay, somehow. Make me believe I haven't ruined everything.

"I'm not wearing that," says Jon, interrupting my thoughts.

He's holding a blue shirt made of a thin, mesh-like material.

"Come on," says Viktor. "You'll look gorgeous!"

"I'll look naked."

"I'll wear it," says Angel, poking his head through an off-white sweater, totally boy-next-door chic. It's sleek and nice, but definitely not sexy. "Let's be real, my grandma would wear this."

Ruben has spun in his makeup chair to watch and is smirking slightly. Likewise, Penny is fully invested, her mouth hanging open. I forgot how much I like that playful smile of Ruben's, and seeing it again, aimed at someone else, rips me apart. Who knows if he'll ever look at me with anything other than cold disdain ever again?

"Boys," says Erin, glancing up from her iPad. "Stick to your assigned outfits, okay?"

"You're asking me to show my body," says Jon. "We've talked about this. I don't feel comfortable."

Viktor frowns. "Don't you want to capitalize off your spot on the list?"

"I don't care about the list."

"It'll help the band, Jon," calls Erin.

"I don't have to use my body to sell music, Erin."

"True," says Erin. "But you'll sell more if you do."

"Well, maybe that sucks, and maybe we should do something to change it."

Erin rubs her forehead and lets out a long, bone-weary sigh. "Can you please choose some other time to be a martyr? I've got so much on my plate right now."

He offers her back the shirt. "Let Angel wear it if he wants."

She sighs again. "Look, if you want to change outfits now, I'm going to have to talk to your dad." She pulls out her phone and unlocks it. "I doubt he'll be happy to be interrupted."

Jon swallows hard, then bows his head. "Fine, I'll wear it. But this is the last time."

Ruben turns, and catches me watching him. He instantly looks away.

"Thank you," says Erin. Jon puts the shirt on. It clings to him, and I can see each ridge of his abs through it. So he had a point. "See, you look great." She turns to me. "Very nice, Zach. You're always so easy, I hope you know I appreciate it."

Once we're all ready, we're shepherded to the front of the set, which is lit by about a dozen lights. The only prop is a pleated brown leather couch, in front of a cream backdrop. We're moved like dolls onto the set by the photographer,

Alecia Mackenzie, who is wearing a flowy back outfit and has a peacock feather in her intentionally messy tumble of brown hair. I keep seeing Ruben rolling his eyes, so I'm lucky none of us are smiling in this photo (as part of our plan to carefully rebrand ourselves as slightly more adult). Not enough to alienate our younger fans, but enough to prevent the people who have liked us our whole career from moving on. Alecia asked us to pose on the couch like we've just gotten to a girl's apartment and we're waiting for her to leave the bathroom after freshening up.

It makes me think of that night. Ruben giving me his playful, confident smile in the seconds before we kissed for the second time. The sense of being overwhelmed by the feeling of his lips against mine. I picture pulling off his shirt, running my hands down his chest, feeling his muscles and the softness of his skin.

"Zach, focus!"

I look down at the photographer, who is glaring at me from around her camera.

"Sorry."

Alecia takes a few more photos.

"Okay," she says, looking at her camera. "Let's change up the order. Ruben, can you come around and stand next to Zach?"

Oh fuck.

He nods, and strides across. We can be professional, but that's all this is. We pose, and the photographer takes more photos.

Suddenly I know, without a doubt, that if I got the chance, I'd kiss him again. I want him to look at me like he did that night, before we realized what we were doing and everything it meant. I want my hands bunched up in his beautiful shirt, and for us both to be breathless, and for me to feel how soft his lips are again. For him to want *me*. For him to know I want him.

So I'm bi.

But is this real?

Or is it just a panicked response to the realization that I might've lost him completely?

Or do I just *want* it to be a response to the realization, because if it's real, that means . . .

Jesus, I'm a mess.

"Hey, Zach," says Erin.

"Yeah?"

"What's going on? You look tense."

I choke on nothing. "Um, er . . ."

"Please don't tell me you're hungover."

"I'm not, I'm just tired."

"Well, get it together, all right? We need to get this done before we head to the meet and greet."

I shake my arms out. "On it."

I try my best to look relaxed and comfortable. Like a guy who hasn't messed things up with his best friend, maybe forever. Like a guy who isn't so confused about his sexuality his head is physically pounding. Like a guy who isn't aware of exactly where his close male friend is in relation to his body. Isn't thinking about how if he moved an inch to the right, they'd be touching.

Alecia smiles. "Got it. Now we need a lighter one. Can you all put your arms around each other?"

I see white.

"Can I?" asks Ruben, his tone casual.

"Sure," I say, shrugging. I'm shocked my voice is still working.

He puts his arm around me, and I can smell the rich, warm, and slightly sweet scent of his cologne. It's amber, patchouli, and vanilla, in just the right amounts, enough to make me want to properly breathe it in. To breathe *him* in.

He moves his arm up, and brings it around my shoulder. The scent is even stronger now, almost overwhelming, taking over my thoughts. His arm is warm and heavy against mine, and my skin is prickling and buzzing under his touch, and I feel like I could spend my life here.

I hold completely still. Frozen.

There's a flash, then the photographer lowers her camera and smiles.

"Got it."

The second I get back to my hotel room, I lock the door behind me and call Mom.

Normally, we set up times for us to talk every few days. We aren't supposed to call for another two days, but I can't wait that long. I don't even know exactly what time it is in the States right now, but I just have to hope that it's okay, and that she'll answer.

Come on, pick up, pick up . . .

The call goes through.

"Hello!" says Mom. I instantly feel lighter than I have all day. "How are you?"

"I'm good, how are you?"

"Yeah, good, what's up?"

"Nothing much, just calling to say hi."

I sit down on the end of my bed. Even though it should be fine, I try to keep my voice down, because I know I'm sharing a wall with Jon right now.

"How was the Sistine Chapel?"

"Really cool. This isn't a bad time, is it?"

"No, I was just getting ready for bed, it's fine. Have you been watching *The Bachelor*? I just got caught up."

"I haven't, I've been too busy. I want to, though."

"You need to work on your priorities."

I laugh, more because I know that she expects it than because I want to. "I know."

"So how is the tour? Fans are saying it's one of your best shows ever."

I rub the back of my neck. "Actually, um, it's been harder than I thought it'd be."

"Oh, in what way?"

"I dunno. I think we're just all really tired. It's nonstop."

"I bet. Your schedule is bananas."

"Yeah. And, um, there's some drama going on with the band, and it's really getting to me."

I tear up just saying it.

"What kind of drama?"

"We're all really tense with each other. Like I keep saying the wrong thing and making people mad."

"Oh. That's awful, I'm sorry."

I force a smile, even though she can't see it. "It is what it is."

"But honestly, Zach, it's surprising that it's taken this long. If you make anyone spend as much time together as you four have there are sure to be disagreements."

"Yeah."

"I'm guessing a lot of the tension is coming from Ruben?"

I freeze. "What makes you say that?"

"Oh! Um. I mean, I saw some talk online, and put two and two together. Is it true?"

"Yep. He won't even look at me."

"That doesn't sound like him."

"I know. I think I might've upset him."

"And now that doesn't sound like you."

"Yeah, but things have been . . . different lately. I might've said something wrong accidentally or something. I don't know."

"Have you tried apologizing?"

"Yeah. He said I haven't done anything wrong. But he's treating me like we're not even friends, and I don't know what he wants from me. Or, I do, but it's not really . . . it's not something I'm sure I can give him."

"Oh, wow. Did he try and hit on you?"

I can tell from her voice she already thinks he did. If I don't cover this up, she's going to figure out what we did. Mom has always been scarily astute; she knew Hannah and I were into each other even when I introduced her as just a friend. This conversation is suddenly a danger zone, and I need to get the fuck out.

"Yeah."

"Okay. Well, if he made a move and you turned him down, then he started giving you the silent treatment, that's on him, not on you."

"But . . ."

"No buts. You don't owe him anything, it's really important to me that you know that."

"I know."

I want to find some way, any way, to fix this conversation. Because now I'm throwing Ruben under the bus when I know he hasn't done anything wrong, and it's making me feel sick. Mom will remember this, and it will forever shape how she feels about Ruben.

"Listen," she says. "I know you, and I know you wouldn't ever say anything to hurt anyone's feelings, and I'm sure you handled turning him down with grace. So if Ruben is being cold to you, it says more about him than it does about you."

"Right."

"Plus, the stress of the tour could be getting to him. People are complicated, it's often more than one thing that's upsetting them."

"Yeah, probably."

"So go easy on yourself, all right? It sounds like you've done nothing wrong. And Ruben will come around. Just make it clear you're there for him, just as a friend."

"I will. Anyway, I'm sorry to vent."

"Don't be. I'm sorry all this is happening. I hope it gets better."

"Me, too. Thanks, Mom. This helped a lot, so thanks."

"Of course! I'm always here for you. And if you ever want to talk more, you can, okay? About anything."

"Yep, I know."

"Okay, cool. Look after yourself, all right?"

"All right. I'll let you go to bed. Night."

"Night. Or, well, morning. Love you."

"Love you, too."

I hang up. The energy leaves my body, and I can't even move. I chew my lip and try to stop the tears from brimming, but I can't help it.

All these lies, and I don't even know why I'm saying them.

I glance around. The room is dark, and still.

I'm totally alone.

NINE

RUBEN

I'm halfway through a workout in our hotel gym in Antwerp when Mom calls me.

In a weird way, I'm almost expecting it when she does. Growing up, working on myself acted almost like a summoning spell for her. She'd just materialize from the shadows in a poof, whatever I was doing, with what she liked to call constructive feedback. Endless, *relentless* constructive feedback.

You're not enunciating, I can't tell what you're saying, it's just "muh muh meh meh muh."

I don't know how you expect to get this move when you can barely even land a box step on the beat. Why are you always in such a rush to get ahead of yourself before you've mastered the basics?

Where's the emotion? You look like you're watching paint dry. I don't care if no one's watching, you need to practice the way you plan to deliver it.

She says I can't take feedback, but I *can*. I take everything our team gives me to heart, and I'm constantly overhearing glowing, whispered exchanges about how well I implement critique. How I *never* need to be told twice. Of course I don't.

I learned early that needing to be told twice came with consequences, and it's not a lesson I'm likely to unlearn now. The thing about Mom is, though, she doesn't judge the finished product, she judges the process. She doesn't seem to believe in "learning."

For example, if you want to increase your upper range—which I worked on just this morning before heading down here to blow off steam—you get there gradually, by pushing your voice past your comfort zone. I'm only following my vocal coach's instructions, and *she's* always assured me that doing it right involves aiming and missing, with cracked notes and flat notes and a ton of other embarrassing sounds, until you're hitting it, consistently and with ease. But growing up, I was shamed for this very process. How could I sound so bad, my mom would ask, when she was paying *so much* on the *best training*? Why wasn't I listening to my teachers? Why wasn't I doing it *right*?

So, I learned to practice increasing my range only when my parents were out and there was no one to hear me mess it up. It helped, doing it in private. At least, at first. It meant I was the only one left who knew just how terrible I could sound. But that meant the only voice that directed cutting jabs at me, cringed when I messed up, and told me I would never get it right the first time, was the voice that lived inside my head.

The only voice I can't ever escape from.

Of course, I know logically Mom isn't calling me from across the Atlantic to tell me I was singing like a starving goat this morning, but my cheeks start burning automatically anyway. Once you've learned shame, it settles into your skin like a tattoo. You can cover it up but you can't scrub off the sense of inadequacy.

The *In This House* album, which I was working out to,

abruptly cuts off as I pick up. "Hey," I say. "You're up late." It's after midnight over there.

When she speaks, I'm hit by the familiar, tangled mess of fondness and fear. The genuine love for my own mother, mixed up with the trepidation of not knowing where this will go. I'm really not in the mood for more conflict at the moment, and I would've ignored the call, but the only thing that irritates Mom more than being spoken back to is being ignored. "Hey, baby. It's good to hear your voice. I went out for dinner with the girls after work and it ran late, so I thought I'd try and catch you before I went to bed."

I don't relax yet. "It's good you called now, actually. We're heading to an interview in about half an hour."

"Oh, having an easy morning, then?" she asks in a bright voice. But I'm fluent in double meanings. Translation: I'm hoping to catch you slacking off so I can lecture you about commitment and wasted opportunities.

"Nope, I'm in the gym. I spent all morning practicing," I say, and walk myself right into another trap.

"Oh, good, are you working on that E in 'Unrequitedly'?"

I start. I've never had an issue with "Unrequitedly." "Oh, um, no." I laugh, but it comes out strained. "Should I?"

Thank god the gym is empty, save Keegan who accompanied me down and is standing guard at the door, idly lifting a dumbbell while stealing glances at himself in the mirror. I have a feeling this is about to turn into the kind of conversation I *really* don't want to have in public.

"It's been a bit inconsistent, yes. I was showing Joan in the office a video yesterday and it was a little embarrassing. I thought you were past an E at this point?"

Wait, what video was she talking about? When the *hell* had I messed up on the E? My parts are too easy *to* mess up, aren't they?

Aren't they?

"I, um . . . I am. I've never had anyone comment on it."

"*I'm* commenting on it." Her laugh has an edge. Forced-breezy with a bite. "Do I not count?"

My mind's racing ahead trying to plan out possible responses, and her possible comebacks to my hypothetical responses, trying to map out a de-escalation. I must take too long to reply, though, because the false cheeriness is gone when she presses on. "You always get so *defensive* whenever someone tries to give you feedback, Ruben. Is this the attitude you give your coaches when they supply notes? Do you think you've made it or something? 'Ruben can't do anything wrong, because he's on an *international tour*.' Because believe me, this is only the *start* of you having to prove yourself, don't think they won't drop you in a—"

"No, you're right," I say hastily. *Please,* I silently beg, *just give me a break today.* "Of course you're right. That's why I'm practicing. I know I can do better. The others hung out and watched a movie this morning, actually, but I chose not to, because I knew I had to get some practice in before we—"

"So, you're being antisocial," she interrupts gleefully. "Ruben, being part of a team means *being part of the team.* You can't just hide in your room every minute you get. You need to be forming those connections and making a good impression."

I can't win. I know there's no point. So why do I even keep trying? "I am part of the team. I'm always hanging out with everyone."

"Well, just as long as it's not *always*. You need to be making plenty of time to practice."

We're full circle again. And she doesn't even notice. "I am," I say weakly.

"I heard there's been some fighting."

There it is. The real reason for the call. Presumably, she saw something while she was out for drinks. Or someone brought it up, and she was embarrassed not to know anything about it. And now I'm thinking of Zach again, and all I want to do is hang up the phone and go hard on the leg press until all the hurt has been replaced by muscle exhaustion.

"Nah, no fighting," I lie. "It's just gossip."

"Good." Not good that I'm not in a fight with my closest friends, of course. Good because—"You can't afford to get a reputation for being difficult. Even if there is anything happening behind the scenes, you have to stay professional."

I'm *trying.* Maybe she needs to call Zach and give him this lecture. *"Totally."*

"What's with the one-word answers?"

"Sorry, I didn't mean to." I rack my brains to come up with a safe topic change. "Where did you go for drinks?"

"Who said I was drinking?"

I roll my eyes at the window. "Nobody. But it's one a.m. I just assumed."

"What, I can't have a nice night out with my friends without being an alcoholic?"

I can save this, I think. "Of course you can. But you *should* have a cocktail or two. You deserve a nice night out to just have some fun. There's nothing wrong with that. I wish I could."

Her giggle is genuine now. "Well, I did have a couple. Do I sound drunk?"

"No, you just sound happy." It's a lie, but it's one designed to make her relax. She gives me *constructive criticism* all the time, but even imagined criticism is enough to raise her hackles. Compliments, affection, and gushing are the only tools in my arsenal to make her claws retract. Enabling is just another word for self-preservation, sometimes.

"I *am* happy. It was a lovely night," she says, and I finally relax. I've successfully navigated into calmer waters.

Someone enters the gym, and I glance up. It's Jon. He heads over and sets himself up on the machine beside me, silently. When he's close enough for me to touch, I grab his arm and mouth "help."

His eyes crinkle and he takes a few steps back. "Ruben!" he calls when he's at enough of a distance that it doesn't blare down my phone speaker. "We've got to *go*!"

"Hang on, hang on, Mom," I say quickly. "I'll be a minute," I call out.

"The bus is *leaving*," Jon sings.

"Jesus Christ," I hiss to Mom, like she's a conspirator.

"Oh no," she says warmly. "Sounds like you have your marching orders."

"I know, I know," I say. "We can talk on the bus? But we won't have much privacy."

"No, you go, I need to get to sleep now, anyway."

It's one of our cleaner conversations. Usually she can tell I'm making an excuse to get off the phone and it starts an argument. Thank god for Jon.

I throw my phone into the holder as soon as we hang up, letting out a guttural groan to the ceiling. A ten-minute conversation and I feel like I've just fielded a high-stakes interview with one of the nosier TV stations.

At least I came into this gig with a lifetime of experience navigating conversational minefields and noticing traps before they're sprung. I should send Mom some flowers in thanks for that skill.

Screw your mom, says the memory of Zach that lives in my head. We're in the bouncy castle, at Angel's party, and he's kneeling in front of me, and his eyes are intense, and I know that it's going to be okay. He's going to make it okay.

Then I snap back to the present. Zach's not here.

"Your parents?" Jon asks, returning to his machine.

"Mom."

"The *worst*," he says. Everyone in the band has their opinions on my mom. They range, politely, from "nope" to "*hell fucking no*."

"She read about The Tension," I say. That's our name for it. Even though neither Zach nor I will give them much of an explanation, both Jon and Angel are fully aware that Zach and I are at odds, and that it's inexplicably bigger than a snide comment made during a livestream. Angel's even stopped making jokes about Zach not finding me sexy, which means shit's gotten *serious*.

"She was gonna find out sooner or later, I guess. Did she give any advice?"

I shoot him a *look*.

"Point taken. You sure *I* can't give you any advice?"

"You don't even know what's wrong, how can you give me advice?" I say.

"Exactly."

"*Jon*—"

"You don't have to tell me specifically what happened! Just give me the vibe. The essence."

"I can't."

"The *seasoning*," he begs. "Not even the main meal. Just, the pepper and paprika of it."

"That's poetic."

"Thank you," he says, straightening with a pleased smile. "I did that on the spot."

There's literally no way to hint to Jon what happened without risking him putting two and two together, though. Even innocent, vague explanations, like, "I did something I shouldn't have," or "There was an awkward moment" risk setting Angel and Jon on a trail that could end in them figuring it out. I might not be embarrassed about it, but Zach sure as hell is. So, it doesn't matter how hurt I am, or how resentful I am that Zach won't even *try* to resolve this with me. That's a line I'm not crossing, period. So I just offer a meek, one-sided shrug.

"Okay, Ruben," he says, and there's an edge to his voice. I bristle.

"Are you asking because you care, or because Erin or Geoff want you to?" I ask.

"*What?*" he asks. "Because I *care*, obviously."

"Really? Because you're pressing the point pretty hard for someone who just wants us to be okay, given I've said we don't want to talk about it."

"I want you to know I'm here to help."

"No," I say, adjusting my position to use the leg press while we talk. "You want to force us to fix things."

"Of course I want you to fix things! You're my friends."

"And it's making the band look bad," I add, raising my eyebrows.

Jon studies me, then shrugs weakly. "What do you want me to do, say that's not true? You *know* it's true."

"There it is," I say. Mom's bite has crept into my voice. This always happens after speaking with her. It's like she infects me.

"For goodness' sake, Ruben, not everything's a conspiracy against you. Not everyone has an agenda."

"I already know you have an agenda," I say. "An agenda's your birthright." Wow, that sounded a lot crueler out loud than intended. I backtrack. "I mean, I didn't mean it like that. I just, like, your dad puts pressure on you. We know he does, and I know you can't help that. But I just . . . need you to not *manage* me right now. I need you to be my friend."

He breathes out long and slow, and I can almost see him counting to five in his head. "I am *trying*," he says slowly.

"Tell me it won't matter if Zach and I are never friends again. Tell me you won't hold that against me."

He seems confused, and I guess I don't blame him. Everything's muddled in my head, and I don't know quite how I got there, but it's suddenly very important to me to know that our friendship isn't conditional based on how well I handle this situation. I need to know it's okay, because I don't think I can control this. It's gotten away from me.

"I'll still be your friend, if that's what you mean," he says carefully. "But I wouldn't say it won't *matter*."

"I need it to not matter."

"But it will. I can't help that. It sucks being stuck between you two all the time. I don't want to choose."

"No one's asking you to choose."

"Maybe, but it kind of feels like it sometimes."

I go harder on the leg press. "I don't know how to fix this," I grunt.

"You could start by being a bit nicer to him."

"*What?*" I ask, pausing. "He's the one who keeps making comments about *me*."

"I'd honestly say it's about fifty-fifty."

I shake my head without speaking, and Jon shrugs. "I'm just giving you feedback. You don't need to take it."

You always get so defensive *whenever someone tries to give you feedback, Ruben.*

Screw this. I throw my hands up, startling Jon. "Fine. Sure. I guess I'm the asshole here. Zach's not doing anything wrong, and it's all on me."

"Ruben—"

"You want me to be *nicer* to him? I'll be super fucking nice. I'll be the nicest goddamn person you've ever seen, and if he doesn't magically become my friend again, maybe you'll finally catch on that it's not actually *me* doing this. I am just *responding*, as well as I *goddamn* can."

"I'm going to go."

I scoff as he gathers his gym gear. "Yeah, okay. Go. Sorry for not being super nice to you, either."

"Okay, Ruben."

"Tell your dad not to worry. The feedback's been *noted*! I'll be *so pleasant from now on*, you won't *recognize me*."

I shout the second half of the sentence to a closed door.

Keegan raises an eyebrow at me. "You know, kid, you probably could've handled that better," he says, lowering the dumbbell to his side. My cheeks burn, and I scowl and turn back to my workout.

It's really, really difficult to keep up a pleasant appearance during the interview. I manage it, though. Because unlike some people, I understand that it's important to leave emotions at the door when you walk into work.

I've been as *nice* as I possibly can be to Zach ever since we left the hotel. On the minibus over here, I asked Zach how he was (fine, thanks). I asked him how he'd slept (yeah, fine). I asked him if he'd heard of the chocolate-covered strawberries they have in Belgium, and if he thinks we'll get the chance to try them (I dunno, maybe).

With every question, he shrank further away from me, staring at me with wary hazel eyes. Like I was threatening him with a weapon, not asking him pleasant conversational questions. Every now and then I looked over to Jon, to see if he noticed. He spent the ride staring pointedly out the window, chewing frantically on his bottom lip. Angel spent the whole ride on his phone.

In fact, the interview is the first time I've had someone properly acknowledge my existence since Jon left me alone in the gym.

Jon and I are sitting on a cream-colored couch, with Angel and Zach taking the armchairs to either side. Against the wall, Erin's sitting and scrolling on her iPad, Keegan's bouncing his crossed legs as he scans the room, and Penny's watching us eagerly. Our interviewers are two women in their twenties, both dressed head to toe in couture. They're sweet and, luckily, don't seem to be trying to lead us with their questions like some others do.

There's not as much banter as there usually is, today. The Tension is sitting over us like a blanket sucking away our oxygen, putting out our fire.

Jon's the best at ignoring it. Right now, he's rhapsodizing about our history. He takes a lot of the "band-centric" questions. He's spent a lifetime in training, after all.

"I actually didn't bond with Angel at first," he says. "Ruben was my best friend, and he sort of squeezed me into the group for the end-of-year concert." He mimes shoving something into a small hole, and the interviewers laugh.

"They didn't want to perform with the son of a famous producer?" one of the interviewers asks, eyes glinting. Ooff. Talk about a touchy subject. But Jon doesn't flinch.

"They didn't know! I kept it a secret, fake name, everything. That's why I know they like me for me." He winks.

"Except, maybe, Angel?" the other interviewer asks.

Angel puts up his hand. "Can I say for the record that Jon is my boy?"

"Your boy?" she repeats, uncertain.

"I'm totally cool with Jon. He's all right." He goes over the top with this "admission," and Jon makes a heart with his fingers to hold over his chest.

The interviewer grins and leans forward. "Now, when you boys all met, they knew you as Reece. That was your name at the time, yes?"

"Yes. Still is, if you ask the government. But what do they know?"

Jon smiles to himself.

"Why did you change it?"

"It's actually a funny story. One day, a girl sees me on the street and she faints, right? Just, boom, woman down, middle of the sidewalk. And she comes to and says to me, oh my god, you're so gorgeous, I thought I saw a real-life angel. And the name stuck."

He deadpans the whole thing. It's a running joke to the fan base that he gives a different story every time he's asked about the origins of the nickname, and I'm pretty sure these women are in on it, because they don't look taken aback at all.

"So, *you two* are good friends?" one of them asks, and I notice the change in tone immediately. I grimace.

"Yup."

"Is everyone friends? We have heard some rumors that maybe there are some who do not like each other as much."

Well, *that* was delicately put. There's no way this question got through by accident. If Chorus didn't want us to comment on the rumors, it would've been a blocked question. They obviously want us to use this question to shut the rumors down.

Jon takes this one, of course. He doesn't seem even a little surprised to hear a question so dangerous. It makes me suspect his dad asked him to discount the rumors before we came. Like this very exchange was planned. "There's just no truth to that at all. We're like a family. Closer than a family. We chose each other, you know? We've always been compatible, but being on tour brings you closer together in ways we couldn't even predict before this. Forced proximity, I guess," he jokes.

Do I look as alarmed by that as I feel? Because if I'd been drinking a glass of water I would've spat it out.

I sneak a lot at Zach, and he's lost all color, like he may faint.

Zach and I are both sitting in stunned silence, so Angel jumps in. "I don't even know which rumor you're *referring to*," he says, hamming up the bewilderment. "Zach, do you know what on earth these lovely ladies may have heard? I'm lost."

Zach startles, and chokes on the first word. "No idea." He clears his throat, and Erin hands him a water bottle. He takes it but doesn't drink. "No, but in all seriousness, it's kind of a silly rumor. I don't think any of us would be mad at each other *just* because some of us got on a list."

It's another one of his digs that's only hurtful in context. I can't even retaliate, because I'm the only one who knows the real meaning. *We wouldn't be mad at each other about* that. *I don't like him because we made out and it meant more to him than it did to me, and he made it weird.*

The edges of my vision are going blurry.

Somewhere in the distance, Angel gestures to Zach with both hands. "This, exactly. I'm not gonna be angry at my friends just because people have no taste."

The interviewers burst out in laughter, and it's in slow motion. Angel's laughing and shaking his head. *I'm kidding. I'm kidding. Kind of.*

I set my jaw, and everything clicks back into place. "Exactly," I say, a little too loudly. All heads turn to me. "I'm sure I speak for everyone when I say I don't believe in wrecking important friendships over things that don't even matter.

But, honestly? Even if we *didn't* get along, we wouldn't be making it obvious. Like, I did professional musical theater for years. Anyone who's been around theater knows how much pointless drama there can be." Both women nod emphatically, and someone laughs, but I can't focus on who. "But the show goes on, you know? You can't throw a tantrum onstage because you have to do a scene with someone you don't like. And personally, you know, *I'm* not a child. I will always treat my colleagues with respect."

There. I can speak in double meanings, too.

I'm so awash with satisfaction and triumph, it takes me a second to realize the interviewers have an odd look on their faces. Smiling, sure, but it's a different smile. A hungry one.

I play my words back in my head, and notice the edge to my voice. The passive-aggressive viciousness.

I sound like my mom.

There's a horrible beat of silence, and Angel laughs loudly. "*Colleagues,*" he says. "See, Ruben's the best, he's always so composed. When you get to know Ruben, you realize that when he says 'colleagues,' he means the best friends he'll ever have in his lifetime. Seriously, like, once he went on a date, and I didn't know that's what it was until afterward because he told us he had an *appointment.*"

That story is a total lie, but I'm dizzy with relief for Angel's ability to make up bullshit on his feet.

"Oh!" One of the women latches onto this, eyes gleaming. "You have a girlfriend, Ruben?"

I can almost feel Erin's eyes boring into me. *Don't you dare.*

Of course, I *don't* dare. I play their game, like I always do, as much as it hurts. "No, not right now. Still looking for the one."

The interview moves on, but I know I've messed up. The

Tension is heavier than ever, and it's wormed its way right into the pit of my stomach, where it's settled like an anvil.

I barely speak for the rest of the interview. All I can do is replay my own words back. I know what the response to that snippet is going to be. And the worst thing is, it's going to be the truth. I snapped, and I screwed up, and now people are going to know. And I can't even blame anyone else.

Fifty-fifty, Jon said.

Was he right? Have I been lashing out this whole time? Delivering little, jagged cuts to everyone around me without even noticing?

Is this what it's like to be Mom? Does she do it without noticing, too?

I think I might be sick.

I can barely look at anyone after the interview wraps up. And I'm not surprised in the least when Erin pulls me aside as we pile onto the bus to head to our next engagement.

"Geoff wants to talk to you and Zach when we're back at the hotel this afternoon," she says. Her voice is apologetic, and careful. A warning.

Shit's about to go down.

TEN

ZACH

I've never been in this much trouble with Chorus.

Or anyone, really.

I can tell this is serious by the cold, distant way everyone's been treating Ruben and me. Like even being close to us will mean they're also in trouble. It started as soon as we boarded the bus to go back to our hotel, and it hung over us the whole journey. Erin is being extremely careful with her words, and Jon and Angel aren't really talking. The worst, though, is Ruben, who is ignoring me again. I almost don't know what I hate more, the way he spoke to me on the bus this morning, in a tone that was actually viciousness disguised as friendliness, or this. The endless, icy silence. In the past, maybe being in trouble together would've brought us closer, but he went straight back to acting like I'm invisible.

I'm in my bathroom now washing my face. The meeting starts in a minute.

He called me a child. And he all but confirmed to the interviewers that the tension between us is real. Being in trouble right now is all his fault.

I splash water on my face. Getting upset now won't help anything, and I can't mess this up.

Ruben is waiting at the end of the hallway for me when I leave my room. Early, of course. What I feel is not anger, though, it's this dull ache. Like something is missing. Like this wouldn't be so bad if we were tackling it as friends.

When we got back to the hotel, Erin gave us half an hour to freshen up and get ready for the call, and her tone made it very clear we were to look faultless *or else*. So now we look more like young businessmen than pop superstars, but that's fitting, because we'll be speaking to Geoff. Pop *is* a business to him.

That's all it is, really. I don't think he gets how music feels to me. How important it is. How it's the quickest way to feel any emotion possible, and how powerful, how *necessary*, it is. It's so much more than something that can be used to make money.

I reach Ruben, and he just tilts his head up in greeting. Right. The silent treatment is still going. Good to know, and good thing two can play at this. We get into the elevator, and ride it up silently. I cross my arms, and lean against the wall.

The air is crackling, though. He's staring forward, his jaw set, his expression plain. He's picture-perfect. If he's nervous, or anything, he's not giving it away. Does he really not care about what could happen? Or is this an act? I open my mouth, and he glances at me, his eyes telling me not to, so I shut it.

I've never seen him act like he did at the interview. Hell, everyone in the room picked up on it. Even though they didn't come out and say so, the interviewers could clearly tell something was going on between us. It's so unlike Ruben to do something that hurts the band, or anyone, but I think he was trying to hurt me.

When the interview airs tomorrow night, it's going to add even more gasoline to the stories already circulating. I've seen it happen before, and it's always scary fast. A story can go from being a rumor to a fact in seconds. Not only that, it can so easily become a *defining* fact. The thing people think of when they think of Saturday.

We could become known as the band that all secretly hate each other, only tied together by our contracts.

I roll my neck, and sense him watching me.

The elevator chimes.

"After you," he says, smiling graciously.

I ignore the fire in my chest and walk out.

Down the hall, Erin is waiting in front of her room. She opens the door for us, and we file in. The air feels heavy and gloomy. The MacBook set up on the desk may as well be a guillotine.

"Take a seat," says Erin, her face grim.

Ruben and I go across the room, and sit down in front of the computer.

On the screen, at a desk, is Geoff.

"I'm assuming you know why you're here?" he asks, his voice deep and gravelly.

Neither of us say anything for a moment too long. It speaks volumes.

"I'm sorry," says Ruben.

Geoff's eyebrows slant down. Even though he's in a different country right now, I still start to sweat. If he decides to stop supporting us, we could fade away and become a band the general public only vaguely remembers.

"*Sorry* isn't good enough in this case. You need to be better. Let me make this very clear, you two are in deep shit. You both understand that, right?"

"I do," says Ruben.

"Definitely," I say.

"No, I don't think you do," says Geoff, his voice rising.

"You two fucked up. You *have* to promise me you'll get whatever is going on under control. You have to."

"We will," says Ruben.

"Seriously, we will."

"I know you will. You've worked too hard to jeopardize everything now." He looks into the camera, and it feels for a moment like he's made eye contact with me directly. "Think about Jon and Angel. How could you let them down like this? You're a band, that means you're supposed to work together."

I bow my head, because he's right.

"And think about everyone that works for you, trying to make *your* dream a reality. Do you even care about them? Do you care that they might lose their jobs because of this? If the band goes down, they go down with you."

"Of course we do," says Ruben.

"Then you need to act like it. Because I'm telling you the truth, if you don't get this under control, people will lose their jobs. Galactic have been calling nonstop, telling me to fix this mess."

I can barely breathe.

I know I have a brain that attacks itself constantly, which means I never know when the negative thoughts I have are the truth or not. Questioning them is one of the best things my child psychologist taught me to do.

But now . . .

Geoff just confirmed some of my worst fears.

The band is in danger because of me. So many people could lose their jobs just because I kissed Ruben and didn't handle it well. I might have caused the end of the band.

My eyes start to sting, but I manage to rein them in. Geoff can't stand tears.

"Now," says Geoff. "Tell me why you two have been fighting, and don't lie."

"We haven't been fighting," says Ruben. "We're just getting on each other's nerves, I guess. We're spending a lot of time together."

"Zach? You're letting Ruben do all the talking."

"Sorry, um . . ."

My voice is shaking.

"Don't say um, you know I hate that."

I suck in a breath to steady myself. "Sorry. Ruben's right, it really is just small clashes that got blown out of proportion. I know we messed up, and we're working on it, I promise."

"Good. If this is not fixed immediately there will be hell to pay. Is that crystal clear?"

Ruben nods. "It is."

"Definitely." My voice is trembling again.

"Good. I need to go, I have a meeting. We'll talk soon."

Geoff taps on his mouse, and the video call ends.

Well. That went about as badly as it possibly could.

"So . . ." says Ruben. "I guess I owe you an apology."

Something flickers within me, something I don't really like. I wouldn't even *be* in this position if it weren't for Ruben. I don't want him to be high and mighty and apologize, I want it to be different; I want everything to have not happened the way it did. I know I'm guilty of avoiding him after the kiss, but I asked him to give me space, and he didn't give me that. And now he's going around poking me in interviews and somehow I feel like I'm in more trouble than he is. I hate it, but I'm seething right now.

No. This is just fear talking. It'll pass.

I just need to keep my mouth shut until it does, because losing my shit at Ruben will make everything worse. So I push the emotions down, and smile.

"It's okay," I say. "You don't need to apologize, it's not your fault."

"Well, it kind of is."

"Yeah, but what would getting upset about it do?"

He stares at me for a long moment. "You know what? Sometimes I wonder if you care about anything." He gets out of the chair and leaves.

He thinks I don't care about anything?

If only he knew what the inside of my head is like.

It's my last night in Amsterdam, and I still haven't seen the canals.

My parents got engaged here, and even though it ended really badly, it's still my favorite romantic story. It was totally spur-of-the-moment. Dad didn't even have a ring. They were on vacation together, and they found this spot they both called the most beautiful place on earth, and right there, Dad got on one knee. He'd already decided he was going to propose once he got home, but then he realized no location could ever live up to where they were, so he went for it.

Mom said yes. She's always said the canals played a big part in that decision, as she was swept up in the beauty of the place. She'd never really planned on getting married in the way some people do, and then it just happened.

I've always wanted to see them, and tonight is my only chance on this trip. But we're not allowed to leave our hotel unsupervised. And this is the sort of thing I want to do without a security guard with me. I want to do it as Zach, not as Zach Knight: bad boy of Saturday.

A knock sounds on my door.

I frown and check my phone, in case I missed a message. There's nothing. So I have no idea who's knocking on my door, especially this late. I open it a sliver.

It's Ruben.

He's dressed to go out, in one of his long wool coats, this one in tan.

"Hey," he says.

"Hey?"

"I'm sorry about what I said in the interview."

I shrug, then move aside, letting him into my room. I obviously wasn't expecting company, so the whole space is messy, with clothes strewn around the place, and my bedsheets all messed up. I pick up a discarded shirt and toss it into my suitcase.

"Look," he says. "I know things have been weird, but this is the one place on the whole tour you wanted to see. If we don't go now, you're going to miss it."

"But . . ."

"Or you can just sit alone in your room all night, I guess. I'm not gonna drag you along." His voice has an edge to it at first, but then he softens. "But I think we should go. Maybe we can try to . . . I don't know, figure things out?"

I cross my arms, and he goes on hurriedly. "I know it's what Geoff wants. But it's what I want, too. I promise. Even if we can't go back to the way things used to be, can we at least try to find a new normal? One that's less weird?"

I pick up another discarded shirt, and twist it in my hands.

"Okay."

"Okay you want to come or okay you want to figure stuff out?"

I just grab my jacket as an answer.

I do want to sort stuff out. I also would like to see the sort of place that would make my incredibly pragmatic mother accept what she knew was a spur-of-the-moment proposal. I think I've spent my whole life hyping up this place, and now I'm here, and I need to see it.

"This is really bad timing," I say, as I put my jacket on.

"Why?"

"If we're caught sneaking out, it could be really bad."

"We won't get caught. I have a way to sneak us out. You out of excuses yet, or . . . ?"

I huff, and pull on a pair of boots.

Ruben clearly doesn't know what to do while he waits. He's lingering by the door, scrubbing the back of his head. And I'm still a little mad at him about the interview, and the fear of Geoff is still swirling around in my gut.

But this is the canals. This matters.

And I miss him, and I want to go do something with just him. Even after everything.

I put on a royal blue scarf and a beanie. And then I'm done. Ready to escape.

"So, what's the plan?" I ask, as I tuck my hands under my arms for warmth. "Keegan or Pauline will be in the lobby, right? I doubt they'll let us out this late."

"There's a fire escape on the roof," he says. "We'll climb down, then we're free."

Like most buildings here, this hotel isn't too tall. We'll be able to get to the street fairly easily.

The bigger issue is still Keegan and Pauline. They check the hallways randomly at night, and if we run into them, it won't end well. They'll have to tell Chorus that they saw—it's part of their contract, and I could never ask them to risk their jobs for us.

"It'll be fine," he says. "Just follow my lead."

The hallway outside is empty, so we go to the end, and get in the elevator. Ruben presses the button for the roof. We ride it up in silence until the doors open, revealing the rooftop. And all around us are the Amsterdam city lights. The stars look incredible. It's brisk outside, but this is so stunning I don't even care.

"Aren't you glad we did this now?" he asks.

"A little."

Ruben crosses the rooftop, his shoes crunching on the gravel. There's a metal ladder attached to the side of the building. With no fear, Ruben steps up to it and then swings out over the roof edge. My heart lurches, but he's smiling.

Seriously: does anything scare this boy?

I climb down after him. The metal is so cold it burns my fingers. When we reach the end, I hear him jump down, landing heavily on his feet.

Shit, it's actually a decent jump. I grip the metal tight.

"It's easy," he says.

I jump. I stumble on the pavement, but Ruben catches me. He holds me there for a moment, his hand on my chest. I wonder if he can feel how fast my heart is banging against my ribs.

"You okay?" he asks.

I step away from him. "Yeah."

He puts his hood on. I copy him. It's cold enough to warrant it, and it'll help us be a little more anonymous.

Together, we set off down the street.

This city truly is gorgeous, like something out of a fairy tale. The streets are wide and spacious, lit by iron streetlamps. Everything is soft and gold and black. The roads are all quiet, but a few of the restaurants are bustling, with people talking and laughing. We go around a corner, and in the distance, I can see the canal. It cuts through the city, broken apart by stone bridges every second block. We go toward it.

"What are you thinking about?" asks Ruben, turning his head toward me.

I shrug, because it's my default response when someone asks me that. But we're going for a new normal. That means I should be different, too.

"I'm thinking about Mom," I say. "I was wondering if I should take a photo of this and send it to her, but then decided against it."

"Why?"

I shrug again. It's a damn disease. "I don't think she'd like knowing I'm here."

"How come?"

"This place probably doesn't bring back the happiest memories for her, after what happened."

"Oh. So . . . why'd you want to see it so bad?"

"I dunno. I just always have."

He gives me a searching look, but doesn't reply.

Up ahead, there's a small stall selling something called stroopwafels.

"What the hell is a stroopwafel?" I ask, as I point at the stall.

"Want to find out?"

I nod, and go up and buy a packet for us from an excessively cheery saleswoman in a blue checkered outfit. Luckily the stall accepts credit cards, and I go back to Ruben with my haul. They look like small, compressed waffles, but sort of seem crispy, and are sold in stacks wrapped in clear plastic.

"I love this word," I say. *Stroopwafel.*

"Please don't write a song called 'Stroopwafel.'"

I grin, and feel my notebook in my jacket pocket. "Don't tempt me."

Up ahead is an iron bench, overlooking the canal. It's lit by one iron streetlight.

It's a perfect spot.

I know we don't have much time, but sitting on the bench, with a stroopwafel, seems exactly right, the kind of moment I've always wanted to have here. I can think about my parents and everything that happened, and hopefully try to understand them both a little better. Normally I just think of my dad as an asshole, but maybe he wasn't always one. Maybe he was a different guy when he was here. He got Mom to like him, so he must not have always seemed like a selfish dickwad.

Golden lights run along the edges of the canal and cross the closest bridge. I can hear the gentle movement of the water and the occasional sound of a passing car.

"Stroopwafel?" I say, offering Ruben the packet, making the plastic crinkle.

He opens it, and takes out one of the waffles. I take one out, too.

I take a bite of my stroopwafel, and then let out a moan, and lean back against the bench. Ruben tries his, and does exactly the same thing. It's sugary and crispy and just the right amount of chewy.

"So, these are fucking delicious," he says.

"Right?"

Silence falls while we eat.

He said we don't have to talk, but if it were ever going to happen, it'd be here. Maybe I *do* get the power of this place, now.

"I really am sorry, by the way," he says, out of nowhere.

"Oh, that's okay. Interviews are stressful, I get it."

"I'm not talking about the interview."

"Oh. What are you talking about?"

"That night."

Oh.

Oh.

Even though it's terrifying, I can't keep running from it. I've done that for long enough. I've known Ruben for years.

He used to be my best friend. I can and should be able to talk to him about everything.

But it's *him,* though. He somehow feels like both the easiest and hardest person to tell.

"You don't have anything to be sorry about." I want to say: *I liked it, because I'm bi.*

"Yeah, I do. We were both drunk, and it wasn't a big deal, and I shouldn't have taken it so personally. I mean, I *know* you're straight. It's not like you lied to me about it. And I want you to know we don't have to talk about this if you don't want to, but I wanted to get that out of the way first." He picks at his waffle, then gives a strained laugh. "We can change the subject now if you want."

I cross my arms. I hope if he notices that I'm shaking, he'll think it's because of the cold, not because of nerves. What I want to say is: *I'm not straight.*

"I'm not upset it happened or anything," is what I actually say.

"You aren't?"

"Nope."

"You've seemed pretty mad."

"I haven't been mad. I've been, um, scared I guess."

"Oh. *Oh.*"

I chew my lip.

"Zach, you know you can talk to me about anything, right? Even if we're fighting. If it's important, I'm here, no matter what."

"Yeah. I guess that's why I've been keeping my distance, because I know we could talk about it, and it freaks me out."

"Why?"

I'm hunched over, and suddenly I'm very distracted by my leather bracelet. "I know it's not normal, but like, talking about this stuff scares the crap out of me."

"What do you mean? Like, your feelings?"

"Yep."

"What's scaring you about it?"

"I have this fear, I guess. Of like, telling someone I care about something about me, and having them stare at me. Or they'll point and laugh and not want to be friends anymore."

"You think I'd point and laugh at you?"

"Well, no, but anxiety isn't exactly rational, you know? I think a part of it is, I think people like me how I am. And if I change, people might stop liking me."

"Right." He leans back. "Well, that's never gonna happen with me."

"That's not true. It already did."

Ruben pauses, and there's something questioning in his eyes.

"Listen," he says. "I might've had thoughts about the way things went down, but I never stopped liking you. I can't promise I'll still like you if you turn into a serial killer, or, like, a neo-Nazi or something, but otherwise you're pretty much good."

"Okay." I stop myself, then push through. "There's something I want to tell you, like, about me, but it's really hard to say."

"You know, I've spent a *lot* of time theorizing about what *might* have been going on in your head over the last week. I can run some theories by you, and if one of them sounds accurate, you can nod or something? Would that make it easier?"

I shove my hands into my jacket pockets and nod.

"So," he clears his throat. "You kissed me because you were drunk and you would've kissed anyone in the same room as you."

I don't move.

"You've had kissing a guy on your bucket list and you saw a chance to get it done but hated it and didn't know how to tell me?"

I keep still again.

"You were so drunk you thought I was a girl and when you woke up in the morning you freaked out because you'd kissed a guy."

"Keep trying," I say. "This is helping."

"Okay." His eyebrows furrow. "You were feeling bad about not being on that stupid list, and I made you feel attractive, so in your drunken state you confused that feeling with actual attraction."

"I mean, maybe that's a little bit of it, but there's more to it."

There's a long pause, and when he speaks, it's basically a whisper. "What if you've figured out that you might like guys, but you've been scared to do anything about it, because then it would become real?"

I can't lie.

Clearly, he gets it. I wonder if he went through a very similar thing, just when he was younger. I wonder if all queer people do.

So I nod.

"Okay, wow," he says. "You think you might be queer?"

"Yeah." I wince. "I think I might be bi."

"Wow. Holy shit."

"Are you surprised?"

"I guess I shouldn't be, given last week," he says with a wry smile. "But I am? I guess I thought I'd have heard about it by now if you were. Obviously I *thought* about it, but I kept deciding I just wan—I kept deciding you probably weren't."

"Right."

But wait, he wanted what? For me to be bi? Why would he . . .

And then I see it. I kissed him and things got weird because I was cold and distant. Which would be crushing, if someone you liked acted like that after you kissed them. How he reacted makes a lot of sense if you factor in that he likes me. Or at least that he started to. God, I'm an idiot. Never in a million years did I think Ruben would care about me like that, but now . . . now it's making sense.

He smiles. "But this isn't about me. Shit, this is huge, Zach. How do you feel about it?"

I look into his eyes. The eye contact is steady, unflinching. It feels a little magical, actually. Having him know, and things not feeling that weird. It just feels *right*. And under it all is this thought that maybe he likes me.

"It's like, terrifying, but in a good way. Does that make sense?"

"Yeah, it does. But, um, are you referring to the fact that you like guys in general? Or . . . ?"

He glances up, a clear signal.

And I really want to.

So I shuffle closer, he nods a little and smiles, so I bring my hands up until they're on his face. Nerves slam into me, and what if this isn't real, what if I kiss him and I don't like it. I move my hand an inch away, and Ruben opens his eyes, and his eyebrows pull together, and I'm ruining the moment oh fuck I'm ruining this like I've been ruining everything lately and . . .

Oh fuck it.

I move across and kiss him, putting everything I have into it. I run my hand up through his hair, his gorgeous hair, and smell his cologne and taste the sugar on his lips.

It's like fireworks in my chest. There's no doubt that this is real.

He brings a hand up and rests it above my heart. "Wait," he says, pushing me back slightly, his hand still resting on my chest. "We shouldn't do this outside. People could see."

"Right."

We rush back toward to the hotel, walking closer to each other than we probably should, our hands occasionally brushing before the other pulls away. Finally we make it to the hotel, and climb back up the fire escape, way more quickly than going down it. On the rooftop I jab the elevator button. Then Ruben grabs me by the jacket, spins me around, and presses me up against the cold brick wall.

"Hey," I say, laughing at the suddenness of it.

"Hey."

He kisses me, and it makes me dizzy. It feels as amazing as I remember. Better, maybe.

"Sorry," he says, pressing his forehead against mine, his hands gripping mine. "I couldn't wait."

"I'm not complaining."

The elevator opens, and we go inside.

As soon as the door closes, we fall onto each other. Our hands are a scramble, and the kiss is frantic, but in the best possible way. He pulls me right to him, so our bodies are flush, his chest against mine.

The elevator chimes, and we spring apart. There's nobody in the hallway, though, so we start up again. Suddenly he's up against the wall, and I'm kissing his neck. Then he spins me around, and I'm up against the wall, and he's kissing me. He presses himself fully to me, hip to hip, and I think we might need to go inside before I lose all sense completely.

"Hey," he says, nuzzling his nose against mine. ""You good?"

"So good."

We reach his door, and he opens it, and we rush inside. Our coats are off immediately. The room is dark, lit only by the light coming in from the balcony's sliding glass doors. I double-check to make sure the door is locked. If anyone at Chorus knew about this . . . holy shit. I don't even want to imagine. Not now.

"Too many clothes," I say, and he laughs, shucking off his sweater.

We go into the bedroom. I start unbuttoning his shirt, all the way to the bottom, so it's hanging open. He takes it off and jumps up onto his bed, now only in his jeans.

He smirks at me, all devilish.

I pull my shirt off and join him.

ELEVEN

RUBEN

"What's better?" Zach asks, reading from his notepad. "'Your smile spills the secret you can't keep from me,' or 'Your smile tells me we're meant to be'?"

We're lying side by side on top of my fully made bed, propped up on a mountain of fluffy goose-down hotel pillows. We have about twenty minutes before we need to head to a choreo check-in, but as much as we all begged Erin to let us explore Cologne for a second, the answer was, as usual, no. She claimed it was because there wasn't enough time to assemble guards for a public outing on such short notice. (When we go out in public, Chorus insists on assigning at least one guard for each of us, as opposed to the more lax ratio they allow for interviews and photo shoots held inside. A part of me gets it, but another part of me resents being treated like we're made of porcelain. We were never kept this holed up on the American tour leg, and Angel and Zach were still seventeen for most of that.)

So, instead, we told the others I was going to help Zach with his lyrics in my room while we waited. I'd low-key hoped Zach understood that was code for "make out until we're dizzy," but it turned out he actually *did* want my thoughts on some new lyrics. Luckily, even lying next to him on my bed is more entertaining to me than anything we could be doing outside, so I'm still fine. More than fine, really. I'm giddy with happiness to be this close to him, knowing he wants to be close to me. That he wants to be alone with *me*.

I glance at the lines scrawled in Zach's neat, tiny handwriting. Above them are some others that he's obviously drafted and decided against, because they're mostly scribbled out. I make out the words *nuclear explosion, billowing curtains,* and *string cheese* beneath the mess of ink.

"That sounds like a couplet to me," I say, then I lean over to run a finger over the page to point to the two legible lines remaining. "Just needs a bit of editing and they match up. Although I don't know why you scribbled out the line about string cheese, I think you really had something there."

He flicks my hand, scoffing. The simplest contact, but time stops for a beat.

How did he get the power to still everything within me through one touch? I've had crushes before. Boyfriends before. But I've always felt in control. Completely separate from them. Me, the individual, happy to be around them, the individual. Content, but not engulfed.

When Zach touches me, though, it's like my skin stops being the barrier that holds me in and the world out. It feels like a boundary he can cross at will, to merge with me and fill me with this *fire,* from the depths of my chest to the surface of my skin. To make me, the individual, bigger, bursting at the seams, surging outward with something both undefinable and terrifying to lose.

All this to say, I think he's turned me into a hopeless fucking romantic. If it wasn't for the fact that I'm loving every second of it, it might occur to me to be indignant.

"Yeah, I think you're right," he says, scrunching his brow.

He's got his serious face on, the one he gets when he's gone somewhere else, some magical land where song lyrics float around in the atmosphere and he snatches them from the sky and transcribes them onto paper. Or, at least, that's how it sounds when he describes his inspiration process. It all comes across as a little sci-fi to me.

As I watch him work, a pang of sadness and trepidation hits my gut. I love our songs already—Galactic Records hires only the best writers for us, and they consistently nail the balance between catchy, relatable, and a little thought-provoking—but I would *especially* love for this to work out. I've seen Zach's drafts, and I know he's talented enough to produce a hit, if only Chorus and Galactic Records will let him.

I just worry he's putting too much stock in Geoff's assurances that they want him to write a song, and not taking the heaping serving of salt he *should* be taking with any promise from Chorus.

I let him go back wherever he was and scroll through my phone. Mom's sent me a link to an article that, from the title, appears to be discussing why I'm actually the worst dancer in Saturday. Some good tips for improvement in here, she's written. Thanks, I type back. I used to beg her not to send me these, but it would just set her off on a tangent about how I needed to grow a thicker skin if I wanted to be in the entertainment industry. Zach's told me more than once I shouldn't let this stuff slide, but there's only so much energy I can put into re-establishing my boundaries again and again, only to get them knocked back down.

Sometimes I fantasize that one day I might bite the bullet and cut off contact altogether. Maybe. If I'm brave enough. If I decide it's worth the loss—and there will be a measure of loss, like it or not. Of her, and the good times, even if they're rare. Of Dad, who I don't want to lose, but comes in a package deal with her. Even of the rest of my family, if they take her side, which they almost certainly will by the time she's done spinning her side of things.

It feels too enormous to contemplate for too long, but that doesn't mean I won't ever do it.

Just not today. I'm not ready for that yet.

"You've been writing a lot lately," I say to Zach, to distract myself.

He doesn't complain about being yanked out of his stupor. Just leans his shoulder against mine and looks up. "I know. I've been feeling inspired."

My eyebrow twitches of its own accord, and he bursts out laughing, turning beetroot-red. "I'm *sorry.*"

"No, no, you said it."

"Ew, I was trying to answer in a way that didn't seem corny—"

"You failed."

"I *totally* failed, that was super corny."

"This is not a good start to the relationship."

I falter at the end of the final word, realizing too late what's coming out of my mouth. He freezes, eyes widening, and my breath catches in my throat as I blink rapidly. Shit. *Jesus.* I did *not* mean to say that. It's like my mouth went ahead and signed off on something without waiting for my brain to review and cosign.

It's been several days since the canals, and though we've snuck into each other's rooms to make out at least once per day—after breakfast, after interviews, before shows—neither of us has made a move to define what, exactly, we're doing.

Zach couldn't look more alarmed if I'd announced I was throwing him out the window to the mercy of the group of fans camped outside. "I mean, I didn't mean *that,*" I stammer before he can reply. "I just mean, you know, relationship, as in, the relationship between two things that exist in . . . relation . . . to each other."

"It's fine, I know what you meant." He relaxes a little, but not entirely.

"Two things that are related. That have a—a relation."

"You're overthinking it, it's really fine," he says, smiling wryly. The last of the tension leaves his posture, and I return his smile, feeling a little sheepish.

It was honestly a slip—and an especially unexpected one at that, considering I haven't thought of Zach as someone I'm seeing. At least, I *hadn't*. Obviously, given Zach's shocked reaction, it's way too soon to explore. More of a thing to file in the "to revisit later" pile.

But, still. Now that the idea is lingering on the peripheries of my mind . . . I'd be lying if I said the idea of having a *relationship* with Zach one day doesn't make warmth radiate from the center of my chest out to my fingertips.

Jon looks like he's about to spontaneously combust.

Our choreographer, Valeria, has singled him out for some brief one-on-one time to slightly alter his dance steps in "Guilty." We're not sure where this sudden change came from, but none of us are impressed with the idea of *any* changes made to the choreo we know inside-out. That's not how it's supposed to be done. And yet, here we are.

"I just need you to go a little harder on the hips," Valeria says to Jon, running her hands down the length of her body, her fingernails dragging on her skin and clothes, resting them just beneath her hip bones.

Jon mimics her, but with about a billion percent less

passion and sex appeal. And Jon knows how to dance better than any of us. It's no mistake.

"Where's this change coming from?" he demands, as Valeria physically manipulates his hands to demonstrate what she wants.

"Just general feedback," she says airily.

Zach glances at me and pulls a face. So, Geoff. It's come from Geoff.

"It's like *this*, Jon," Angel says, running his hands from his neck to his crotch, then falling to his knees on the stage, pulling his shirt down at the neck to bare his chest, panting like he's in the middle of a porno shoot.

Valeria scowls at us. "You three take a break while I work with Jon."

The three of us have been standing around with nothing to do for over ten minutes now while Jon resisted the new moves, so we gladly hurry off to the wings to grab our water bottles.

"Do you think Geoff's punishing him for something?" Zach asks, popping his bottle open with his teeth.

"Nah," I say. "Geoff doesn't do anything he thinks will make us look bad. He just . . . seems to want sex, lately."

Zach gives me a weird look at the word *sex*, then becomes very interested in the label on his water bottle.

"Hey, if he wants sex, I've got sex," Angel announces, shoving his phone in his pocket. "Speaking of which, I'm running to the bathroom. Be right back."

"Speaking of which?" I repeat. "What do you—*Angel*, what are you doing in the bathroom?"

Out on the stage, Valeria's showing Jon how to accidentally-on-purpose knock his jacket off of one of his shoulders. Until this moment, I've never seen this expression on his face, though I've seen it on mine in family photos.

This particular expression is best described as "silently begging for the sweet release of death."

"Do you think we can save him?" Zach asks after a while.

"What are you thinking? An intervention with Geoff?"

"I was leaning toward something quicker. Like, a distraction?"

"*Phantom of the Opera* style?" I perk up. "There aren't any chandeliers to crash, but maybe—"

"*No,* you don't have my permission to wreck the set," Zach says quickly. "Maybe a scream or something?"

"You want me to stand here and scream? I think that'll just annoy them, honestly."

"Nah, go down the hall a little bit. You can pretend to be kidnapped."

Wait. Speaking of kidnapping. "Hold that thought. Not that it's any of our business, but Angel's been in the bathroom *awhile* now."

Zach tears his eyes away from Jon, who's now mid-body-roll. "You don't think he was being serious?"

I start off down the hall backstage, Zach at my heels. "Look, I'm *assuming* not. I'm more concerned a group of fans have squirreled him away or something."

"You talk about him like he's a collectible item."

I raise an eyebrow. "You can't stand there and tell me you've never felt like a collectible."

"Can I count the first time I ever saw the creepy-as-hell Zach doll?"

"I would've gone with the time you lost that Band-Aid in the crowd and it ended up on eBay."

He barks a laugh. "Oh, man, I forgot about that. Touché."

I poke my head inside the men's bathroom. "Empty," I announce.

Zach pops his head over my shoulder. "You wanna

double-check?" I joke, stepping inside so he can enter. But he has no interest in checking the empty stalls. Instead, he steps into me, forcing me backward until I hit the closed door.

"Not really," he says. "I just want to kiss you."

Oh.

That might be the best thing anyone's ever said to me.

He kisses me quickly and fiercely, his hands flying to my neck, his fingers pressing into my hair. Then he pulls away to kiss my jaw, and he runs his lips down my neck, warm as he kisses me, followed by a shock of ice as air hits my skin in his wake. Then, just as my knees start to give out, he straightens and pulls back. "Sorry for the ambush," he whispers. "I've just been wanting to do that for *hours*."

I'm speechless for the next full thirty seconds. For once, it's me following *him* out the door, adjusting my jeans as well as I can, and praying we don't run into anyone before I can get my blood pressure back under control.

He checks the women's bathroom—also negative—then we swing past to peek at the stage again just in case Angel returned while we were, ah, *preoccupied*. Still no luck. I send him a text, and even try calling him, but he doesn't respond.

"Maybe we should ask the guards if he went out somewhere?" I suggest uncertainly as we hover in the empty hallway.

"Maybe . . ." Zach shrugs. "Give him a minute, though. He hasn't even been gone for ten. I don't want to get him in trouble over nothing if he's just gone to take a look outside."

"You think he's outside?" I ask skeptically. "There's no way he could've gotten past Keegan."

Then it hits me. Of course. Zach and I aren't the only ones who know how to work a fire exit.

We find it in less than a minute: follow a stark white

hallway with a concrete floor, then open a second door, letting the midafternoon sun stream in.

"Wait-wait-wait, hold it open!" yells a familiar voice. I pull the door back a little more to find Angel on the other side. "That thing shut behind me—I couldn't get back in!"

He has sunglasses on and his hood pulled up, at least, but it's still a small miracle he wasn't mobbed. Although, now that I peek outside, there's no one around. Just some guy I don't recognize in sweatpants and a T-shirt, walking briskly away from us.

"What were you doing out there?" Zach chides. "Erin would've murdered you."

"Nothing important," Angel says, which makes me think it probably *is* something important. "Come on. Let's get back before Jon starts doing Hail Marys in penance for touching his thighs in public."

He takes off his sunglasses and shoves them into his pocket.

I can't help but notice he leaves his hand over those sunglasses *very* protectively as we walk back to the stage.

We're about halfway into that night's performance when I become quite certain that Angel was outside meeting a dealer. He is, fairly obviously, high off his face.

Luckily for us, I don't think it's noticeable to the audience. They probably just think he's really, *really* into the songs. But up as close as I am, I can see the manic look in his too-open eyes, the way he's chewing on his lower lip, and the restless trembling of his legs.

As soon as we get a break between songs, I make my way over to Zach, and duck my head in. "Keep an eye on Angel. I think he's taken something."

Zach's face clouds as I pull away, and in the back of my

mind I can already see the headlines. *What insult did Ruben whisper to Zach onstage last night? Inside source gives us the catty details on the latest in their dramatic feud.*

It's time for us to perform "Guilty," complete with Jon's updated choreo. Impressively, even though Jon was only taught the new moves a few hours ago, he nails them, and injects them with enough passion and charisma that I'm sure Valeria is side stage somewhere beaming. Jon's like all of us in that way. He'll resist where he can, but, ultimately, he jumps when and how he's told to jump. I guess he can reconcile this with his morals by reasoning that he was forced, and that he's doing it for everyone's good.

I can relate to that.

I'm so busy focusing on my own moves, and glancing at Jon to admire his new set, that it takes me several seconds to notice Angel has changed up the way he's dancing. He's supposed to be in time with Zach and me—a symmetrical unit at the back of Jon's front-and-center dance solo—but tonight he's adding in . . . *stuff.* More than just the usual flair he pushes boundaries with. I catch a pause and a wink at the crowd, then a pop of his collar when our hands are meant to be down, then a lip bite and a kick out when we're meant to be standing still with our heads to one side.

Is this how he's decided to prove his "I'm actually the sexiest one here" case to Valeria? Or is he so out of it that he's doing this without an ulterior motive at all?

It's a good thing I'm not trying to pull off new moves tonight, because I'm so distracted I'm relying completely on muscle memory to make it through. I plaster a smile on my face and start praying—to Jon's god, out of convenience, because I figure He knows enough about us by now to not need extra context—that Angel makes it through this performance without doing anything he can't take back.

By the end of the concert I'm relieved to say it could have been worse. He doesn't stage-dive, or hurt himself, or yell anything inappropriate that could get us in headlines. But, still, I'm so tense I can barely breathe right up until the moment we say goodbye to Cologne and run off the side stage, plunged out of the laser lighting and into the darkness.

Erin's there to greet us, as usual, but this time, so is Valeria.

"Great job," Valeria says to Jon, squeezing his shoulder. "No notes. I knew you could do this. It wasn't so bad, was it?"

He gives her a tight smile in reply. Personally, I'm just glad that look isn't being directed at me. He's only just started warming to me again since my tantrum earlier this week, despite saying we were cool after I pulled him aside to apologize to him the next morning.

I catch Jon's eye and mouth "you okay?" He goes purposely cross-eyed in response. Yup. That about sums it up.

Valeria turns to Angel now. From Angel, she receives an enormous, sloppy grin. He's apparently very pleased with himself.

"Next time," she says icily, "stick to the choreo. You made everyone look bad tonight. You looked like you didn't know what was going on."

"I knew what was going on," he says. "I was dancing Jon's part with him."

"Dance *your* part."

"I like Jon's part better."

Valeria looks to Erin for help, and Erin waves her off. "Angel," Erin says as we walk. "I know everyone's tired, but you're embarrassing yourself. Stick to what we've agreed on, okay? You're a legal adult, now, I expect you to act like one."

I brace myself for her to press him about the drugs. Hell, even right now it's obvious. His pupils are so dilated the iris is almost engulfed, and his jaw is working frantically. But she doesn't. Does she . . . not *notice*? Or does she just not care?

As we go about the usual routine of stripping and handing our clothes to our team to organize, Jon leans in to Angel and says under his breath, "What did you take?"

"Didn't you hear Erin?" Angel asks brightly, but with an edge. "I'm just *tired*."

I can tell from the glare Jon gives him that the conversation isn't over. But while we're surrounded by our team, there's not much we can say to him.

If they ignore it, we have to.

Synchronized, choreographed denial.

TWELVE

ZACH

Today, 10:36 a.m. (12 hours ago)
Geoff <geoffbraxton@chorusmanagement.com>
To: me

Dear Zach,

Great news! I've had a talk with Galactic and they've decided they would love to get your input on one of our upcoming songs, "End of Everything." We're thinking it might be a strong second single for *The Town Red,* and having you as a songwriter would give it a narrative edge that will really push it over the line and make it a hit. Have a tinker with the lyrics and get them back to me and I'll pass them on—we'd love for this to work out, and to get you a songwriter credit on the LP!

Best,
Geoff

Things lately are . . . wonderful. Completely and utterly wonderful.

Sure, the email is great, and I've already been brainstorming lyrics. But being with Ruben blows that out of the water. I can't recall the last time I've smiled this much.

We just wrapped up another show in Cologne, and it felt like my best performance in ages. I was on *fire*. I hit every note perfectly and I had so much freaking fun onstage. The crowd responded, cheering louder than I can recall in months, so much so that the applause at the end felt endless.

Right now Ruben and I are sitting in the back seat of yet another dark, anonymous minibus, sharing one of the blankets Erin got us. We're partly doing it because it's cold out—but also partly so that we can touch each other without anyone else noticing.

I'm trying to be careful about how obvious we're being, though, more than I think Ruben is. He's resting his hand on my inner thigh, and keeps inching upward.

The only issue is, I *want* to be touching him back. Everywhere. So even though it gives me heart palpitations to be doing this, especially so close to the others, I'm not stopping or moving his hand off my leg. It should be fine. We're both looking out our opposite windows, pretending to be captivated by the city, and it's not like we've never shared a blanket in the back seat before. We're a band. We share pretty much everything. If anyone looked at us, they wouldn't see anything out of the ordinary.

Ruben moves his hand off my leg, and I miss it, but then he runs his fingers down my arm and starts drawing circles on my wrist. I turn my hand, and our fingers interlock, so I can feel the heat of his palm against mine.

"Hey, boys," says Erin, from the front seat.

As casually as I can, I pull my hand away. I glance at Ruben, trying to silently apologize. But if anything, his wide eyes make it seem as if he's just as alarmed as I am.

"Get off your phones and look out your window for one second," she says. "The Cologne Cathedral is coming up."

The minibus turns a corner, and through the front window is a view of maybe the most badass-looking building I've ever seen. It's a towering gothic building, one that would probably be right at home in a horror movie, honestly. Its stone spires are lit up by hundreds of yellow lights underneath. I'm not sure if this is offensive to think or whatever, but it kind of looks like a castle a monster would live in. Like Dracula or some shit. It's just so over the top in a cool, freaky way.

I'm obsessed.

The driver pulls over, and I start smiling. Again. God damn it. Even though it's a struggle to keep my eyes open, I feel hope catch on in my chest. If the outside is this cool, who even knows what will be inside? I bet it's amazing.

"It's something, right?" says Erin. "I knew you'd like it, Zach."

"I love it."

"Same," says Jon, awestruck. It might have some big importance to his religion. It might matter to him as something much more than a cool-looking building, I don't know. "I can't believe I didn't know this existed."

The rest of us just murmur in agreement. Angel takes a photo of it on his phone, and I see him Snapchat it to someone. Probably a model.

Ruben was taking it in before, but now he's focused on his phone, the screen lighting up his face. His frown tells me all I need to know. His mom must've messaged him again. He's getting multiple texts from her a day now, and they're never just checking in. It's always a link to some article online criticizing him.

"Hey," I say. "Ignore her."

He presses his lips together and slides his phone back into his pocket. I know him, though, and I know he'll read whatever article his mom sent him as soon as he's alone. He can't help but scratch that itch.

Erin nods at the driver, and we move away from the curb.

Wait, no.

I lean forward, to ask if we can go inside. "Hey, Erin."

"Yeah?"

Everyone is staring at me, and the answer is going to be no anyway. I know that.

"Doesn't matter," I say, falling back in my seat.

I should've known better than to get my hopes up. It was such a long shot.

"We'll come back," says Ruben, his voice just above a whisper. "We'll see it then."

Under the covers, he reaches out. I put my hand on his, and he squeezes.

I wonder if he means "we" as the band, or like, *us* as a we. He used the word "relationship" to describe what we are doing, but that was a slip of the tongue—at least he swears it was. I'm pretty convinced there was a grain of truth in it, though.

The weirdest part is the thought doesn't freak me out at all. Something like this is what I've been waiting for ever since Hannah. Something that just clicks. The thought of Ruben and me as a couple, not only dating but going on our own European vacation together, feels great. We'd have to do things mostly in private, at least for the time being, but I know it'd be so worth it. Plus, I like doing *things* in private with Ruben. Like, a lot.

For us to travel here as a couple, though, we'd need to come out publicly at some point. Ruben hasn't even done that yet. I know people will care, but right now, the thought of us as a couple just seems nice. To be there for him and for him to be there for me, and for us to have a good time together, making out whenever we get the chance . . . it sounds nice.

Ruben and I hold hands secretly all the way back to the hotel, only breaking apart when we have to get out. Like everywhere we've stayed on this tour, this hotel, the Excelsior Hotel Ernst, is one of, it not *the,* best in the city, and it shows. This time, though, it irks me a little. While it's nice to see a new place, hotels always start to look the same after a while. This isn't really Cologne, it's just another fancy hotel. We could be anywhere right now. Maybe I'm being a brat, but this is all starting to feel a little anonymous. Like we may as well still be touring at home.

Ruben nudges me. "Still upset about the cathedral?"

I freeze. I sort of forgot that I can still say *words* in public to Ruben.

"It just looked so cool," I say. "I love that gothic stuff so much."

"You're so weird."

"Says the musician who only listens to one album."

I notice Angel and Jon are watching us. Jon seems quietly pleased, and Angel is grinning. I wonder how they'd react if they found out. I'm sure they at least will be supportive, but I guess there's no way of knowing until it happens.

Bone-deep exhaustion has turned me into a grumpy troll by the time we get to our hallway, and I just want to get into bed and put headphones in and listen to music. My kind of music. I'm probably the most even-keeled in the band, save for maybe Jon, but I'm still human and I have my moments where I'm a nightmare and I hate everything. I just make it a point that people don't see them. Angel and Jon go into their rooms, and I see that the hallway is empty.

Ruben is loitering in his doorway. He tilts his head back toward his room.

Okay.

This is way better than my original plan.

I go up to him, and move in a little too close as I slide inside his room. Only it's *not* too close. Because this is okay now. Ruben often does this tiny little semi-smirk before I'm about to kiss him. I don't even know if he knows that he does it, but seeing it is enough to make me hard. Already. Damn. I'm self-conscious that he might see, and skinny jeans were definitely a mistake right now.

He closes his door, and the second it latches shut I move forward to press him up against it. I put my hands on his hips and grip him tight.

"Hey," he says, looking up at me with wide eyes.

I kiss him so hard he rocks up against the doorway. I was tired, but not anymore. I want this. I need it. Any frustration I had before about never being able to see any of the places we've visited goes away; this is the only place I want to be right now. I lose myself for a moment. Ruben runs his hands up my forearms and then back down. Then he's taking off my shirt. He tosses it away.

He touches my bare chest. I go to take his shirt off, to even up, but he stops me. "You're beautiful," he says. He runs a finger up my stomach. He kisses my neck, and I close my eyes, enjoying the sensation. He starts kissing harder, so it's just below the limit of painful, but also it's so, so not.

"So are you."

To distract him, I kiss him again, pressing my body against his. He puts his arms under mine, and touches my back. Then he lifts his legs up and wraps them around me, so I'm pinning his back to the wall.

"I didn't know I could do this," I say.

He laughs, and rests his head on my bare shoulder. "You're a natural."

My breath catches in my throat. Nobody knows about this. This is one of the first things I've had all of my own since Saturday started.

He tilts his head, and I tease my tongue against his skin and breathe in a little. He lets out the softest moan, and I like it so much it's kind of wild. I want to go harder, but I don't want to give him a hickey. Or, I do, I just don't want the questions that will follow if anyone sees. Instead I bring a hand up and run it over his chest then up through his hair. Knotting my fingers through, I move his head to the other side, and I kiss his neck there.

He starts laughing.

I move back. Even though I'm supporting most of his weight, it feels comfortable. "What?"

"Nothing."

"No, what?"

"I used to think you were *really* straight."

"So did I," I say, laughing, too, now.

I lower him back to the ground and put my hands on the hem of his shirt in a question. He raises his arms so I can pull it off, my fingers scraping lightly against his skin.

I gently push him toward the bed.

He falls back, grinning. I fall, too, so now I'm on top of him, cupping his face, and I can feel that he's obviously having as good a time as I am.

I need a second, so I move sideways, so I'm lying next to him. We're both breathing heavily.

He's gorgeous.

His bare chest is rising and falling rhythmically. It's still a novelty for me to allow myself to stare, without pulling my gaze away in embarrassment or distracting myself to fuel my denial. His chest is toned, and his skin looks so perfect, smooth, and tanned.

Ruben starts rubbing my arm with the back of his hand. It's kinda scary, but I'm getting very close just from the contact and the kissing, and I think I should slow down but I don't want to. I lean across and kiss him, trapping his arm between us.

"Have you done this before?" he asks.

His eyes are half-closed.

"What do you mean?"

"Like, have you ever . . ." He trails off, searching for the words. ". . . done . . . much with a guy?"

My cheeks start burning. "Oh. Nope. Is that a problem?"

"No, not at all. Just checking."

I lie back down, and rest a hand behind my head. "Cool."

"So . . . if we did anything else, it'd be totally new."

My breathing gets shallow. I think I know what he's getting at, and I know what's happening. "Yeah." My voice comes out thin and high-pitched, and I swallow.

"How would you feel about that?"

I barely manage to force the words out I'm so breathless. "Really, really good."

"Good," he whispers.

I unbutton my jeans with trembling fingers, trying and failing not to stare at Ruben as he slowly pulls off his own. Once we're just in our underwear, we both pause. Somehow, this feels like the tipping point. We've never been fully naked around each other.

"What?" he asks. He seems almost self-conscious, which is weird, because he's like, perfect.

"Nothing, you just look good."

"Well." He grins. "Thanks. So do you." He pauses. "Seriously, are you sure you're okay? I know this is new to you, so I don't want to rush you . . ."

"You're not rushing me. I've done stuff before, just not with a guy."

"And how does it feel?"

"Not that different."

His face falls.

I press a kiss to the top of his shoulder. "Not like that. It just feels natural. How does it feel to you?"

"Ah, yeah, pretty sure I'm fine right now. I have Zach Knight in my bed. You know how many people would kill to be in my spot right now?"

"This bodes well for me." I start kissing toward his neck. "Be careful, I might decide to play the field. What's that Grindr thing everyone is always talking about?"

"Shut up," he says, kissing me, his hand going lower down my chest. "Besides. I can think of a reason why you shouldn't get Grindr."

The world falls away.

I sit up and go into the bathroom. As I go inside, I see myself in the mirror. My hair is messy and my cheeks are flushed.

I just had sex with a guy.

I know it was just hands, but I'd say it still counts. Ruben comes in and presses himself up against my back. Then he spins me around and kisses me.

"I should go," I say. "So nobody is suspicious."

"No, stay."

"I want to . . . I just . . ."

"I get it," he says, bowing his head. "Go."

I press a kiss to his lips, and then leave the bathroom to get dressed. I make sure I have my keys and wallet.

Then I leave the room, flush with joy.

Oh no.

Outside, down the hall, is Keegan, doing a routine sweep. Seriously, *again*? Somehow, I've managed to run into either him or Pauline *every* time I've snuck out of Ruben's room. I'm starting to think it's the universe playing some sort of cruel joke.

Keegan is staring at me.

I make my way back to my room as nonchalantly as possible.

"Ruben was showing me a . . . thing," I say, as I reach my door.

"Again?" says Keegan in a voice that's a little too casual to really be casual. "I'm surprised you two are functioning at all during the daytime."

"What do you mean?" I ask, my voice squeaky. It always betrays me. I shouldn't have spoken. I should've just nodded, and left, and—

"This is, what, the third time Ruben's *showed you something* in his room at one a.m. in as many days? Don't you all get up with the sun?"

I should ignore him, I should ignore him, "I—What do you mean?"

"Oh, I don't mean a thing. Just that I don't know where you kids get your endless energy from. The two of you have barely slept a wink lately. If you're not in his room all hours of the night, he's in yours."

I stare at him, and he shrugs. "Bet you're glad you've worked out whatever you were fighting over, at least?"

I shouldn't be trusted with anything.

I'm just going to make this worse if I stick around, so I go into my room and close the door behind me.

Fuck. He knows. I just gave us away. And now he's going to tell Geoff and everything is going to suck.

I flick my light off, and fall back onto my bed. Everything crashes down around me.

What have I done?

I'm experiencing a lot of clarity right now, and with this clear-mindedness has come the fear. I just had sex with my best friend, but also a guy who is effectively my coworker. This is going smoothly now, but if things change, it could be catastrophic. And I was *caught*.

Someone other than us knows now.

I start messaging Ruben.

> Hey. Keegan knows. He
> seemed really suspicious
> when I ran into him just now.

Wait, what??

> Yeah. He said we've been
> spending every night
> together, basically.

Shit.

Okay.

Shit.

So what do we do?????

I don't know. Do you think
he'll out us?

I chew my lip while I wait for a reply.
My phone lights up.

If he's caught on, it's not going
to be long before the others do. I
guess we were optimistic to think
we can hide it forever.

I have a bad feeling they're going
to find out sooner or later. The
question is do we want to take
control of how they find out?

I know what he's getting at. My hands shake as I type out:
I'd rather they hear it from us. If they find out in any other way
we'll be in so much trouble. Maybe we tell them tomorrow?

I don't send it, though. If I do this, people will know
about me, just like they know about Ruben. But also, not a
single part of me is ashamed about what I'm doing with him,
and thinking of myself as bi is getting more comfortable with
every passing day.

And Chorus has made it very clear what they think about
secrets. They need to be told about everything going on in
our lives, so that they can plan accordingly, and our narrative can never get wrenched away from us. If I want to keep
hooking up with Ruben, it can't remain a secret. Otherwise
someone will out us and it will blow up into a massive thing.
We need to be ahead of it.

Plus, Angel and Jon are two of my closest friends. I want

them to know about me. I just thought I had more time than this to come out.

But . . . I guess I don't.

I hit send.

Are you sure??

Yeah. I wish we had more time, but you're right. I don't want them finding out from anyone else but us.

Right. Well maybe sleep on it, and if you still want to, we can tell them at breakfast tomorrow.

Sounds good. Night.

Night. Sleep well. 😊

NOOO I MEANT TO SEND THIS ONE 😊

Sure you did. 😊

😄

Unsurprisingly, I didn't sleep well last night.

I'm in the shower now. I should've gotten out five minutes ago, but I haven't yet. I keep telling myself just a few more minutes.

I'm not even sure why I'm stalling. Being out to Ruben has been so utterly wonderful, and now that one person knows, coming out feels so much easier. Not effortless, no way, but definitely easier.

But Ruben has showed me how great it is to have people know about this side of me.

Ruben has asked me multiple times if I'm sure, and I honestly am. It might not be exactly what I want to do, but I know it's the right call. I think he's surprised by the speed of this, and I completely get that. I think I learned from my time keeping my feelings a secret from him that not talking can be even more devastating than just saying the truth.

So yeah. As far as I can tell, I have no reason to not come out to the team, and maybe a lot to gain if I do.

But at the same time, I can't get myself to get out of the shower. I think it's because once I've said it I can't take it back, so I want to be sure.

Last night, I spent hours reading every article and Reddit thread on coming out that I could find. I discovered a subReddit called Gaybros, which had a bunch of great advice. Seeing countless guys just like me on the Internet talking about their coming out experiences really comforted me. The only people whose families seemed to have major issues with it were the religious ones, which did freak me out a little, considering how Catholic the Braxtons are. Then again, Jon is a huge ally. He's never treated Ruben any different from the rest of us, and I know Ruben and Jon have had plenty of deep conversations about the intersection between religion and sexuality. Jon's stance has always been that the God that he believes in loves all. Ruben has some issues with the way the church has treated gay people throughout history, but he knows that Jon, and a lot of other Christians, have his back. He just says he wishes Jon and others like him would challenge the status quo a little more, and for the most part, Jon agrees.

Geoff, though . . .

I don't think he's going to be mad at me for being queer. But this will definitely change the narrative of the band once it becomes public knowledge. As far as I know, two members in the same boy band have never dated before. Or have been out at the peak of the band's success. If it's found out, it will become a *huge* news story. It could easily become Saturday's defining characteristic.

Plus, I'm not dumb. I know who listens to our music the most, and it's teenage girls. Our fans are very liberal, and are normally very on board with LGBT+ people. But a big part of our appeal has always been us posing as fantasy boyfriends for our fans. There's a reason each of us fulfils an archetype, and it's so the widest variety of girls will have one guy that's their type that they can crush on. It's a science; Geoff built us to be as mass-appealing as possible. If half of us are queer, that maybe could mess with that. We have some straight and queer male fans, sure, but without straight and bi girls we'd lose the lion's share of our audience.

Okay.

I need to stop stalling.

I shut the water off.

I can do this. This doesn't have to be about my brand and Saturday. This can be about me telling two of my best friends something about me I've finally figured out. I'll tell Mom the next time we talk, which will probably be in a few days. At least I don't have to do that right away, because I have enough on my plate right now.

As I'm picking my clothes, I pay a lot more attention to them than I normally do. Is this the sort of outfit that a bi dude would wear? I end up settling for a black T-shirt, ripped jeans, and a studded belt, because it makes me feel like the most quintessential Zach. Which I guess means it is the kind of outfit a bi guy would wear.

I check my phone. I have a new message from Ruben.

Hey, are you coming? The rest of
us are at breakfast. And seriously,
are you sure you want to tell
them??

> Yeah, on my way, sorry. Lost
> track of time. And I am, trust
> me.

I just want you to know this is your
call, Zach. Chorus shouldn't take
this from you.

They kind of already have. But whatever.
I type back: They're not, I want to.

I go down to the restaurant at the bottom level of the hotel.
The boys of Saturday are seated at a table at the back of the
room, each with carefully portioned high-protein plates from
the breakfast buffet. I load up my own plate, with a whole-
wheat roll, some natural peanut butter, scrambled eggs, and
some sausage, then join the others.

"Guten Morgen," says Angel, as he takes a big bite of a
sausage.

Nobody seems to think anything is amiss. Angel is swip-
ing on his phone as he stuffs his face, and Jon has brought
the chunky *Wheel of Time* novel that he's been reading whenever he gets a second of free time. I bite into my roll.

Now is as good a time as any, I guess. We're far enough
away from everyone else that I can just tell these two.

"Um," I say. "I have an announcement."

Jon looks up. Angel doesn't.

"What is it?" asks Jon.

Here we go . . .

"Um, so, yeah, there's this thing I think you two should know about."

That finally gets Angel's attention. "What'd you do? Hook up with a prostitute? I've got it, you shoplifted, didn't you?"

"What? No, nothing like that."

"Damn," he says, then he peers at me. "Holy shit, you like guys?"

Well, that's one way for this to go down.

"Um, yeah, actually. I'm bi."

"Called it," he says, then takes another bite of his sausage. Jon goes really still.

"I'm sorry I didn't tell you two sooner, I was just figuring stuff out, and then . . . well. Jon, you're being really quiet."

"Am I? Sorry, I'm just listening." Something must cross my face, because his eyes widen. "You know I love you no matter what, right?"

"Yeah. I love you, too."

He grins, then lightly punches me on the shoulder. "This is great. Good for you, Zach."

Angel glances at me, and then at Ruben, who's pointedly avoiding eye contact with him. *"No."*

"What?" says Jon.

"They're hooking up."

Jon whips his head around so fast I'm worried he's going to hurt himself. *"What?"*

Ruben asks me a question with his eyes: *Can I tell them?*

I nod. Here we go.

"Angel's not off base," he says.

"Holy shit," says Angel. "This is *huge.*"

"Keep your voice down," hisses Jon. "Have you told Erin?"

"Not yet, but we kind of have to," I say. "Keegan caught us last night."

"Scandal!" says Angel. "Ugh, I love this. You two got busted having sex by security, the drama of it all."

I start blushing.

Jon frowns. "That means they're basically forcing you out, Zach."

"No, I mean . . ."

"That's what it sounds like to me."

"Agreed," says Angel. "It's bullshit."

"I'm okay with people knowing," I say. "Seriously. Sure, maybe this isn't the timeline I would've picked for myself, but it's fine. I'm not ashamed of being bi."

"You shouldn't be," says Ruben.

"You do know that Dad's going to freak out about this?" says Jon, glancing between Ruben and me. "But I'm happy for you, though. I promise. You make a cute couple."

Ruben goes red. "We're not a couple."

"Friends with benefits, then, whatever," Angel jumps in. "It's still cute." He stands. "You know what this calls for, right? Group huuugggg."

"Do we have to?" Ruben grumbles, but as Angel tugs us up, a tiny smile breaks through.

It's funny. Group hugs used to be such a thing with the four of us. I didn't realize how much I'd missed them.

I knew Angel and Jon would be supportive, but it's so cool to know that's not just a theory anymore. My instincts have been proven correct.

Across the restaurant, I see Erin walk inside. Soon, I need to tell her, too. But I can wait a few seconds.

I can have this moment just for me.

THIRTEEN

RUBEN

"Well, obviously, this is wonderful."

Out of all the things I expected to hear from Geoff on this call, this ranks somewhere down the bottom, smack between "We're passing complete creative control on to you, boys" and "I've decided to become the fifth member of Saturday."

On the chair beside me, Zach's face lights up. I'm not sure he has a suspicious bone in his damn body. "Really?" he asks.

"Of course!" On-screen, Geoff leans back in his chair, his already wide-set features spreading further into a smile. It's a dangerous smile. The smile of someone watching their opponent make a fatal move in chess. Of someone watching their enemy sign their own death warrant.

Or—*or*—I'm paranoid as hell after growing up in a house of dangerous smiles, and it's impossible for me to trust that an authority figure is genuinely happy for me when I, personally, feel like I've gone against their wishes. One or the other.

Erin is perched on the edge of her bed so we can take the two seats by the table. She gives us a thumbs-up, and *her* smile definitely doesn't seem dangerous. So maybe I should relax.

"Young love is a beautiful thing, boys," Geoff goes on, a

regular romantic poet now, apparently. "Although, I'm sure I don't have to impress upon you the importance of maintaining a professional working relationship, no matter the outcome, here."

I wish he hadn't used the word "love." This is all feeling a little intense. But I nod firmly, shoving my embarrassment aside. "Absolutely. The band comes first, for both of us."

"I'm very glad to hear that." There's that smile again. My arms pull into my body against my will, like they're putting up reinforcements.

Zach straightens, putting his hands on his knees. "Um, I need to let you know, though, I'm not ready for . . . there's a lot of people who don't know. Like, my parents. Can this stay on a need-to-know basis, for now?"

For once, Geoff looks sincere. "Zach, of *course*. I wouldn't dream of overstepping like that. Your private life is your business."

Zach seems to melt into himself, and he flashes me a relieved smile. I try to return it, but my lips are weighed with lead.

Then Geoff continues. "In fact, I think you should take your time. This isn't the sort of thing we want to make public right this second, anyway."

"No?" I ask, trying to keep my voice light.

The thing is, this is all feeling like déjà vu. From the fact that interviewers who *must* be aware that I'm gay never seem to ask about this, as though they've been instructed not to, to the "insider sources" who continually "leak" stories about my latest girlfriends, to the dozens of gimmicky articles they've run with us where we're encouraged to share what our ideal *woman* is like. It doesn't take a genius to read between the lines to the implication. In public, you're straight. In private, your life is your business.

Zach's got to be aware of this. He's seen me go through it. But maybe I've rolled with the punches too efficiently, because he doesn't seem to notice any red flags here. If anything, he seems thrilled.

But then, maybe he should be. I've never particularly wanted to keep my sexuality a secret; for Zach, though, it's new, and confusing, and discretion is likely exactly what he wants. So, is it the end of the world if Geoff wants this to stay on the down-low for now? If it's what Zach needs, who am I to kick up a fuss?

Still, for clarity's sake . . . "I agree," I say with false cheer. "There's no rush. But when you say right this second . . . ?"

"I'm just thinking about Russia," Geoff says. "Given the political climate over there, it's our priority to keep you boys completely safe. We have a duty of care. I can't say exactly what would happen if this gets out before that tour stop . . ."

"Right," Zach says. "They might cancel the show."

"They might," says Geoff. "There are anti-propaganda laws in place, especially in regards to minors, which constitute the majority of your audience. But even if we were to find a way around that, traveling there amidst a likely media storm about your relationship . . . well, some people might object to our presence strongly enough that we end up in a dangerous situation."

"Our" presence, he says. Like he'll be there alongside us. Good joke.

Zach's eyes widen. "Shit."

"Exactly. But in the grand scheme of things, that stop's only seconds away. Once it's over, we can all have a conversation about the next best steps. Sound good?"

Zach nods enthusiastically. I hesitate, then give a single, curt nod.

There's a fairy tale Dad used to read to me before bed, about a gingerbread man who needs to cross a river. A fox offers to give him a ride on his head while it swims.

Then the fox rips the gingerbread man apart while he's still conscious and screaming for his lost limbs.

"I'm a quarter gone. I'm half gone. I'm three-quarters gone. I'm all gone."

When Erin lets us out of her room, we find Jon and Angel standing right outside the door. Jon holds a finger to his lip and ushers us into his room. We all tumble onto the bed, and Zach falls backward to lie down with his legs over the side, a blissful grin on his face. "It was fine!" he says. "He was *so good* about it."

Angel's eyebrows shoot up, and Jon looks to me for clarification. I shrug and give a half smile. Something in his eyes goes hard. If anyone knows what Geoff's like, it's Jon.

When you're raised by a fox, you know better than to climb on its head.

I should've known better, too. Jon's not the only one who grew up in a fox's den.

"That's . . . great," Jon says.

"Yeah!" Zach tips his head back farther to look at me, and reaches a hand out. I give it a squeeze. I think I might squeeze a little too hard.

Angel hops up and goes to the window to look down at the crowd. "Well," he says. "Screw it. If Geoff's gonna act like a human for once, take it, I guess."

"Exactly," says Zach.

"So, when are you telling everyone?" Jon asks.

"To be determined," I say shortly. "Probably after the tour."

Jon lifts his chin slowly in comprehension, wearing a bitter smile. I shrug a single shoulder. *I know.* We announce when Geoff decides we announce. Not when we're ready.

"So, secret dating?" Angel asks, turning away from the window and leaning his hands back against the pane. "Scandalous."

"For now," Zach says. "We're just taking it as it comes. Who knows what'll happen."

"Right," Jon says delicately. "Just . . . be careful, okay? If you two break up and it gets weird, it could go bad real quick."

"What are you basing that on, Jon?" Angel deadpans, kicking off from the wall to stroll around the room. "It's not like we have *any* examples of Zach and Ruben turning into mortal enemies the second things get weird between them."

"We can't break up," I say. "Because we aren't in a relationship. We're just two people who exist in relation to each other."

Zach ducks his head to hide a laugh.

Angel widens his eyes innocently. "Oh, I'm sorry, were you in a relationship the *last time* your 'feud' became a trending hashtag?"

"We get it," Zach interjects, hoisting himself to a sitting position. "Promise. We won't let it get weird again. You can hold us to that."

"We will," Jon says. There's not a trace of playfulness in his voice, either.

"Just don't get *too* cutesy, okay?" Angel says, turning slowly in the middle of the room like he's performing a dance solo for us. "I don't like it when I'm not the center of everyone's universe, so I'm gonna need you to be mindful of my feelings."

"Don't worry," Zach says. "You'll always be the center of Jon's universe."

Jon rolls his eyes and Angel doesn't look impressed. "Yay. But for real. No dates without me, okay? I get an all-access pass to dates."

"Watch what you wish for," I say. "Some things work better with two people."

Zach suddenly becomes very interested in the ceiling, and shuffles away from me on the bed, his entire face deepening into an unflattering shade of ketchup-red.

Angel blinks, looks between Zach and me, then mimes gagging. "Nope. This is already too much for me. Jon, it's not them we need to worry about. This is weird for *me*."

I shrug. "Well, don't talk about our dates if you don't want to hear about it!"

"Keep it PG, at least," Angel moans. "*Jesus.*"

"What dates did you *think* you'd be joining them on?" Jon laughs. "It's not like they can go for brunch at a local café at the moment."

I try to keep my face neutral, but apparently I fail, because Angel pounces on me immediately. "What don't we know?" he demands, grabbing the head of the bed frame.

I look over at Zach helplessly. This seems like something I shouldn't share on his behalf. He only told me about the canals, after all.

Luckily, he doesn't look uncomfortable. In fact, he's wearing a conspiratorial grin. "We *may* have snuck out in Amsterdam one night."

"*What?*" Angel yelps. "*How?*"

"Are you for real?" Jon asks at the same time. "You could've gotten *caught!*"

I catch Zach's eye and we grin at each other. His smile is

soft and affectionate. "Ruben thought to use the fire escape," he says. "Nobody saw us, it's fine."

Jon looks stricken, but Angel bursts out laughing. "Holy shit. I feel like I'm seeing a whole new side to you two."

"I feel like you're more shocked about us sneaking out than us hooking up in secret," I say dryly.

Angel folds his arms. "Well, neither of you have *ever* asked me to sneak out with you."

"Presumably," Jon says, "neither of them has ever asked you to make out with them, either, though?"

"Unfortunately, you'll never know the answer to that one," Angel says with dignity. "I don't kiss and tell."

Zach glances at me and raises a questioning eyebrow. I shake my head no, biting back a laugh.

"And to be fair, Zach didn't *ask* me to make out with him, per se," I start, but Angel shoves his fingers in his ears and starts singing his part in "Guilty" loudly enough to drown me out.

I can't say that it didn't occur to me it was a bad idea to put the idea of escaping the hotel in Angel's head.

It seems unlikely that it'd never occurred to him, given we literally caught him using a fire exit only last week. But I guess ducking outside to meet a dealer for five minutes is a different ball game than escaping at night to go on an adventure. Still, it's been *days* since we told him about our escape, and as far as I can tell, he hasn't tried it himself. Or, at least, if he has, he hasn't been caught.

In fact, Angel has been pretty low-key since he got into trouble for messing with the choreo in Cologne. I have no idea if it was escalated to Geoff, or if Erin's disapproval was inexplicably enough to set him straight, but he hasn't made a peep.

Which is why, when he sends a group message to us telling us about the "few friends" he has in his room tonight, I'm actually a little taken aback.

Zach, whose phone buzzed the same moment mine did, pulls his blanket to his chin and burrows deep into his mountain of pillows. "I don't want to, I just want to stay in and watch movies." Suddenly, his head snaps up. "Unless you want to? We can totally go if you want to. I'm easy."

"No, I'm happy to stay in," I say, putting my phone on his bedside table and snuggling in beside him to steal his body heat. It's an especially cool night in Berlin, and even though the rooms are all climate controlled, the steady pattering of light rain on the windows is enough to make me feel sleepy and cozy. I feel sorry for the group of fans huddled outside the hotel hoping to catch a glimpse of us. I hope they have blankets. And umbrellas.

"I can't hear any music," Zach says. "Maybe it's actually only a few friends."

"Yeah, totally," I say, walking my fingers across his bare shoulder to his collarbone. He shivers and his eyes go dark as he watches me. "I'm sure he's having one or two buddies over for a rousing game of Monopoly."

He swallows and touches my fingers, tilting his head back. The sight of him like this, shirtless and languid, sets something alight within me. The thing is, I'm quite sure he's the most impossibly beautiful thing I've ever seen. I'm about to lean forward to kiss him on his lips, or his neck, or anywhere and everywhere he'll let me, when he closes his grip around my hand and pushes me away to prop himself up. He suddenly looks worried. "Do you think he's okay?"

I let out a short laugh. "Ah, yes, I'm sure he's having a great time."

But Zach doesn't laugh. Instead, his eyebrows draw closer together, and he presses his lips thin. I haul myself up into a half-sitting position to match him and lean forward. "Hold on, what do you mean?"

"I don't know. He's just . . . he's been high a couple of times recently, and if he's having friends around . . . I'm probably overthinking it."

The thing is, though, that up until now Zach's been much less concerned about Angel's well-being than Jon and I have. If even Zach thinks something's off enough to want to take charge here, I'm inclined to pay attention.

"Do you think we should check in on him?" I ask.

His eyes flicker to mine. "Would you mind?"

I roll my eyes and launch forward on the bed to grab his discarded shirt and throw it to him. "One day you're going to do something without permission from everyone in the room, and I'm going to pass out from shock."

"Am I that bad?" he asks as he pulls it over his head.

I head over to his side of the bed and offer him my hand to pull him up. "The worst. But don't panic, you're still the best."

Jon's already in Angel's room when we get there. Like Zach had hoped, there's only a handful of visitors this time. Nothing like Paris. But unlike Paris, I don't recognize anyone, and everyone seems to be buzzing. The conversations are all happening in double-time, with most conversation partners both speaking over each other. And whether they're standing by the window, or kneeling on the bed, limbs are trembling and postures are odd and eyes are a little too wide.

Angel, who was speaking earnestly with Jon by the bathroom door, flings himself at us when we enter. Beads of sweat are glistening on his forehead, and his hair is hanging in damp strands. "You *made it*," he cries out, flinging his arms around us both so our heads knock together. "I thought you were gonna ditch us and do your *own thing* tonight."

I rub my head while Zach grabs Angel to hold him steady. "Angel, you haven't told anyone here about . . . that, right?" he whispers.

Angel narrows his eyes and pouts. "That's a secret," he says. "I'm not stupid. Or a piece of shit."

His voice hardened at that last part, and I wonder for a second if he's offended Zach suspected him. But there's no time to ask, because he's bounded off to talk to an unfamiliar, petite girl with long dark hair styled into twists.

Jon joins us by the door. "I think I'm gonna go to bed soon," he says in a heavy voice.

I know just how he feels.

Two guys dressed head to toe in gaudy designer clothing head in our direction. They're covered in logos and insignias, just in case anyone missed that they are, indeed, *very rich*—ironically, the exact sort of outfit that announces to the very people they want to fit in with that they've only been rich for five minutes, tops. The taller of the two reaches out to shake each of our hands and introduce himself as Elias, like we're heading into a goddamn business meeting. "It's so good to see you three," he says warmly.

He talks like we're old friends, but I'm perfectly sure we've never met before. My guess is he'll probably spend the next year of his life talking to anyone who'll listen about the time he hung out with the guys from Saturday and changed our lives forever through the sheer power of his charisma and wisdom or some shit. God only knows how he knows Angel. How *any* of these people know Angel.

Elias holds out a clear baggie of what can only be cocaine,

as casually as if he was passing a cigarette. "Want some?" he asks cheerfully.

The three of us glance at each other.

"Oh, no, *thank you*, though, that's so nice."

"Huge day tomorrow."

"That's extremely illegal."

Everyone turns to look at Jon, and the two guys hesitate, their expressions unreadable. I wave a hand at them in the hopes it'll diffuse any tension. "You two go on ahead," I say with a forced smile, and they disappear into the bathroom, pulling the door closed firmly behind them. My guess is they were initially aiming for the surface of the wooden stand beside us. If I ever have the inclination to snort a line of coke, I wouldn't want to do it under the judgmental eyes of Jon, either, though, so I don't blame them.

Angel waltzes back over, holding hands with the pretty long-haired girl. "We're going to the roof," he says.

"The *roof*?" Zach asks. "It's freezing."

"It's fine. We're going to say hi to the fans!"

"From the roof?" I repeat.

"Yes. Lina wants to greet them." He mimes waving like the queen, pursing his lips together, and the girl, who I assume is Lina, bursts into too-loud laughter. "And our window doesn't look down upon the crowd, Ruben, my love."

"We'll come," Zach says, giving me a meaningful look. "We can all say hi together."

"No offense, Zachy, but I don't need a third wheel." Angel pinches Jon's cheek, then mine. "Or a fourth. Or a fifth. I'll be back in a minute, get a *drink,* have some *fun,* for god's sake. It's not like we get many fucking opportunities."

Before we can protest further, Angel steers Lina past us and out the door.

The three of us stand in a group, uncertainly, staring

after him. I steal a glance at Zach. He's biting his lower lip so hard it's disappeared.

"They aren't going onto the roof, are they?" I ask.

Zach shakes his head slowly. Jon looks confused, then comprehension dawns. "Oh, *no*."

By the time we burst into the hallway, Angel and Lina are nowhere to be seen.

"Let's get Keegan and Pauline," Jon says.

Zach looks over his shoulder, alarmed. "But he'll get in so much shit!"

"Um, not as bad as they will if they get into an accident because they're high off their faces."

They turn to look at me as one. Oh. I guess it's my call. "Come on," I say, already moving. "If we can catch them now, no one has to know. We'll call the team if we need to."

It takes us longer than it should to find the fire escape in our panic. Which, to me, seems like the sort of thing they should account for when providing directions to an *emergency escape door*, but I digress. We could try the elevator, but we'll only lose time trying to figure out where the fire escape opens into. Not to mention if we take the elevator we'll have to pass the throngs of fans gathered by the main entrance, as well as our Berlin guards stationed in the lobby.

"Should we check the roof first?" Jon asks as we file in. We pause. It probably does make sense to check there first before we go running into the night. But if we go all the way up, we'll lose any hope of finding Angel if he *has* left the hotel.

"No time," I say. "Zach, spam his phone. See if you can get him to pick up. If he *is* on the roof, he won't ignore you for long."

We take the stairs at a run, which isn't an easy feat, given we started at level forty-one. Thank god for our oppressive workout schedule.

Zach peeks out the door at the bottom to check where we are before we tumble out. Luckily, the door emerges into a parking lot. Enclosed enough we won't be spotted by the crowd camping out in front of the hotel, but open enough we can already spot a way to get onto the street.

The air rakes at our faces with icy fingers, and the wind blows with enough force to snatch words away, carrying frigid raindrops that slam into every bit of exposed skin. I'm wearing a crew-neck cashmere sweater—fine for a hotel party, less fine for these sorts of conditions. I wish to hell I'd had time to grab a coat. We run along the paved concrete, close to the row of towering masonry buildings, and my heart skips a beat every time a car passes. Will someone recognize us? Then what?

"Angel!" Zach calls, looking desperately around the streets. The only people nearby are an older couple huddled under an umbrella, and they don't even glance back at us.

"Don't call his name," I whisper. With the amount of fans camped out at the hotel, being overheard is more of a *when* than an *if*. And Angel isn't exactly a subtle name.

Zach nods and slows us to a stop, then turns in a circle. "Reece!" he shouts to the sky instead. "REECE!"

"It's still attracting too much attention," Jon murmurs.

Zach looks back down and scowls. "How am I supposed to attract Angel's attention without attracting attention?"

We start walking again, and Jon shakes his head. "I'm calling Keegan," he says.

"Wait," Zach says. "*Please,* Jon. Can't we just—"

"They could get *hurt,* Zach!"

"Just let me try his phone one more time?"

We round a corner and turn onto a busy main street. The relative anonymity of the previous alley is lost as the orange glow of streetlights and headlights washes over us. I scan our surroundings, taking in the rows of uniform trees, bustling outdoor dining spots, and ancient stone buildings decorated with towering cream columns. Then I grab Zach's shoulder excitedly. Separating two multi-laned roads is a wide pedestrian strip lined with park benches and shrubs, and walking down the middle of that strip are Angel and Lina.

We break into a jog again. They have their backs to us, so they don't hear us approach until we're upon them. When he finally does notice us, Angel doesn't exactly look pleased for the company.

"Can't I have five minutes to myself?" he snaps, ripping his hand away from Lina's. She gives him a wounded look as he raises his voice further. "Not even five minutes?"

We slow to a stop, and he takes a few steps back. His eyes are wild and unfocused, and he's breathing heavily. Jon was right. We shouldn't technically be out here alone for a variety of reasons, but Angel, in particular, should *not* be out right now.

A prickling on my peripheries tells me there are already curious eyes fixed on us. I ignore them for now. Time's slowed down, measurable by tasks on my to-do list. Task one: try to calm Angel down. "You invited everyone over to your room," I remind him in a measured voice. "Everyone's missing you."

He looks from me to Zach to Jon and plants his feet apart. "I spend all day, every day, with you three," he says in a rush. "*No one else.* Aren't I allowed to have some fun with some friends sometimes? Can't I have that?"

"Of course you can," Zach says. "That's what we're saying. All your friends are in your room, waiting for you."

"They're not my friends. Lina is my friend. And Lina and I want to explore Berlin. You know, given I traveled five thousand fucking miles and haven't seen *any of Europe.*"

"We know," I say, stepping forward. Angel takes another step back. His knees are slightly bent, like he's poised to run. "It's shit. It's *totally* bullshit. Maybe we should ask for a meeting with Erin, see if we can—"

"*You two*," Angel cries, interrupting me, "already *went out*. You've been *having* fun. And you won't let me do it? What makes you so special?"

"Angel, people are looking," Jon pleads. And they are. We've attracted the full attention of several people on the street, as well as some people drinking in front of cafés. A few phones are already out.

Angel throws his arms to the side. "*Let them look, Jon!* You're so fucking preoccupied with what people think of us. Relax, pull the goddamn stick out your ass, *please*."

"He's worried about *us*, not himself," I cut in with a firm voice. "You're embarrassing all of us right now."

"Oh, now I'm an *embarrassment*, Lina," Angel shouts. "I'm the only one of us who doesn't act like a goddamn robot, and I'm an embarrassment! Oh, Geoff says I have to make people wanna fuck me, so I'll strip. Geoff says I can't write my own music, so I'll write *his* music. Geoff says I can't tell anyone about our secret—"

"*Angel*," Zach cries.

"GOD-FUCKING-DAMNIT, ZACH," Angel roars. "I LITERALLY JUST TOLD YOU I WOULDN'T TELL ANYONE. Why do you all think I'm an idiot?"

There's about two dozen phones, now. And down the street, there are people running toward us. A lot of them look like young girls.

Shit.

They'll be on us in a minute or less. Word spreads fast.

"Jon," I say under my breath. "I think you can call Keegan now."

"You *think*?" he hisses.

Zach's spotted the approaching hordes. "Angel, we've got to go," he says.

They're calling our names. Screaming our names, really. Louder, and louder, as they get closer. Our onlookers turn from the girls to us, putting two and two together. More phones are whipped out, like a ripple. The lights glow brighter and brighter until I feel like I need to squeeze my eyes shut before my vision closes in.

Zach steps forward, arm outstretched, and that's a step too far for Angel. With a strangled noise that doesn't sound quite human, Angel grabs Lina's arm and breaks into a sprint, launching onto the road.

Time slows down even further. Headlights flash in the distance. Far enough away that Angel and Lina can make it across both lanes. Just. But then Zach moves. Darts forward to chase Angel.

The headlights are too close for him to make it.

I don't make the decision to move. But I move.

I grab Zach in a bear hug and wrench him back onto the pedestrian strip. Headlights flash, and horns blare, and they're screaming our names. They're screaming for Angel. I think I'm screaming, too.

Zach and I stumble together, and I catch us before we hit the ground.

Finally, time catches back up.

"*Jesus*, Zach," I'm shouting, still gripping him. "Watch what you're doing!"

Angel's made it to the other side of the street. He falters, as he realizes there are fans closing in from both ends of the street. Lina is looking around at the cameras like a cornered rabbit searching for an escape route that doesn't exist.

I remember when the sight of that many photographers

freaked me out, too. Now they only worry me if they're recording, oh, a heated argument between our group, in the middle of the night, while one of us is obviously off his face and getting dangerously close to publicly defaming our management team. *That* would be the sort of contract breach that'd see us bankrupt in a finger's snap.

One of the blinding headlights pulls to the side of the road, beside Angel. My heart jumps into my chest as I let Zach go. Is it a fan? Or someone who knows who Angel is, and also knows how much money he can get if he pulls him into his car? It probably wouldn't be a difficult feat with Angel in this state.

But the driver steps out, and I almost pass out with relief. It's Keegan.

"That was quick," I say to Jon.

Jon shakes his head. "I couldn't get ahold of him. Guess that's why."

Thankfully, Angel doesn't kick up a fuss with Keegan. Whether it's because he knows Keegan can overpower him, or he's realized he wants to get off this fast-filling street, I can't say. Zach taps me on the arm, and I turn to see Pauline's pulled up in another car, and is sitting with the hazard lights on by the strip.

We don't need to be asked—we clamber into the back seat as quickly as we can, slamming the door against the rising crescendo of people calling to us. My heart thrums in my throat, and I seek out Zach's hand the moment we're hidden. He holds me in a death grip, obviously as shaken as I am.

"Not exactly hard to find you," Pauline's saying to Jon when my mind starts processing words again. "Your photos were all over Twitter. You boys can't *cough* without it being recorded online, why'd you think you'd be able to go out without us? If you wanted some air you could've *asked* us, we could've gone for a walk around the grounds. We wouldn't have even needed to tell Erin! Now look!"

Of course they found us. We've been missing for barely fifteen minutes, and they tracked us down.

We've been missing for barely fifteen minutes, and we'd come a hair's breadth away from being mobbed. Or worse.

I've never been quite so aware of how monitored I am. But at the same time, I've never been so grateful to be closely monitored. Of course, the downside is, they're taking us back to the hotel, where our whole team is going to find out what we did.

Climb onto my head. I'll swim you across the river.

FOURTEEN

Saturday is still trending.

I keep waiting for it to die down, for something else to take over. God, please let a Kardashian do something, *anything*, to get the spotlight off us.

But no. It seems like the whole world has decided to pause so everyone can give their opinion about what is now known as Angel's Meltdown.

And boy, people sure are enjoying giving their opinion.

Today is supposed to be a rest day before our second show in Berlin tomorrow, but nobody can sit still. For most of the day the four of us have been stressing in Jon's room, because it's the cleanest, honestly. I'm at the desk, trying to tinker with the lyrics in "End of Everything." Ruben, Jon, and Angel are on the bed, trying to watch TV or browse on their laptops.

Chorus changed the passwords on our social media accounts, a temporary freeze, they promised us, so we can't post anything that could get us in even more trouble. I have been checking, though, and the Saturday account has posted a selfie of the four us we were asked to take a few days ago. In it, we're all smiling, and it seems like everything is fine.

Angel picks up the remote, and changes the channel away from the nature documentary that was on.

"Hey," says Jon. "I was watching that."

"You need a life." Angel flicks through to find a trashy news show.

They're talking about us. In German. It's really weird.

"Why?" moans Jon, resting his head back against the headboard as Angel turns on the subtitles.

"Just checking in," says Angel. "If they're talking about me, it's only fair that I hear what they're saying."

Jon pretends to fake cough. "Narcissist," he says, between coughs.

"Takes one to know one. I'm just not coy about it."

The show is a glossy panel show, the sort of thing that would air on E! at home. Behind the panelists is a screen with the words ANGEL: DURCHGEDREHT? in big white letters, along with a photo of Angel mid-tirade.

We read the subtitles: "We've seen this all before, it's very Hollywood. They get famous too young, the power goes to their heads, and then this happens. Is it inevitable? Opinion?"

"Look, no, I wouldn't say it's inevitable. There are hundreds of kids who have grown up under the spotlight who never do anything like this. I wish we talked more about them."

The audience applauds.

"Angel clearly has two paths ahead of him. One is he gets his act together and gets his life back on track. The other . . . well, I don't want to think about that, but we've seen it before."

"What could stop it, though?"

"He's the only one who can. Until he makes the connection that he's ruining his life, there's no helping him."

"Fuck off," says Angel, turning off the TV. "I bet they're all using the second they get backstage. Hypocrites."

I turn back to my computer, and check Twitter. If anything, it's worse. I don't know what I expected.

Fucking Twitter. If it got taken down à la Vine I wouldn't be mad about it.

Footage of Angel's outburst has taken over the site. Angel Phan is trending alongside the main Saturday hashtag. A still of Angel screaming has become a meme, and a reaction shot of Ruben and me looking horrified has become a popular reaction GIF.

Naturally, Chorus has been freaking out. We're being kept in here until further notice "for our own safety," which really means until they figure out what our next move is. Like always, we'll only be told when they come to a decision, because they know best.

I click on the Saturday hashtag, which is still number one worldwide. I'm not sure why I keep checking it. It's like I think if I keep my eyes on it, it might slow down or go away. It hasn't yet, though.

The top tweet is fucking TMZ, with the caption: FALLEN ANGEL: formerly squeaky-clean Angel Phan of Saturday is GUILTY of getting wasted in Berlin! Watch his drunken tirade now!

I start reading the comments.

Yikes.

They're all saying what I feared. That his rant is confirmation that we all secretly hate being in Saturday. That we hate the band, and all want to escape. Even the people who have us as their avatar seem to be having a field day with this. One with over three thousand likes just says I KNEW HE HATED SATURDAY LMAOOOOOO.

I keep reading.

who cares omfg???

Honestly, I wish they'd quit and go solo already, we
all know they're going to. Maybe then my boy Ruben
can get out of this mess okay

They haven't even been good since self-titled, stream
REDZONE

I want to remind people that it's legal for the boys
to drink in Berlin! Like, who hasn't gotten messy
occasionally? Jfc

Where is Jon?? His bottom is in trouble #anjon

He's probably just mad "Signature" flopped
hahahahaha.

My eyes start to sting. It's all bad. It's just all criticism,
never-ending.

We're a boy band, so getting hate comes with the job de-
scription, and after two solid years of constant online abuse,
I've gotten as used to it as possible. I've learned to avoid
social media as much as I can and I try never to read comments. For one thing, I think the music we make is good,
even if it's not really my thing, and that helps.

Second, every famous person I know has dealt with this.
Some more than others, sure, but nobody is liked by everyone. It's impossible. Before they get big everyone thinks
they're going to be the *one* artist everyone loves, but it never
works out like that. Never. Every single person has at least
one thing about them a lot of people won't like. Hell, even
Beyoncé gets hate for being *too* perfect.

The thing is, haters and trolls don't matter, even if it seems like they do. Sales are the most important thing, and we're still breaking records. While we still have that, the trolls can talk their shit, but we're safe. I know that.

I exhale.

As long as we haven't upset Geoff too much, we'll survive this. His opinion is the one that really matters.

I run a hand through my hair, pushing it up and away from my forehead. It keeps falling over my eyes lately. I'd definitely cut it if I could. I read more comments, trying to find one positive one. Or one that is positive enough to drown out the dreck. Further down, there are actually a lot of fans standing up for Angel, but those seem a lot quieter than the haters for some reason. They shouldn't be, though. They should matter just as much.

Ruben slides out of bed, and comes up to me. I minimize the browser.

He starts rubbing my shoulders. I hadn't realized how tense they'd become. "What were you looking at?"

"Porn."

"Fun, show me."

I roll my eyes and load the page.

"Oh God, were you reading comments?"

"I can't help it."

"Zach."

"I know."

Angel bounces off the bed, and comes up to us. "What are they saying?"

"Are you sure this is a good idea?" asks Jon, then he pauses, having a moment of self-realization. "Am I always such a buzzkill?"

"Only most of the time," says Angel. "We still love you."

The four of us huddle around my computer, and scroll

the feed, before Angel makes me click on #angelphanisover-party, which is, unsurprisingly, extra toxic.

"This is wild," says Angel. "Am I canceled?"

I'm actually so curious to find out how he feels about all this, but he isn't giving it up. If anything, he's grinning and his eyes have lit up. I'm not sure I trust this, though. Sometimes I feel like Angel is playing a character even when he's not onstage. It's just different from his Saturday role.

A knock sounds on the door.

We all scramble. Jon jumps onto the bed, and changes the channel on the TV. I focus on my frustratingly unaltered page with the "End of Everything" lyrics, and Angel pretends to look out the window. Ruben goes over to the door and casually opens it.

"What's up?"

It's Erin, and she surveys the room. We all look totally casual, though. Nothing to see here, folks!

"Phew," she says. "I'm so glad you're all here."

"We're in lockdown," says Angel. "Where else could we be?"

I write down *lockdown* in my notebook. It's a cool word. *My heart is locked down by you?*

"Knowing you, anywhere," she says, smiling fondly as she sits down on the edge of the bed.

"So, what's happening?" asks Jon, tucking his legs up. "Is Dad mad?"

"Yes, but more than that, he's worried, we all are. Anything could've happened to you while you were out there."

Everyone goes quiet.

"It's my fault," says Angel. "I can call myself out, I know I lost my shit for a minute there. Nobody else should be in trouble, they only came after me."

"That's good, but that's not going to be enough."

Ruben's eyes narrow. He's definitely a lot more skeptical than I am, which I've always liked about him. It means he's a lot harder to mess with than I am, because I tend to accept things at face value. I can see his point now, though. I'm starting to think Geoff is actually beyond furious, but Erin is watering it down. Why would she do that, though?

"So, how much trouble am I in?" asks Angel. "Give it to me straight."

"I won't lie, it's bad."

"But hey, a little controversy never hurt anyone, right?" says Angel.

"Planned controversy is okay. This is a nightmare for Chorus. Everyone thinks that you hate being in the band."

"I don't though!"

"Doesn't matter. What the public thinks is what is important. And they're taking your video and running with it."

"What can we do?" asks Jon.

"Just give us time to figure out how to spin it. And we've had to make a change to our security. It's become obvious things with Keegan and Pauline had become too lax."

"What do you mean, 'had'?" asks Jon.

"They've been let go," says Erin.

No. No way. Keegan and Pauline have been our security guards for two years now. I am actually friends with them. I know about their families. I care about them.

"It's become clear they've become too close to you to do their jobs properly," she says, like it's no big deal. "We've terminated Tungsten's contract. They're on their way back home as we speak."

"We can't even say goodbye?" asks Angel.

"We decided it would put unnecessary stress on you all."

"You can't do this," says Ruben.

"It's already been done. We've hired Chase Protective Services, they've come highly recommended. They'll keep you safe."

"Keep us prisoner, more like," says Angel under his breath.

Erin ignores him. "Another thing. You can't have visitors anymore. We can't trust them."

"You can't be serious," Angel says.

"Hey, don't use that tone at me. We did this because *you* snuck out. We trusted you and you showed us that was a mistake."

A hard look settles in Angel's eyes.

"I'm sorry," she says. "It's been a long day. Just try and behave yourselves from now on, okay? I'll let you guys get some rest. Big day tomorrow."

She gets up off the bed, and leaves. As soon as the door clicks shut, Angel gets to his feet and starts pacing.

"This is *bullshit*."

"She does have a point," says Ruben.

Angel whips around to face him. "What?"

"You were high off your face in an unknown city with no protection," he says. "Anything could've happened."

"Don't start with me."

"What does that mean?" Ruben shoots back.

"I'm just saying you have your ways of letting off steam." Angel glances at me. "And I have mine."

"Whoa," says Jon. "Take that back."

I cross my arms. Is that all I am to Ruben? A way to let off steam, to make it through this tour? No, Angel is just being mean.

"Let's not fight," says Jon. "Let's just . . ."

"Be good boys," says Angel, now turning on Jon. "So

your dad can sit in his office and make more than each of us combined."

"That's not . . ."

"Don't you think it's weird that *you're* the one who wants us to be the best behaved? You're just thinking about your inheritance."

"Fuck you, Angel."

"Ooh, so he does know how to swear, how spicy. I . . ."

An idea crosses my mind, and before I can really think it through, I get up and go over to the mini-fridge, then swing it open. I retrieve every single mini bottle, and then dump them on the bed, silencing everyone.

"That's it," I say, as I pick up a mini bottle of Fireball. "I'm calling a truce. We need a night off."

The others are all watching me now.

"There's no way you can drink that without choking," says Angel.

I close my eyes for a second, and let it pass. If I snap back, this will just go on and on.

"Maybe we can't leave the hotel," I say, as I twist the bottle open. "But we can still have fun here. Plus, Chorus is paying."

"I'm in," says Angel. "If there was any doubt."

"You sure about this?" asks Jon.

To answer him, I lift the open bottle and take a shot.

Oh my god. This was a mistake.

It *burns*.

I cough and splutter, and the others all laugh at me while I thump my chest to get the burning to stop.

"Here," says Ruben, grabbing a can of Diet Coke from the mini-fridge and pouring it into two glasses. Then he takes the bottle of Fireball from me and pours what remains into the cup, before giving it back.

I take a sip. I can still taste the whiskey, but it's nowhere near as overwhelming as it was before. It's actually nice now.

"Better?" he asks, as he makes his own.

"Much."

"Admirable attempt at taking charge," he says. "I was intimidated until the shot."

"You were not."

"No, not really, but you *are* cute when you try to be bossy."

I grin, already a little woozy from the shot.

"And I'm in," says Jon. "I can't handle this sober."

"Amen," says Angel.

"Who'd have thought," says Ruben, as he starts massaging the top of my head. "All we had to do was hook up to get them to get along."

"Maybe we should've done it sooner."

"You," says Angel, pointing to me before taking a vodka shot. He drinks it like water. "Stop being adorable and start playing music."

"On it."

I load my Spotify. I've been listening to a compilation album of B-sides and rarities by one of my favorite bands, which isn't really the best hype music. What I want is a song we can drink to that lets us forget everything. I end up picking a hyperpop song I know Angel loves. I hit play.

"Nice choice," says Angel, who starts bopping along. "Seems like you have *some* good taste."

"Hah."

Ruben sits down beside me.

"You failed, by the way," he says, keeping his voice low.

"At what?"

"You're still being adorable."

I pretend to dry heave, because I'm pretty sure I legally

have to whenever someone says something that cheesy, even though it makes me feel all warm inside.

Still, it's nice.

We're all wasted.

Turns out, Fireball is *strong.*

Ruben and I are sitting on the floor at the foot of the bed, our legs stretched out in front of us, our hands entangled. Angel is in the bathroom, throwing up. I'm so drunk I'm only barely conscious of the sound over the music and the ringing in my ears. Jon is beside Ruben, his eyes closed, the back of his head resting on the bed.

The room is constantly lurching, and the edges of my vision are fuzzy.

"Are you o . . . kay?" asks Ruben, then he laughs. "I'm so . . . drunk."

I smile. Wherever Ruben gets drunk, he always tells people.

"I'm okay. Just drunk."

"God, same. Like, so drunk." He lifts my hand and kisses the back of it.

The song changes, becomes slower, a little sleazier. The lights of the room are off, and everything is blue and black, all swirly. Oh! I know this song. It's really sexy. Songs can be sexy. Saturday songs can be cute, but I like songs that are hot sometimes. Songs that are about sex or whatever. Maybe I could write a song about sex. That might be awkward to hand in to Geoff, though. Like, here you go, here are my thoughts on how it feels to hook up with a guy, hope you like it.

Speaking of, Ruben is beside me.

"We should go back to my room," I say, bopping him on the nose. "I want to sleep."

We've never actually slept in the same bed before, and

holy shit, I can't believe drunk me just invited him to sleep with me.

"I don't want to sleep, but your room sounds good."

In the bathroom, Angel throws up again. Gross.

Ruben and I stumble to our feet, and Jon opens his eyes.

"You're leaving?" he asks.

"Yeah, it's late," says Ruben.

Jon gets up, and we huddle together like a tripod, using each other for support.

"Okay," says Jon, pouting, and then he presses his forehead to mine, and rubs the back of my neck.

"You two are so good together. Like, really, don't mess this up, because it's special. Now go, I'll look after our resident mess."

"I heard that!"

Ruben and I leave, going out into the hall.

And holy crap.

There are two unfamiliar security guards standing at the end of the hallway. They're wearing light gray suits, with white ties. Their stoic expressions don't change when they see us.

I feel like I'm in trouble, even though I haven't done anything wrong. Drinking at eighteen is legal here. And surely these guards have been told about Ruben and me, and have signed an NDA.

Ruben and I go to my room, and we go inside. Ruben's been coming over a lot lately, so I've been keeping it cleaner than I usually do.

We fall down onto the bed, our hands entangling.

"You're really hot," I say. "You know that, right?"

"Where'd that come from?"

"I dunno. I just feel lucky, I guess. And I get what Jon was saying. This is . . . you know."

He gives me a kiss on the top of my forehead, and I close my eyes. "I've been thinking about a thing, today," Ruben says. "It's been bothering me."

"What is it?"

"It involves something I never told you. And I kinda want to tell you, but I also don't want you to think I'm an asshole."

Even though I'm completely and utterly wasted, this opening is enough for me to try to snap back into focus. "Tell me."

"You sure?"

"Yep."

"Are you sure you're sure?"

"*Yes.*"

"Okay, story time. The first day at Camp Hollow Rock, Mom and I get there stupidly early, and there's no one else there. Then a fancy car rolls up, and Mom says, 'That's Jonathan Braxton. His dad's Geoff Braxton. Make sure you get to know him.'"

I blink. Jon signed up at Hollow Rock under a fake last name every year to avoid that exact situation. If people at camp knew he was Jon Braxton he never would've been given even a second of peace, and he never could've trusted why people wanted to become friends with him. I didn't find out he was the son of Geoff Braxton until Geoff called us and our parents into a meeting the night after the final show. "So you knew who Jon was when you met him?"

"Yep."

"Does he know?"

"Yeah. God, yes, he knows. He asked me not to tell anyone who he was, and that's how we became friends. And I loved him once I got to know him. But do you think you can ever know . . . like . . . what's the word I'm looking for,

Zach? What am I saying?" He stares into the distance. "*Biased!* Can you be unbiased when you know something like that about someone? Like, I *think* that when you and Angel asked me to be in the final show with you, I would've been all 'No, Jon, has to come,' even if I didn't know who his dad was. Zachary, I would *like* to think that. I'd *like* to. But maybe I wouldn't have. Maybe I would've been like, 'Hey, Jon will find someone else to be with. He and Angel *really* don't get along, so it'll just make things awkward, blah blah.' Who knows?"

My drunk brain tries to keep up with this. "But he grew on Angel. They're fine now."

He sighs. "That's not the point."

"What's the matter, then?"

"What if I used him?" Ruben whispers. "What if I made sure we were friends so I could get in front of his dad to sing?"

"You didn't. It was obvious you liked him."

"Yeah, but I *knew*. And I couldn't, like, un-know it. So this, all of this, it didn't happen because we were good people, or because we worked harder than everyone else, or even just because we got fairy-tale lucky. It happened because my mom is ruthless, and maybe I am, too."

I study him. "You're not ruthless. You're a good person."

"Hold on, hold on. I have a point. My *point* is, when you kissed me, I thought you were using me. I think I told you that. Have I told you that? Whatever. I thought you were using me, like *everyone* uses me. Every guy ever, right? They're always straight and experimenting, or they're gay but they want to be a pop star. But then I thought *you* did it, and it was like, *fuck*. This has got to be karma at this point. I was an asshole with Jon, and now I have to pay for it forever. No one's ever going to like me for me. They're always gonna use me. So *that*," he finishes, his head lolling to one side, "is why I was so upset. Mostly."

I slip my hand under his shirt. "No offense," I say, "but that's stupid. You're not getting bad karma, because you're not a bad guy. All you did was make friends with someone after your mom gave you a shove; it happens. And even if you *were* cursed or whatever, I must've broken it, because I'm not using you for anything." He slides his fingers up my thighs, and I tip my head back. "Although I wouldn't mind using you for *some* things . . ."

"You're drunk."

"You're hot."

He smiles sadly. "What if I'm turning into my mom, Zach?"

I pull him closer. "Listen to me. Your mom is the worst person in the world. You're the best. You're nothing like her."

"Thank you." He groans. "Wow, okay. I'm in bed with a hot guy and all I can do is talk about my mom."

"What would you rather be doing?"

"Not sure. But I think it'd be better if your shirt was off."

I laugh, then pull it off and toss it away. I drop back down, sliding my hand back to the spot it was before, under his shirt.

"Better?" I ask.

He kisses me, his hand flat in the middle of my chest. He lies down, and I move across, so I'm on top of him, his legs over my hips. He's still dressed, and I'm in jeans, but still.

I think I like being like this.

Ruben pauses. "Thanks for being so cool. I never thought I'd tell anyone what I just told you."

"I'm so glad you did," I say.

He touches my silver necklace, which is hanging down between us.

"And like, I get it, you know?" I say. "I know how horrible being used feels. I really want you to know it was never that for me, and I'm so sorry that Adonis guy treated you like that."

"Mm-hmm. One very shitty example among, like, *a million of them.*"

"He was hot, though."

"Oh, you *noticed*?"

"Definitely," I say. "I didn't know it at the time, but I was jealous."

"You're more my type. Plus, importantly, you're not an asshole." He closes his eyes for a moment. "Hey, do you remember the first time you met me?"

"It's sort of hard to forget."

I was running late for camp, and I burst into my cabin to unload my stuff before rushing to orientation. I accidentally burst in on Ruben, who had returned to his cabin in order to get his inhaler. He shrieked and then threw a pillow at me, and told me to *never* do that again. He later told me he freaked out because he'd watched *Friday the 13th* just before coming to camp.

"What was your first impression of me?" he asks.

I think back. I can actually still picture it so clearly. Me, rushing to my cabin, and then my blood going cold when I realized I'd just burst in on a boy I'd never met. Even at my first sight of him, I knew Ruben was someone I wanted to like me.

"I remember thinking you were special," I say. "I knew right away you were going to be a big deal at camp, you just had that vibe."

"That's nice," he says softly.

"Do you remember the first time you saw me?"

"Yeah."

"And?"

"I remember thinking: how am I going to stay chill sharing a cabin with a guy this hot?"

I can barely contain my smile.

"And now?" I ask, kissing the spot below his ear.

"I think I handled myself okay."

"Me, too."

I'm so drunk, but I still can't help but dwell on it. Has Ruben liked me for longer than I thought? And how long have *I* liked him? What I drunkenly admitted was true; I was jealous of the guy he was flirting with at Angel's party. I've always felt intensely about Ruben, but the ease with which this has become something more makes me think that there has always been something romantic in those feelings.

Maybe I just wasn't ready to accept them until now.

"Hey," he says. "Have you ever thought about us as . . ."

I fill in the blank for him. "Boyfriends?"

"Yeah."

"Definitely."

His eyebrows lift. "And?"

"Well, I have no intention of stopping seeing you like *this*, so it feels a little inevitable."

"Same."

"So like . . ." I laugh. "Yeah."

He chews his lip. "Being boyfriends would be cool, though. Just saying."

"It would be," I say, keeping my voice low and measured.

"We don't have to or anything," he says. "But for the record, if you asked me, I'd say yes."

"If you asked me, I'd say yes, too. For the record."

That hangs between us.

"That settles it, then," he says, grinning. "We both want it, so one of us just needs to ask the other."

"Yeah. Do you want it to be me, or do you want to do it?"

His eyes light up. "What if we ask at the same time? Or is that really cheesy? It is, oh god, I'm drunk, ignore me."

He covers his face with his hand.

"Hey, Ruben," I say.

He moves his fingers, so he's peeking out. "Yes?"

"Aren't you going to ask me something?"

The smile he gives me kind of makes my life.

What he asks next totally does.

RUBEN

I'm sitting in Penny's hotel room in Prague, getting my hair trimmed and styled for tonight's concert, when Mom's message comes through.

> Interesting article on how heavy
> metals in tap water can kill the
> good gut bacteria and cause
> breakouts. Worth looking into re.
> your skin issues?

"Skin issues?" Penny reads over my shoulder in disbelief. "What skin issues?"

Zach, who's already had his hair blown out into his precisely messy and windswept style and is sitting against the wall with a notebook, slams his hand on the carpeted floor with a thud. "Seriously?" he asks. He doesn't need any context, apparently.

Angel and Jon, both sprawled on top of Penny's made bed waiting for their own cuts, groan in unison, while Angel performs a convincing mime of wringing someone's neck. It seems they don't need any, either.

Penny, who has zero context and very clearly needs it, lowers her scissors. "Am I missing something?" she asks.

I exit the offending message and shove my phone back in my pocket. "It's just my mom. Apparently there was some sort of article about how we're stressed out on tour and that's why the Berlin thing happened, and it said my breakout is more evidence."

She'd sent it to me a couple of days ago, and, of course, I couldn't help but scan it. It'd been super harsh, too, zooming in until the handful of pimples on my forehead and chin were pixelated as hell and taking up most of the screen. That's what I get for swapping my rigorous, stage-makeup-melting cleansing routine for make-out sessions with Zach, I guess.

"What, these two little things?" Penny asks, coming around to view my face with a critical eye. "That's not because you're stressed, or because you're drinking tap water. It's because you're a teenage boy."

"Well, in Veronica's defense, we also happen to be stressed," Angel says, bicycling his legs in midair while he lies on his back. "We aren't allowed downtime anymore, in case you haven't heard."

"'In Veronica's defense,'" Zach repeats, slapping the notebook on his legs for emphasis. "Not a sentence I was ever hoping to hear."

"Hey, that's your mother-in-law now," Jon jokes. "Show some respect."

"Oh, I'll show her respect," Zach grumbles. "I've even been writing a song for her."

Angel perks up at this and rolls on his side to look at Zach. "Is that the one you were writing yesterday? Something something 'I'd throw you to the wolves but you're too gross for them to eat'?"

"It's 'the rot in your soul might've spread to your flesh,' but yes, actually."

"Aww, Mom got a song written for her before I did?" I blow away a strand of hair that lands on my face. "Where's the romance?"

Zach hesitates, all innocence. "I . . . did you want a song?"

My heart swells. How anyone can be so freaking sweet and eager to please, I'll never know.

"Do it." Jon laughs. "You guys are just sappy enough Dad might let it appear on the next album." Then, he launches into Zach's part in "Unsaid." "You're the explosion that tore me apart, and I'm sorry to say that you've reclaimed my heart—" He glances at Angel and gestures for him to join in. "*Ruben,*" they sing together in perfect harmony, in place of the word "baby."

Zach looks like he wants the ground to swallow him up.

"Personally, I like the wolves song," I say. "We should petition for it."

"If that song gets on the next album, then they have to use my song, too," Angel says, dragging himself to sit upright with his legs crossed.

"You wrote a song?" Zach asks, his tone half interested, half wary.

"Yeah, this morning." Angel clears his throat. "A lady from South Carolina, shoved garlic up her vagina. She claimed it was natural—"

"*And* you're done," Penny says quickly, tapping me on the shoulder to vacate her chair. "Angel, you're up."

Angel glares at her as he rolls off the bed. "Rude."

"Keep working on it," Zach says drily, going back to his notebook as I sit on the floor beside him. "Sounds like it has real potential."

"Some people," Angel says in a wounded voice as he lowers himself gingerly into the chair, "just don't appreciate the avant-garde."

I think I'm a little exhausted.

I think maybe we all are.

It's not that the energy of this concert is horrible, per se. More that the vibe backstage was flat. I guess it's not that surprising, considering how long it's been since we had a break, but I have to admit I'm grateful that next week we're mixing it up a little. No live shows for almost a week while we film the music video for "Overdrive." It'll still be work, but it's a change from the robotic monotony of promo, show, hotel room, repeat.

All we need to do is get through a few more shows, tonight included.

So, I force a spring into my step as I sing the same lyrics, with the easy-to-hit notes. I dance the same steps. Look out into the same faceless crowd. Read the same posters (I LOVE YOU RUBEN. ZACH KNIGHT, BE MINE FOR THE NIGHT. AN-JON!). Squint against the same light display, and breathe in the same stage smoke at the same moment I do every night. Beat by beat, planned down to the millisecond.

Then we move onto "Unsaid," and I return to my body. Jon wiggles his eyebrows at me at the start of the song, and I can't fight a grin. Sure, the song has nothing to do with Zach and me, but now it kind of feels like *our* song.

Suddenly, the flashing lights and colors lose their luster. I wish to my bones, to my *core*, for the freedom we deserve. To be able to talk to the crowd about things that haven't been preapproved. To share this story with them, a tender little moment between our group, and the newfound significance of the song we just sang to them. To tell them about Zach and me. To hear them scream, and cheer, and let them into our real lives, so they can love *us*, and celebrate with *us*, not the curated images of us we're forced to put on display.

I'm tired of being in so deep we can't even call it false advertisement anymore, because what they see *is* what they get.

I'm half gone.

"Unsaid" is a particularly choreo-heavy song, so I can't dwell on this for too long before I'm throwing myself into the music, spinning and stepping and ducking and turning in time. But the steps bring me over to Zach when his part comes up, and I can't help but stare at him as he sings.

"You're the explosion that tore me apart," he starts in his gritty, strong voice, staring straight into the audience without noticing me, "and I'm sorry to say that you've reclaimed my heart . . ."

Then—*hah*—his eyes flicker sideways to me. "Baby," he finishes, eyes sparkling as he bursts into a toothy smile. I return it and let out a delighted, choked laugh. He purses his lips in an attempt to kill his smile, but it's no use—sunlight is practically streaming out from him. We're so busy looking at each other we almost, *almost,* miss our cue to return to the choreo. But we don't miss it. The song goes just as it does every night, but tonight it feels different, because on top of the lights and the crowd and the moves and the smoke and songs and the steps is Zach's smile, and the way his eyes locked onto me, and saw me above all the noise.

I have a giddy smile on my face, and a giggle threatening to burst from my lips, for the next few songs. And it feels *good*.

So, I'm caught off-guard when we pour off the stage at the end of the night to find Erin and Valeria waiting for us with stern expressions. It's almost like I can feel the band shrinking into ourselves as we try to figure out what we did wrong, and who they're mad at.

Erin makes eye contact with me first, and that answers that question. Lucky me. "Walk and talk," Erin orders, and we move, with me falling into step beside her. Zach appears at my shoulder immediately, and though he doesn't touch me while people can still see us, his elbow bumps against mine and I'm pretty sure it's not an accident.

"What was so funny?" Erin asks without looking at me.

For a split second, she's Mom, and I'm several years younger, trapped in the car beside her while she gears up to scream at me about my behavior that day. But she's not Mom, and I don't need to panic, because this is business, and we're all professionals, and it's just professional feedback.

But then, why is my stomach rolling, and why have my fingertips gone cold? Why are my eyes darting around to pinpoint an escape route, just in case? "Nothing," I say. My voice comes out uncertain.

"You know," she says. "I get that everything feels very exciting right now. I *remember* what it's like to be in your first real relationship. But you two are going to have to work on remaining professional."

Something very much like fear stabs behind my heart. "Oh. I thought we were."

"You thought giggling like schoolkids throughout three and a half songs, onstage, during a concert people paid good money to attend, was professional?" Erin asks, finally looking at me. She's not smiling. "I know you better than that, Ruben. That's not you."

I feel like dying. Finding a small, quiet hole somewhere

and crawling into it and curling into a ball to wait out the day, or maybe even the week. She's right. Mom would kill me if she found out I did that. I should've cleared my mind better. We're not up there for fun. We're up there to put on a show.

How could I let myself forget that?

Zach's arm brushes against mine again, more firmly this time. "We were singing fine, though," he says. "It's not like we messed up."

I catch his eye and shake my head. The last thing I want right now is to make this worse. I just want Erin to drop it, so we can forget about it, and I can do better next time, and prove I *am* professional. That I don't make stupid, silly mistakes, like a kid playing around in drama class.

Erin turns on him sharply. "You don't become the best by putting in the bare minimum," she says. "You're not earning what you're earning to tick the boxes. Those people in that audience? They worship you. For a lot of them, this is the only time in their life they ever get to see you. Some of them have been waiting years. Don't disrespect them by getting up there and going through the motions, or slacking off because you have a new distraction. If it happens again, we'll need to put you on different ends of the stage for the rest of the tour."

Wait, she's threatening to separate us like kindergarteners who can't pay attention if their friend is too close to them? Maybe we did screw up today, but I hardly think we deserve the patronizing way she's talking to us. My shame mixes with indignant anger, but anxiety intervenes long before I form a response. *Just smile. Nod. Apologize. Don't give her a reason to punish you.*

So I bite my tongue and give a curt nod. "Sorry. It won't happen again. Don't worry."

Erin brightens dramatically. "Good. That's all I wanted to hear."

Just behind us, Valeria speaks up. "Zach, can I grab you for a sec?"

I watch as he hangs back, eyebrows drawn together with concern, so they can talk. She slows them down so they're trailing several feet behind the rest of us, so I can't hear a word. But I already know from the look on his face I don't like what's being said.

When he finally pulls away from Valeria and rejoins us, we've started stripping in the dressing rooms. I raise a questioning eyebrow at him, but he gives me a forced smile and shakes his head as he takes off his jacket to hand to Viktor. *Later.*

Later doesn't end up being until we're back at the hotel.

Zach spends the rest of the night pulled into himself, quiet and distant. Even on the bus he sits next to me in silence. It's obviously nothing like the last time he went quiet on me, though, because when I stroke his arm with my thumb, he leans his body so hard against mine he squashes me into the window. He clearly needs something from me, but doesn't want to say what that might be in front of everyone else.

So, as soon as we get out of the elevator and the guards from Chase Protective Services take their stations around our doors, I give him a faux-enthusiastic grin. "Wanna come over for a movie or something?" I ask. He nods eagerly, with a look of relief.

"Oh. Are we not invited?" Angel asks in a funny voice.

Jon sighs. "Angel."

"I'm just saying, you and I are stuck sitting alone in our

rooms because we can't have anyone visit, and no one's asking Zach and Ruben to stop *their* visits. And you like being alone. So, essentially, I'm the only one who has to change my behavior."

Zach's face is falling further by the second, and I officially run out of patience. "No one's stopping you from hanging out with Jon if you're lonely," I say, "and no one's stopping you from inviting us over to chill *without* a party going on. But don't take it out on us because you got yourself banned from having visitors, Angel. We tried to stop you."

"They wouldn't have known about it at all if you three didn't chase us down and make a scene," Angel says coldly.

"You don't know that," Jon says, looking between us, his eyebrows rising in alarm. "It probably wouldn't have been good either way. And it's done."

Zach hugs his arms to himself. "Come hang with us?" he asks, a little desperate. I'm pretty sure he doesn't actually want to hang with Angel and Jon, or he would've spoken on the bus. But trying to get Zach to prioritize his needs over anyone else's is like trying to beg a bee not to sacrifice itself for the hive.

I glare at Angel. Angel looks between Zach and me, then tosses a hand. "Nah. I'm tired."

He and Jon head to their rooms, and Zach frowns. "Tomorrow?" he asks.

"Sure. Maybe." He couldn't sound less enthusiastic if he tried, though.

When we get inside my room, Zach hovers by the door, rising onto his tiptoes and lowering himself again like he's bracing to take flight. I land heavily on my bed with a creak of springs. "What happened?"

He takes a few slow steps across the room, looking out of the windows down at the blinking lights of Prague. "Nothing. Valeria was just giving me some notes on my dancing."

Somewhere deep within me, my sixth sense pricks up. When you've survived a lifetime of passive-aggression and veiled threats, your stomach starts to recognize them before your mind quite knows why. This, I can already tell, is one of those moments. "What kind of notes?"

He shrugs, like it's no big deal. But it is a big deal, or else he wouldn't be so quiet. "She said you were distracting me tonight and it made me really out of time. Apparently I'm actually out of time a lot, and I need to work on it with her in our filming breaks next week."

Valeria is fucking lucky she's not in the room with us right now, or I'd have a word or two to say to her. "You're not out of time," I say, trying to keep calm.

"How do you know? It's not like you can see me when we're dancing."

I get to my feet and stride over to him. "Um, because I've been working with you for three years now? And I've seen you dance a million times?"

He fiddles with the curtain. "Yeah, but it's Val's job to tell us if we're doing something wrong. And I *am* the worst dancer out of all of us. I'm just really frustrated at myself. I'm *trying*. But I'm not the one with the perfect body, or the charisma, or whatever. I just want to write music and sing, and they've known that since the start, but they want me to be a pop guy. I'm just not . . . as good as . . ." He trails off, a muscle in his jaw working.

I take his hand. "Well, you are," I say. "You're great, actually. And that whole meeting had nothing to do with your dancing."

He squeezes my hand, but keeps looking out the window. "What do you think it had to do with, then?"

Honestly? I think we pissed them off by daring to interact onstage even a little, and they're freaked out about rumors but don't want to say it in as many words. I think they're laying the foundation to find an excuse to separate us as much as possible, and they think if they blame it on professionalism and distractions, we can't accuse them of doing anything wrong. I hadn't noticed it when Erin was yelling at me, because a part of me had figured I deserved it.

But hearing them come for Zach? No. That I can't accept as deserved criticism.

I should say so to Zach, but instead, I hesitate. He's only *just* come out. He's still processing, for god's sake. He hasn't even told his *mom*. So, yeah, a part of me wants to protect him from the realities of what it means to be queer, and how it changes things in a million subtle ways. How it always leaves you a little uncertain if things are fair, or if there's a tiny shred of hate underlying it all. How, much of the time, you can't even call it out without turning people against you and calling you overly sensitive, because it can be so insidious, you're the only one who notices it for what it is.

If I can keep him shielded from the dark side of reality, for just a little bit longer . . . I will.

So, despite some reservations, I drop his hand and step back. "We're all just tired. And they were paying more attention to you and me because we were laughing, so they noticed. If it wasn't for that, they would've missed it, guaranteed."

Zach finally turns away from the window. "Can you help me? Now?"

I blink. "Zach . . ."

"Just let me show you. Tell me if I'm out of time, and you can't lie."

We stare at each other for a few moments, then I give in and pull out my phone to search up our discography. "Fine. Which song?"

"'Unsaid.'"

A corner of my mouth rises at this while I search. I'd had a feeling he'd say that.

I kick off my shoes and settle on the bed while the music blares through my phone speakers, and Zach moves to the center of the room. He launches into the dance easily, flying through the moves we both know inside out and back to front. There's no stumbling, or awkwardness. Not that I expected there to be; they put us through boot camp over these songs before the tour began. It feels like a lifetime ago, now. Back home. Before . . . everything.

In fairness, it actually has been a while since I've stopped and watched Zach dance. For weeks, months, even years now . . . he's right. We've been side by side, in synchronicity.

Back at the beginning, he'd needed more help than me. I had a lifetime of musical theater experience and jazz lessons thanks to Mom. Zach had . . . soccer. So, my memories of Zach dancing are of someone competent, but maybe not so fluid.

Now? He makes it look as easy as breathing. There's no stiffness, no look of concentration. Just skill. After one particularly smooth turn, he catches my eye, and smiles self-consciously, but doesn't stop.

I'm glad. I don't want him to stop.

He's mesmerizingly beautiful.

When the song finally ends, he stands still, waiting for feedback. He's not even out of breath. I guess this kind of thing is below our skill level, now. Once, we could barely get through a song without dying on the floor, begging for water. Now, we do it while belting song after song, night after night.

"So?" he asks impatiently.

I get up slowly and cross the room to him. "So," I say,

scanning from his socked feet all the way up to his eyes, which have darkened to a deep gold in this light. Burnt caramel melting into honey. With a soft smile, I place my hands on either side of his waist to line him up with me as I drop my voice to a murmur. "You're in time."

He pauses while he stares at me. For signs that I'm lying, or going easy on him, I guess. Then, breathing out with a heavy gush of air, he kisses me hard and deep, his arms flying around my shoulders. His chest presses against mine and I can feel the heat of his skin through the thin cotton of his shirt, and the rapid thud of his heartbeat, and suddenly I can barely hold myself up.

He's kissing me like it can erase the frustrations and hurt of today, deeper and more frantically by the second, until I can't keep up with him. I walk backward, pulling him, until my leg hits the bed and we fall together, crashing into the soft layers of blankets with a gasp. He doesn't even pause, just cups my face and kisses me between his hands.

It's zero to a hundred, but my body hasn't skipped a beat. My breathing is hard and fast, and I grab his hips and pull him firmly down against me. The weight of his body flat against mine wipes my mind blank. All I know is him, and the smell of him, and the satin of the skin of his back as my hands slip under his shirt and lift it over his head.

Then we're shuffling backward, still horizontal across the bed, and I'm gripping his middle with my knees for stability while I take my own shirt off, and his hands roam over my legs with a firm pressure. My breathing gets thicker and harder until it's embarrassingly loud, and I can't keep quiet anymore, and I want to be cool about this, but I can't be. It's not possible to be chill and detached with him. I change positions slightly, so I'm the one touching his legs, then, slowly, I crawl off the bed so I'm on the floor looking up at him. It's a power dynamic I'm used to. I've given blow jobs before, to boyfriends in the past.

He must figure out straight away what I'm implying, because he swallows, and says, "I've never done this before."

"Do you not want to?" I ask.

"No, I do. I'm just . . . sharing."

I start on the buckle of his jeans, and he fidgets. "Can I ask you something?"

Okay. Something tells me this is not the moment for me to undress him. I rise back up and sit next to him on the bed. "Okay?" My voice comes out uncertain. It's never a *good* thing if someone cuts you off mid–make out to have a Talk, capital T.

"It's nothing bad. I just . . . I know you've had boyfriends in the past. And I don't need to know every detail or anything. But pretty much everything I'm doing with you is a first for me. I was wondering if you've . . . ever . . ."

"If I'm a virgin?" I finish for him. "No."

"So, you're all out of firsts?" he asks.

"I'm sorry."

"No, don't be. I just wanted to know if I should expect to always be the newbie out of us. That's all. I don't *mind*."

I hesitate, and look away from him. "Well, technically, I still have one first left."

He cocks his head in a question.

It shouldn't be hard for me to say, but suddenly I feel a twinge of embarrassment. Stomach clenching and cheeks flaming, I get the words out, still careful not to meet Zach's eyes. "I've never actually been given a blow job."

It's not an accident.

Nathaniel, a guy I was seeing for a while once, kind of expected me to be the one giving, and even though it was never said out loud, it felt like I was doing the *right thing* if I instigated it. Like I was the good boyfriend, thinking about the other person before myself, like I *should*. I guess it stuck, because every time I've reached this sort of stage with a guy, I've made sure I was the one giving. Out of all the things there is to do, that's remained the most vulnerable for me. To just lie there and not give anything back. To somehow trust that I'll still have worth to the other person if I'm not earning it.

Even though my mind knows that's bullshit, I'm not sure my heart's climbed aboard the self-assuredness train just yet. I'm just so used to conditions. My whole life's been filled with them.

To my surprise, Zach actually smiles. "I could change that."

"Uh. I guess? You could."

He picks up on the slight note of panic in my voice. "Or not," he says. "That's fine."

I relax again, and he kisses me gently on the lips. The taste of him, along with his calmness, makes me feel safe and steady. We end up back against the pillows, the kissing growing harder and more breathless. Then he moves his knee over my thigh, and a small sound escapes my throat before I can stop it.

And I realize with a spark of clarity that I feel completely safe. I'm not afraid of what will happen if we do this.

Something in my gut kicks up. Eagerness. Excitement. A longing to be touched like that.

"Actually, okay," I whisper, my heart hammering. It feels like it's dropped somewhere inside my stomach. "If you, um . . . as long as you still want to?"

Zach's hair tickles my forehead. "Yeah," he murmurs thickly between breaths. "I want to. I want to."

I grip the blankets beneath my fists and tip my head back.

The moment feels enormous. The last thing I've never done. But the nervousness evaporates within seconds, replaced by anticipation.

And then that's replaced by something else entirely. And it might be the heat of it all, or the adrenaline rush, but somewhere in my swirling mind, a thought flickers. A thought about Zach, and how *necessary* he's started to feel in such a short span of time. Like he's the thing keeping me tethered to the ground. Like if I were to lose him, I might have lost the most important, urgent thing to ever happen to me.

But it's just a swirling thought.

When it's over, and our breathing slows down, Zach rests his red-hot cheek against my damp chest. His chestnut-brown hair is sticking into clumps from perspiration, and his bare shoulders are covered in freckles that are becoming as familiar to me as my own, and he has a soft smile playing on his full lips, reddened from kisses.

I press my lips into the soft canopy of his hair. "I'm not going to let them mess with you. Okay?"

He doesn't ask who *they* are. He doesn't have to. "Okay."

"I mean it. They can come for me all they want, but the second they come for you, it's war."

"Sounds serious."

"I am serious."

His smile disappears. "Well," he whispers. "Hopefully it won't come to that."

I have the same hope.

I'm just not sure if I believe it.

SIXTEEN

ZACH

I'm so thankful for dance rehearsal.

That is definitely not something that fifteen-year-old Zach ever would've thought, not in a million years, but now I'm so damn grateful for them. I'm with Valeria, in a dance studio an hour earlier than everyone else, to go over my moves for the show before the others arrive to learn the "Overdrive" music video routine. So right now it's just us in this massive, mirrored space.

I need this, though. Because earlier, I got an email.

Today, 1:17 p.m. (1 hour ago)
Geoff <geoffbraxton@chorusmanagement.com>
To: me

Hey, Zach,

Galactic had a read of your "End of Everything" suggestions and decided that they're maybe not as strong as the original draft. As a thank-you for your help, you will still be receiving songwriter credit on the song. Don't be down about this, they liked your suggestions, and hope to get you more involved on the lyric side of things in the near future!

Best,
Geoff

"Okay, Zach, go."

The chorus of "Yours, Mine, Ours" starts, and I dance, as hard as I can go.

Don't think about it. But as hard as I push myself, the thoughts come back. I'm getting credit, but the song is in no way mine. It's Galactic's song, but it will have my name on it, and now everyone out there is going to think that I wrote "End of Everything"—a sappy, slow ballad, nothing even remotely like the kind of music I enjoy listening to or writing.

Songwriting was *my* thing. And it feels like it's been wrenched away from me, just like my appearance and singing style has. The whole thing is moving too fast to stop. We're recording it tomorrow.

Stop. Thinking. About it.

I hit each of my movements on time, harder and faster than I usually dance. Turns out, frustration is one hell of a motivator. I finish off with a body roll, the last move of the routine. I'm done now, and panting to catch my breath.

"Perfect!" says Val, giving me a high-five. "Dude, that was absolutely perfect."

I rest my hands on my hips and try to get in some much-needed air. "Really?"

"If you do that onstage you could cause a riot."

I grin.

I retrieve my water bottle. Maybe I'm overreacting about

the song. It's just one track, and who knows, it might be the start of something. Geoff did say they want to get me more involved on the lyric side of things. It's a foot in the door.

Val calls "Be right back!" and walks out, leaving me totally alone.

The room goes quiet. I use my tank to mop some of the sweat off my face, and then I check my phone. Oh shit, we went over by ten minutes. I must've kept the others waiting.

I've got a new message from Ruben.

Hey hey, how's it going?

> Great! We just finished and
> Val said I was perfect!!

I haven't told him about the email yet. I haven't found the right time. I hear the door open, stopping me mid-response.

Ruben and Angel walk in. Ruben is dressed in a football jersey that shows off his arms, black workout pants, and squeaky-clean Nikes. The world stops.

He should only wear this.

"Hey," he says, doing a cute little wave and tilting his head up.

I want to jog up to him, pick him up, and kiss him. I don't know if there are cameras in this room, so I don't. It's tough, though, because Ruben in workout clothes . . . damn. Just, damn. I don't know how he keeps getting sexier to me, but he keeps finding a way. Seriously, when did his arms start looking like that? When did he start being able to make me feel like this?

We make eye contact, and his eyes sparkle. I want to press him up against that mirror and feel him run his hands down my back. I want him to whisper my name. I don't care that anyone could see us, because I know with everything I have that it'd be worth it. Screw the world. Screw everyone but Ruben.

Or, maybe screw Ruben. If he wanted that.

"What are you thinking about?" he asks. He chews his bottom lip, like he knows I'm thinking about screwing.

I scrub the back of my head. Keep it together, man.

"Nothing."

"Nothing, huh?"

My chest tightens, making it hard to breathe. Does he even know how much him looking at me makes me feel? Does he even know how bad I have it for him?

I catch Angel rolling his eyes. "You two really need to learn the meaning of 'secret relationship.'"

"Whatever, Angel," says Ruben. "You wouldn't know subtle if it hit you in the face."

"Last I checked I'm not the one keeping a huge-ass secret from . . . *fromage,* ah yes, that was the word I was thinking of."

He changed tack as the door opened. It's just Val, though. Now her bubblegum-pink hair is loose. She scans the room.

"What'd I miss?"

"Nothing," says Angel.

She scoffs. "Like I'd believe that for a second. Where's Jon?"

Good question.

"He was talking to Geoff," says Angel, who is mid–calf stretch. "He asked for some privacy. I was more than happy to give it to him, of course, because I'm a stand-up guy."

"Pfft. He better hurry up. The backup dancers get here in half an hour and we've got a lot of ground to cover before then."

The door swings open again, and Jon rushes inside.

"Sorry!" he says, rushing to dump his bag and unzip his

hoodie. He's actually showing the least skin of all of us, in a plain black tee. I wonder if that's intentional.

I stand next to Ruben, in our usual formation.

"Actually," says Val. "I was thinking we could switch things up for this video? To keep things fresh. Ruben, can you stand next to Jon?"

"Sure."

He walks around, so he's at the other end of the lineup. It feels weird. We never perform like this.

Something is up.

"Great," she says. "Let's get started."

It's official.

They're keeping Ruben and me apart.

I first noticed it on the first night of our shoot. The theme for the video is that we're futuristic race car drivers, who dance for some reason, and they've built us a few massive sets at the studio.

During that first dance rehearsal, Ruben and I were positioned at opposite ends of the lineup. I thought it might be Val just trying something different.

Now though? I'm sure something malicious is happening.

We've spent the past two days shooting our solo scenes, each in front of a partially built set backed by a green screen. I posed with a futuristic sky-blue Aventador, and I was put in a custom black-and-blue leather racing jacket that was so tight it was like a second skin. My hair was spiked up and a few of the front strands were temporarily dyed blue by Penny. Each of us has a color motif for the video: Ruben is red, Jon is gold, and Angel is white.

For each chorus, we have a group choreo scene. In the first one, Ruben and I were kept apart, at opposite ends of the band. We're halfway through filming the second group number now, and it's happening again. This whole video, we're as far apart as we can possibly be, when we always used to be side by side.

We go through the number for what's got to be close to the five-hundred-thousandth time. Erin is on set, watching us carefully, her arms crossed.

"And, cut," calls the director. "I think we got it."

"Home time, boys," says Angel.

The energy in the room quickly changes, as now it seems like all anyone wants to do is get away from here. Lighting guys turn off the dozens of lights pointed at us, sound guys start packing up their equipment, and our director slumps down in her chair.

"Hey, Zach," says Ruben. "Got a sec?"

I nod, and follow him through the set, to a quiet spot.

"Have you noticed anything weird about this video?" he asks.

"Are you talking about how they're keeping us apart?"

"I am. Tell me I'm not the only one who thinks that was see-through?"

"I don't know. Maybe? It could just be a coincidence."

"You haven't been dealing with this stuff as long as I have, and trust me, there are never any coincidences when it comes to Chorus."

"Right."

"But I dunno, maybe we're overthinking it."

That seems unlikely. I trust Ruben's judgement. If we both noticed it, then chances are high that it is actually a thing. That they actually are keeping us apart to try to keep our relationship a secret.

"I have an idea," I say. "Do you want to find out for sure if they're up to something?"

He pauses for a moment.

"I do."

My plan is kind of simple, but I think it will work.

At the end of this video, there is a "candid" moment. It happens when we're done with the routine, and the plot is wrapped up. Angel's character has won the race, and there is a shot of us all celebrating for him.

The plan is for us to interact while filming this, and see how they respond.

The set we're on is another green screen. This time, we've been told it will be set up to look like we're at the finish line.

"And, action!"

Angel, who is holding a neon trophy, beams while Jon applauds. I go up to Ruben, and put my arm around him.

I can feel the tension on the other side of the camera. Erin's clearly biting her tongue.

"Nice work," says our director. "Let's go again."

Penny rushes over to me, and starts dabbing my face with a makeup sponge.

"What are you up to?" she asks, whispering under her breath. "I think Erin is about to snap her iPad."

"That would be like murdering her child, no?"

Penny laughs. "Just be careful. They're watching you."

She moves away to fix Angel's makeup.

Once take two is rolling, I move over to Ruben, only this time I don't touch him, I just stand next to him, to applaud Angel.

The shift in the room is immediately noticeable.

But we're just standing next to each other. It's not like I'm kissing him or even holding his hand or proclaiming our mutual love of Lady Gaga. Why would they have an issue with this? In a way, I get staying closeted until after Russia, but right now, this feels excessive.

Our director rubs her forehead. "We'll go through one more time, then we'll have a break."

Now comes the time to properly test our theory.

"Action!"

This time, Ruben and I don't interact at all.

"And, cut! Great work, boys, I think we got it that time!"

My stomach sinks.

The video shoot went almost half an hour overtime, which means we're rushing to make it to the meet and greet.

At this point, meet and greets aren't a super common thing for us. They used to be: with every show people could buy a VIP ticket and get the chance to meet us. I always felt a weird mix of excitement and awkwardness during them. It was so great seeing fans, but the rushed nature of it made me feel uncomfortable. Plus, people often told me deeply traumatic things that had happened to them, before the photo was taken and they had to move on. I never knew what they wanted me to say back to them, and felt guilty I couldn't properly respond to the devastating news they told me.

So I'm not exactly disappointed that with our increased celebrity came increased security risks, so meet and greets ended, save for special occasions.

This special occasion is a contest run by Prosper, the mega-conglomerate that owns a share of Galactic Records as well as a few dozen other companies. A magazine owned by a different subsidiary of Prosper ran a contest in which the winners would get to meet us, and in order to keep them happy, Geoff sent us.

Our bus pulls into the back lot of the theater. Two Chase guards climb out first, to check the area, and once they say it's safe we all get out, and go into the backstage area of the theater. We're led straight down the hallway, toward the stage.

Erin turns around, blocking our path.

"Hey, boys. Given our situation, we're going to do this a little differently for group shots. Ruben, you're going to stand next to Jon, and Zach, you'll be next to Angel."

Ah.

Our new formation.

It seems it's extending even past the video.

"Okay," says Ruben. "This is ridiculous. We can all see what you're doing."

"It's just until Russia," she says. "For your safety, we want to make sure word doesn't get out until then."

That sucks, but it does make sense.

Ruben crosses his arms, but doesn't say anything. Erin spins, then leads us out onto a stage. In the seating area, a line has formed, made up of about fifty contest winners, mostly teenage girls and their parents. They're fenced in by dozens of security guards, like they're dangerous.

The screaming starts.

It's almost deafening. Some of them start crying. A bunch of them have brought homemade signs, along with bags filled with things to give us that I know we won't be able to keep. They must know it, too, but they still bring it. Maybe it's because the thing that matters to them is the act of giving it to us. Or maybe they think their present will break through the slush, even though, honestly, it never does, which is another thing I feel guilty about.

The cameraman is already in position, so the four of us line up, in our new, freshly approved order, with Ruben and me standing as far apart as possible.

The first girl comes up onto the stage. She's in all black, and her hair is clearly dyed raven-dark. Her mascara is thick, and she has leather bracelets on.

I would die for her.

"Hey," she says, nodding at the others before coming right up to me. "Zach, I made you something."

"Oh, that's so nice! Thanks."

She hands me a paper bag. I open the bag, pulling out a hand-stitched piece of art, with the lyrics from the chorus of "Fight Back," my favorite song. I relate to every single line Randy Kehoe wrote for it. I answered an interview question *years* ago asking what my favorite lyrics are, and she's clearly remembered.

"Oh my god," I say. "I love this!"

"Really? I'm not the best at stitching, and it's a bit wonky in the corner, I'm sorry."

I clutch it to my chest. "Don't be sorry, I love it, thank you."

"Falling for Alice is my favorite band," she says, before her eyes widen. "Besides you guys!"

I laugh. "They're my favorite, too."

Erin clears her throat.

"Sorry," says the girl, and we line up for the photo. The camera flashes, and she leaves the stage. "It's so nice to meet you!"

"It's nice to meet you, too!"

I know I'm going to get scolded by Erin for what just happened. By giving this much time to her, I've set up a precedent that every other person in the meet and greet is going to expect that much attention. And we can't have that, because we have a show tonight, and that means we need to be at the stadium in an hour. So people are going to be upset, and upset fans upset Chorus.

I get all of that. And making Erin mad at me is terrifying.

I'm just not sure I did anything wrong.

SEVENTEEN

RUBEN

"The next question we have for you boys is about romance within the band!"

As the word leaves our interviewer Elisa's lips, time screeches to a halt. Beside her, her very-blond colleague, Moritz, tents his hands, apparently eager to see where this is going.

We're at *Array Magazine* in Vienna, the four of us sitting in a row of single metal chairs, with Zach and I placed on opposite ends of the row, as per Erin's instruction. While cameras are fixed on us for recording purposes, none of the footage is making it to the public eye, so until this moment our postures were relaxed. But now, I shoot up straight, feet planted on the floor and my hands on my knees. I see the others stiffen similarly in my peripherals.

"I'm sure you know all bands receive their fair share of shipping and rumors—"

This can't be happening.

"—and our readers want to know the truth!"

We'll deny it, of course. But how did they hear about this to begin with? Who leaked something? Or did we slip up? I sneak a glance at Erin, who's typing frantically on her iPad, her expression livid.

"Are you familiar with the term 'Anjon'?" Elisa finishes.

I am extremely happy this footage isn't going public, because I'm pretty sure the expression on my face went from "stricken terror" to "utter bewilderment" a little too obviously just now.

Jon, who's sitting to my right, laughs. "Uh, I've seen a few people mention it in comments."

Angel, who's been slumped over throughout the interview with bags under his eyes, perks up for the first time in an hour. "We have a ship name? Why wasn't I informed of this?"

Jon holds a finger up to the interviewers. "Hold on, this is off the record for a second." Then he tilts his head and turns to Angel. "We have access to the same posts. They're under every group photo. Why don't you pay attention to anything?"

"I thought there was some guy called Anjon a few people were obsessed with! I figured they wanted him to join the band or something, I don't know."

"Oh, so, essentially, you thought it wasn't about you so you didn't process it?"

"Yes, exactly that, thank you."

Jon gives him a long, tight smile, blinking rapidly, then returns to a front-facing position. "Okay, we're ready to answer. We—"

"No, you're not *going* to answer," Erin cuts in, brandishing her iPad as she storms over to Elisa and Moritz. "Here. Your magazine agreed, in writing, to this list of blocked topics. This question is off-limits."

Elisa is unperturbed. "We were told that any question

about Zach and Ruben and romance was blocked. We were not given any directions about Jon and Angel."

I glance at the others. Zach's shrunk in his seat, fiddling with the zipper on his leather jacket. All I want to do is reach across Jon and Angel and take his hand—or at *least* squeeze his arm—but the three feet between us might as well be an ocean for all we're allowed to interact outside of hotel rooms.

"*Obviously* any questions about romance within the band are going to encourage online speculation, though—"

"I'm not sure what you mean," Elisa says with an innocent shrug. "I do not understand."

"But, really, '*Anjon*'?" Angel whispers, rubbing a palm across his eyes to wake himself up. He looks like he's recovering from a particularly bad bout of the flu. "I guess we are the hot ones, but still. Why are they shipping *us*, of all people? Jon's Catholic!"

Jon sighs. "I'm pretty sure you can be Catholic and gay, Angel."

Angel does an exaggerated double-take. "Are you trying to tell me something here, buddy?"

"No!"

Moritz has jumped into the fray now. "If you ask me, it could be a good idea to focus on Anjon," he says. "This could take the focus off of the other boys, no?"

"Nobody did ask you," Erin snaps.

"Why are they asking about shipping at all?" Zach asks in an urgent whisper. "We've never gotten those questions before."

"Yeah, but if in-band romance becomes a blocked question, it's going to be pretty obvious why," I murmur.

Zach pales. "So, what, everyone's going to know? What the *fuck*? I haven't even told my mom, I haven't—"

I lean forward as far as I can, right up in Jon's personal space. "Hey, breathe. It's okay. They don't *know* know. And they won't tell anyone because they'd get *so* fucking sued. My sexuality's been a blocked question from the start, and the public still thinks I'm straight."

Zach nods, but he's breathing rapidly, and his eyes are too wide. Jon does what I can't, and reaches behind Angel to touch Zach's shoulder briefly. And as much as I want it to be me doing that, I'm endlessly grateful to Jon for giving him a brief moment of comfort.

Erin steps back from Elisa, shaking her head with a scowl. Elisa and Moritz don't look any happier about things, but they force smiles as they go back to their question list. "Okay," Elisa says. "Um . . . What are you all most excited to do in Europe?"

Jon's ready. "To see all our amazing fans. I'm *super* excited for our concert tonight. I've heard Vienna has some of the best music fans in the world."

Elisa laughs, then turns to Zach for comment. He's staring into the distance with a look of sheer panic on his face, and he doesn't notice her indicating to him. Angel jumps in, though his voice is hard. "We don't have very much time to do much of anything," he says. Erin's face clouds. Wrong answer. Angel notices her expression, and something in his posture changes. "We're just focused on giving the best performances we can. But I've seen so many incredible things, I'm definitely planning on coming back to see Europe with more time."

That's better. Much more rehearsed. For a moment there it almost sounded like he had a negative opinion.

Now it's my turn. "The Burgtheater," I say, trying to keep my voice upbeat. "I've heard it's spectacular, and I've always had a love for the history of theater."

I don't tell them that Erin approached me a few days ago to gently let me know we wouldn't have time to see it after all.

I hadn't really hoped for it too much, anyway.

Just a little bit, I guess.

"I'm gonna get David on their ass," Erin rants from her spot on the minibus as we pull out of the parking lot. "Imagine the nerve . . ."

Zach is sitting across the aisle from me, both of us alone. Last week, Erin asked us to keep our distance better whenever people can see us, and the minibus definitely counts as public. Even now, we're driving particularly slowly to avoid the writhing crowd of fans who have gathered at the gates outside, hoping to catch a glimpse of our faces through the tinted windows. The screaming and shouting is muted by metal and glass. I can only imagine what it must be like to stand among that crowd without walls up.

We roll through the automatic gates and it—*somehow*—grows even louder. I wave at the people who make eye contact with me, and they shriek with ecstasy. I'm hit with the familiar, conflicting feelings of gratitude and love for them and their support, mixed with the sense that if I stepped out of this vehicle they would rip me limb from limb to get close to me.

As individuals, they're all wonderful to begin with, but there's something awe-inspiring about them as a group. Banded together, they have more power than the four of us and our team ever could. That's how they managed to raise us as high as they did, I guess. But the flipside is they also have the power to destroy us, if they choose to.

Once we get on the street and join the traffic of Vienna,

Erin precariously walks down the aisle, swaying with the van's movements, and stops before Zach and me. "You two okay?" she asks. "Zach, I know that caught you off guard."

Zach's wearing his too-cheerful smile, the one he turns on whenever he lies about being okay. And, as predicted: "It's fine," he says. "I get it."

"It's not, fine, actually," Erin says. She strikes me as a motherly figure in this moment, full of concern and rage on Zach's behalf. But there's something off about it, something that's niggling at me. The thing is, Erin isn't a bad person. But she is a person who values her job more than anything. On the plus side, it means we couldn't find a harder worker to be our tour manager. But on the other hand, it means that if she has to choose between us and what Chorus expects of her, she'll pick Chorus.

I don't know where her line in the sand is. What she wouldn't do to us if Chorus asked her to.

It scares me to consider that maybe she doesn't have one.

"We'll be making ourselves perfectly clear moving forward," she goes on. "No romance questions, no shipping questions, no questions about who's closer to who. Period. Ever again."

I cock my head. "Well, not *never*," I say. "Right? Just until Russia's over and we're ready to announce? Right?"

Erin hesitates. I *see* her hesitate. Then she smiles. "Yes. Obviously, Ruben, we wouldn't keep the block on once you're ready to announce. But, Zach, there's *no* rush there, okay? We want you to wait until you're absolutely, completely ready to bring things to the public eye. It doesn't matter how long it takes you, in the meantime, we'll make *sure* you get your privacy."

I glance at Zach, who looks wary. So, he caught that undertone, too? The sudden narrative that they're keeping this a secret for Zach's sake, so he can retain his privacy? When last week, they were keeping it a secret for the *band's* sake, and for the sake of our safety?

So good of them to be so very worried about every aspect of our well-being. So thoughtful, so responsible.

It's a pity I don't buy it.

"Hey, so," Angel announces, oblivious to any tension on my half of the van. "I'm looking up ships. This is wild."

"The bigger question is how you missed the whole shipping thing," Jon says. He's sitting sideways on his seat, back against the window and legs sticking out into the aisle.

Angel props himself up on his knees so he can see us all while Erin makes her way back to the front. "I knew it was a thing, *Jonathan*, I've seen stuff with Zach and me before. But people are, like, *really into* you and me."

"Yup." From the way Jon says it, it's not a surprise to him.

"Has it always been like this?"

Jon sighs and lets his head fall back against the window. "I guess? But it took off after the bouncy castle video at your party, I think."

"Oh my *god*." Angel actually looks pleased. "This is so flattering."

"It's creepy," Jon answers in a singsong voice.

"It's . . . oh, holy shit, look at this photoshopping. I'm sorry, Jon, but I've seen you in your underwear and they got you *all* wrong. But props for creativity, I guess. Wait. Woof, this next one might be accurate for all I know, actually, I haven't seen *that* much of you." Angel raises his eyebrows at his phone, then holds it out to Jon. "*Do* you have a mole there?"

Jon yelps and squeezes his eyes shut.

"What about us?" Zach asks.

Exactly what I want to know. I'd googled Zach and me together several times, but it was mostly to keep an eye out for any possible leaks—not that I think David and the rest of the publicity team would let anything like that slide, but still. But I'd always scrolled the news page results. I try to avoid any fan content I'm not tagged in online, and even then, it'd take hours out of each day to read everything anyone ever says about us.

Angel looks at his phone, still wearing a self-impressed grin. "Let's see . . . Anjon . . . Zachathan . . . Zangel . . . Jonben . . . Rungel . . . Zuben. You have your shippers," he announces after a pause. "But it's niche. You guys don't hold a candle to the sweeping romance that is Anjon."

"¡Salud!" I say. "To the happy couple."

"It's funny, don't you think?" Angel asks. "That Zuben is one of the smaller ships?"

"I don't think it's an accident," I say.

From the front of the bus, Erin's eyes flicker to me. I hold her gaze with a blank expression.

She should be proud. So should all of Chorus. The damage control—or rather, the damage prevention—has worked like a charm.

We're in the green room a couple of nights later when Zach pulls me aside to speak privately. We're styled and ready to go on in twenty minutes, and after a day filled with interviews and photo shoots, it's the first free second we've had to talk all day.

We find a corner of the room that's removed from the bustling of our team and plonk down on the carpet with our backs against the walls.

"So," Zach murmurs, pressing his arm flush against mine. "I think I'm gonna come out to my mom."

"Oh wow. Shit, that's huge."

"I'm thinking maybe, like, tomorrow? Ish? Or maybe on the weekend. I don't know. When I'm brave enough, I guess." He gives me a sheepish smile, and I resist the urge to wrap him in a bear hug.

I take a second to find the right words. "That's . . . look, it's great, but . . . are you doing this because you want to? Or because you're worried? 'Cause . . ."

"No, I want to." He sounds unsure, but then he gives a firm nod. "I've been thinking about it for a little while and I don't want her hearing it from somewhere else."

I hesitate. "I get that, but . . . I dunno, to me that sounds like you feel pushed into doing it."

He shrugs. "Not really. It's nothing like when we came out to the band."

I pause. "What do you mean?"

"Well, we were backed into a corner then. I didn't want to come out, but if the only other option was being outed, I figured we kind of had to. I guess this is similar, in a way? But it feels different. It feels like my choice this time."

I stare at him, my blood going cold. "You didn't want to come out?"

He falters at the horrified tone in my voice. "It's fine. It's not a big deal. I'm just saying."

"Zach, it is a big deal. I had no idea. If you'd told me, we would've figured it out, talked to Keegan, or hidden it better, or whatever we needed to."

"Please don't worry about it. I made my own decision. No one forced me."

I blink, gobsmacked. Because now I kind of feel like I must have forced him. I replay everything I can remember from that night. What did I say that made him feel trapped?

Did I give him enough space to give his own opinions? Did I check in with him? Or did I assume he was on board with my opinion and steamroll him? I genuinely don't know anymore, and the thought that I might have dragged my boyfriend out of the closet, even if I didn't mean to, makes my stomach churn.

Did I hurt him?

He reaches for my hand. "Ruben," he says with a nervous laugh. "Breathe. Everything's fine."

I push those terrifying thoughts aside and try to refocus on the present situation. He wants to come out to his mom. Okay. What does he need from me, then? Does he need me to talk him out of it, and reassure him that he can wait a year to tell her if needed? Or does he need me to congratulate him and talk him through it?

At the best of times, I find it hard to tell if Zach's doing something because he wants to or because he wants to make as few waves as possible. Now, with this new information, I feel less confident than ever I'm reading the situation right. He needs me to understand what he wants, but I don't, I just *don't*, and how can I help him if I can't read him?

In the end, I just ask, "Do you need me there while you do it? For support?"

He shakes his head slowly. "I think I need to do this on my own. But thank you for offering. Seriously. That means a lot."

We sit in silence, then Zach sucks in a deep breath. "Ruben?"

"Mm?"

"This is going to be okay, right?"

Screw personal space. It's not like anyone in the room right now doesn't know what's going on, anyway. So I swivel around to kneel in front of him and put my hands on his shoulders. "Hey. Yes. I promise it'll be okay. No matter what happens, you have me. That's not gonna change. Not as long as you still want me."

His eyes are glassy, bringing out the shock of green that borders the irises, but he clenches his jaw to steady himself. "I'll always want you."

"Then you'll always have me."

The rest of the room blurs away, until he's the only person sitting in it. I stay still, letting him steer us, unsure how comfortable he is with public affection in this situation. But then he leans forward with his head down, to—hug me? Just be close to me?—and I bend my own neck to meet him, and touch my forehead against his.

"Okay," he whispers, his breath falling softly against my face.

Okay.

We rejoin Jon once Zach's collected himself, falling into the stiff armchairs placed around a coffee table holding sliced fruit and bottles of expensive spring water and a selection of every Doritos flavor except for Cool Ranch (Angel's request).

"Angel's gone to the bathroom," Jon says.

"Uh, thanks for the update," Zach says, grabbing a water. All traces of vulnerability are gone, and he's back to his lying smile.

"No," Jon says. "He's gone to *the bathroom*. For the second time in fifteen minutes."

Ah. So, he plans on being high for another performance. Wonderful.

"Also," Jon says. "I got a bunch of comments on the selfie we posted earlier."

He's referring to a shot of the four of us in the halls backstage we took after we'd been set free from the stylist's chair. *Ready for Round Two, Vienna!!!*

254 SOPHIE GONZALES & CALE DIETRICH

"And they were all asking about the same few girls, so I googled us, and this went live today."

He hands his phone over to me and I skim the article, Zach reading over my shoulder.

Romance Is in the Air! A Peek into the Past—and Present—Romances of the Boys from Saturday!

There's a photo of Jon as a kid, alongside some girl I don't recognize. God, he must be, what, fourteen here? Following this is a photo of him and Imani Peters, a childhood friend of his, walking on a street somewhere. From his haircut, I place the photo as somewhere shortly before our tour started back in America.

Not much is known about Jon and Imani Peters, although our source confirms they definitely had a fling a few months back. Could it be serious? We don't know— but we're sure thousands of girls around the world are praying it isn't so!

Well, that would be a categorically shitty thing for Imani to read if she *was* with Jon. Which I'm damn sure she isn't, given Jon's brought her up exactly zero times in the last few months.

Next are a few photos of Angel and various girls. One is Rosie, a girl he dated for a month or two when he was sixteen—they've stolen a nauseatingly cute couple photo from her Instagram, which isn't creepy at all—one is a girl I don't recognize, and one is a blurry shot of Angel and Lina on the street during our confrontation in Berlin.

Sources tell us that Angel and Lina Weber have been inseparable for the last month, and that he's flying

across Europe for the second half of Saturday's Months
by Years tour! Could this be an endgame couple? Time
will tell. But we sure haven't seen Angel give heart eyes
this obvious to anyone before! Sorry, ladies. He's taken!

Those weren't heart eyes, they were the over-dilated eyes
of someone high, panicky, and paranoid. An easy mistake to
make by all measures.

Next is a photo of Zach, out to lunch with—

"That's my *cousin*," he cries, aghast. "What the *fuck*?"

"Cousin, 'mystery girl,' potato, potahto, I guess," I say,
curling my lip.

"Which 'sources' say they saw us on a whirlwind date on
a horse-drawn carriage?" Zach demands. "We caught up for
lunch so she could show me her *ultrasound photos*. Because
she's *pregnant*. With her *boyfriend's baby*."

I'm too busy scrolling down to my section to reply,
a brick sitting in the pit of my stomach. Yup, I'd thought
as much—me and all my "girlfriends." There's a photo of
Amaya, the girl who played Mimi alongside me as Roger in
Rent a year before Saturday was formed. Me and Molly, a
girl I'd been friends with at Camp Hollow Rock, who I've
more or less fallen out of touch with. Me getting my hair
"lovingly pushed back" by goddamn Penny, *Penny,* because
apparently whoever wrote this article either didn't bother to
research who our *hair and makeup* artist is, or they simply
didn't care.

Angel rejoins us, buzzing with renewed energy. He has
a bounce to his step and he's running his tongue over his
teeth. His eyeliner is already smudged. "Whatcha doin' over
here?" he asks, sitting on the back of my seat and reaching
for Jon's phone.

"Just reading an article about every girl we've ever been in the same room with and why that means we're dating them," I say.

Angel flicks through the article. "Oh man. Oh *man*. I— well, you know what, at least they're *fucking* acknowledging I'm fuckable," he says loudly. Then he throws his arms back to address the room. "Breaking news! Chorus realizes it's actually possible for someone to find Angel attractive! Call the press, this changes everything!"

A few of our team members, including Erin, glance our way, but no one replies or approaches us.

Zach hums. "So, you think the source is David, too, huh? I wondered if it was just me."

Angel laughs at top-volume, and for several beats too long. It sounds more like a villain's cackle. "No, Zachy, not just you. If this isn't David's doing I'll jump off the stage and surf the fucking crowd tonight. This is real obvious. Zach and Ruben are super super no-homo, just super straight, everyone."

"And I'm probably available, with just enough of a question in there to make me seem more appealing," Jon says dully.

"And I'm also definitely straight, but not the one the fans should be dreaming of," Angel adds, a vicious edge to his tone.

"So, there's no reason to even *think* about shipping anyone with anyone," I finish, and Angel claps me on the shoulder in approval.

"David sent in a photo of me with my *pregnant cousin*," Zach says, indignant, and Angel howls with laughter until he falls right off the chair.

Jon helps Angel to his feet, and I stand to meet him. "Hey, you okay?" I ask.

Angel claps his hands. "Absotively fantastic. I am so, *so* ready. Let's fucking *go*, let's get on*stage*, I'm *pumped*!"

He's jumping on the spot now.

Not one member of our team seems to mind. They've got to have noticed; it's impossible for them to have missed it. But if they don't mind, what can be done? It's not like Angel listens to us.

I hand Angel a bottle of water and force a smile. "Okay. Well. As long as you're okay, I guess."

His face clouds and he rips the lid off the bottle with his teeth. "I'm *fine*, Ruben. Don't ruin it."

I glance at Zach and Jon. They're wearing matching concerned expressions. But their eyes tell me I'm right. There's nothing we can do that we haven't already tried. And frankly, between our schedule, and the weirdness over me and Zach coming out, and Zach's worry about his mom, and my mom texting me with critiques every second of the day, I don't have the capacity to deal with this. It's all too big for me to know where to begin.

So, when Erin calls us to head to the stage, I do the only thing I can. I tell myself that Angel's fine, and it isn't the end of the world if he has some extra energy onstage, and I push him to the back of my mind, and I get on with the show.

Because I don't know what else I *can* do.

EIGHTEEN

ZACH

It's time.

I need to tell Mom about what's been happening with Ruben.

I've got everything set up for our scheduled FaceTime. I've done my hair, pushing it down instead of up, and I'm wearing a shirt I've only been wearing lately as PJs: a long-sleeved Falling for Alice one. I guess I've done all this to show Mom that even though she's about to find out something super personal about me, I'm still me. I'm still her weird kid who loves pop punk bands with everything he has. Nothing about me has changed, and I want to show that. I glance at the fan's embroidery with the 'Fight Back' lyrics on them, the one thing I kept from the meet and greet.

My phone starts ringing.

Oh crap.

Oh freaking crap.

I'm frozen. As soon as I answer the phone, I'll have to have *the* conversation. And right now, my stomach feels completely twisted. I'm wrung out, honestly. Coming out to her should be fine; Mom is extremely, I mean extremely, liberal.

And after coming out a few times now, I've learnt how good it feels.

All the good feelings come once the conversation is over, though. And right now, it feels like everything is going badly. Saturday is spinning out of control and I can't stop it. Having Mom on my side is one of the few constants, and this could change that. It shouldn't, but that's the thing about people— sometimes they do things that you don't expect. Plus, it's possible Mom is cool with queer people as long as they're not me.

But with everything going on, I want her to know about me, even if I can't predict how she'll react. I am bi, and I have a boyfriend. She should know. And it's not like I'm ashamed about being into guys or dating Ruben.

I just don't want to let her down.

The call ends.

I missed it.

I let out a breath, and shake my shoulders. I've performed in front of thousands of people and haven't felt even slightly nervous, but I'd pick a concert over this any day. I'd even pick one where I have to perform in my underwear and I don't know the lyrics.

I lift my shaking hands, and call Mom back, starting a video call. We didn't do this until the start of this tour, but speaking face-to-face is just nicer now that we're so far away.

It rings once.

"Hello!" she says. She's still dressed in her work uniform, but her hair is loose, hanging around her shoulders in messy light-brown curls. She must've called me the second she got home from her shift. "How's it going?"

"I'm good, how are you?"

Mom frowns. "All right, what's up?"

"What?"

"You're wearing your moody shirt and you're being weird."

"I'm not being weird!"

Mom's time working in healthcare has given her zero tolerance for crap. Patients who keep secrets from her out of shame or whatever piss her off because they make her job way harder.

"Okay, you're right. I actually do have something I want to tell you."

"I'm shocked."

"Can we be serious for five seconds?"

"I'm sorry, I'll put on my serious Mom face. What's going on, sweetums?"

"You're the worst."

"Come on, tell me. Let me guess, you're dating someone?"

I pause.

"Er . . ."

"Oh, you are! That's so great, who is she? Look at you, you're blushing, this is precious. You know, I thought this would happen while you were overseas, you scoundrel."

"Mom, stop. Um . . ."

Tears fill my eyes.

Just saying this is really hard. Way harder than I was even expecting. And I want to say it because I know if I don't do it right now I'm going to talk myself out of this and telling her is the whole point of this call. I should just do it so that it's done.

"Mom, the thing is, I kind of like guys. I'm bi."

"Oh."

I know for the rest of my time on this earth I'm going to remember what she says next.

"How long have you been feeling like this?"

"A while."

"All right, wow. I had no idea."

"Really?"

"Okay, maybe I had some idea. A few of my friends said it could be possible, but you never gave off a vibe to me. I had no clue."

"But you have thought about it?"

"As much as any mom does."

"Then why did you say you had no idea?"

"I thought you'd want to hear that."

"Why would I want to hear that?"

"I don't know, Zach. I wasn't expecting to have this dropped on me right now. I'm exhausted."

"Oh. I'm sorry. I just thought now would be a good time because . . ."

I don't know how to finish this sentence, because I'm not even sure why I thought this was a good time. Clearly, I thought wrong.

"Don't be sorry, it's okay." She tears up. "I feel like I've let you down. I don't care about you being bi or gay or anything, I just wish you'd told me sooner. I could've helped you through this. Jesus, Zach, we're not even in the same country."

"I know. I think this is one of the things I needed to figure out on my own. Being overseas helped, I think."

"Oh. But you know you could've talked to me at any point, though, right?" Her voice has an edge to it.

"Definitely."

"How many people know?"

"Um, the band, and I had to tell Chorus, because it's my job, you know?"

"Right." She sniffs. "I'm sorry, this just reminds me of

your dad. You're so like him these days, it scares me some-times."

"How am I like Dad?"

"I thought I'd made it clear to both of you that you could talk to me about *anything*, but you both kept huge secrets from me, and I don't know why."

Whoa.

It sounds like she just equated me being bi with him cheating on her.

"Listen, Zach, I'm really tired and I'm worried I'm mess-ing this up. So I think I'm going to go, can we talk about this later?"

"Sure, that's fine."

"I love you so much, you know that, right?"

"Yeah."

"Okay. We'll talk later."

"All right, bye."

She hangs up.

That wasn't how I was expecting it to go. At all. I sit still, totally numb.

I can't believe she said I'm like Dad.

I didn't even get to tell her about Ruben. Dating him is one of the most wonderful things that has ever happened to me. Maybe that's for the best, though, given her reaction. Al-most every article I read about coming out online mentions that it's a bad idea to come out by introducing your parents to your partner. It's better to tell them about your sexuality, and then talk about your partner once the dust has settled.

Suddenly, everything catches up to me, and my eyes fill with tears. I never thought she'd say I'm like Dad and mean it, but I guess she thinks that now. I'm just like him. Just an-other guy who kept things from her.

Ruben asked me to message him as soon as it was done, so I send him a text.

Hey, it's done.

How'd it go?

Could've been better honestly.

Oh. Do you want to talk about it?

If you're free, yeah.

A few moments later, I hear a knock on my door. I open it, and let Ruben in.

"So, it was rough?" he asks, as I close the door behind him.

"Yep."

"Hey, have you been crying?"

"Maybe a little."

"Oh, Zach."

He moves in close, and hugs me. I squeeze him, gripping the soft material of his shirt. I don't want to let him go.

"I'm so sorry it didn't go the way you were hoping," he says. "It'll get better, I promise."

"It's okay."

He puts his hand on my shoulder, and I look up into his eyes. There's a sureness there. Something unflinching. "You know it's okay if it's not, right?"

I sniff, wipe my eyes, and shrug.

"Hey, look at me," he says, putting a hand on my cheek.

"I'm here for the tough stuff, too. This isn't just about us hooking up. If you want that."

"You're sure I'm not annoying you? You can say if I am."

"I'm sure. I'll stay as long as you want."

"Cool. Can we cuddle for a while or something?"

"Of course."

We move to the bed, and lie down together, with him as the big spoon. He pulls me to his chest, so our bodies are pressed together.

"You never annoy me, you know," he says, as he presses a kiss to the back of my head. "You don't need to pretend to be happy if you're not. You're perfect just the way you are."

I close my eyes.

I'm so lucky I have Ruben. Without him, right now . . . I don't know what I'd do.

I do know I'll do whatever I have to do to protect this.

We've finally been allowed out of our hotel rooms. It's just for a magazine interview and lunch, but still. At this point, I'll take anything.

Now the four of us are walking along the Langelinie promenade in Copenhagen. It's supposed to seem like we're here for fun, just checking out the sights, but it's all fake. Erin has been making sure we all take lots of "casual, candid" selfies and the like, that will get posted if Chorus deems them good enough. She even called Jon out for not taking enough.

I'm walking beside Ruben, but it feels different. An entire squadron of Chase guards is around us. But hey, at least we're out of the hotel. Finally.

Ruben catches me looking and smiles. I really wish I could hold his hand.

My phone starts buzzing in my pocket. I check, and see that it's Mom, so I let it ring out.

I know I'm being a little immature, and I should just talk to her. Or, at the least, I should call her back. I type out a text message instead, and try not to feel bad about the short, clipped replies I've been giving her ever since I came out to her.

> Sorry. Going to an interview.
> Will call later.

Okay good luck. U will crush it.
Love mom.

"Hey, Ruben, Zach?" calls Erin, from behind me. "A word?"

"Sure."

We fall back, so we're walking with her, out of earshot of the others. Just behind us, scarily close, are the guards.

"You guys are being really obvious right now," she says, under her breath.

We were just walking.

We weren't doing anything.

But whatever. This isn't just about me. It's also about Angel and Jon. And, honestly, I don't want to fight right now. I don't have enough fight in me to.

Ruben and I move apart.

Jon sees this happen, and he falls back, so he's walking beside me. Ruben shoves his hands into his pockets, but doesn't say anything, pretending to be taken in by the sights.

"You okay?" asks Jon.

I press my lips together. I don't want to lie.

"Zach, wait," says Erin.

What now, I think.

"You're up," she says, handing me a phone. "You and Jon look great together. We'd like a selfie of you throwing up a peace sign with Jon in the background. Think you can manage that?"

"Sure."

I take the phone. Erin holds up a portable ring light, giving me perfect lighting, and I take a few shots, then give her the phone back.

A few minutes' walk later, we reach the café. There are guards positioned out front. We go inside, and a reporter stands up. He's a bigger guy, dressed in a button-down and a bow tie. He's really cute.

A few of the other tables are occupied. I sense someone looking at us, and I turn to see a girl with long brown hair and faultless makeup, sitting with a guy with messy black hair in an oversized jacket that hangs off his muscular frame. They could both be models, honestly. I've gotten pretty used to what it looks like when fans look at us, and I get a completely different, colder vibe from the two of them.

We all shake the interviewer's hand, and then sit down. A waitress comes by.

"One Bloody Mary, please," says Angel.

The reporter writes a note down.

"Scratch that," says Erin. "He'll have a Pepsi Max."

The waitress clearly has no idea who to listen to, and she turns from Angel to Erin.

"Unless you brought your passport, of course," says Erin, to Angel. "The law here is you need to provide identification if you look underage, I believe."

"Er, yeah . . ."

Erin nods, as if it's settled. "Then a Pepsi Max it is. I'll have a latte, please."

Angel crosses his arms, only speaking to say he's not hungry when asked if he'd like to order food.

The interviewer is clearly thrilled by this display. The poor, poor man. He obviously has no idea that he won't be allowed to write about any of this. Chorus would never have agreed to the interview if they didn't have that kind of power in writing. He thinks he's going to do a big splashy piece right now about how we're treated like children, but that's not how this story is going to go.

"So, boys," he says, barely able to hide his grin. "Are you enjoying Copenhagen?"

"So much," says Ruben. "It's such a wonderful city, and we're so happy to have the opportunity to see it for ourselves."

Outside, through the glass doors, I see a small crowd of fans has assembled. Holy shit, already? That was fast. I know they're all connected on Twitter, but damn. A few of them press their faces to the glass, and I'm not sure I've ever felt this much like a zoo animal.

The interviewer hits all the familiar beats, asking about our clothes, how we're handling our schedule, and how we're hoping fans feel when they see us live. He doesn't seem to be aware that the questions they come up with are always the same. Or maybe because our team has so many topics that are off-limits, he's only asking what he can.

As Jon is reciting his response to "So what's next for Saturday?" I see the guy with dark hair stand up. He crosses the café, and goes into the bathroom. I look across, and see the girl with him. She's drumming her perfectly done fingernails against her white leather handbag. She catches me looking, and her stare is dark, like it won't end well for me if I keep looking.

I return my focus to the interview.

"Zach, I've heard you have a songwriting credit on the new album? That's so exciting! Can you tell me a little about that process?"

I spout out the line Geoff told me to say when asked this question.

"Um, well, I wrote a song, and I showed it to our team, and they were into it. The rest is history. It's called "End of Everything" and I'm really proud of it."

We started recording the song last week, without any of my tweaks put in. I'm trying not to think about it.

"That's so exciting! I know fans are dying to hear it."

"Well, I hope they aren't *dying,* no song is worth that. But I'm excited for them to hear it. I think it's good, and I think it's something a little different for Saturday. Plus, it's nice to have a song that's a little more personal, you know? I want our listeners to get to know this side of me."

"Excuse me," says Angel, and he stands up, and goes toward the bathroom, leaving his untouched Pepsi. A guard follows him across the café, but he goes into the bathroom alone. A few seconds later, the model guy I noticed walks out.

It could just be a coincidence.

But my instincts are telling me Angel is up to something.

NINETEEN

RUBEN

The night our whole world falls apart, I spend most of our concert lost in thought.

It starts with Zach. Since watching him that night in the hotel room, I've tried to catch more glimpses of him onstage. I have to do it with a measure of subtlety, though, in case it gets too obvious and someone from Chorus reprimands us.

So, as surreptitiously as possible, I steal glances at him, marveling at the way he bites his lip unconsciously when the tempo picks up and the choreo speeds with it. His little smiles at the audience. The damp strands of hair he pushes back from his head with spread fingers.

And while I'm doing it, a black ball of bitterness coils in my stomach. Because I shouldn't have to train my eyes to look anywhere but him, when they simply want to trail back to him and his magnetic pull.

I try to picture how Chorus will announce our relationship.

I try to picture us holding hands on this very stage.

But I can't.

Then I turn my attention to Jon. The way he bites his lip on purpose, seducing the crowd like he's been taught to. His lust-ridden, crooked smiles, directed at whichever lucky girl he can find in the nosebleed section. The way he spreads his fingers apart as he runs his hand over his thighs, sending a ripple of charged electricity through the audience.

And the bitterness grows. Because he's an unwilling puppet.

Then I look to Angel. The way his lips are parted as he drags in labored, exhausted breaths—he's not high tonight, but he looks like he had a hell of a time *last* night. The way his smiles resemble smirks, like he can't quite commit to them. The way he balls his hands into fists whenever we stop dancing, like he's laden with tension he can't get out any other way.

And the bitterness surges. Because I just don't think he's okay. And there's nothing I can think of to stop this train from derailing.

The bitterness must show on my face, because people give me a wide berth backstage. Zach asks me a couple of times if I'm okay, while we change, and on the drive home, but I just smile tightly and say I'm *fine*.

I get a message from Mom, and I send her a quick response. After a few back and forths, I give myself a quick break. I don't have the capacity right this moment. I'll message her in twenty or so, before she gets too worked up, and tell her my phone ran out of battery or something.

At the hotel, nestled in the bustling center of Budapest, Angel disappears to his room, and Jon disappears to his, and Zach and I escape into mine. Once we're alone, I feel the bitterness start to uncoil just a little. Things always seem more manageable when I'm with just him.

Zach kicks off his shoes and sits on the bed, holding his arms out. "Do you wanna talk about it?"

I shrug and climb onto the bed beside him, letting him

wrap me into a cocoon of a hug. The pressure of his touch melts some of the tension from my back. We sit in silence for a long while, Zach scrolling his phone with his free hand, me breathing in the scent of his chest until the rhythm of my heartbeat slows to match his. Usually, we'd be tearing each other's clothes off around about now. But tonight—for now, anyway—I just want quiet closeness.

After a while, Zach lowers his phone, and runs his fingers through my hair. I could fall asleep like this, resting my head on his chest. But I think we need to talk.

"I'm just worried about the whole coming-out thing," I say finally. "What if they don't let us tell people after Russia?"

He pauses mid-stroke. "They said they would."

"I know. But what if they *don't*?"

Zach pulls away from me. He leaves behind the ghost of his touch on my skin. I wish I hadn't said anything, and I'd let him hold me for hours.

"Well," he says. "I don't know. What *can* we do if they don't?"

I chew on my thumbnail. "That's not exactly a comforting response."

Zach's smile is soft and warm. "Hear me out, okay? So what if they don't ever let us come out?"

Hah. He did not seriously just say that to me, did he? "What do you mean 'so what'?" I ask thinly.

"I mean, let's say they don't. That doesn't mean we lose each other. You'll have me no matter what. Whether the world knows or not."

I try to process his words. Where the hell has this come from? "It's not about that. It's about being controlled."

"We've kept things private before."

"But this is about who we *are*," I shoot back. "It's the principle."

"I don't think you're this upset about a principle, Ruben. What's really worrying you, here? Like, *really*?"

Well. I don't exactly think I need a reason to be mad about being forced to hide my sexuality from the world indefinitely. But I'll bite. "Where do we draw the line? It's not just about what we say in interviews. What if people start wondering why we don't ever have girlfriends, and they make us pretend to have them to shut down the rumors? What if one of us gets sick, and they won't let the other visit us in hospital without the whole band because people will ask questions? This will affect a *lot*, Zach."

"Oh." He goes quiet, and stares at the bed, his brow furrowing. I can't read his face.

Oh my God. Is this like when Zach came out to the band? Is he just going along with this? "Do you . . . not want to go public?"

"No, I do. It's not that. I just wondered if it'd be that big a deal if we didn't."

"If you don't want to come out publicly, that's different. You know that, right?"

"Right, totally. I just . . . forget it. I hadn't thought about all those things you said. You have a good point."

I study him. "You sure?"

"I'm sure." He squeezes my hand. "I hope we're able to, then."

Something seems off about this. Zach's weirdly detached, and I can't quite tell if he's agreeing with me because he agrees with me, or because he knows I *want* him to agree with me. On something this monumental, the thought that he doesn't feel like he can express his own opinion worries me. He has to know that this is the one area where he can't just agree with everyone else to keep the peace and call it a day, right?

Frowning, I pick up my phone to find a stream of messages from Mom and Jon.

Mom's are expected.

Why aren't you answering?

Hello? I can see you're online.

Okay, now you're offline.

I guess you don't like my new dress
then, haha!

You know, we can talk about
something that isn't you, Ruben.

Maybe next time you want to talk
I'll be too busy for you!

I get a familiar stab of fear in my gut, seeing these. My first instinct is to rapidly reply to calm her down before she gets *really* mad. But then I open the messages from Jon.

Are you watching this?

Angel's livestreaming alone. He's
acting weird.

I think he's high . . .

I'm going to check on him.

Are you coming?

Ruben?

Is Zach with you? Can you two
come when you see this?

NOW?

Zach's checking his own phone. I assume he's reading a similar barrage of texts.

"Come on," I say, getting to my feet.

"What do you think he said on the livestream?" Zach asks, following me.

"No idea, but it doesn't sound good."

I get another message. Not Jon. Mom.

I can see you've read my last
message.

For once, something's scaring me more than the threat of Mom's wrath, though.

Sorry, not ignoring you. In
the middle of something.
Will explain when I'm free.
Nothing to worry about.

We nod at tonight's unfamiliar Chase guards as we pass them, exchanging tight smiles. Jon lets us in when we knock on Angel's door. His expression is grave. "What took you so long?" he demands.

Inside, Angel is pacing back and forth. He's visibly shaking, and he's wringing his hands while he chews on something. It takes me a beat to realize he's not eating anything at all. Just clenching his jaw, over and over.

"We have to get out of here," he's saying, half to himself. "Now. Tonight. It's our last chance."

"What do you mean?" Zach asks him.

Jon sighs. "He's paranoid about Chorus."

"You should be!" Angel yells at Jon. "They've brainwashed you. But just because they've wrapped you in their little web doesn't mean they're gonna get me. I'm not gonna let them. They aren't gonna have me."

"Angel," I try. "How about we sit for a bit. Maybe you can tell us what you're upset about."

"All of it. I'm upset about . . . can't you *see*?" he cries, still pacing. "They want to take everything away. They don't want us to exist anymore. They're murdering us. They're going to kill us, until they only have our bodies left. That's all they want from us. They don't want . . . they won't let us stay alive. We have to go. Tonight. It's them or us. I'm choosing me. They aren't gonna have me."

"Where are we gonna go?" Zach asks.

That's when Angel pivots, yanks the balcony door open, and darts out.

"Angel!" Zach cries as we race after him. "What are you doing?"

"I'm not gonna let them take me. They can't have me," Angel keeps repeating in a trembling voice. Then he climbs onto the balcony ledge, and everything inside me jolts like I've slammed into a wall.

"Angel, don't!" Zach screams, and Jon starts whispering *no, no, no,* under his breath in a frantic litany.

None of us make any sudden moves, though. We don't dare. You don't rush at a suicidal person when they're about to jump. I expect to hear screams of terror echoing from the streets below, but then I remember our rooms face the hotel grounds rather than the main road.

No one will see.

"I'm fine," Angel says, looking directly down. Not at the grounds, but at the balcony below him.

That's when I realize he's not jumping.

He's escaping.

Angel lowers himself slowly, hands clenched on the bars. The wind whips his black hair around his face, making him look wilder still. He wedges his feet in the gaps between the bars on the balcony. Then he smiles at us.

Jon reacts first. "Come back up," he says, extending a hand. "We can . . . hey, how about we all bring some drinks over? We can have a party. Just us."

Angel bends his knees. Jon strides forward.

"*Stop*," Angel barks.

Jon stops. "You can get me drunk?" he tries. "How about we find out how many shots it takes to get me to . . . to . . . Angel, please, *please*."

One foot leaves the balcony. Then the other. He hangs there for a second, holding onto the bars halfway down, then one of his hands slips. He's thrown off balance. His free hand falls to his side. There's only one left holding on.

Jon sprints forward. Zach and I follow at his heels. Jon slams into the bars and throws his hand down.

But Angel doesn't take it. He hangs, legs dangling into midair. Then he swings himself up with a grunt and grabs onto the bar.

Then he lets go altogether.

The three of us let out a singular, strangled cry as he falls.

But he lands safely on the balcony below.

"*Shit*," Zach hisses.

All at once, it clicks into place. The last time we let Angel go loose, we almost didn't find him. And he'd been nothing like this. Then, he'd been high. Tonight is different, though. This isn't just high. This is erratic paranoia. We can't lose him in the streets like this.

And if we turn around, we'll lose him.

"Get the guards," I say to Zach and Jon, before hoisting myself onto the ledge.

"Ruben, don't," Zach cries, but I've already flipped around. My phone begins to buzz against my leg repeatedly. Presumably Mom calling.

"I'll be okay," I say. *"Go."*

"Come back up, holy shit," Zach begs. "You'll fall."

I won't fall. If Angel could do this high off his face, I can.

As long as I don't look down. As long as I don't think of how many floors we soared past on the elevator ride up half an hour ago. Of what would happen to a body if it fell that far. And how easy it would be to misstep.

Maybe I should go back up after all.

But then I sneak a peek down. Angel's standing flush against the balcony wall, watching me. He's poised to run.

From this angle, I can also see what he must have seen when he hung here. The balcony below us sticks out a little. I won't even need to swing in to stick the landing. I just need to drop.

So, before I can second-guess myself, I suck in a breath and drop, serenaded by Zach's scream.

I hit the balcony hard, and stumble, but I'm safe.

Angel's smile is lopsided and manic. "You're coming with me?" he asks.

"Yeah. I'm coming, too."

"I knew you got it. They haven't sucked you in yet."

His eyes trail past me as he speaks. I think he's looking at the sky, but then Zach calls for me in alarm. I turn around to see a pair of legs dangling from the upper balcony.

"Jesus, Zach!" I dart forward and stand between his legs and my balcony's ledge, so I can steer his landing. Jon's worried face is peeking over the balcony ledge, and his hand is outstretched toward Zach just in case.

"Okay," I say. "Drop. I've got you."

Zach lands between my arms. We both turn to Angel, who's decided to try the balcony door. To my relief, it opens. One terrifying balcony leap was enough for tonight.

He stumbles inside, and Zach and I follow into the pitch-dark room. The bed is unmade, but the room is empty. Thank god for the thriving Budapest nightlife. *Saturday Breaking and Entering* is the last headline we need right now.

"You know," Zach says loudly. "I think Jon's idea was good. Let's go up to his room and get him drunk!"

Angel either doesn't hear him or ignores him, still muttering to himself about Chorus. He bursts through the front door into the hallway, with Zach and me on his heels. I already know where we're going. The fire exit.

Zach pulls out his phone. I expect him to message Jon, but instead he starts a FaceTime call with him. Of course—so Jon and the guards know exactly where we are. I'm impressed.

Jon answers as we start down the fire escape stairs, but before he speaks, Zach holds a finger to his lips. Then he taps the screen to turn the video around and film us as we run.

The escape opens into a dimly lit underground garage filled with cars. Angel turns in a circle, looking for an exit, and I wonder if Zach and I should just tackle him. Together, we could surely take him. But I'm not sure how violent Angel might be in this state. I don't want to hurt him. And if he hurt Zach because of a call I made, I'd never forgive myself. So, I decide, we just stall him. Jon and the guards can't be more than a minute off. The guards will know how to dees-calate this.

"So, where do you wanna go?" I ask Angel in the calmest voice I can muster. My phone starts to vibrate again, and it speeds my heart rate even more. Focus, I need to *focus,* and I can't focus with Mom trying to reach me, because when Mom's mad at me, bad things happen. I try to ignore the buzzing. I *try.*

Angel stops turning and blinks at me. "Far. We just need to get far away. Somewhere they can't get us. Come on."

At the last word, he breaks into a run, sprinting through the rows of parked cars. Crap. "Wait," I say. "Where's the exit? Where are we going?"

"It's . . . there's gotta be one. Help me. We've got to find one. Now. Ruben, hurry. They're going to find us, and they'll lock us away. We need to get away."

"It's just a temporary restriction, Angel. It's not forever."

"It *is* forever. They'll never let us go, Ruben."

"Come on. You know that's not true."

Angel slows to catch his breath and swings around. "You're not dumb. You know. You . . . you know, and you don't say it. But I know you see it. You can see what they're doing to us."

Zach tugs on my coat sleeve as he reaches me. "They're in the fire escape," he says below his breath. I nod with as much subtlety as I can muster.

"What are they doing to us?" I ask gently. I know the answer, but keeping him talking nonsense is the only way to stall.

Angel's laugh is high pitched and frantic. It bursts out like a howl. "We are their prisoners! And they won't stop, so we have to run. Help me find the exit. Quick!"

Zach lowers his phone and steps forward. "We've only

got to get through the rest of the tour. Then it'll be back to normal."

"Normal?" Angel spits. "When's it *ever* been normal?"

"Before. It wasn't so bad."

"Before." Angel runs a hand through his sweaty hair, and glances around us to check for spies. He looks afraid. Terrified, really. "Three years ago I was called Reece."

"Angel—" I say.

"*I was called Reece,*" he shouts, his face contorting. "They took my *name from me*! And you think they're going to let you come out on your own fucking terms? You're both *fucking deluded*!"

A door slams with a heavy clang of metal behind us. The three of us snap our heads up. Beyond the rows and rows of cars are Erin, Jon, and four guards.

"No," Angel says, turning on his heel.

Zach, who was still catching his breath, lets out a frustrated sigh as we give chase again. "I'm gonna kill him in the morning," he pants to me. "Making me . . . jump off a fucking balcony . . . run laps around a freaking garage . . ."

We round a corner, and suddenly an exit sign comes into view. Erin's yells echo through the garage as she pleads with Angel to slow down. Angel stumbles through the door, and Zach and I follow him. Erin's voice is abruptly cut off as the door swings closed.

The night air has a fierce bite to it. Not cold enough for snow, but the wind still stings my cheeks, and I can feel my breath as it travels down my chest, the frigid air scraping against my lungs. I button my coat with prickling fingers and brace myself against the chill. Zach hugs his arms to his chest and stands behind me to take shelter from a gust of wind.

Angel's not wearing a coat. I doubt he feels the cold at

all. His eyes dart around rapidly, then he rushes toward the street. Toward light.

I don't like where this is going.

"Angel," I say urgently. "Not this way. That's the main street."

He ignores me.

"There are people camped out here."

"We can hide in the crowd. Yeah. We'll . . . they won't be able to find us in the crowd."

"No, we'll get *mobbed* by the crowd."

Angel's voice is shaky, desperate. "Shut up."

"He's right, Angel," Zach says.

"SHUT UP!" He starts to run again, and takes a right onto the street.

The others are outside, too, now, and they're running. They'll catch up to us before anything too bad happens. We just have to make sure we don't lose Angel.

Zach groans as I pick up speed. As I predicted, an ocean of fans are surging and swarming toward Angel. When they see Zach and me round the corner, their screams of excitement and surprise turn into a roar. Angel runs toward them, and they run toward Angel, and they collide. And he's engulfed.

It's like they've consumed him.

Zach and I exchange glances, wary. I want to take his hand so I don't lose him. He needs to be tethered to me for safety, in case something happens.

But I don't. I don't, because there are cameras, and witnesses, and because Geoff and Chorus said not to. And even in this moment of sheer panic, with this mounting fear, and the crowd about to hit us, I don't disobey Chorus.

Maybe I'll never be brave enough to. Maybe I only want to think I am.

So, when the crowd hits us, I find myself standing alone, surrounded by dozens of strangers.

Ruben.

Ruben.

Ruben.

Ruben.

There's no malice in their eyes. There's only love in their touches. Admiration in their voices. But they press against me until they're breathing my air. Their hands, dozens of hands and hundreds of fingers, claw at my body wherever they can touch me. My neck, hair, lips, arms, legs, chest. A hand slips inside my coat. Moist lips press against my wrist.

My name gets louder, and *louder*, and LOUDER.

Some try to push the others back from me.

Give him some space.

Back up, guys.

He can't breathe.

Their voices are swallowed up, though. Just like I am.

"Please, let me get through," I beg. "Please. I need to go. I need to move. Please. Just—just let me, *move*, let me *go*, I need to get THROUGH!"

Someone hears me. Hands take mine. A small group of them pulls me, and the group grows as the word spreads. *I need their help. I need them to save me from themselves.*

The sea starts to move, and it's like being dragged through quicksand, but, gradually, its grip on me loosens, and I'm collectively yanked out before I can be sucked back in the depths.

And the freezing air is back on my face. And lights. Blinking, flickering streetlights, headlights, neon lights on storefronts. I'm chanting *thank you, thank you,* to everyone and no one while I search for Zach, Angel, Jon.

"*Ruben!*" Zach finds me first, tearing his way from the

crowd. He throws himself at me, and I grab his upper arm, because that's okay, I think, that's safe, and I need to touch him,
I can't not. The crowd is still there, and it's still swarming, but
it's split in two. The half trying to reach us, and the other half
holding it back. It wrestles with itself, seething, crushing.

"Angel!"

It's Jon, standing with his feet planted firmly apart, fifty
feet away from us. I follow his eyes and find Angel, hovering
at the edge of the crowd. Angel's skin flashes orange and
white as he stares at the lights around us with unseeing eyes.
The traffic is thick and furious. Even though it's night, the
city is alive and blaring. The shouts, and the crowd, and the
blinding headlights whipping and whipping and whipping
past, must be disorienting him beyond belief.

"I'm not going back there!" Angel yells, but he isn't looking at Jon. He isn't looking at anyone.

Erin and the guards appear from within the thronging
crowd. They weren't consumed. They're immune.

Erin stands beside Jon. "Angel," she says, in the world's
most casual voice. For the cameras. For the onlookers. "We'd
better head back up now, don't you think? We have to be up
so early."

It's a show. Just a performance. The performances never
end with us. They just go on and on and—

"She needs to stop talking," Zach says. "She's freaking
him out."

He's right. Angel's looking between Erin and the crowd,
like he's considering diving in. He's running his hands over
his face and down his neck, scraping and dragging at his
skin. His chest rises and falls like a drowning man gasping
for air he can't suck down.

"He's known you the longest," I say, squeezing Zach's
arm. "If anyone can calm him down, you can."

He nods grimly and takes a few steps forward. "Hey, dude," he says. "It's fine. Honestly. But it's way too cold out right now, so why don't we all go out together tomorrow? I want to see Budapest, too!"

It's a good attempt at talking him down without making it obvious to our hundreds of witnesses what the problem is. But I don't think he'll buy it. It needs an endorsement. He needs something substantial to grasp on to. A promise that things will be different, if only he comes back.

As I suspected, he starts shaking his head.

"Erin," I call. "We can go out and see Budapest tomorrow, right? Maybe we can visit the castle?"

Just say yes. Just play along until we can get him home safely. He just needs to ride this out safely.

But she doesn't. Instead: "Angel, if we go back now, we won't need to involve Geoff. He doesn't have to know."

A veiled threat. Angel stiffens. Tears roll down his reddened cheeks. "No," he says.

Then Erin takes a step.

And he flings himself backward, screaming through a raw throat. "NO!"

But backward is into the street.

I see what's about to happen an instant before it does, my hand flying to cover my mouth. Horns blare, and rubber screeches on concrete. The car hits him with a thud, and his body goes over. He spins in the air. *Thud,* against the roof. *Thud,* against the trunk.

Then he rolls, limp and lifeless, onto the black road.

The screams rise in a swell around us.

Angel's lying on the road, and he's not moving.

Zach falls to his knees.

My phone starts to buzz again.

Angel's lying on the road, and he's not moving.

I fight against the wave of the crowd as it reaches me again, because I have to get to Zach, I have to.

The buzzing won't stop.

Angel's lying on the road, and he's not moving.

I reach Zach, and get my arms around him. This close, I can differentiate his screams from the others. He's not screaming Angel. He's screaming "Reece." Over and over again, to the ground, hunched over with his eyes squeezed shut so he doesn't have to see.

Then there's nothing to see anymore anyway. Just a wall of bodies, as the crowd closes over us to share in our grief. Everything is distant, and floating.

I think they're suffocating me.

I think they're drowning us.

The weight of the crowd on us is crushing. I can't get air in. I can't focus, I don't know the answer, I can't think, because—

Angel's lying on the road, and he's not moving.

I don't want to stand. I just want to kneel here, holding onto Zach, keeping him steady as he screams out the name of someone he knew as a young boy. I don't want air, and I don't need it. I don't mind being crushed.

Then strong hands grab me, and pull me free from the fray. It's one of the Chase guards. Another guard strides over and stands between me and the crowd, so I can suck in air. Before I can fear for him, I spot another guard emerging from the crowd with Zach. He's safe. Okay.

But—

Angel's lying on the road, and he's not moving.

I can't cry. I want to, but I can't. I feel nothing. I see nothing, except Angel's motionless body, even though he's blocked from sight by the swarm. I can't see Erin or Jon. I call for Zach, but the guard shakes his head. "Not now," he says.

"Is Angel okay? We need to go back."

"Not now."

"Let me go to Zach, then. I need to be with Zach."

"Not now."

The screams don't fade as the guard steers me firmly to the refuge of the hotel.

It doesn't matter how far away we get.

The screams don't fade.

TWENTY

ZACH

They won't let us see Angel.

Erin has been messaging us updates, that he's alive and okay, so we at least know that much. Well, he's as okay as you can be with a compound fracture, some bruised ribs, and a bunch of scrapes and a possible head injury. They're not sure how bad it is yet.

But he's awake, and is mostly okay. He got lucky, that's for sure.

If they're telling the truth, that is. We can't know for sure, because all we have is their word; we aren't allowed to be with him. Apparently that will cause a scene and will draw even more attention to what's happened, which Chorus wants to avoid at all costs. Footage of Angel's accident has spread around the Internet as fast as anything involving us does, but Chorus is really trying to make sure this only lasts one news cycle. That means no visits until it's all blown over.

Normally, I somewhat get why they keep us out of the loop of big stuff, and I trust that they know how to handle whatever situation is going on best. This is so far from being normal, though.

He's our friend, and he's hurt. We should be with him. Being here feels wrong.

Ruben and Jon are in Ruben's room, waiting for more news, but I left about an hour ago to try to get some sleep. "Try" being the operative word. I can't get comfortable, as everything feels cloying and too hot.

I get out of bed, and start pacing. The clock on the bedside table says it's just past four a.m., which makes me think sleep at this point is going to be impossible.

The accident replays in my mind. It's vivid, down to every minute detail. I can still hear the dull thud of him hitting the hood and tumbling over, before finally hitting the road facedown.

And then the silence.

Until the screaming started, anyway.

He was so still, his body bent awkwardly with his arm jutting out. In that moment, everyone who was there thought he was dead. I know it. I could smell blood. His blood. I saw it, stark red, on his face before the guards dragged the three of us away. Jon tried to fight them, to stay with Angel, but he wasn't strong enough. I just went with them. I didn't have the energy to fight back. Maybe I should've. Maybe then I wouldn't feel like this, and Angel wouldn't be alone.

I press my fingertips into the corners of my eyes, to stop the tears. I'm not ashamed of crying, I'm just sick of it. But I just can't help but think I should've been more aware. I should've seen this coming. I should've been there for Angel, and stopped this.

I go into the bathroom and lean against the sink. My reflection doesn't really look like me. Not lately, anyway. My eyes are red, and I have puffy bags under them. I splash some water on my face, then go out and see the empty room. It's dark and messy.

I feel an ache. I need to be with the others now. Maybe I can't see Angel, but I can see Ruben and Jon.

In the hallway, there is a whole squadron of Chase guards, more than I've ever seen, blocking each end. The stares the guards give me are cold, utterly devoid of emotion. I'm sure they have orders to stop us by any means necessary if we try to leave.

I knock on Ruben's door, and Jon lets me in.

"Can't sleep?" asks Ruben.

"Nope." I sit down beside him on the end of the bed. He puts his hand on my leg, his touch reassuring. "Any news?"

He shakes his head.

"I can't get ahold of Dad," says Jon. "I think he's ignoring me."

I grimace. Jon has just seen one of his best friends get in a horrific accident, and Geoff's ignoring him.

I wonder if he even cares about Angel. Or any of us, beyond our value to his company.

I wish I could tell myself that he does.

But I don't think I can anymore.

It takes five more hours for Geoff to call us to a meeting for an update on Angel. Eight hours, since Angel's accident.

Eight. Freaking. Hours.

Honestly, during this time I've started to feel as if the four of us are the least important members of Saturday. We're just pretty props that the Chorus bigwigs can move around however they like. They can dress us up, or strip us shirtless if they want, to satisfy the public's desires. We're sold as dream boys. Anything human about us only makes us more difficult in their eyes. Anything real is ugly and breaks the illusion.

We file into Erin's room.

A laptop is on her desk, showing Geoff, in his office at Chorus HQ. A board of suits is already in the room, mostly publicists and other people like that I don't generally have much to do with.

"Well," says Geoff. Clearly, we've walked in on him mid-conversation, and he just glances at us, then continues. "We don't know when he's going to be able to go back onstage yet, but there are options. We can change the choreo to accommodate his injuries."

"Hold on," says Jon, before we even sit down. His chest puffs up. "You're not considering going ahead with Angel on the tour, are you?"

That finally gets his full attention. "Respectfully, Jon, this isn't your decision to make. Just focus on helping each other through this trying time and leave the logistics to us. Now take a seat."

Jon huffs, his eyes on fire. He moves toward an empty seat, but then stops, standing his ground.

"You know what? No. Angel needs help. You do know he's been high almost every day, right? He's not coping. Dad, he almost died!"

"We are well aware of the grievous nature of his accident, but we've been assured it is safe for him to perform once he has recovered—"

"What is it going to take for you to care? This tour can't continue. Angel only needs to be one place now, and that's getting the best help money can buy. Otherwise there won't even be a Saturday for you to pick at much longer."

The room goes silent. A PR manager tugs at her shirt collar.

"All right," says Geoff. "We wanted to include you in our

discussions about the immediate future, but emotions are clearly too high right now. We can talk about this later."

Geoff moves to end the call.

"What about the tour?" asks Ruben. "We have a show in two days."

"We'll discuss, and get back to you soon with a plan."

The screen goes blank.

And that's it, I guess.

I look to Erin, I guess searching for some sort of comfort, or at least some answers.

"So what's going to happen?" I ask. "Are they going to make us perform without Angel?"

"I'm really sorry, Zach," she says, frowning. "But I can't talk about this."

Wow. Okay. So that's where she stands.

Ruben and I go back to his room.

"This is fucked," he says.

I nod. Because yeah. Guys in Saturday might not be allowed to use that word in public, but it's the only appropriate one for this current situation.

"Do you want some space?" I ask. "I can go, if you want?"

He shakes his head. "Stay."

We move to the bed. I lean back against the headboard, and Ruben sits in my lap, his legs curled underneath him. I look him in the eyes and push a strand of hair back into place. He smiles softly at the contact, which makes my stomach fill with butterflies. I wonder if he even knows how cute he looks when his hair is a little messed up. Or how beautiful I find him.

"Are you okay?" I ask.

"Not really. Are you?"

"Same."

"I keep thinking about last night. I keep *seeing* it, like it's on a loop. And I can't stop thinking about what he said."

"Which part?"

I put my hands on his hips, holding him close to me. Maybe I'm not the best at saying exactly what I want sometimes, but I hope maybe I can show him by doing this, by listening. Maybe that will be enough for him to just know. I start rubbing him with my thumb, feeling how warm he is through the soft material of his shirt.

"All of it, I guess," he says.

"I'm sorry they're being so shitty."

I reposition, lying down and putting a hand behind my head. Ruben starts touching my necklace, like that's all he wants to be doing, but I know from his furrowed brow that he's going to ask me one of those questions he's wanted to ask for a long time, but has held back, waiting for the perfect moment.

"Zach, how do you actually feel about coming out after Russia?"

"What makes you ask?"

"You know *I* want to come out, and you know they're saying we're allowed to after Russia, but what about you? Just because we're allowed to doesn't mean that's what you want."

I sit up, my brow furrowed. "I want to."

"Do you really though? Or are you just going along with it because you think it's what I want? You know you don't have to, right?"

"That's not what I'm doing. I'm not scared of coming out."

"Not being scared of something and wanting to are very different things."

"I know, but like . . . I don't mind being out. In a lot of ways it's been a relief. It's fine."

His stare drops down, and his shoulders slump a little.

"What?" I ask. "Did I say something wrong?"

"You never do."

"Wait, what?"

"Sorry, that sounded harsher than I meant. I'm just really tired and crabby."

"Do you need a nap?" I grin, but he doesn't return it.

"Yeah."

"It's okay, I get it."

He frowns, and turns over on his side. I lie back down and I shuffle closer, so we're spooning, our bodies pressed together. I press a kiss to the back of his head.

"I just never know what you want," he says quietly.

I hear alarm bells.

"What do you mean?"

He sighs. "Nothing. Don't worry about it."

It sounds like I should worry about it, but I'm tired, too, and I'm really not in the mood for an intense evaluation of my feelings and motivations right now. Not *now*. "Maybe I should go, so you can get some sleep?"

There's a heavy pause. When Ruben replies, his voice is small. "Don't."

I pull him closer, trying to ignore the fact that, clearly, I've done something wrong, and I don't know what it was.

"Okay."

"Hey, guys," says Angel in a black voice.

The three of us are sitting on Ruben's bed, with a tablet on Ruben's lap. To be honest, I was sort of expecting him to crack a joke, or at least smile, but he seems like a totally different person right now.

His arm and leg are both in a cast, and there's a bandage stuck to the side of his temple, but he's awake, and that sight relieves at least some of the tension I've been feeling these past few days.

"So," says Angel. "Which one of you told them I have a drug problem?"

I glance at the others, who are all avoiding Angel's stare.

Finally, Jon speaks up. "I told them I think you need help."

Angel rolls his eyes and leans back. "Knew it. I *knew*—"

"And you do," Jon says over him. "You almost *died*, Angel."

"That could've happened to anyone."

"It happened because you were *high*. You jumped off a *balcony*, Angel. Because you were *high*."

"So did Zach and Ruben."

"And if they got hurt it would've been *your fault*."

Angel startles at this, staring at the camera in wounded shock. "You must enjoy this, right?"

"What's that supposed to mean?"

"Come on. You're always preaching about doing the right thing, and being *mature*, and how *awful* it is that I wanna have some fun while I still can, and the first chance you get, you throw me under the bus to Chorus. I don't even have a problem, I just had one bad night."

"You've had a lot of bad nights lately."

Angel laughs, sharp and bitter. "You know what, fuck you, Jon. You're such a stuck-up, pretentious dick. You know people only put up with you because of your dad, right?"

"I'm not going to fight you."

"You know why I think you're so against me? It's not

because you're all *moral,* and *in with God.* It's because you know if you actually joined in and had fun with everyone, they wouldn't want you around, and you don't want to give them the chance to shut you out. You're just another obnoxious rich boy who goes crying to his daddy every time he doesn't agree with someone, and everyone *hates you.*"

Jon's face is completely blank. "You don't mean that."

"Yes, I do. I hate you."

"You're mad at me because you *know I'm right* and you don't want to face it—"

"I think I might've hated you since I met you."

"—and I am not apologizing for this. I am not apologizing for getting help so I don't have to sit there and watch you kill yourself."

"You know we're done after this, right? I don't want anything to do with you. We're *done.*"

"Better us done than you *dead,*" Jon shouts at the screen, his voice raw and strangled.

The screen goes black as Angel ends the call. Jon's breath is labored, and he covers his mouth with a trembling hand.

It's only now that I realize I'm squeezing Ruben's hand, so tightly his fingertips are turning purple. I relax my grip. "He didn't mean that," I whisper. "I know Angel, okay? He's just mad."

Jon doesn't reply. He just stares at the screen.

Ruben lets go of me and wraps Jon into a bear hug from behind. Jon grips onto Ruben's arms, his knuckles turning pale.

A knock sounds at the door, and I open it to let Erin in.

She takes in Ruben and Jon on the bed. My stricken face. The tablet set up.

"Angel called, huh?" she asks.

We all nod. None of us say a word.

"Well, as I'm sure you've figured out, Chorus and Galactic have made a decision about the tour."

"And?" Jon forces out.

"They've decided you're right, Jon. Angel needs time to recover. It's been postponed."

I wish it felt like a victory.

It doesn't, though.

Not even close.

TWENTY-ONE

RUBEN

The flight home is all but silent.

I'm hoping to get some sleep on it, because god knows I haven't had much lately, but as usual, even with my eyes closed, my mind refuses to still. It bubbles and crackles, jumping from topic to topic with the high-strung energy of a hummingbird.

Angel, and his recovery, and how we still don't know enough about it beyond vague platitudes.

The media, and its now-sympathetic discussions of Angel and his apparent fatigue-driven stumble into traffic.

Jon, and the way he's burrowed into himself since finally standing up to his dad. How I recognize the fear of the fallout of putting your foot down to a parent.

Zach, and the way his smile began to flicker when he came out to his mom, and how it's disappeared completely since the accident. How he's about to face his mom for the first time since coming out to her, and I'm going to be in a completely different state, unable to hold his hand, or rush right to his side if it goes wrong.

My mom, and how she'd seemed less concerned with what happened to Angel that night than how it'd affect the tour.

That, and the fact that I'd *left her on read*. How, apparently, the trauma of what I'd been through that night hadn't been a good enough Get Out of Jail Free card for my behavior.

How I have to try to go back to normal in their house. Around her. Without the band. Without Zach.

Topic to static to topic. As though my brain's trying in vain to tune into the correct radio station. I try to drown it out with headphones and *In This House*, but it only half works.

It feels like we're in the air for a lifetime—to the point where I start to seriously consider that maybe Geoff was never planning on setting us free, and that he's secretly diverted the plane to head to a last-minute media opportunity or something. Or maybe it's less complex than that. Maybe we're just hanging motionless, suspended in one place, and we'll never get back home at all. Maybe waiting, and sitting in our grief, is all there is now.

But then the pilot announces we're about to land in LA, and I finally open my eyes. Zach, whose shoulder has been pressed tightly against mine the whole flight, locks eyes with me, but he doesn't speak. Doesn't smile, either.

Usually Angel and Zach stay on the plane together while the rest of us disembark here. Today, though, we're leaving him to go on alone. The team files past Zach, saying their goodbyes with forced cheer. Jon gives Zach a tight hug, and a lump lodges in my throat as I watch. The seconds tick away.

And now they're gone. It's time for my own goodbye.

I'm not ready for it.

I haven't been apart from him for more than a few hours since we began this leg of the tour. Now, I feel like I'm being wrenched away. How am I supposed to get off this plane alone, and go home without him, and fall asleep without his scent on my pillow, and wake up to only the echo of the symphony we made together?

I feel like life is about to enter the off-beat. That leaves me out of sync.

Gritting my teeth, I pull him roughly against me, breathing him in and gripping his hair between my fingers, to refresh my memory of holding him, so I can live off that until I see him again.

"See you soon?" I say as we break apart.

He swallows, and the corner of his mouth quirks. "Soon. Message me when you get home safe?"

I nod instead of replying, because I'm worried if I open my mouth, the words will crumble.

With a deep breath, I head out the door with Jon, and down the steps to the tarmac. I try to comfort myself as I walk. We have our phones. We have WiFi. This is going to be fine. It's just a break.

There's no fanfare as the team is steered by the two waiting Chase guards into the airport this time. Instead, we're ushered through a back entrance into a private area, away from the crowds with their photos and videos and screams. Just an empty, low-level buzz punctured by airport announcements and practiced greetings by efficient airport staff. I barely have time to rub my eyes and shake the stiffness from my limbs before I'm saying goodbye to Jon by the curb. Then he's whisked into his own car, and I'm directed into mine, and it's over. I'm alone. Going back to my parents, with no way to avoid them. Nothing standing between me and them. No time difference.

Was it only a month ago I was upset to be leaving their time zone?

I steady my breathing as the car rolls out of the parking

lot. After half a minute, I whip my phone out and turn off flight mode to message Zach. But as soon as my phone signal returns, a message comes through from him. He must have sent it while the plane was still grounded.

Hey. I miss you.

And despite the heavy ache in my chest, I smile.

TWENTY-TWO

ZACH

Now that I'm home, staring at Mom's front door, it's become obvious I can't keep doing this.

Mom's weirdness has finally gotten to the point where I can't ignore it anymore. It's turned her place from a safe haven into a spot that, honestly, I don't even want to be.

I'm so sick of it.

I've been trying my best not to let the wall she's put up bother me, because I thought that was the best move. I thought it was a good idea to give her some space, so she could come around to my sexuality.

Now, though, I've decided that that's bullshit. My mom is starting to make me feel like I've come out as an axe-murderer, not bi, and I'm dreading seeing her. That means it needs fixing.

I unlock the door and go inside.

"Hey," Mom says, turning the TV off. She's in an oversized top and sweatpants, and her hair is messily tied back.

We hug. It's cold, both of us keeping a safe distance.

"How was the flight?" she asks.

"Okay."

"Really? You look tired."

I wince. "Yeah, I am. I'm going to crash."

"Sorry about the mess," says Mom, picking up a cardigan from the couch and folding it. Mom, like me, can generate huge amounts of mess in record time. "Work was hectic today."

"It's not even that bad."

"See, now I know you're lying."

I think she meant it as a joke, but it sounds harsh. I chew my lip.

She keeps cleaning, like I'm not even here.

I could just go to my room, but I can't help but think about the time I came back from the first leg of our tour. Now she's acting like I'm a bother. An annoyance. I know she has a life and it doesn't revolve around me, but like, I can't help but think this is because I came out to her. It's the biggest difference I can think of between then and now.

This can't go on.

I need to talk to her about it.

"Hey, want a coffee?" I ask.

"Oh, yes, please."

I turn on Mom's coffee machine. I bought this for her one Christmas, the first one after Saturday started making serious money, and Mom and I both spent an enormous amount of cash on each other. Back then, every big buy felt scandalous, and they still kind of do. That's the thing about being poor, it never really leaves you. I still weigh the worth of every dollar, even though I don't need to do that anymore. My first impulse is to get the cheapest thing available *because it's just the same.* I remember wanting new clothes or a video game or even something from a coffee shop but having them be off-limits because they cost too much. Even if I did get them, guilt always followed. And for her whole life Mom had always wanted, in her words, a "fancy-ass coffee machine," but she held off, focusing what she had on other, more practical things, like rent and bills.

That Christmas was honestly one of the biggest highlights of the first year of Saturday, and maybe my life. This coffee machine was the crown jewel; she flipped out when she saw it in a way I don't often see from her. She lost her shit, basically.

I put some coffee beans into the grinder and blitz them, which makes the whole place smell like a coffee shop.

I want to bring up the weirdness, to finally talk this out, but the words get stuck in my throat.

Talking with Mom about how I'm unhappy with the way she handled my coming out is invasive, almost. Maybe akin to showing her one of my late-night incognito searches. It feels like something I would never do.

I put two mugs under the nozzle. Then I get to work. The machine rattles, the entire thing shaking. I don't remember it ever doing that. Maybe it needs to be repaired. I hate that, because I bought this in the golden days, back when things with Saturday were more fun than stressful, and now it's breaking. Given everything going on, that feels fitting.

"How's Angel doing?" she asks.

"He's fine."

She huffs. "Okay, Zach, what's going on?"

"Huh?"

"You've been giving me one-word answers for weeks now. What's up? Have I upset you, somehow?"

"I'm not upset, exactly. I just . . ."

Come on, Zach. Say it. Say you're not happy with how she responded when you came out. It's what Ruben would tell you to do.

"Ever since I came out to you, you've been treating me so weird, and I want you to know it's not cool."

"You think I've been treating you weird?"

"I do."

"Zach, lately you've been a different person. You've pulled away, I can tell."

"That's your fault, not mine."

Oh jeez, that was clearly the wrong thing to say, as her eyes widen. "How exactly is your behavior my fault?"

"Because I told you I'm bi and you got weird and mad, and then never talked about it again."

"I thought that was what you wanted!"

"For you to be mad at me?"

"No, gosh, for us to treat it like it's no big deal."

"I only said that because I could tell you were being weird."

She rests her hand on her hip and studies me. "Hang on, is this why you've been ignoring me?"

"I haven't been ignoring you."

She pulls out her phone, and shows me the screen. She has been messaging me almost constantly, and my responses have been sporadic at best.

"I've been busy," I say.

"You've been busy since camp. You made time before."

"Well, maybe that was before I came out to you and you treated me like I was betraying you."

"I did no such thing."

"Can you please stop telling me how I feel? I felt like you didn't accept me, and I . . ."

"Oh, Zach," she says, stepping closer. "You really felt that?"

I nod, and I feel tears prickling.

"You do know I go to Pride every year, right?"

"Yeah, but . . ."

"And you do know that some of my best friends are queer?"

"Yep."

"And have I not always told you I'm going to support you wherever you fall on the gender and sexuality spectrum?"

"Well, yeah. But then why were you weird when I came out?"

That catches her off guard. "I didn't mean to be weird. I was just surprised, that's all. And for a second, just a second, I started to question our whole relationship. Like, I always thought you told me everything."

"That's what I was *trying* to *do*."

She starts smiling.

"What?"

"Nothing?"

"No, what?"

"Oh, it's just you're being such a teenager right now. It's adorable. Okay, back to our serious talk. All right. Mm-hmm, yes, queer teen angst, go on."

I shake my head and laugh. For the first time in weeks, this feels right. "You're the worst."

"I know. But, just so it's obvious, I think you being into guys is both wonderful and a non-event at the same time. All right?"

"Fine. And, like, you should know I haven't known for that long, so I did tell you pretty early. I only really figured it out for sure on tour."

"You must've had an inkling, though, right? Being bi isn't something that comes out of nowhere."

"Yeah, but I thought it was just a phase, I guess. Like it might go away at some point."

"I think that's problematic."

"Am I going to get canceled?"

"Now you definitely are."

"Damn it." I scrub the back of my head. "Seriously,

though, I do tell you pretty much everything, the other guys think it's weird. I just wanted some time to figure this out before I told you. I'm sorry, I just convinced myself you were upset and honestly, it scared the crap out of me."

"Oh, Zach," she says, giving me a hug. "I had no idea, and I'm so sorry for fucking up so badly."

"Let's just agree we both messed up and move on. Deal?"

"Done."

We take the coffees, and go over to the coffee table. Cleo hops up and sits between us. I scratch the top of her head, and she stretches out.

"So," my mom says, sipping her coffee. "Have any boys visited you backstage?"

I almost choke on my coffee. *"Mom!"*

"Come on, fill me in. What made you figure it out for sure? Or, should I say *who*?"

I drum my fingers on my legs. "Er, so you know how Ruben is gay?"

Her mouth drops open. *"No."*

I grin. "Uh-huh."

"Shut up. Zach, he's *hot*."

My mom calling my boyfriend hot is kinda weird, and I hope it never happens again. But this time, I'll let it pass.

"I know."

She nestles down, getting comfortable. "Go on, tell me ever-e-thing."

I wasn't expecting to do this now.

But you know what?

I think I'm going to.

TWENTY-THREE

RUBEN

I pounce on Dad the second he gets back from work.

"They finally told us something," I say as he removes his coat by the front door. "Apparently it's the Armstrong Center they checked Angel into. They said it's too early to know if he'll be back up and running when he's out, but he *is* having daily physical therapy there, so, that's something, right?"

It's not much information, but compared to the vague updates we've gotten from Chorus over the past two weeks since arriving home, it's practically a gold mine. Much more helpful than "Angel's doing well," and, "we can confirm narcotics rehab will be going ahead," and "we'll be back up and running as soon as possible."

As for Angel, we all FaceTimed him a couple of times from his hospital bed, but the last time we spoke, right before he was discharged, he was almost as in the dark as us about how long his recovery would take. Then, once he left the hospital, we stopped hearing from him altogether. Logically, I know it was because he was checked into rehab somewhere, but without knowing exactly where he was or how long he'd be there, it's felt a little like he's been "disappeared" by Chorus.

Dad quirks a bushy eyebrow at me. "Hi to you, too. My day was great, thanks for asking."

"Sorry. Hi." I walk with him through the spacious, clean-lined hallway to the living room. "I got excited. What do you think?"

Until now, the perks of having a physiotherapist for a father have mostly involved having a useful set of warmup exercises to stay safe during dance training. But having him here to offer his uncensored thoughts on Angel's recovery makes me appreciate his knowledge bank in a whole new light.

"What do I think?" he repeats. "It's not much to go off."

"But we know he's been out of the hospital for a week, and he's already started working on getting his movement back," I press.

Dad shrugs and flops onto the sofa as Mom comes into the living room to greet him. "It depends on a lot of factors," he says. "How extensive the injuries were, how they heal, whether he follows the hospital's instructions, if there were any injuries missed in the initial screening . . ."

"But if he was really, really injured, he wouldn't be up to therapy yet, right?" I ask, lowering myself to sit beside him. "So, he must be okay?"

Dad takes my hand and squeezes it. "Yes. It might take a couple of months or longer, and I would imagine it'll be a long time before he's back dancing with you all, but . . ."

"But he'll be okay," I finish. The relief makes me feel lighter, brighter. Sure, Chorus has been assuring us he's been doing better, but they've been in denial about the severity of things enough times now that their platitudes are worthless.

"So, three weeks until he's out," Mom says.

"How do you know?" I ask.

She just gives me a wry smile. "I must be psychic."

Ask a stupid question, get a stupid answer, I guess. I *know* how she knows. She spent half her career choreographing movie musicals before opening her jazz studio here after I was born. You can't work a job like that without hearing about a few rehab stints. Or, more accurately, a few dozen.

"I can't imagine he'll need longer than twenty-eight days, from what you've told me," Mom says. "The bigger concern is how you'll resume the tour with him out of commission. Media sympathy will only get you so far, and it can't replace the publicity you'll lose here. Or the ticket sales, for that matter," she adds.

"I dunno," I say.

"I guess you'll have to stand Angel in the middle while he has a cast. But it'll look odd once the casts are off and he's still not participating," she adds.

"I guess. But people will just have to understand."

"You can *hope* they'll understand," she says. "But the general public have a short memory. They might not be forgiving of a lack of showmanship for the next year. If you ask me, you'd be better off replacing him for the next year while he gets his full range of movement back."

In other words, she's advocating for the racehorse route? The horse injures a leg, so he gets shot and replaced? The words bubble up, tempting me, but I don't dare say them. I'm offended enough to push back as far as I can get away with, though. "We wouldn't do that to our friend."

Mom tries to exchange an exasperated look with Dad, who has one of his *really*, right *after I finish work?* expressions on. They've both made multiple comments over the past couple weeks about how abrasive I've been since I went on tour. How much less *agreeable*. Well, Mom's made comments, and

Dad's *hmm*ed, which is close enough to count. "Don't be so dramatic, Ruben," she says. "It's just business. The band matters more than the individuals."

"He's not replaceable."

"Everyone's replaceable. And if you have to choose between Angel and your career, I hope you make the right choice."

Everyone's replaceable. Just like Zach and me, if we dare to show ourselves to the world. Just like Jon, if he pushes against his dad's wishes one time too many.

Good to know I can't count on my parents for support if I lose everything I have for being a little too gay. In this house, we put up walls to block the atrocities from the eyes of the paying spectators and shoot the limping horse. Call it exhaustion. Move on with the race.

"It's not like it's up to me," I say dully.

"That sounds like a convenient excuse to not have to think about your future," Mom shoots back.

"Do you think I want to be here?" I ask. "It's not like I've loved being left out of the loop like this. But if Chorus doesn't want us to know the long-term plan yet, it either doesn't exist, or they don't want our feedback. Either way, it's not up to us."

Mom rolls her eyes. "Uh-huh. And swanning around the house for two weeks is definitely doing your best."

"It's not a vacation."

"But you're treating it like one!"

"I'm *not*. I'm still working out, I'm rehearsing . . ."

"You've barely been on social media."

"Chorus doesn't *want us to be on it* right now."

"Ruben, stop talking to me like I'm your enemy. I'm trying to help you bounce some ideas around! What about when Zach visits tomorrow? I'm sure you can do a livestream or something to keep the band on the radar. If you message David tonight, you'll have approval by tomorrow. It's called being proactive. You're an adult now; familiarize yourself with the concept."

I ignore the dig. "That's the last thing they'll ever approve. They're terrified of the public finding out about Zach and me. They won't even let us get photographed standing next to each other, let alone film ourselves without Jon at my house."

It's the first time I've mentioned the censorship to my parents. I say it with as much emotion as I can, so they can't possibly miss how I feel about it. I guess, in a way, it's a test. I want them to probe. To lean forward, and say, *What do you mean? That's not okay. Do you want to talk about it? How can we help?*

Instead, Dad takes out his phone and mutters "work email," and Mom's face clouds. "Well . . . do you think it's wise for him to come over at all, then? Maybe you should wait until the next gathering . . ."

I stare, aghast. "Are you serious? Mom, seeing Zach in private is all I have. He's my *boyfriend*."

"The question is, how serious are *you*, Ruben? You have the opportunity of a lifetime. Don't throw it away on a high school relationship."

I'm so hurt, so outraged, I can't form a reply. Even Dad must think it's gone too far, because he stretches, and gets up. "All right. I'm gonna have a shower before dinner."

Mom and I face each other down. She chews on her bottom lip, doing her best to tell me how *extremely disappointed* in me she is with her face. It's not exactly an unfamiliar expression to me. I can read her perfectly.

"We've already eaten," she says to him finally, following him out. "There's some *ensalada Rusa* in the fridge, and I can reheat you some tortilla from last night, if you don't mind having that twice in a row . . ."

"I'm sure it'll be great," he says, his voice fading as they leave the living room.

That's Dad's usual contribution when Mom and I face down. Changing the subject, distraction, or escaping. It has a pretty good success rate as a de-escalation technique. Though it'd be nice if, just once, he had my back instead of shutting the conversation down. But he does like to take the easy, nonconfrontational route wherever possible.

Holy shit, did I just describe Zach or my dad?

I pull a face and turn to my phone to distract myself. I'm not in the mood for Freudian introspection tonight, thanks all the same.

There are messages from Zach and Jon waiting, as well as a missed FaceTime call from Zach. Obviously, they've both read the update email from Chorus.

Jon: Dad said Angel's not allowed to take any calls while he's checked in, but we can send him a message if we're happy for it to be read by the staff there first. I'm going to put something together tonight. Anything specific you want me to say from you?

Zach: FINALLY!?!?

I smile, shoot Jon a get-well-soon message for Angel, then head to my room and call Zach.

"Hey," he says, breathless. The floor behind him is littered with clothing. "So, I'm packing for tomorrow. Do I need to bring anything special?"

I raise an eyebrow and grin. "You're only coming for one night."

"Right, but I thought I'd check . . ."

"Anything you forget you can just borrow from here."

He hesitates. "You sure?"

"Of course."

"I don't want to assume . . ."

I'm confused now. "Just bring whatever you could possibly anticipate needing. If you forget something, we'll figure it out. I think you're overthinking it."

"I'm totally overthinking it. You're right." He lets out a breath that's way too heavy for a conversation about packing enough socks and underwear. "So, possible activity suggestion: we make s'mores, then collect Jon from the airport and storm the Armstrong Center to check on Angel?"

"I wish."

"I'm totally serious, dude. I have a whole break-in planned."

I snuggle into my pillow while Zach summarizes the proposed crime, a plan that somehow includes chain saws, bubble gum, *and* an impromptu a capella performance of "End of Everything." He's talking total crap, and we both know it, but I don't cut him off. It's just nice to hear his voice, and pretend he's lying beside me, whispering into the dark while we put off falling asleep. In the end, it's not me who cuts him off, but a knock at my door.

Mom pokes her head in as we hang up. "I thought you were asleep already," she remarks. "Then I heard voices."

"I wouldn't go to bed without saying good night."

"Hmm, you better not." A smile plays on the corner of her lips. "I've had too many nights without any kid to say good night to. It's good to have you back."

This is the thing about Mom. The thing that makes it so hard to know how to manage her. She's got a nasty streak, but it's not because she hates me. It's just sort of . . . how she is. She has a soft side, too. In a lot of ways, the soft side makes it harder. If she was awful 100 percent of the time, it'd be easier to cut off contact without guilt. But knowing that to lose all the bad stuff, I lose the few good moments in the middle, where I have a mom standing in my doorway implying she missed me . . . even though the good stuff isn't worth all the bad, it does make it tougher.

"Mom?" I ask.

"Yeah?"

What I want to say is, *Zach and I want to come out. I'm worried they won't let us. I'm worried what they'll do to all of us if something doesn't give.*

But then our chat in the living room comes back to me, and I think better of it. "Can you take a photo of me tomorrow before Zach comes for my stories? If I can get Chorus's permission?"

Her eyes sparkle. I feel dirty. Like I somehow just took responsibility for tonight's disagreement. But sometimes, it feels worth it just to placate her. "Sounds great. Want the light on or off?"

"Off's fine. I'll go to bed soon. Night."

"Good night, sweetie."

See? To hear her voice like that, all happy and warm, is worth the dirty feeling.

Kind of.

My phone lights up, and I grab it to find a message from Zach already.

Hey so . . . you're still on PrEP,
right?

The message slams into me as I finally understand the context of our chat tonight. I mentioned that I'm on PrEP, a preventative medication against HIV, to Zach a few weeks ago. Not as a nudge, but just as a, "Hey, here's something you might not know exists, given you only just came out."

But this text feels like a lot more than a nudge. It's closer to a shout.

Zach's coming over to sleep tomorrow. And he wanted to know if he should *bring anything*. I now have the feeling that "anything" might have been more along the lines of "condoms and lube."

Heat pools in the pit of my stomach and starts spreading downward, and I climb beneath the covers. My fingers slip beneath the waistband of my pajama pants as I replay Zach delicately broaching the topic of tomorrow's visit in my mind. Then I think of him next to me again, without any guards on the other side of the wall, in my own bed, with no alarm clock in the morning. I think of him reaching beneath the covers, and pressing his lips against mine.

I hold that image in my mind even after I finish. Then a strange feeling washes over me. A draining sensation, like everything's slipping away from me, sand in an hourglass.

We have tomorrow. But I don't know what lies beyond that.

And I don't know if I'm quite ready to find out, yet.

I pull Zach into me roughly the moment his driver is out of sight. I feel ridiculous, given we've barely been apart for two whole weeks, but I've missed him with a ferocity that's stunned and, to be honest, frightened me.

Thankfully, my parents are both at work, so we don't need to worry about forced pleasantries.

"I forgot how fancy your house is," he says as we traipse upstairs to dump his stuff in my room. He's practically bouncing. I try to match his mood, but I'm still laden down with the feeling of dread from last night. If anything, it's been growing today. "It makes me want to get my mom a

T-shirt," Zach goes on. "'My son's an international pop star and all he bought me is this apartment.'"

"*Penthouse* apartment," I remind him. "She's not exactly hard done by. How are things with her, anyway?"

His smile is immediate, enough to dispel any lingering worries I've had about his reassurances over the phone these past two weeks. "Good. They're really good, now."

Thank god.

"I'm glad," I say. "At least one of us has had a good time at home, then."

"Are you moving out anytime soon?"

I lean against my bedroom doorframe. "Why? You have a better offer for me?"

"That's not what I meant. I'm just curious."

The most honest answer is that I haven't made plans for the future, because I'm not sure what the future is, yet. The more I think about what's to come, the more certain I am that I can't rely on everything working out for the best. "Probably. I was planning on looking after the tour, but it's on hold for a sec while we figure out what the next steps are."

"LA still?"

"Yeah. Maybe Santa Monica."

Zach looks a little disappointed. "Oh."

"It's only a short flight away, remember," I say, but I realize as I say it that being a two-hour flight away from Zach has already been way too hard. I don't want to think of a life where he's not by my side.

"I'm not married to the idea," I add.

"I like Santa Monica," he says at the same time, totally casual.

I study him, my chest warming with affection. For a moment, I let myself pretend that this could be our future. Both of us in the band, both of us together, both of us free to live without secrecy. By the beach, under the sun. Happy. "Me, too."

We hover in the bedroom for a beat. Suddenly, his message from last night replays in my brain, and my heart starts to race. What does this pause mean?

The silence feels heavy, and significant. So, naturally, I panic and fill it. "So, we can watch a movie or something," I say, kicking off the doorframe as I step into the room. "Unless you're hungry? I guess you would be, huh? We have some leftover tortilla but it's probably pushing it to reheat it again. Have you ever had Spanish food? Tortilla's great, it's kind of like potatoes, and eggs, and onions, all fried up together. Or we can do takeout?"

"I'm not hungry."

"Cool. Well, then, movies are fine. I guess I already suggested that. Or we could go for a walk? It's, you know. It's, um, pretty?"

Zach blinks. "We could?"

"Only if you want to," I add.

Zach steps toward me. His expression says *don't*. It says *stay*. It says . . . Jesus, it says *kiss me*. "Do you?"

I swallow thickly. "No, not really."

Having him up this close, smiling a funny half-smile, is agony. Because all I want is for this moment to last forever, and I feel like it's already over, somehow, even though it's barely begun. It's a paradox, because *we're* a paradox. We're Schrödinger's boyfriends. We both have a future together, and we're about to crash and burn, and until Chorus decides once and for all whether to remove our chains, we can't know which reality is the truth.

So, for now, I'll pretend I know the answer. I'll pretend everything's going to be okay.

I grab his wrist, tug him toward me, and kiss him desperately.

We keep the door open as we kiss, him pressing me hard against the wall, even as more and more clothing falls to the floor. There's something so exhilarating about having so much open space around us. About being completely ourselves, outside of a cramped, boxed-in hotel room. And though we have a million things to talk about, from Chorus to his mom to Angel, it's wonderful to let go of it all, for just a moment, and indulge in something *happy*. Even if it's only briefly.

He has brought condoms, as it turns out. Even though he's the one who's never done this before, and it should be me checking with him, he hesitates before opening the box and asks me if it's okay. And of course it's okay, it's more than okay, it's everything.

He's shaking a little at first, until I kiss his lips, and his neck, and his collarbone, and then he scrapes his fingers down the skin of my back until his hand is steady.

When he whispers my name, there's nothing uncertain in his voice.

When his eyes lock onto mine, so dark with *wanting* they're almost chocolate, he holds my gaze.

After it's over, and we lie tangled up in each other's bodies, his head resting heavy on my chest, I think through a fog of happiness that I don't want to sleep with anyone but him ever again. And even though I know that one day I might look back on this moment and think it was a naïve thing to hope for, right now, it's the entire truth of it.

One day, I might not have him anymore. But right now, he's the only thing that exists. So, I push away all of the other fears and grief for just a few minutes longer.

I pretend it's just us, and that forever will be just like this moment, for a few minutes longer.

TWENTY-FOUR

ZACH

It's been six weeks since I've seen the rest of Saturday.

I've visited Ruben, and let's just say we had a, ahem, great time trying out all sorts of things. We're being very safe, as he's on PrEP and we're using condoms, just in case, and mostly it's nice that we don't have to think too much about STDs and stuff.

So I'd be lying if I said I didn't want to see Ruben for *that* reason.

But I do also miss the band. I get to see them today, and I can't wait.

Angel was released from rehab a few days ago. Like always, it turns out Veronica's instincts were scarily accurate, and he was released at exactly the one-month mark. As a celebration, we've all arranged to meet at Ruben's place now that Angel has had enough time to catch up with his family. We also want to watch the "Overdrive" music video, which arrived without warning in all our in-boxes a little over a week ago, but watching it without Angel felt sacrilegious, so we've waited for him. People at Chorus asked for our thoughts, but we all know they don't really care about that, and they haven't pressed us.

320 SOPHIE GONZALES & CALE DIETRICH

I go up to Ruben's front door, and knock. A few moments later, the door opens.

And Ruben is there.

My boyfriend.

I start smiling really hard. He does, too. I press a quick kiss to his lips, then go inside. Ruben lives in a private, guarded subdivision, so I know we're not in any danger from paparazzi, at least inside. Even on the slim chance someone has a long-distance camera, if we're indoors, they can't sell the photo or they'd get the crap sued out of them.

"I missed you," he says.

"I missed you, too."

He rubs my arm. "Want a soda?"

"Yeah, please."

We both grab Diet Cokes, and we go onto the deck. The others, including Angel, are already here, and Ruben's dad is grilling on the barbeque. It smells smoky and delicious. Jon and Angel are seated on the outdoor furniture, looking out at the pool. Angel beams, before awkwardly getting out of his seat, mindful of the gold-and-black Versace-pattern cast he still wears on his arm, where the compound fracture was. I didn't even know they made those. Maybe it's custom.

"There he is!" he says. "Finally."

"Hey."

He gives me a sideways hug as Jon comes up, his hands shoved in his pockets. The graze on Angel's temple seems mostly healed, which is good, but I do see he's still walking with a limp. Aside from that, though, he seems back to normal. I also get a hug from Jon and then a handshake from Ruben's dad. Veronica just nods at me.

So here we are.

Saturday is back together, for the first time since the tour was called off.

"How are you?" I ask Angel, as we sit.

"Never better. You?"

I'm a little taken aback to see him acting like himself, after the way we all left things the last time we spoke. But it is Angel, I guess. I glance at Jon to see if he shares my opinion, but he's not looking at me. "Can't complain."

"I bet," he says, glancing between Ruben and me and wiggling his eyebrows.

"And, food is ready," says Ruben's dad, clearly wanting to change the subject. "Come and get it."

He's made a bunch of mushroom burgers, along with a selection of meatless sides and sauces, because he's a vegetarian at the moment. According to Ruben, he always cycles through diets, and they only ever last a month, max.

After lunch, we all go into the home theater to watch the "Overdrive" video. Without even needing to ask, Ruben's parents leave the four of us alone, so we can watch it as just us. It's been our tradition ever since our very first music video. Jon swipes on his phone, and the title page comes up on the projector screen, showing the word "Overdrive" in neon red against a night sky.

"Ready?" he asks.

"Wait," says Angel. "I want to say something, first."

We all fall silent.

"Come on," says Angel. "I just went to rehab, it's not like I'm dying."

Jon crosses his arms. "Just rehab, huh? Not a big deal?"

"I'm getting to that. But first, I want to apologize to you, Jon."

Jon straightens in his seat and raises his eyebrows, waiting.

"I was . . . really shitty to you. My therapist calls it misplaced anger, which apparently is a thing. Who knew?"

Jon is lingering by the TV, clearly unsure of what to do, or what to even do with his hands. I get it. I am not exactly sure Angel has ever apologized before.

"You said you hated me," says Jon.

"I don't hate you." Angel chews on his lip. "I love you. I love all of you. I was just . . . everything was so fucked up. I was angry, and fucking terrified, and I thought you were just doing it to hurt me. I didn't get it. It took me weeks to get it, actually. I guess I had a lot of time to think." He gives us a weak smile. "It's not an excuse, and you don't have to forgive me. I probably wouldn't forgive me. But I'm so fucking sorry for what I said."

Jon looks at him for a long while, scanning him from head to toe. His expression is so unreadable, I actually start wondering if Angel pushed it too far. Maybe this was unforgivable to Jon.

Then Jon's expression crumples. "I missed you," he says. "It's so good to see you, man."

Angel springs to his feet—as quickly as he can with his limp—and the two of them pull each other into a rough hug.

Arms around Jon, Angel looks at us over his shoulder. "And you two. Shit. I know I wasn't cool on tour, and I know I lost my shit, and that messed with you both. I'm sorry about that, too. Fuck, I'm sorry about all of it."

"It's okay," says Ruben. "But thank you for the apology."

"Yeah, thank you. You shithead," I add with a grin.

Angel steps away from Jon. "The thing is, the drugs, it wasn't even for fun. It started out as a way to stop feeling so criticized and controlled all the time, but it got out of hand, and I couldn't stop. Once you get a break from it it's so hard to go back to dealing with it sober."

I don't want to do drugs, but I get it. If I could take a pill and stop the feeling of constant, overwhelming pressure, if only momentarily? I can see the appeal.

"Hey, serious question," I say, turning to Angel. "When you were high, you said something about wanting to be called Reece. Is that what we should be calling you? Because we can?"

He seems taken aback. "I did?"

"Yeah."

He considers this, then shrugs. "I don't know. I actually like being called Angel. I just don't love that I didn't get a say in picking it. I was just told I had to."

"Are you sure?" asks Ruben. "We can call you whatever you'd like."

"Oh, no, I'm sure. What kind of pop star is called *Reece*? But anyway, let's watch the video now, no more confessions from me."

Jon laughs, and he hits play.

The camera zooms past the word "Overdrive," showing a sleek, neon-drenched city at night. And then there's a shot of Jon, Ruben, and me, in our futuristic racing jumpsuits, getting ready for the race to start. Jon is talking to a ridiculously hot racer. Ruben is sitting in his front seat reading a book called *How to Win at Racing,* while I am tinkering with my engine, my jumpsuit hanging down so I'm just in a black tank, and I have grease smeared on me.

"You look hot," whispers Ruben.

"So do you."

He snuggles against me as it cuts to Angel, who has just reached the racetrack, seemingly late. His suit is all white.

"First time?" asks a guard, whose eyes are obscured by a shiny visor.

"Um, yeah," stammers Angel.

"Boy, you sure you're in the right place?"

"Er, yes?"

"Well, you better hurry up, the race is about to start."

Angel rushes past a lineup of cars, to an all-white Mercedes. The camera lingers on the logo for a beat. Angel climbs inside, and closes the door, just as the flag girl walks out.

Angel makes eye contact with her, there's a beat, and then the song starts.

I watch the rest of the video in a kind of awe. It's *amazing*. They've edited all the individual pieces we shot together into one sleek, cool piece of art. It's the perfect Saturday video, fun and exciting and, let's be real, a little silly. The CGI is also seamless, which makes me wonder how much they spent on it. It's got to be a fortune. They usually spend the most on the video for the first single, but this might be the most expensive video we've ever made.

The video ends on the "candid" scene we shot at the end of the race, and they used the take where Ruben and I totally avoid each other. It's the one moment I don't like in the whole video. Would it have been so bad if we had stood next to each other?

I see a glare settle in Ruben's eyes. I know what he's thinking. I know how upset he is about this, that any hint of intimacy between us has been completely cut out, yet again. And how, even though it's maybe our best video, there's still a sting at the end.

I'm getting really sick of that sting.

TWENTY-FIVE

RUBEN

Tue, 4:46 p.m. (3 days ago)
David <davidcranage@chorusmanagement.com>
To: me, Zach, Jon, Angel, Erin, Geoff

Hi all,

Boys, an update. TBC, but two possible options for the remaining part of the Months by Years tour are:

1. We return at the end of next year for a special mini-tour. We allow attendants to keep their tickets or return for a full refund (we still anticipate this will be sold out, so nothing to worry about here), with an eye to adding in some additional bonus shows/countries to "make up" for postponing the shows.

2. We offer a full refund and provide anyone who missed out with a code for special pre-sale access to your next tour (tentatively scheduled for 2023. Will confirm at a later date).

326 SOPHIE GONZALES & CALE DIETRICH

Nothing is finalized yet, so no mention of either option to anyone outside of this chain.

In the meantime, there will still be plenty for you all to do. The focus for the next few months will be to promote "Overdrive" and *The Town Red* overall. Early buzz is promising, and we want to capitalize on this. Which leads me into a piece of good news: we can confirm that your scheduled live appearance on *Good Afternoon United States* will be going ahead as planned prior to the drop of "Overdrive," with some alterations. Being mindful of Angel's recovery, there will be no choreography during your performance, but I know the four of you have the stage presence to put on an amazing show regardless. This will be the public debut of your new single, and we're extremely excited to utilize it as our official kickoff into promo season! Teaser scripts and assets for social media to follow shortly. As usual, any questions, feel free to shoot them through! (And enjoy your break while it lasts: we have a busy few months coming up.)

Best,

David Cranage
Publicity Director
Chorus Management

Tue, 6:13 p.m. (3 days ago)
Ruben <rubenmanuelmontez@gmail.com>
To: David, Zach, Geoff

Hey.

Zach and I actually have some questions (not strictly about
the above, but more in relation to the fact that we're not
going to be touring Europe for another year at the earliest).
Can we organize a time to speak? I don't think this
concerns Jon and Angel (not yet, anyway).

Thanks,
Ruben

Wed, 10:21 a.m. (2 days ago)
David <davidcranage@chorusmanagement.com>
To: me, Zach, Geoff

Hi Ruben.

Absolutely. Geoff and I can meet you for a video chat on
Friday. How does 11 a.m. suit?

Best,

David Cranage
Publicity Director
Chorus Management

Our four faces fill the screen in equal boxes.

Small talk is done, and it's time for Zach and me to bring
up the reason for today's call. David and Geoff are pretending that they have no idea where this is going, but they have
to know what we're going to say. In fact, I'd bet a *lot* of my net
worth that they were chatting together to finalize the plan
right before calling us.

None of us are smiling.

Zach looks down at his lap, and I take it as my cue to kick us off. "So, Geoff, when Zach and I told you about our relationship—"

"Oh, it's official now, is it?" Geoff cuts in with over-the-top enthusiasm. "Congratulations!"

"I—yeah, it is. Anyway, at the beginning, you said—"

"It must be hard to be apart right now," Geoff interrupts again. "I trust you're practicing discretion in regards to visits?"

He's trying to buy time. That, or he's hoping if he changes the subject enough, or puts me on the defensive, I'll lose my nerve. "Yes, we are. You said that we could come out publicly after Russia."

Both Geoff and David keep their expressions carefully blank. Zach peeks up at them, then turns back to his lap.

David answers first. "Russia is still a year away at this stage."

I'm ready for that. "It's unconfirmed. We aren't going to stay a secret because of theoretical trips to certain countries we might take years in the future. That's ridiculous." I sound confident. Like a fully grown man, capable of holding his own in this meeting. Which is the opposite of how I feel, if I'm honest.

Geoff leans back in his chair. "Ruben, as I'm sure you're well able to recall, we made no promises about announcing your relationship immediately after Russia. The conversation as I remember it is that we could begin to think about the plan for it after Russia. And I agree. It's the perfect time to have this conversation."

Zach glances up. I set my jaw, waiting.

"Of course, this is a conversation that affects the whole band, so nothing will be settled on before we run it past Jon and Angel."

Zach nods. "We get that."

I blink. "Um, *no*, we don't 'get that.' We'll take them into account, but we don't need their *permission* to say we're queer."

Zach considers this. "True. Fair point. But, I'm sure they wouldn't have a problem with us doing it?"

"That's not the point."

"This sounds like a conversation the two of you might want to have in private," Geoff suggests. God, anything to shut this talk down before he has to commit to anything.

"It's a business conversation," I say briskly. "There's no need for privacy."

Geoff, David, and I stare each other down. Zach's looking at the screen, but the crease between his brows tells me he's not a participant in the face-off, but an observer.

David shrugs first. "Okay. Well, on my end, the first obvious thing to consider is the promotion of *The Town Red*. We're still snowed under managing the media's coverage of Angel, here. We're on top of it, but the last thing we need is another scandal."

"Well, 'scandal' is the wrong word," Geoff jumps in quickly.

"Right, of course. Sorry, haven't had my second cup of coffee yet." David laughs. No one else does. "We just need the narrative to be more focused on how Saturday is returning to business as usual. Not another significant change. People need time to adjust after a hiccup like Budapest. The best time for an announcement like this will be when things are steady and predictable, and Saturday's regained its image."

"But this could be good for the band's image, right?" Zach asks uncertainly. "If we spin it, it could pull attention away from Angel's accident and make the narrative about, like . . . love?"

330 SOPHIE GONZALES & CALE DIETRICH

I want to smack David's patronizing smile—directed at Zach—right off his face. "As I said, not in a period of instability like this. There's a ton of ways the media could spin a revelation like this, and if it suits them to tie the announcement in with Berlin and Budapest to theorize that Saturday is a bad influence on its vulnerable audience . . ."

"Why, because we'll turn them all into gay drug addicts?" I snap.

"You know as well as I do how some groups will take this news, Ruben, don't be obtuse. Just because the official narrative for Angel is exhaustion doesn't mean journalists won't revisit the substance abuse theories from a few weeks ago to boost their story. We need you to be realistic, here. Maybe a little less selfish?"

"He's not being selfish," Zach jumps in, uncharacteristically firm. "This is important to us."

"We understand. How about we pencil in a group discussion about this, say . . . January?"

I think my heart stops. "January of next year?"

"Well, I don't mean January five months ago." David laughs again.

"But it won't take seven months for the Angel story to become old news."

"Yes, but we're about to go into album promotion for *The Town Red*. We have a real shot at breaking some massive records with this one, guys. I don't want you to get too preemptively excited, but we think this one will be career-changing. But for that to happen, we need *all* of our current audience, and then some. Your younger fans might be largely progressive, but it's mommy and daddy who control the purse strings. When this happens, you *will* alienate a portion of your would-be sales, and an even bigger portion of their parents. We lose support in the red states, and we lose a *lot*. You do this now and who knows what'll happen. The band might not recover."

Zach's nodding, and I feel a flicker of frustration toward him. "That makes sense," he says. "So, January, then?"

"Yes! We can revisit in January," David says.

"In January," I say, "there will be another reason we can't come out."

"We can't predict the future."

"No? I can. Either the band collapses and you won't have any opinion on what we do, or the band does well. And if the band does well, there will *always* be something. Another international tour. Another record. Another upcoming award voted on by homophobes."

Geoff rolls his eyes. "Don't you think you're being dramatic here, Ruben?"

Dramatic. He sounds like Mom.

In that moment, I hate him. But it also makes me doubt myself for a split-second, simply on the basis of being the common denominator here. If two people in my life think I have a tendency to overreact . . . could they be right?

Or is that just the easiest way to shut me down, and they've both figured this out about me over time?

It works, too. In my brief moment of self-doubt, while I reel backward in my chair with my mouth hanging open, Geoff pounces. "I have another meeting to get to now, but to wrap up. Our tentative next steps are meeting again in January to review the situation. Ruben, as much as you have doubts, you will understand the need for caution. The right time will come, and when it comes, you'll have a united team behind you. And that's if you two are together still, come January. And if not? No harm done!"

"I don't believe you."

"Well." He looks directly into the camera, and it's like he's locking eyes with me. "You're just going to have to."

While David, Geoff, and Zach mumble goodbyes to one another, I remain silent, glaring at the camera. David's face disappears. Then Geoff's. Only Zach's left behind, his face filling the screen.

That's it, then? It's over?

I'm three-quarters gone.

I'm all gone.

Zach pulls a face. "So. That went well."

I'm suffocating with rage. It's bubbling, a cauldron of acid sitting in my chest, pressing against the inside of my skin until I feel like I'm about to burst with the pressure. But the rage at David and Geoff can wait for a second. I need to clarify something with Zach, *now*. "How come you agreed with them about January?" I ask.

"Oh." He blinks, looking taken aback. "I don't know. They just put us on the spot, and they seemed like they were looking out for us. But then you said you didn't believe them and, totally, you're definitely right. I hadn't thought of it like that until you said it. But no, I'm with you. They're not going to let us come out."

"Right," I say. "And I don't care what they say. It's enough."

"What do you mean?"

"This is—I—it's *enough*. I'm not going to sit here and listen to this over and over again for the rest of my life. I have been asking to come out publicly since I was sixteen."

Zach looks shocked. Honestly, I'm taken aback to see this look on his face. I mean, I've never discussed my frustrations about Chorus indefinitely closeting me with the other guys, but I figured they knew it wasn't my choice. I'm out to everyone I possibly *can* be out to, after all.

And yet. "You've . . . been asking to come out all this time?"

"Yes. It's never a good time, though. They make me lie, and lie, and lie. Every single time I get on that stage. Every interview. Every event, they force me to be someone I'm not. And it's always temporary. It used to be 'there's no need to disclose until you have a boyfriend.' Then I dated Nathaniel and I had to keep it quiet because I was nominated for that bachelor of the year thing, and then we broke up anyway. You know that magazine that got a photo of Nathaniel and me in Michigan? We saw the paparazzi, and I kissed him anyway so I could say it was an accident. When Chorus shut it down before the magazine could run the story, they made me *thank them* for it. Then there were those rumors about me dating Kalia, and it was all 'even if it's not true, let them talk, we've seen a sudden increase in sales.'"

Zach's staring at me like I've mutated right in front of him. "Wait, so it's . . . like, for sure. They'll *literally* never let us come out?"

"I wanted to give them the benefit of the doubt because this is different, it's so much harder to hide *us* than it is to just ask me to keep my mouth shut, but it's no different to them. They will *never* let us come out, Zach. *Ever.*"

Zach slumps. "Oh my god."

But my mind is racing now. "I'm calling you back. Just in case they're recording this. Hold on, let me—" I hang up, then create a meeting of my own, which Zach joins instantly. "Okay," I say excitedly. "Hear me out. Let's just do it. Fuck them. They don't own us, no matter what they'd like to think. It's easier to apologize than ask for permission, right?"

"But . . . what about the record sales?"

"That's just an excuse. Do you really, *really* think we'll lose that many fans if we come out? Think about them all. They'll have our backs on this. I *know* they will."

"But, the thing about the parents makes sense."

"Sure, but that's going to happen regardless, whenever we come out."

Something about Zach's face catches me off guard. "Okay, Zach," I say. "One second you're agreeing with David about waiting, and now you have a weird look on your face. I need to make sure we're on the same page here before I drag you into something you don't want to do." *Again.*

"No, like I said, I'm okay with it."

Right, but, yet again, being okay with something isn't the same thing as wanting it. Why is it so impossible to get a handle on what Zach actually, truly wants? Why do I feel like I'm alone in making this choice, a choice that's going to affect *both of us*? "Zach, if you're not ready just yet, that's fine. It's one thing if Chorus is forcing us, but it's another thing if you need time. Do you want to press pause on going public?"

"Honestly, I'm fine either way," Zach says. "I'm just worried about all that stuff David said . . . I . . . if we screw everything up for Jon and Angel, I'll never forgive myself. It's not just about us. We should involve them."

I shake my head in wonderment. "In case you haven't noticed, they're not exactly thriving right now, either. I think if we push back against Chorus it'll help those two see we don't have to just take everything they throw at us. And, hold on, what do you mean you're fine either way?"

"I just don't want to let you down. But I don't want to let the band down, either."

"Me?" I repeat. "It's not just about me. And you coming out publicly or not is *definitely* not about me. What do *you* want?"

"For everyone to be happy."

I try to process this. "So . . . you don't want to come out?"

"Do you want me to?"

"No, *no*. You can't do it for me. That's too big a decision to make for someone else's sake."

"But you being happy will *make* me happy. So, I'll do it."

"Zach!"

"I'm telling you what I want!"

"No, you're telling me what *everyone else* wants." I'm trying to stay calm, but the fury from the meeting has simmered into a swamp of fear. It's settled into the pit of my gut, and it's pulling on me like quicksand. I feel like everything is about to collapse down and in. Because I *know* Zach is a people-pleaser. Sometimes, his kindness and thoughtfulness, the way he can read you and find *just* the right thing to say, is my favorite part about him.

But there's a dark truth behind that. It's not always easy to pinpoint exactly what matters to Zach, other than keeping the peace. And right now, that's not good enough. He can't just sit there and shrug and say "whatever." Not about this. Not about us.

Us. A sudden thought hits me like a speeding train. Does Zach . . . want to be with me?

I insisted we talk after the kiss.

I asked him to be my boyfriend.

I suggested we tell the band about us.

It was all me.

Could it be possible he's only with me because he thinks I want to be with him, and he feels swept along by the tide?

That's a ridiculous thought, right? Total paranoia territory, now. Right?

But it's *possible*.

This can't go on. I *need* him to give his honest opinion, even if it's contrary to mine, because at least then I'd know where we stand. It's better than me making decisions for us that are quietly hurting him. The thought that maybe I somehow talked him into doing this with me, into *being* with me, and that he's gone along with it this whole time because it was easier than saying no, is paralyzing.

But saying all of that is too terrifying. So, instead, I say, "I don't understand why you're being so passive about this. Be really clear with me, Zach. Do you want to come out now? Do you want to wait? Do you want to never come out?"

"It depends. This decision doesn't just impact me. I want everyone to be happy, I guess."

"*That's not an option.*" I don't mean for it to come out so harshly, but I'm starting to feel panicky. "Why can't you ever think about yourself? Why does it *always* have to be about everyone else?"

"Well, maybe you should *start* thinking about everyone," he snaps.

It's the last thing I expect to hear. "What?"

"We're a *band*. We make sacrifices for each other. Look at Jon and Angel. Like you said, they aren't happy, either. But they've been putting up with it all for *us*."

"And that's *wrong*."

"Is it?" Zach asks. "Or are they just the sacrifices we need to make?"

"Sacrifices are supposed to be things like missing out on parties, and being away from your family for longer than you want to be. Not *losing* yourself."

"Well, maybe that's too optimistic," Zach says. "I've been making sacrifices, too. This? Is *not* my kind of music. I grew up writing *my* songs, and listening to *my* music. I didn't ask to be in a boy band. Our performance at camp was just meant to be for fun. Then everything started happening so fast, and we had a band name, and Geoff had all these plans for us, and the rest of you were so excited, and I realized, hey. This isn't what I wanted for myself, but I'm part of a whole, now.

If I focus on what I want, we all lose. So I *sucked it up*. I asked
Geoff if I could write some songs, and I even tried to write
stuff I thought he'd like, and I still didn't get the *one* thing I
wanted. I just get to put my name on a song I had no hand
in that I barely even like, and that's my consolation prize."

I play his words over and over in my head, to be sure
I've heard him right. "Wait, you . . . don't want to be in the
band?"

"That's beside the point."

"No, it's the *whole* point," I argue. "If you don't want to
be in this band, you shouldn't be."

He looks wounded. "You want me out?"

"No. I don't want you giving up your entire life to do a
thing that's making you miserable because you think the rest
of us need you to."

"It doesn't make me miserable. I just wish I could be a
songwriter. And that I could write my style of music."

"Okay, but 'not miserable' is a low bar."

"I'm *fine.*"

"So, you want to stay in the band? You're happy?"

He shrugs.

"What does that mean?" I ask.

"I don't know what you want me to tell you."

Holy *shit,* getting a simple answer out of Zach is agony. "I
want. You to tell me. What you want."

"I don't know, okay? I don't know what I want. I haven't
thought about it."

"Well, I need you to go and think about it," I say. "Because I am *terrified* I'm going to make the wrong decision
on your behalf one day. And also, it's actually important to
me that you care, like, *deeply* care about our relationship and
what happens next. We need to be in this together, even if
it gets messy. If you tell me right this second that you never

want to come out to the public, that is *fine,* and we'll figure it out. *Together.*"

"I *do* care about you," he says. "And I care about our relationship."

"Okay, but, honestly, if we're going to work, you have to learn how to care about *you* as well. Because I don't want to be in a relationship with someone who sees it as something that's happening *to* him."

"Ruben . . ."

"Also, just so we're clear," I add. "I'm coming out to everyone, soon. I don't know how I'm going to do it, but I am." Even if the thought of doing it alone, without Zach by my side, makes me feel like I've stepped into an empty elevator shaft where I expected there to be a floor. If I don't do this now, they'll wrap us even tighter in their web. And even though I feel sick at the thought of doing this, *knowing* that it will turn Chorus against us, and *knowing* that if Geoff is right and the world turns on us I'll have ruined this for everyone, permanently. Our team. Jon and Angel. Zach. Even if that makes me feel like the most selfish, disgusting person who ever lived.

Even then.

"And I don't need Geoff's permission," I add, my stomach churning. "Or Jon's, or Angel's. So, don't get it into your head that if you don't come out, you'll be holding me back. Whatever you choose, whether you want to stay in the band, or leave it, or you want to come out publicly, or stay private, or even if you want my help with figuring it all out? I'll be right here, and we will work through it together. But if you can't give me anything more than 'I want everyone to get along'? Then I just . . . I don't think I can . . ."

"Okay," he whispers.

". . . do this anymore," I finish.

He swallows, and we sit in a lengthy silence before he finds the words. "Does this mean we're over?"

Even hearing the words makes me nauseous. My mind scrambles to catch up. How did we get here? "I hope not," I say. "Just . . . let me know when you figure out what you actually *want*, okay?"

He nods without speaking.

I think I've just destroyed us. And I don't know how to undo it.

Even worse, I'm not sure undoing it is even the right choice. Because even if this argument was fueled by frustration and panic, I'm pretty sure I meant every word.

We end the call and I leave the study, but I don't know where I'm going. My ears are ringing with the echo of the conversation, and my mind refuses to address what's just happened.

It's only Mom and me at home right now; Dad's at work, and Mom's studio doesn't open for class until midafternoon. A puffing sound down the hall tells me where she is, and I follow the sound of her heavy breathing to our in-home gym.

It's a sun-drenched room with floor-to-ceiling windows, so we can work out inside while imagining we're out in nature, I guess. Mom's on the treadmill, with her headphones in, staring at herself intensely in the floor-length mirror in front of her. She catches sight of me in the mirror as I lean against the doorway, and she slows to a stop. "Hey," she says. Then, after studying my stricken face, "You okay?"

I know if I tell her what happened, she'll take any side but mine. She'll lecture me on being selfish, and immature, and I'll be equal parts furious at her for the implication and terrified that she's right, so I'll go on the defensive. And we'll scream at each other until my sadness turns into rage.

But if I don't tell her, I can pretend I'm a little kid again, back when my little concerns were worth her comfort instead of her scorn. When I'd scraped a knee, or gotten into an argument on the playground, or knocked over a glass of water, and she'd stop whatever she was doing to wrap me into a hug until everything was okay again.

So, when she holds out her arms to me, I let myself forget that more often than not she's the one who makes me feel like nothing's okay. I ignore the fact that she's mid-workout, and covered in sweat. I just go to her, and she pulls me into an embrace, and whispers, *Sweetie, what happened? Talk to me,* and for a second I pretend that I *can.*

But I don't say a word.

TWENTY-SIX

ZACH

The call ends, and I can't move.

His words slice me apart. They end me.

"I don't think I can . . . do this anymore."

I know he said other things, but that was by far the loudest. It's practically screaming in my mind, over and over again.

From his voice, it sounds as if he's already given up on our relationship, already decided that this isn't something that I can give him. That means what comes next is just a gradual descent. This means, soon, he's going to break up with me, all because I don't know what I want.

I sit still, starting at the blank screen of my computer, my eyes filling with tears.

That really just happened.

After what happened with Dad, I've known that if someone opens the door to leave, it's only a matter of time before they walk out.

So maybe Ruben didn't say he was going to break up with me over this, at least not now, but he opened the door.

I go into the bathroom, lock myself in, and pull my shirt over my head. Every movement feels slow and laborious, like it's costing more energy than I have. What I need is a shower. To take a second to myself, to wash everything away and reset.

I turn the taps on and step inside. I bow my head and let the water run down my face, messing up my perfect Zach Knight tousle. Good riddance. I don't even want my hair to be this long. I never have.

Oh boy, maybe Ruben does have a point.

I thought I was doing the right thing, trying my best to be a team player, but maybe I've gone too far. Maybe I've lost myself, and now it's costing me.

Things with Ruben were wonderful, *so* wonderful. Easily more perfect than I'd ever dared to let myself dream of, especially after what happened between my parents. He's fiery and brings out the best in me and also has an incredibly caring side and more drive than I've ever seen in anyone. He's inspired me so much, and I never told him. I also never told him having him as a boyfriend makes me feel like the luckiest guy on the planet.

Instead, I let him down.

I tilt my head back, so it's under the water. This is all too familiar. Hannah suggested we break up because we weren't "connecting" and she encouraged me to do some soul-searching. I thought I had, but I guess not, because I'm right here, yet again.

The emotions surge up, and suddenly, I'm crying.

It's an ugly, hacking affair, one I try my best to keep quiet, but it doesn't really work. I press my hand to my face, trying to hold it back, or at least to muffle it enough that Mom doesn't hear me. The last thing I want to do is to try to explain this to her, or to anyone, ever. This is too personal, it cuts too deep, especially because it's my fault. If I could just be different, be stronger, and more assertive, then I wouldn't be in this situation.

Once the worst of the emotion has passed, simmering down to just a major, energy-sapping depression, I turn the taps off, and step out. The steam has fogged up the mirror completely. Cool, I don't even want to look at myself right now. I wrap a towel around my waist, and plod back to my bedroom. I slam my computer shut, as if it's to blame, then get dressed in the softest clothes I can find before slumping down onto my bed. I don't have enough energy to even get under the covers. It's mental exhaustion. All I can do is wallow. Anything else is too much effort.

"I don't think I can do this anymore."

Just him saying that, hearing the resignation in his voice, makes my heart ache so badly.

I wish I knew how to get people to stick with me.

I stay in my room for hours, undisturbed, until a knock finally sounds on my door.

"Yeah?"

"Can I come in?"

I sit up as Mom walks inside, not even waiting for an answer. "I'm going to take a swing and guess something happened between you and Ruben?"

I shrug.

She comes in, and sits down on the end of my bed. "What do you need? Chocolate? Ice cream? Wine?"

"Won't help. Nothing will."

"That bad, huh?"

"Worse, probably."

"What happened?"

"He's sick of me." Just saying it makes the tears prickle again.

"Oh, sweetie," she says, throwing her arms around me and pressing a kiss to the top of my head. "Nobody could be sick of you."

"He is."

"Why?"

"He basically said I'm a pushover and he doesn't know who I am."

She pauses. I thought she was going to deny whatever it was that he said about me, but him saying *that* made her pause. Which makes me think there's at least some truth in what he said.

Damn. Even my mom thinks I don't stand up for myself enough.

"Do you agree with him?" I ask.

"No, of course I don't. I'm going to be on your side, no matter what. The thing is, though, I don't think Ruben is a cruel person."

"I don't, either."

"And you know one of the things I love about you the most is how considerate you are."

I roll my eyes. "Yeah."

"Ever since you were a kid you've put others before yourself. I still remember you'd always let the other kids beat you in athletics, even though you could've won, because they would've gotten upset and you didn't care."

"I thought that was a good thing. You said most people only care about winning."

"I know, and it is. But I can see what Ruben is saying. You can't spend your whole life trying to keep everyone happy. You need to stand up for what *you* want."

I wipe my eyes on the back of my hand. "I know. But it's hard. I feel like I barely even know what I want anymore. I know I want to be with him, but he doesn't want to be with me, so, yeah."

"Can I ask something?"

"Sure."

"Did he explicitly say he's breaking up with you? Because if he did, you need to respect that, and give him space."

I shake my head. "He said: 'If you can't give me anything more than "I want everyone to get along," then I don't think I can do this anymore.'"

"Well, if I can teach you anything, it's that you should actually listen to people. Ruben is telling you exactly what he wants. It's not that he's done with you."

It sinks in.

"He wants to know what you want," she says. "So tell me: if you could have anything in the world, what would it be?"

"I want to be with him," I say. "And I want to work on this."

I think I get it.

No, I know I do.

"I have an idea," I say. "I think it'd work better face-to-face, though."

I know it's a long drive to the airport, so it's a big ask.

She smiles. "I'll grab my keys."

I have a whole thing planned.

First, Mom drove me to Penny's apartment. I texted the situation to her, and she was on board, so now I've got a brand-new haircut I can't stop looking at. It's short and textured, with the front pressing down over my forehead. Penny is calling it a modern spin on emo, and she's pretty confident it's going to start a trend. If Chorus let the public see it, that is. Maybe they'll ask me to keep it hidden until it grows out.

After the haircut, Mom and I drove to the airport and we both got on the next flight to LA. Once we landed I picked up a bouquet of flowers from a gas station near the airport, and they're now sitting in the back seat of the car Mom rented. I ignored the voice telling me he might not like them, and that he might think it's weird. Even if he does, I want to do this.

So I'm doing it.

Ruben knows I'm coming over to talk things through, but he doesn't know I'm coming over for this. I might be making a mistake, but at least it's *my* mistake. It's a risk, sure, and I could fall flat on my ass in front of the guy I pretty much love, and I could've made Mom come all this way with me for no reason.

We reach Ruben's house, and Mom parks. My instincts tell me to double check about this with her, to make sure this is okay, that it's a good plan. But I'm sure about this. For better or worse, this is my idea, and I'm going to see it through.

"Wish me luck," I say, as I grab the bouquet of flowers from the back seat.

It's dark out, lit only by streetlights.

"You don't need it. Just tell him you listened, it's all he wants to hear."

I step outside, and walk up to the front door. I ring the doorbell. My palms have gone really sweaty, slick against the plastic wrapping of the flowers. The door swings open, and I see it's Veronica. She glances down at me, and for maybe the first time ever, I see her break into a tiny smile.

"Oh, Zach, hi," she says. "Ruben didn't tell me you were coming by, come in."

Ruben appears at the end of the hallway. "It's okay, Mom," he says, sliding past her to stand in the doorway.

Crap. Crap crap crap.

He glances at the flowers as Veronica walks away, then back up at my face. "Holy shit, your hair."

"Do you like it?"

"I love it."

We go inside, and I offer him the flowers. He takes them, then brings them to his nose. "These are nice."

"They're from a gas station," I say, then wince. "I wanted to get you something nicer, but everywhere else was closed."

My palms are seriously sweating now.

"Right," he says. "So, you wanted to talk things through?"

"I do. I'm here to say that I've heard you, and I'm going to work on what you said. I know I'm too passive. But I don't want to be anymore. I know what I want, and it's you."

"Okay, but what does that *mean*?"

"I want to be *with* you. To work through exactly this kind of thing, just, with you. And if you want to end things, that's fine, and I'll respect your decision. But I want to be with you more than anything else. All in. For the world to see. No more hiding. And, yes, ideally, I want to stay in the band, too. But if I can't have both, then I pick you."

He kicks at the ground. "That's one hell of a speech."

"I try. And listen, I am going to work on actually saying what I want. It's not going to happen right away. It'll take effort on my end. But I'm going to do it. Not to be with you, but because I need to. It's what I want to do, and if you want to do it with me, that's your decision."

"So, what if I don't?"

I falter. "Don't what?"

"Want to do it with you. What would you do then?"

My voice is steady as I reply. "I've thought about it, and even if you don't want to be with me, I'm still going to come out. I'll never make it as a songwriter if I'm not allowed to write what I actually care about; I'll always have one hand tied behind my back. And all that stuff I said about Saturday isn't about Saturday. It's about Geoff. I don't want to leave the band, I love it, but I want to leave *him*. Maybe we can't, I don't know. But I do know it's what I want."

He drops the flowers to his side. "Wow. This is the first time I've actually known where you stood."

"Well, I mean it. I should do this more often, it feels great. I'm like, unstoppable."

He laughs, finally smiling. "That sounds like a lyric you'd write in your notebook."

"Ouch. Fair, though. Know any words that rhyme with unstoppable?"

"None come to mind." He takes a deep breath, and his shoulders relax. "Thank you. You have no idea how badly I needed to hear all that."

"So, we're back on?"

"Zach, we weren't off. I just needed to know you were walking by my side, not being, like, dragged along kicking and screaming." He smiles, and steps closer. "Although, is it just me, or does this feel like the part in a movie where the music starts swelling and we make out in the rain?"

I glance around. There's no music, just the faint chirping of crickets outside. I've always loved the sound.

"Oh really?" I ask. "So, should we, you know, do that?"

He grabs me by the shirt, pulls me to him, and kisses me.

Now that Ruben and I have decided to come out publicly, we made the joint decision to tell the rest of the band our plans.

It's the morning after my big declaration, and we're in Ruben's bedroom with a Zoom call set up. Jon is already waiting, but Angel hasn't requested to join, even though he's seen the link in the group chat.

"You're sure about this?" he asks.

"Completely. Are you?"

He nods.

Angel accepts the call, and then Ruben starts the meeting.

"Oh hey, nice hair," says Angel.

"Thanks."

"What's up? Surely you didn't just set this up to show us a haircut."

I clear my throat. "Er, no, um, we have news. We've decided we want to come out publicly, even if Chorus won't let us."

"Oh shit."

"Yeah," says Ruben. "It's become pretty clear they aren't going to let us do it on their terms, so we're making our own."

"Right," says Jon.

"But we wanted to check with you all first," I say. "Because this will impact you all."

"I'm so in," says Angel. "I say you fuck 'em up."

"Jon?"

Jon's brow creases. "I think it's a great idea. You should be able to be yourselves. It's garbage that they asked you to keep your sexuality a secret."

A rush of relief fills me. I knew Angel would be down to do something this chaotic, but Jon is much more of a risk when it comes to this sort of thing.

And then he surprises me further. "I have an idea," he says. "If we're going to do this, we should do it right."

We talk it over until we're all on board.

"It's perfect," says Ruben. "I'm in if you all are."

I offer my hand, and Ruben grabs it. I don't need to say anything. It's obvious I am completely and utterly in.

That just leaves Angel. He grins. "Let's wreak some havoc."

TWENTY-SEVEN

RUBEN

The crowd's been lining up in Central Park for two days.

While we get our hair and makeup done by Penny—who goes out of her way to lament how bedraggled we've all let ourselves become without her regular care—our team sends hundreds of bottles of water into the crowd. It makes it look like they care, but realistically, they just don't want anyone collapsing from heat exhaustion or dehydration on their watch. Of course, neither do I, but I have a feeling that while my feelings stem from "god, that would be *horrible*," theirs are closer to "god, that'd interrupt the whole concert."

We're set up in a heavily guarded tent behind the pop-up stage, surrounded by standing fans, harried staff hissing into headsets, and the low hum of nearby generators. Zach and Jon have ditched their jackets, laying them over the back of the nearest plastic chairs. Luckily for Angel and me, the two of us have been styled in T-shirts for the concert. The afternoon sun has a bite to it today, but at least we won't be out in it for too long. We'll go out, participate in an interview, perform "Overdrive" for the first time, launch into a quick message from Jon to the fans, then two more songs. Easy.

At least, that's the *official* plan. Reality is going to play out somewhat differently.

I poke my head out of the tent to catch a glimpse of the crowd. I can't see much through the security detail, but the chatter tells me they've started filing in to stand in front of the stage. My stomach plunges. It's the first time I've been nervous before a show in years.

A hand rests on my shoulder, and I turn to find Zach. He doesn't say anything, but the look on his face tells me he knows something's up with me.

"What happens if my mom turns on me after this?" I ask.

Zach tips his chin away from the tent entrance, and I follow him to a secluded corner. Well, at least, as secluded as we can pull off under these circumstances. No one should be able to hear us over the din, but he keeps his voice low. "If she turns on you for telling the world who you are, she's lost the right to call herself your mom, if she didn't lose that right a while ago already. She doesn't get a say in this anymore, Ruben. You're not a little kid. You're an incredible, inspiring person, and it should be her who's worried about losing her place in *your* life."

A sad smile tugs at the corner of my mouth. "Logically, I know that. But this isn't theoretical anymore. Specifically, what do I *do* if she calls me after this and tells me not to come home?"

"The house *you* paid for, you mean?"

"Yes."

"Then you get off the plane in Portland with me, and we go straight to my mom's, or a hotel room, or wherever the hell we want, and we figure out what the next steps are together. No matter what happens, you'll never be alone, though. You know that, right?"

"Thank you," I whisper. I'm not afraid of losing my home. Money might not be able to buy everything, but with as much of it as I have, I can buy everything I need to live in a heartbeat. I can wake up tomorrow and put in an offer on a sprawling mansion in the Hollywood Hills, fully furnish it, and be set up in the time it takes to finalize the paperwork. I know that, in that respect at least, I'm blessed. But what I am afraid of is losing my family. For better or for worse, they're still mine. And even if I *am* getting more comfortable with the idea of leaving them—or, at least Mom—behind, that doesn't mean there won't be a tidal wave of grief.

Zach continues, gentle but certain. "And that doesn't just go for today, okay? If you *ever* decide you're done, even if it's four in the morning, you can come straight to me. I know she's your mom, but that doesn't make it a compulsory relationship. We're your family, too."

I sink against the wall of the tent. "I don't think I'm ready for that, yet."

"I know. But if you ever are, you don't have to be afraid. That's all."

I nod, but don't reply.

Zach lets his thumb brush mine, blocking the touch from sight with the angle of his body, and adds, "Plus, there's more options than 'living at home' and 'no contact.' You can try creating some space, and see how that goes."

"True."

"You should hit up Jon and Angel, see if they're ready to move out yet. Someone's gotta keep an eye on Angel."

I think he means it as a joke about Angel's personality, rather than a reference to his ongoing recovery, but the words jolt me. What *is* going to happen with Angel when things pick up again? When we go on our next tour, for example?

Will Chorus keep an eye on Angel? Will he be looked after, and supported to stay sober—a feat that's going to be difficult enough for him to begin with, without added stressors? Or will they put him right back in the pressure cooker that triggered all of this to begin with?

I think I know the answer, and it fills me with a rage I try to shove back down. I can't think of all the reasons I hate Chorus right now. I need a clear mind for what we're about to do. So I focus on Zach's suggestion. "Just the three of us living together?"

"Well, if all three of you did, I'd obviously want in on that. You're not leaving me out of all the fun." I raise my eyebrows meaningfully, and he scowls. "Not like a 'move in with me' type thing. I'd want my own room, still."

"Right. I don't like you *that* much," he says, rolling his eyes, but his scowl is turning into a smile despite himself.

"Mm-hmm. Waking up with you every day. I'd *hate* that."

"Eating meals together, sharing a shower with you. It sounds awful."

"I hate you."

"I hate you, too." His voice is low and thick.

A producer in jeans and a red shirt strides over to us. "Sound check in a minute, guys. Time to head on up."

Zach looks to me, takes a deep, heavy breath, and we exhale together. We head to the lockers to deposit our phones, and as I take mine out, almost as if on cue, it starts to vibrate with a call from Mom.

My stomach drops. Not now. Not when I'm already feeling this on edge. The last thing, the *very last thing* I need is to try to navigate a loaded call with her about what I should and shouldn't remember to do onstage.

"She wants to wish me luck, I guess," I say to Zach.

He just watches me, expressionless.

The phone buzzes once more, twice, three times. And I dump it in the locker.

"Not now," I say to him. "I just . . . can't right now."

He brushes his thumb against my shoulder. "It's fine. You can call her back after. Just say you'd already dropped your phone off."

I nod, then shake my head. "Actually. I think I might just tell her I was about to go onstage and wanted to keep my head clear. Because that's actually not an unreasonable thing to do, and I don't need to lie about it so she accepts it. I think?"

Zach makes a show of dropping his mouth open in shock. "Wow. You know that's bordering on *healthy*, right?"

"I know." I pause. "I shouldn't text her right now, should I?"

"No, you definitely should not. Come *on*, we need to go up."

Angel and Jon meet us near the entrance and we make the short trip to the stage flanked by guards. A few people on the edges of the audience catch a glimpse of us, hands waving frantically.

"I still think you three could've kept the choreo," Angel says as we walk. "They could've hooked me up to wires and had me fly above the stage. That would've been way cooler."

"You could've been our hype man," Jon agrees.

"Exactly!" Angel says. "You get it. I would've been an excellent hype man."

"Of course, it helps if you can raise both your arms above your head," I say drily.

Angel glares at me and wiggles his right arm. "I'll have you know I've regained a full eighty-five percent of my original swivel range, thank you very much."

"You have a great swivel," Zach reassures him.

"See, Ruben, your boyfriend likes my swivel just fine."

"Whose side are you on?" I ask Zach, elbowing him playfully as we ascend the stairs.

"No one's!"

"Pick a side," Angel says.

"Yeah, Zach, pick a side," I echo.

"No!"

"You can do it, Zach," Jon joins in. "You've done it once; you can do it again."

"That depends how today goes," Zach says. "If I regret it, I might go back to being neutral forever."

Angel pouts. "Why pick neutral when you have the whole rainbow?"

Zach shoots Angel a look so sharp he shrugs and mimes zipping his lips as one of the sound technicians approaches us.

"All right, here are your mics," he says. He's not much older than us, short, built, and blond. "Remember your number, because you have to make sure you get the right one onstage."

I have number four. Zach has two. I can't exactly muster up shock at finding us separated again.

They have us run through a few lines of "Unsaid" as they adjust the levels, then our mics are taken from us. Zach starts hopping on the spot to shake out his nerves, and I pace back and forth, my arms hugged close to my chest. Even Jon and Angel go quiet as we wait. Then the hosts are announcing us, and I'm walking onto the stage in a haze.

We take our spots in a row—me, Jon, Zach, and Angel— to a cacophony of screaming. Angel lifts his bad arm, still in a cast, and gestures at it with a cheeky grin. The screaming gets louder still somehow. I squint against the blinding

356 SOPHIE GONZALES & CALE DIETRICH

sunlight and take in the rows and rows of people, all here to see us, a crowd pulsing with the frenetic energy only a concert can produce.

The interview is a blur. They don't ask us anything groundbreaking; the banned topics list is three feet long at this point. No shipping. Nothing about Angel's accident. Nothing about rehab.

How was your first international tour?

Which was your favorite city?

Are you excited to get back to Europe at some stage?

We're so glad to see you're feeling better, Angel. What did you all get up to on your rest break?

What are your plans for the rest of the year?

I answer the questions directed at me on autopilot. David's walked us through what to say to which question enough times that I don't have to think, which is how they want it. During the interview, I just want it to end, so we can get this over with, and I can stop anticipating the biggest moment of my life. Then, as soon as the interview's over, my heartbeat goes into overdrive and I regret wishing for its end. I want to go back. I'm not ready. I can't do this.

But there's no going back, now. The intro music to "Overdrive" has started.

We've never performed without choreography. Even years ago, when we were fifteen and performing together for the first time at the camp's final performance, with Geoff watching us through calculating eyes in the audience, we had choreography. It was terrible choreography that we crudely put together by ourselves by watching YouTube videos of bands and altering the moves to fit our ability levels, but it was choreo. Without it, I feel naked onstage.

Valeria walked us through how to act onstage. Jon's meant to flirt with the audience. Angel's meant to keep his microphone on his stand, and to smile as much as possible. I've been instructed to take mine off and hover toward the back of the group, with an emphasis on moves like kicking off the floor to propel myself backward and running my hands through my hair. Zach's meant to wave to the nosebleed section and reach out to them while crouching down.

But Valeria can't make us do anything right now.

We scatter. Angel pulls his microphone away and heads straight to the edge of the stage, jumping as he sings, causing a chunk of the crowd to jump in time with him. Jon clasps his microphone in both hands, his stage presence strong as he rocks to the rhythm, but not a single thigh stroke or lip bite in sight.

Zach and I move to the center of the stage, a few steps back from Jon, and turn to each other as we sing. If Zach's nervous, he doesn't look it. In fact, he seems to be having the time of his life. His eyes sparkle as he catches my gaze, and he raises his eyebrows at me. As though he's reminding me of our secret, and how it's only going to be our secret for a few minutes longer. It hangs in the air between us, pulling me toward him like a magnet, and I do something absolutely forbidden. I throw an arm around his shoulder as we launch into the chorus.

Somewhere, members of our team are watching this. Definitely Valeria and Erin. Probably David. Maybe Geoff. Are they frantically messaging or calling each other? Is our grand punishment being planned on the other side of the country? In the tent fifty feet behind us?

If so, they'd be better served holding off. There's no punishment big enough for what's coming.

I'm riding high on adrenaline as I remove my arm from Zach, still tingling where we touched, and when my solo comes, I figure, *screw it*. Instead of singing it straight, I throw everything I have into it: fifteen years of professional vocal coaching, eight years of musical theater experience, and eighteen years of critical feedback from my mother. My voice soars past my high note, up another note, and another, my vibrato resonating perfectly in my throat as I engage my core and bend back. I can tell even before I hit the peak that I've got this, and I punch the air in victory as I finally, *finally* show them I can actually *sing*.

They scream and clap for me, and my gaze sweeps past several shocked faces in the audience. Onstage, Zach and Jon are both giving me thrilled expressions, and Angel's encouraging the crowd's reaction by mouthing the word "what" as wide as his mouth will allow him.

There. Now, even if I never get the chance to show my range again, the world knows what I can do if I'm not gagged. I'm not a stencil. I'm not rigid.

I'm fucking *good*. And now it's on record.

The song ends, and we catch our breath. It might be a lot less demanding to sing without choreography, but damn, you get unfit fast after a couple months off. The light on my microphone flicks from green to red. It's time for Jon to address the crowd.

I make eye contact with him. And we step into each other's places.

Now I'm standing in the middle with Zach. And my microphone's on.

I need to move quickly. Jon went over this with me last night as I shared my written speech with him. *Get to the point. If Chorus figures out what you're going to do, they'll make them switch your mic off. If* Good Afternoon United States *realizes something huge is happening, they won't obey that order. Don't. Fluff.*

"Thank you so much, everybody," I say. The crowd roars

in response, and I don't wait for them to finish. We don't have time. So I plow over them, against every instinct in my musical-theater-trained body to *wait until they can hear the line clearly.* "We've missed being onstage, being with our fans—with *you*—but today is particularly special. Not just because we have Angel back up and running." Another cheer—damn it, I should've anticipated that. *Get to the* point, *Ruben.* In my mind's eye, I can see Erin running from the tent up the stairs. Finding the blond technician. My heart gives a panicked *thud.* "But because today, we weren't choreographed. And the thing about choreography is that in the wrong hands it takes something as expressive as dance, and it reins it in, to make you a cohesive group. It's still a display of skill, and it's beautiful to look at, but today we're hoping that instead of seeing us as the group, you'll learn more about the dancers."

I had more of a lead-in written, but onstage, this feels a million times longer than it did last night in my room. I need to say it, now, before I lose my chance. *Come on, Ruben. You've got this.*

Mom's face flashes in my mind, and I push it away. *No. Ignore her. Focus on the words. Say it.*

I.

"I . . ."

Am gay. Go on.

"Wanted to tell you all . . ."

I'm GAY. Spit it out, Ruben.

"That Zach and—" But I cut off, because my voice has lost 99 percent of its volume.

I took too long. I hesitated.

Jon told me not to hesitate, and I hesitated.

I stare at my microphone in shock as I try to process this. Even though I can't bring myself to look up, I know how the others must be looking at me. How Zach must look.

The audience murmurs, confused and curious. A few people yell out from the crowd in protest. *Turn his mic back on!*

The producer from the tent says something into her headset, then gestures at the crowd. "Just some technical difficulties, everyone!" she calls.

"I'm sorry," says Jon. He knows as well as I do that this is it. They'll claim they can't get any of the mics to work. They'll apologize to the audience and send them on their way. Wrap up the segment early, march us off the stage, then we'll face the consequences.

I'll take full responsibility. Tell them no one else knew what I was going to say. Tell them Jon thought he was switching with me because I wanted to say happy birthday to someone on-camera or something. I won't let them take it out on the others, though. This was my mistake, not theirs. I should've been faster. I should've asked Zach to speak.

The producer walks to the edge of the stage and beckons to me. I kneel, already knowing what she's going to say. *The show's over. We've been instructed not to continue. We're sorry.*

She leans right in to whisper in my ear. "We were given a list of banned topics for today's interview. Were you about to . . . address one of those topics?"

I nod, hardly daring to hope.

When she steps back, her eyes are blazing. "My wife was *very* jealous I got to meet you four today," she says. "She's your biggest fan."

Holy shit. She's going to turn the mics back on.

I meet her eyes, and a charge of shared understanding runs between us. "If you want to bring her backstage after we finish all our songs," I say, "we'd love to meet her."

She smiles conspiratorially. "She couldn't get the day off work. But I'll tell her you said hi."

I straighten and return to my microphone as she hisses into her headset. A second later, my green light is back.

Now, it seems, I have all the time in the world. And unfortunately for Chorus, I'm angry. Real angry. They've tried to silence us for the last fucking time.

I was raised by a fox. To cope, I became the rabbit lying limp in the fox's mouth, shutting down to minimize the agony of being eaten alive.

But I'm not going to be a rabbit anymore. Today, I'm a fucking wolf.

For once, I'm going to be the vicious one. For all the times I chose to whisper when I needed to roar.

"The best part of our job is you," I say, my voice booming over the crowd again. "Seeing you all, meeting you backstage, reading your messages to us. You don't hold back with us. You show us everything, every vulnerable bit of yourselves. You trust us with that. Do you know how powerful that is? Because it's a gift, and it's one we're beyond lucky to receive. The wildest part is, you don't even demand anything back. We don't deserve the love you give us. We're just four guys who met at music camp one year, and now we have the world, because you saw us, and you decided to give us the world. Just because."

Jon's nodding emphatically. Zach isn't taking his eyes off me.

"The worst part of our job," I say, willing the sudden shake out of my voice, "is how long we've been forbidden to give the same back to you. For years now, we've been boxed in and told who we're allowed to be. We've had our names taken from us, and we've had our dignity taken from us. We've been forced to cross moral lines we aren't comfortable with. We've been dressed in clothes we don't like, and we've been taught to say lies as naturally as if they were the truth. And the more we've tried to reach out to you, and recover ourselves, the more we've been reined in. But we want you to see us. Deep inside, I think we've all hoped that maybe, you saw us anyway. Like, the Angel you just saw? The one jumping all over the stage? That's about a *quarter* of the energy we get from him." Angel pretends to shoot me a dirty look, and I narrow my eyes right back at him. "On a *quiet* day," I add, and the audience laughs. "And Jon? He's always got his eye on other people, constantly ready to help them, and tell them what they need to hear. He's sweet, and he's gentle, and he's someone you want there for you in a crisis. And Zach—" My voice cracks, and I steady myself. Here goes nothing. "Zach—"

"Ruben," Zach whispers. I pause, and turn to him. He holds his hand out for the microphone. I draw my eyebrows together in a question as he takes it from me. "I don't want this to be something that just happens to me," he whispers, before bringing the microphone up. At first I misunderstand him, and think he's changed his mind. Then my words from our fight last week come back to me, and I realize.

"Ruben and I have been forced to hide things, too," Zach says. "The biggest one being that Ruben is my boyfriend. We're together, and we have been for a little while now."

The noise that comes from the crowd isn't one I've ever heard before. I can't pinpoint the emotion, or even if it's positive or negative overall. The best word for it is probably, simply, *shock*.

"We're telling you this because the freedom to be ourselves, and express whatever truest version of ourselves we know of to the world as we see fit, is the most important freedom we have. We want that freedom back, even if the truth is something not everyone wants to hear from us." Zach blinks, looks at the microphone like he's just noticed he's holding it, then hastily passes it back to me. I guess what he's just done has hit him all at once.

I finish for him. "We're standing here sharing it with you, sharing *ourselves* with you, because we love you. We trust you. We respect you. Most importantly, we think you deserve more from us than just a well-choreographed show. And so do we."

I place the microphone back on the stand and look at the cameras with my head held high. There's nothing to hide behind, now. No persona. Just me—*us*—and the crowd, and the millions of eyes that will pore over the clip of this very moment today, tomorrow, and for the rest of our lives.

Taking Zach's hand in mine, I turn to the crowd. At first, I see it as a whole. It writhes, and cheers, and yells. Then I look closer, and focus in on some faces. Someone in the third row is covering her mouth with both hands as she jumps on the spot. Fifth row center, a girl stands still, staring at us with a slack jaw, while the girl next to her waves their clasped hands in the air. In row two, toward the left, two boys hug each other. One seems to be crying into the other's chest, but he turns his head just enough for me to confirm they're tears of joy.

I drag my gaze across the rows slowly, meeting the gaze of as many individuals as I can. There's nothing between us. For the first time, I don't feel like I'm looking down on them from unreachable heights with an impenetrable wall separating us. Suddenly, I belong to the crowd. I'm part of them. We all are. All four of us.

The band plays the opening chords to "Unsaid," and Zach lets out an exhilarated breath and turns his head to look at me. He swings our linked hands up between us, hailing the crowd, and a cheer swells up to greet us back in return.

I smile and lift my mic to start the first verse, Zach's hand still in mine.

TWENTY-EIGHT

ZACH

As soon as the cameras turn off, chaos breaks out.

We're pretty much pulled offstage by security guards. The crowd starts to boo, at them, not us. At least it seems that way.

"Zach, we love you!" calls someone.

Backstage, Erin is waiting for us.

"What have you done?" she asks, her eyes wide. "I can't fix this."

She brings her phone up and charges off down a hallway, I guess to get some space. Seems Angel definitely got what he wanted.

We've wreaked havoc.

I close my eyes, and see the fans assembled outside. They know, now. They finally know. I saw a young guy in the crowd, and from the look on his face when we said it, I knew he got it. He saw someone like him, up onstage, and we gave him hope. That alone makes what we did so worth it. Screw Chorus. If we made someone feel good about themselves, then that's so much better than breaking another record or making Geoff more money. This is what Saturday should be about. I've never been prouder to be in a boy band.

The host of *Good Afternoon United States*, Kelly, comes

up to us, with her co-host, Brendon. We're in an ad break. They were supposed to talk to us after the performance, but clearly, that plan has changed.

"Well, that was unexpected," Brendon says.

"You can say that again," says Kelly. "Nice work, boys. You know, my nephew is gay."

"A heads-up would've been nice," interrupts Brendon, his usual sunny disposition changing to something acidic. "So I didn't look like a gaping fish on-camera when they cut to me."

"Sorry, but if we warned you, Chorus would've blocked the interview," says Ruben, and my chest fills with pride. "It had to be a surprise."

He sneers, and steps toward him. "You do know what happens after this, right? You're done, kid. You all are."

"Well, good," I say. "If people are mad at us for being together then we don't want anything to do with them."

"Yeah!" adds Angel. "Zach, I might love the new you."

Brendon laughs, but it's harsh. "You're all smiles now. But when you're washed-up has-beens begging for attention, you'll change your mind. Trust me."

"Easy, Bren," says Kelly.

"No, the boys deserve to know. You betrayed your team. Nobody will work with you ever again. You think you're heroes, but you don't see that you've ruined yourselves."

Erin comes up to us. Her face is red, flustered.

"Well, Geoff wants a meeting with you all, obviously."

"When?" asks Jon.

"He hasn't said," she says. "He wants to talk to his lawyers before he talks to you."

Chorus's headquarters are a gleaming, modern building in downtown LA.

Out front, a huge crowd has assembled, lining up on either side of the road. Chase Protective Services has set up barricades to fence people in, and to keep the road clear from the swarm of fans that has appeared, predicting this move. As we slowly drive down toward the building, the screams of the fans become almost deafening. Some are openly crying, and I don't think it's because they're overwhelmingly happy to see us.

In contrast, there are also a few rainbow flags in the crowd, being waved proudly.

We reach the front door, and our security team climbs out. The roar of the crowd becomes even louder, hurting my ears, and cameras start flashing violently. In my pocket, my phone buzzes again. It's been going off nonstop, but I haven't really wanted to check it. But I do now, to deflect from the situation outside and what's about to happen. I have countless notifications, from my Instagram and also from people who have my number, like Dad (A buddy texted and told me the news, I think it's fantastic! Love you no matter what—Dad) to Leigh, one of my friends from middle school who I haven't talked to in years (YASSS BUDDY WERKKKK, WELCOME TO THE RAINBOW FAMILY). I even have one from Randy Kehoe (Nice work today, man. Proud of ya.).

Wow. We might not sing punk songs, but I guess what Ruben and I did is pretty punk.

We climb out of the car, and I'm blinded by the camera flashes and deafened by the sound. There are just so many people here, and the speed at which they've assembled is mind-blowing. I see reporters and news teams and countless paparazzi, all scrambling to get our picture or footage of us.

Shielded by a Chase guard, I am hurried inside, into a grand white foyer. It's spacious and cold, designed with minimalist white furniture.

Once we're all inside, the doors are closed and locked. Two Chase guards step across, blocking it. It's like we're trapped.

The receptionist glances up at us, then gets up out of her seat. "Follow me."

We follow her down a hallway, her heels clicking on the polished cement floor. On the walls are posters of the other bands that Chorus also manages. We nearly reach the meeting room at the end of the hall when we finally see the Saturday one. It was taken just after our first album came out, and we look so young. I remember I had a pimple that day, but they photoshopped it out. We're onstage, with our band name in golden lights underneath us. Each of us is smiling, and it looks genuine, because it was.

The receptionist opens a frosted white glass door for us, and we go inside.

Inside, there's a number of suits sitting at a long desk. Geoff sits at the head of the table.

"Take a seat," he says.

The four of us go in, and sit down at the end of the table. The lawyers all watch us, their expressions cold.

"Now," he says, a tone of smugness in his voice. "I want to make it clear that what is about to happen is not because Zach and Ruben announced their relationship. We at Chorus pride ourselves on building a supportive environment for all, regardless of nationality, sexuality, or gender expression."

"Right," scoffs Ruben.

"*However,* in the process of announcing your relationship, you have defamed us, and done irreversible damage to our brand. You signed a contract stating you would never publicly speak against Chorus, and you couldn't fulfill your end of the bargain. So, it is with great sadness that I have to inform you that we will be taking legal action against all of you. There will be extreme punishment for what you just did."

"Wait, Dad, what?" says Jon. "You're doing this all because Ruben and Zach came out?"

"This has nothing to do with Ruben and Zach being together," he says, his voice finally rising. He quirks his head to the side, like his emotions surprised him, and he needed to wrestle them back into submission. "This is *business*. You signed contracts agreeing to boundaries we set, and one of those boundaries was that you would not defame us. People are already calling us homophobic and the media is already running stories falsely accusing our company of homophobia due to your words, when we never said either of you couldn't come out. You have proven you can't be trusted. You went against us, have shown you are unreliable, and have done huge damage to our brand. This is the consequence."

"You can't be serious," says Angel. "You know this is going to look like you truly are the homophobic assholes everyone is calling you, right? Because that's exactly what you're being."

"I repeat, we at Chorus have always prided—"

"Oh, don't give me that!" says Jon. "Ruben told us everything. He told us you pressured him to stay closeted for *years*."

"We did no such thing. We simply advised Ruben and he agreed to wait for the ideal time—"

"Which never came! Dad, do you even see how messed up this is? You made him deny who he is, and then you tried to do it to Zach!"

Geoff clenches his fist, and then releases it. "I won't argue with you about this, Jon. By saying what Ruben and Zach did on live television, in what was clearly a premeditated ploy, you have defamed us, and we will be seeking compensation."

We have a five-album contract with Chorus, with two remaining. That means, for our next two albums, they will get their huge commission no matter what, and we can't get new management, since the new team would need to take us on for free. So Chorus can make our lives a living hell while suing us for everything we have. And from the sound of things, Geoff is planning on doing all of that.

"You can't do this," says Ruben. I can hear the defeat in his voice, because he's smart, and he knows that's not true.

Geoff grins. "You'll find that we can."

I look around the room.

Geoff is backed by an entire team of the best lawyers in the world. Jon, Ruben, and Angel all look so young compared to them.

We lost.

And we're trapped with the very people who are going to break us.

TWENTY-NINE

RUBEN

"What were you thinking?"

I raise tired eyes as Mom greets me at the door with a red-faced glower. "I don't know," I say, truthfully. The only answer I can give is a useless one. I wasn't thinking about our contract terms, or being sued, or what finally standing up for myself would mean for the band. If I had, I would've stuck to the script, and simply announced my relationship with Zach.

Instead, I've ruined everything. I've destroyed us.

"I'm sorry," I say.

"You're sorry. You're *sorry*? You went up on that stage and you recklessly . . ."

Her words fade into muffled humming. My eyes trail past her to take in the living room while she shouts. It's empty. Dad's not here. Not that he'd step in if he was.

So, who will?

Who's going to have my own back if my parents won't? If management won't? If my friends aren't here?

I drag my gaze back to Mom. She's sneering at me, throwing her arms up while she bellows loudly enough for the neighbors to hear.

The words bubble up.

Then the dam bursts.

"STOP IT!" I roar, snapping back into focus. "I know, okay? I know I did something stupid, but it happened, and it happened for a *reason*."

"You stand there and you *dare* to—"

"I don't need this," I cut her off. "I need support right now. I'm not a fucking idiot. I know what happened! The last thing I need is to hear it again from you!"

"Well, guess what, Ruben, this isn't just about you—"

"Today it is," I yell over her. "Today I just came out to the world and I'm getting sued by my management team, which means today it's *all about me*."

"Just like the rest of your life is, huh?"

Three things strike me simultaneously.

One: it feels wonderful to say what I'm really thinking, for maybe the first time while my feet are planted on these floors.

Two: shouting back at her hasn't made things worse. She barely seems to notice I've fought back. The room didn't catch aflame. She isn't going to physically hurt me. She's simply screaming, exactly as she always does. Terrible, but no more terrible than it was when I didn't stand up for myself.

Three: I don't need to stand here and be screamed at if I don't want to.

So, I turn on my heel and go right back out the front door. "I'm going for a walk."

I slam the door in the face of her reply.

I sit in the park for a while, watching the sun slowly set. As the darkness creeps in, fear starts to scrape at my chest with shadowy fingers. *Maybe yelling back only went okay because she was so shocked. Maybe you've made it worse. Maybe when you go back, she'll have something planned to make you regret what you did.*

But if that's the case, I can leave again. I can go to a hotel, I can go to Jon, I can even go to Zach in Portland.

It's okay for me to leave.

So, psyching myself up with this mantra, I walk back home.

Mom and Dad are both on the couch watching TV when I enter. There's no yelling. Mom looks up at me with a cloudy face, but all the redness is gone. Dad places a hand on her arm, and neither of them speak.

"I've been wanting to come out publicly since I was sixteen," I say, by way of a greeting. "Chorus never let me. Whenever I tried to push back, they pushed me further into the background in the band. They make me dress plainly. They won't give me any good solos. They never wanted me to be too big, just in case people saw too much of who I really am. When we got overseas, it got bad. They didn't let us leave the hotel. They stopped allowing us to have visitors or speak to friends. They didn't make time for us to eat every meal. Then, when Zach and I happened, they turned on us even more. They basically told us we could never make it public. They lied to the media about our personal lives, and forced us to lie, too. They separated us in public, and they punished us if we even looked at each other onstage."

My throat is tightening, and it's getting hard to force the words out. Usually, I'd swallow the sensation down, and breathe until everything loosened up. Instead, now, for the first time in a long, long time, instead of my emotions coming out in a tangle of anger and anxiety, I don't fight them.

"I decided to come out anyway," I say, the words fractured. "Which is *not* against our contract terms. It was so, so important to me that I don't have to lie about myself anymore. I want to be *myself*. I want to be allowed to have boyfriends without hiding them. And then . . . I . . . started . . . and they turned my mic off."

The anger has disappeared from Mom's face. Dad's nodding, but it's a severe sort of nod. A funeral nod.

Finally, tears well up in my eyes. And I don't fight them.

For the first time in a long, long time, I just let them fall.

"They turned my mic off," I repeat helplessly.

Mom rises to her feet and wraps her arms around me. I fall against her chest, and everything feels hot and humid and wet. The tears flow more freely now, and I break into sobs as she rubs a flattened palm over my back.

At least she's stopped screaming at me. It won't be the last time she does it, but at least, in this moment, I don't have to deal with her fury on top of everything else. Right now, I'll take it.

"It's going to be okay," she murmurs.

I don't know how to believe her. But I try.

Jon's mom calls a group meeting at her sister's apartment in Orange County the next day.

When Mom and I arrive, Zach and his mom, Laura, are already there. Dad wanted to come with us, but he had to work and Mom convinced him she'd give him the rundown when she got home.

I make a beeline for Zach as soon as we step out of the private elevator, which opens into a hallway attached to the main living area. We throw our arms around each other while our moms give each other pleasant, if detached, greetings. All of our parents know each other, of course; they met during our performance at Camp Hollow Rock years ago, and have sat together at numerous concerts and events since. I suspect that Laura isn't the biggest fan of my mom, though. I also suspect that's mostly because Zach's told her *his* very strong opinions about my mom.

Mrs. Braxton is a petite woman, shorter than Jon, with a halo of dark brown, curly hair, and a smile that's usually beaming, but today has a tired, tight edge to it. Jon messaged us last night and told us by the time we'd landed back in LA, she'd already packed his stuff and taken it, as well as herself, to stay here for a while. I doubt either of them got much sleep last night.

She nudges a pizza box toward us. "Hungry?"

Mom blinks like she's been assaulted with something hideous and confronting. "Oh. Pizza. Maybe later." Her smile is convincing, now. Smooth recovery. "Thank you so much for hosting, Shantelle," she says. "This was a wonderful idea, getting everyone together to strategize before we have the chance to be bowled over."

"Help me move the boxes?" Jon asks Zach and me. We set about transporting the pizza from the kitchen counter to the coffee table and end tables. The dining table is only big enough for four people, so setting us up in the living room on the couches and armchairs was the best call.

"It's good of you to squeeze us all in," Mom's saying to Mrs. Braxton. "If I'd thought of it, I would've offered our house. There's more room for guests, and it has LAX."

Zach's head snaps up. He's gripping a pizza box so tightly it's buckling. He stays silent, though. Jon merely rolls his eyes.

"It's no trouble," Mrs. Braxton says. "I just wanted this done as quickly as possible. I'm so furious I could just, *argh*. I figured we need wine, and pizza, and an action plan."

"Well," Mom says, taking a seat at the kitchen counter. "I think we're all furious. Chorus Management has *no right* to do this," Mom says, repeating her heated words from last night. In her rage, she seems to have forgotten that Mrs. Braxton's husband is our manager. "Our boys are the hardest workers I've ever seen, and they're talented, and they're *good kids*. And as for whether they come out or not, it was never management's decisions to begin with."

Exactly what she said to me last night, after I collected myself. Then she placed her hands on my shoulders. *You're my son. If they mess with you, they mess with me.*

The words were meant to be supportive, but I was left feeling confused, and a little empty. Because the message received was, *I'm the only one who's allowed to hurt and limit you.* And as grateful as I was to ultimately have my parents' support, and for things to not be made worse than they were, it didn't feel the same as real support. It didn't feel the same as unconditional.

As she let go of my shoulders, I was reminded of the night of Angel's accident, when I'd gotten sucked into the crowd. It was the crowd that'd almost drowned me, and then it was the crowd that saved me. It hit me that it had felt awfully familiar. It was the same sensation as receiving my mom's version of love my whole life.

The elevator dings, and the doors open to reveal Mr. and Mrs. Phan, as well as Angel, and the noise levels in the apartment suddenly seem to quadruple. In the midst of the bustling as everyone relocates to the living room to get started, Mrs. Phan comes face-to-face with Jon, and she stops in her tracks, staring at him.

Jon cocks his head as he seems to realize she has something to say. "Hi," he says, a question tingeing the edges of his tone.

"Hi," she says warmly. She hesitates, then powers forward with her arms out and wraps Jon in a hug. He keeps his eyes open, wide and confused, as she squeezes him. "Reece told us you're the reason he got help. We wouldn't have known. Anything could've happened. *Thank you.*"

Mrs. Braxton watches with wobbling lips. When Jon's released by Mrs. Phan, Mrs. Braxton holds her arms out from where she's sitting in an armchair, and he sits on the armrest so she can wrap her arms around his middle.

Angel dives straight into the pizza, and Zach and I follow his lead. "I'm starving," he proclaims, shoving a slice in his mouth as he scrolls his phone. "Hey, we're trending."

"*Reece,*" Mr. Phan admonishes. "How about you try swallowing?"

Angel ignores him. "Anjon, Zuben . . . Save Saturday is a hashtag now. Chorus is trending, too! Mind you, they're probably enjoying the publicity boost . . ."

"Who are Anjon and Zuben?" Laura asks.

Zach turns bright red. "They're our ship names."

"And what's a ship name?"

"Aren't ship names usually female?" Mr. Phan asks.

"No, Dad, that would be a literal ship," Angel says. "I feel like if you thought on that for more than a second, logic would tell you that Twitter is not collectively discussing a literal ship."

"Reece, don't talk to your father like that," Mrs. Phan chides. "And tone down the sass, please, we adults don't speak your nonsense Internet talk, remember?"

"It's short for relationship, I believe," Mrs. Braxton says sweetly. "Jonathan, would you like to tell me more about 'Anjon'?"

"Actually, there is nothing I would like less in the world than to talk about Anjon with you, Mom," Jon says. "All you need to know about Anjon is that it doesn't exist."

"It exists in people's hearts," Angel says, placing a hand over his chest. "So, you could argue—"

"*It doesn't exist,*" Jon practically screeches.

"We believe you, Jon," Mr. Phan says. "Although, rest assured, if you *had* ended up as our son-in-law, we would've been thrilled to have you."

Angel holds his hand up for a high-five. His father leaves him hanging.

"*So,*" Mrs. Braxton says pointedly. "Good news on the Internet front, then, Angel?"

Angel's smile fades and he turns serious as he scrolls through the hashtags. "I mean . . . yeah. It looks promising. Oh, shit, 'End of Everything' is trending, now, too."

"I've always known there to be truth in the phrase 'no publicity is bad publicity,'" Mom says.

I glance at Zach, who's barely able to hide his lip curling at her about-face from the "don't look bad in the press" stance she's taken for the last . . . oh, eighteen years.

Laura's watching Zach, too, and she jumps in to change the subject. "So, Shantelle," she says, turning to Mrs. Braxton. "You said something about a lawyer on the phone?"

Mrs. Braxton smiles grimly. "Not just one. Several."

Laura stands. "That tone calls for wine. I brought sparkling and red."

"*Great* idea," Angel deadpans.

His mom snorts. "Nice try. You're underage again."

Angel rolls his eyes until only the whites show. "This country *sucks.*"

Not in spite of his joking, but *because* of it, I'm suddenly all too aware of how uncomfortable this must be for him. How every time he's around people drinking socially, he's going to have to make a choice a large part of him won't want to make. Again and again. It's not over for him because he's out. It'll never really be over.

If it weren't for Chorus.

If it weren't for *fucking* Chorus.

Mom places a hand on my arm. "Sweetie, would you like some wine?" she asks. She probably wants it to appear like she's making a point about wine at the dinner table being part of Spanish culture, but, more likely, her real point is something much crueler. Either she's trying to prove that she's *way* more relaxed than the other parents in the room, or she's trying to highlight the fact that *her* son hasn't got a substance abuse problem. Whichever it is, I'm pretty certain the underlying vibe here is that my mom is, most of the time, still the absolute worst.

My smile doesn't meet my eyes. "No, thank you."

Zach's holding his head up with both hands, his fingers outstretched so they're spanning across his face. His fingertips are digging into his cheekbones so hard they've formed dents in the skin. He's doing a valiant job at keeping his opinion to himself. Verbally.

Mrs. Braxton accepts a glass of sparkling white and leans back in her chair. "My husband might be their manager for now, but don't think I have no hand in Chorus Management. Everything he thinks he can throw at this, I can do one better. *Our* payrolled lawyers are good, but there are better ones out there. I can think of at least three who would be happy to represent us, and I have verbal confirmation from one already. Jane Sanchez?"

The name doesn't seem to ring a bell to anyone in the room but Mom. Her noise of approval tells me all I need to know, though. Mom still has her ear to the ground when it comes to the entertainment industry.

Up until now, our lawyers were Chorus's lawyers. Geoff

recommended them to us when we signed with him, and everyone we asked at camp said they were pretty sure that was normal. It's only a bad thing to share lawyers during disputes.

For example, if one party sues the ass off the other.

"Do we have a leg to stand on?" Mrs. Phan asks as she takes her glass between two hands.

"The defamation claim is a load of crap," Mom says. "Ruben wouldn't have said a single untrue word on that stage."

"Oh, I believe it," Laura says, sitting back down and placing a second bottle of wine on the coffee table. "Zach's told me *plenty* since he got back. In fact, it sounds to me like they were often held against their will. Is that kidnapping? Because *I* think it's kidnapping." Mom and Mrs. Braxton make similar "eh" motions with their hands. Laura takes a defiant sip of wine. "Doesn't sound legal to me."

"I'd like to have Jane review the morality clauses in the original contract," Mrs. Braxton goes on. "I had a look last night and there were some extra lines put in about speaking against management or revealing insider information. Lines I know for a fact aren't in Geoff's boilerplate contracts. I want to know exactly what that's all about."

"And there's always the discrimination angle," Mom says. Lucky me, to be an angle.

"And what about duty of care?" Mr. Phan asks. "My son almost *died* thanks to their incompetence."

"They'll just say they didn't know," I jump in. "They always pretended they didn't notice. They have plausible deniability."

Mrs. Braxton smirks. She looks very pleased with herself. "Well, we may have a thing or two in writing. When Jon came home from the tour, we had a talk, and he shared some . . . *concerns* with me about the way some things were handled. I took it upon myself to take a look at Geoff's emails, and sent a few through to myself so I'd have copies."

"*Mom*," Jon says, a smile spreading across his face.

She giggles. "What? It's my company, too, Jon. The content of some of those emails was quite enlightening, though. For example, the boys' hair and makeup artist lodged some formal concerns regarding Angel's well-being, *long* before Budapest, and as far as I can tell none of the processes that are *supposed* to happen in those situations were followed. I found *years* of emails regarding Ruben's sexuality, and I'm sorry to say a large number of them firmly cross multiple legal boundaries. Especially concerning the relationship between him and Zach."

"We'll sue them back for all they're worth," Laura hisses. "I'll make him wish he wasn't—" then she catches herself. "Sorry, Shantelle. This is awkward."

Mrs. Braxton laughs. "Oh, it's awkward. But not between anyone sitting in this room, I promise you."

The worst part is, the awkwardness is only just beginning. Even if we manage to win the lawsuit Chorus is preparing against us, that won't magically free us from their contract. If this Jane Sanchez is as good as Mrs. Braxton says, she *might* be able to free us, but I'm not hopeful about it. As long as our contract stands, Chorus is our management team for the next two albums, and as long as they're our management team, they'll do everything they can to make our lives a living hell short of ruining our careers—and that boundary will only be there because our profit is their profit.

We could technically find another management team, as long as Chorus still gets their contracted commission, but our options would be to pay them nothing, or pay them their fair commission as well as paying Chorus, which would leave so little over for the four of us we'd almost be working for free by that point. And no company in their right minds would work for us for free. Maybe for one album cycle, if we got lucky, but not for *two more*.

"I have to ask," Mom says. "Chorus Management is your company . . ."

The question is implicit in the statement. Mrs. Braxton doesn't seem surprised to hear it. "Let me make two things very clear. One, I am appalled at what our boys have gone through. *Appalled*. If I'd been aware of it earlier you can *believe* I would've shut that down in its tracks. As it is, all I can do is apologize sincerely for any complicity I had."

"It's not your fault, Mom," Jon whispers, but she shushes him.

"Second," she goes on. "A company is a company, and money is just money. Geoff and I had a very clear understanding when it came to Jon and his involvement with the label. His responsibilities as a father were supposed to trump work, *always, period*. I didn't think for a second he would breach those boundaries, which, I suppose, is why it took me so long to realize what has been happening. But he did. My family comes before anything, and he's going to find out what happens when you cross my family."

The parents raise their glasses, and Mom clears her throat. "I'd very much like to see the emails concerning my son, please."

The others nod in firm agreement, and Mrs. Braxton promises to send them around tonight. That's when Zach excuses himself, looking a little green. Concerned, I follow him, and find him by the private elevator with his back pressed against the wall.

"Are you okay?" I murmur. There's not much privacy here—we can still hear every word being said by the others.

"Yeah. Yeah, I just . . ." He shakes his head. "Everything's happening so fast. Yesterday morning we were a secret, and the band wasn't in any danger. Now we're out, and everyone's talking about us, and we might be losing everything, and there are *lawyers,* and *emails,* and . . ."

"Do you need some air?"

"Yes, please."

After dashing back to gesture to the group, we escape into the elevator. Zach lets his head fall against the mirror, but his body is angled toward me. He presses level three—the pool and gym level—and tilts his head back, sucking in a deep breath. When he's done, he lowers his head to look at me, eyes dark, and stretches out a hand to beckon me in. I step between his legs and crash my lips against his roughly. It's our first moment alone since the concert, and suddenly I realize how desperately I've wanted to feel his skin beneath my fingertips, to pull him hard against me and hold him until all the adrenaline and tension seep out of my muscles.

"God, finally." He breathes between kisses, and I just about lose my mind, cupping the back of his neck and pressing us back together. When the elevator dings, it takes me a full couple seconds to register what it means and reluctantly step back.

We stay a chaste few feet apart from each other as we walk past the mostly empty pool. There's only a single family using it, and they aren't paying us any attention, but the habit is ingrained now. It's not until we sit on a swinging love seat overlooking the pool from a distance that I take his hand in mine.

He looks at it in surprise, then it seems to dawn on him. We aren't a secret anymore. Holding hands in public isn't a punishable offense.

Wordlessly, Zach takes out his phone. Apparently he's as interested in exploring the aforementioned hashtags as I am. I watch over his shoulder, then move to my own phone. What I find is pages and pages of photos of the two of us. One, taken when Zach lifted our linked hands, is particularly popular, and has been shared again and again, on individual posts and on major media outlets. But there are other photos, too. Some of the band posing at awards shows, some of Zach and me smiling at each other at events, and some of us interacting onstage on the American leg of the Months by Years tour.

Before Chorus tore us apart, we used to look at each other a *lot*, it turns out. In hindsight, I probably should've figured out there was maybe something there long before I did.

Of course, it's not all support. Dotted here and there are cruel words, and threats. Sometimes attached to faceless accounts, sometimes attached to real ones. Seeing those feels a lot like being gut-punched. And even though they're rarer than the nice ones, they seem louder, somehow.

I try to train my eyes to drift past them as I scroll. As soon as a red-flag keyword pops up, stop reading, move on. Focus on the kindness.

We love you. We won't let them treat you like this #SaveSaturday

zach and ruben you're the best people and also jon and angel, the four of you saved my life. now we're returning the favor #SaveSaturday

Everyone make sure you buy and stream End of Everything. If you can't afford to buy, stream on repeat (turn the volume down if you need to do other stuff, we just want the hits up). YouTube helps too! #SaveSaturday

#SaveSaturday KEEP TWEETING ABOUT OVERDRIVE AND SATURDAY. KEEP IT TRENDING. SHOW CHORUS WE WANT TO SEE THE BOYS AS THEY ARE. SHOW #ZUBEN WE CARE.

"They're making us trend on purpose," I murmur out loud as I realize it. It's not the first time they've done something like this. But to have everyone band together for us *now,* when we're at our most vulnerable? At the precipice of losing everything? When we're waiting to see whether our coming-out narrative will be positive or scathing overall?

All this time, I've been intimidated by the power this group of wonderful people has. But they were never the ones we had to fear.

Yes, they made us. But that doesn't mean they'd hurt us. Even if they *could.*

It's been so hard for me to believe that being adored doesn't mean I'm one mistake away from being despised. But between Saturday, and Zach, and our fans, I think I'm starting to view things differently.

They love us. And I love them right back.

But more importantly, I think I *trust* them.

Zach's voice is high and funny as he says, "Oh." I look to find his eyes glassy, and I brush my thumb along his jaw. "I can't believe they all . . ." He looks to the sky and sucks in a breath to steady himself. "I wasn't sure. I wondered if they'd be mad at us for hiding it. Or for doing it in the first place."

I understand the fear. I think I'm less surprised than Zach is, though. After years and years of wanting this, I've had ample time to study how fans react to celebrities coming out. Deep down, I did trust our fans to have our backs, for the most part.

What I wasn't braced for was the sheer euphoria of seeing myself reflected back at me. *Me,* not a curated character with my face on it. It's now hitting me, properly, that I did it. I came out. After all these years of wanting it, it's happened.

At the crux of it, everyone wants the world to see them as they are. The truth isn't the problem. The problem is that the world doesn't always make the truth safe for us to share.

A splash as one of the kids cannonballs into the pool grabs my attention. The two children, maybe three- and five-ish, are too young to recognize us. And if the parents recognize us, they sure aren't that interested in staring. We're just two guys chilling by the pool, like our entire worlds didn't implode less than twenty-four hours ago.

Suddenly emboldened, I open a live video.

"What are you doing?"

"We've gone silent. They're out there supporting us, and we're silent. I don't want to be. For the first time in my life, I don't have to be."

In response, he takes the phone out of my hand, checks himself over in the video preview, then presses Live before we've even had a chance to plan out what we're going to say.

Okay, well, at least I appreciate his confidence and commitment?

He elbows me. Oh, great, so he can take the initiative with starting the recording with no warning, but I'm the one who has to kick off the speech. Got it.

"Hey, everyone," I say. "It's been . . . a weird day. This isn't going to be a long message, but we wanted to check in with you and tell you we've been seeing the hashtags. We've seen the support. And . . . it means more to us than you'll ever know. Yesterday was probably the most challenging day either of us have ever been through, and knowing you had our backs, and you still have our backs, is everything. We have so much love for every one of you."

The view count is going up so quickly I can't keep track of the numbers. Comments have started pouring in.

Omg omg omg omg

We love you too!!!!!!

Is EOE about zuben? Its zachs song right?????

SO GLAD YOUR BOTH OK

"Thank you all for speaking," Zach says. "Thank you for being here from the start. And thank you most for being here when we needed you."

"We don't want to ask for more from you when you've already given so much," I say. "But there are some people who might expect Saturday to fade out of the spotlight after yesterday. If the opposite of that were to happen? If you can help us? You could change everything. Right now, today, you have the power to change everything. You always have."

Zach must like that as a note to end things on, because he shoots the camera a mischievous grin, leans in, and kisses me on the cheek as he ends the video.

"Subtle." I laugh.

"I thought we were done with subtle."

I lean my head against his shoulder. "Thank you for being the one to say it, yesterday," I say suddenly.

I don't think I need to tell him what it means to me to know for certain that we're in this together. To not be sitting here analyzing his words and expressions, wondering if he secretly resents me for telling the world about us. Even with all the fear and anxiety prickling at my skin right now, having him be all-in, no hesitations, helps. It means I'm not in this alone. That's everything.

"No regrets?" he asks.

"None. You?"

"None."

He kisses me gently, his fingers tracing the bottom of my earlobe. We're interrupted by Angel's voice calling from the elevator. "Found them!"

We break apart to find Angel and Jon striding over to us, watched by the pool family, who are now all acutely aware of our presence.

"How did we know you escaped to make out?" Angel demands. *"Typical."*

"Is it typical?" I ask. "You've literally never caught us escaping to make out before."

"Or maybe you've just never caught us catching you," he shoots back, tapping his nose.

"Your mom was worried, Zach," Jon says. "You looked pretty upset before."

"He's fine," Angel says, waving a hand. "Ruben gave him mouth-to-mouth."

"Can you *not,* for, like, five seconds?" Zach asks.

"I'm good, actually."

"Also, Ruben, your mom's starting to convince everyone she's known from the start that Chorus was abusive and that she's been trying to convince you to set boundaries with them for years," Jon says. "I figured you might wanna go back and defend yourself."

"Oh is *that* what she was doing?" I say. "And there I was thinking she's been telling me to follow their rules and not screw up our opportunity this whole time. My *mistake.*"

"Hmm. Zach's mom tried to shut her down a few times but she needs backup."

Zach looks pleased. "Good."

"You'd better hope she doesn't lose her temper," Angel says. "That'll make the wedding awkward."

Zach kicks at him and he jumps out of the way. "You're lucky you have a cast on," he grumbles.

Angel spreads his arms to the sides as best as he can. "Oh yeah? Ignore it. Come at me. Go on."

They face each other down for a few seconds. Suddenly, Zach jumps up and Angel tears off toward the elevator, screaming for help at the tops of his lungs. The pool family looks on in alarm.

"Okay, for real, though, are you two all right?" Jon asks me as we follow after them.

"Yeah. I think we will be." I take a deep breath. "What about you?"

He shrugs a single shoulder. "I don't know whether I'm happy we've moved out or . . . I don't know. I never thought my parents would ever separate. And they haven't, officially, I guess, but I don't see where else it could go from here."

"You wanna talk about it?" I ask. "We can hang back for a second?"

Jon thinks, then his eyes blaze. "Not really. What I want is to go back in and find out how we're going to make Dad regret everything he's done to us this year."

I fold my arms and raise my eyebrows. "Let's do it."

THIRTY

ZACH

"Zach!" says Ruben, shaking me awake, ending my sleep-in early. "Look at this."

I open my eyes slowly. We're both in my bed, and the last thing I recall was having my arms wrapped around him as we drifted off.

He's been at my place for the past few days, ever since the family meeting, when Mom offered to let him come home with us. And honestly? It's been the best. I don't know how I'd be handling things if I didn't have him here. He just has a way of making everything so much better.

Our families are still in constant contact, figuring out a way to make Chorus pay for what they did. Mom is pretty much always on the phone to the other moms now. They call themselves the Mom Squad, and they get shit done. Geoff should be terrified.

Ruben is sitting upright, his back pressed against the headboard. His face is lit up by the blueish light of his phone screen.

I shuffle upright, so I'm beside him, and he shows me his phone.

It's the *Billboard* email, with the recently updated Hot

100 chart. I knew it was coming out this morning, but I've been trying not to think about it. Ruben is practically humming, though, which makes me think this isn't going to be as upsetting as I thought. I scan the list. "Overdrive" is number one, but seeing it stings. I may have given my vocals to it, but it doesn't even remotely feel like my song anymore. Geoff may as well be listed as the artist.

Plus, its success can be attributed to the endless news coverage we've gotten lately. Our relationship has been dissected by pretty much every major magazine and site out there. The *New York Times* did a piece on it. It's *still* being talked about almost nonstop, twenty-four-hour news cycle be damned. I guess that's just what happens when two boy band members reveal they've been dating in secret. It demands attention.

I've been trying my best to avoid all the online discourse, which is about me but is being used as a launching pad for a variety of other things, like criticism of the boy band formula in general and many much-needed examinations of the music industry.

A lot of it is good. The fight is good. But right now, this early, I just want to be with my boyfriend. I don't think that's too much to ask for.

So I offer his phone back. "Great. Maybe Geoff can buy himself another yacht."

"Look down," he says.

I scroll.

"End of Everything" is charting at number four.

I stare at it, like if I even blink, it'll disappear. "End of Everything" isn't a single yet, it was released as an additional track with "Overdrive," as Chorus and our label wanted to see how the public would react to it before deciding on a second single. It's not supposed to chart. It hasn't even had a music video, and it hasn't had any real label push. Yet there it is, the fourth most popular song in the country.

It's all from the fans.

"Keep going," says Ruben.

"Guilty" is at number nine, which could be a record as that song came out more than two years ago, and now it's in the top ten. Normally, only holiday songs appear on the charts years after they've been released.

"What is happening?" I ask.

Our lead single charting well could be attributed to the scandal. But this, having two songs, one that hasn't got any radio play and one that's two years old, in the top ten? It's something else entirely. I do a keyword search.

Zuben.

Zuben's song.

Zach's song for Ruben.

Then I figure it out.

"People must think I wrote 'End of Everything' about you," I say, the realization dawning on me. "They're buying it to show support."

"Oh my god. You're right."

"But I didn't even write it."

"Your name is on the credits, so I guess that's all they need to hear." He laughs wryly. "You're not done, by the way."

I scroll down.

At number twenty-one is "Unsaid."

And then coming in at thirty-three is "His, Yours, Ours."

"Signature" is at number fifty-eight, higher than it's ever reached.

We have *six* songs charting right now. Our fans are dedicated and hardworking, but they've never done anything like this. This is undeniable. Huge numbers of people are showing up for Ruben and me as a couple.

Ruben's phone screen changes. It's a call from his mom.

His expression shifts, dimming just a little. I already know it, and I know this isn't going to be good enough for her, for some reason, because even when Ruben does something completely extraordinary, like getting *six* songs to chart, it's somehow still not good enough. He goes to answer it.

"Don't," I say.

We've spent a lot of the past week talking about setting up a healthier boundary between him and his mom. I know it'll be a long process, but we've got to start somewhere. Hopefully I can help him with it like he has helped me with my assertiveness.

He glances at me, like: *I wish,* and he swipes to accept it, putting her on speaker.

"Ruben," she says. "I take it you've seen the Hot One Hundred?"

"Hey, Mom, Zach's here."

"Oh hi, Zach. I take it you've seen the chart?"

"I have."

I mouth the words *hang up* to Ruben.

"'End of Everything' is overperforming, which is good. I just wish it were a better song, Ruben, we really should've ironed out the flat you hit on the bridge . . ."

Ruben swipes across, ending the call.

"Oh god," he says, tossing away the phone as if it burned him. "Oh fuck."

"Hey," I say, laughing. "It's fine."

"It's not, she's going to kill me."

"She was ruining it. You did *great,* Ruben. Full stop."

"You know I'm going to have to call her back, right?"

"Yeah." I lean closer, and start kissing his neck. "It can wait, though, right?"

His eyelid flutter closed, and he moans softly.

"She's going to be so mad at me."

I grin. "Probably."

He starts blushing, and it drives me wild. I start kissing down his chest, each kiss going lower. He brings a hand up, running it through his hair, and closes his eyes. He's turned on, and it's making me want to tear off his boxers.

"And she . . . oh fuck, who cares. Don't stop."

"There we go."

I kiss back up, until my lips meet his.

A little while later, we're in the shower. He has his back to me, and I'm using the new loofah he got to wash his back.

"What do you think this means?" I ask.

He looks back at me. "In what way?"

"Well, our numbers must be incredible to chart without much radio support."

"Yeah. It's all streaming and pure sales. Our fans are the best."

"*Plus* 'Overdrive' is still number one. So Geoff's big worry about us coming out hurting our numbers is certifiable bullshit, and we can prove it. It puts us in a pretty strong position."

He turns around. "What are you saying?"

"I just think, maybe this could be good, if we ever want to make more music as Saturday."

We know from the meetings our parents have held that we don't really have an option of getting rid of Chorus until our contract is done, and no management company will take us on when Chorus still gets paid. But given our earnings at the moment, maybe, if nothing else, it'll give Chorus an extra incentive to keep pushing us. After all, the more money we make, the more money they make. Even if they despise us right now.

Ruben puts his arms around me and smiles.

"Can you imagine if we could be in Saturday," I say, "but without Chorus controlling us so much?"

"You could finally write a song."

"That'd be sweet." I lift the loofah. "A song about loofahs would be cool, yeah?"

He slaps me in the chest. "If your first song is about loofahs and not about me, I swear to god."

I grin. "I have a feeling it will be."

After our shower, we get dressed and go down the hall, to the living room.

Mom's sitting on the sofa, reading on her tablet. "I take it you've seen the news?" she says. "It's all Twitter is talking about. And nice work hanging up on Veronica."

"She told you?" I ask.

"She demanded I break your door down and make you call her back." She grins. "I left her on read."

Mom's already made three coffees, one for each of us. She's learned exactly how Ruben likes his—with just a tiny amount of creamer and one sweetener to cover up the bitter taste. I grab mine, which is straight black. Ruben said *like your soul* once, which made me giddy.

"What does the rest of the squad think?" I ask.

"They're pretty excited. You boys have real power now."

"And how about you?"

"I just wish those bastards at Chorus weren't getting rewarded for this. Save Saturday has shirts now, by the way, with all the proceeds going to GLSEN. I bought three."

Ruben's face quirks. "That's great. But hey, I'm going to

grab my phone." He runs his hand down my arm. "I'm not calling her back, I promise."

"Okay."

I give him a peck, and then he goes down the hall. I go and sit down across from Mom.

"So, things are going well?" she asks, her semi-smirk horrifyingly making it seem like she somehow knows what we did twice last night. And then again this morning.

"Yeah, he's the best."

"Oh, young love," she says. "There's nothing like it."

There are fireworks in my brain.

Young love.

There's a song there. I know it. I just need to get my notebook and write it. It all starts clicking into place, the melody coming out of nowhere. I think this is what I've been waiting for this whole time. It'll actually be from me, the perfect blend of what I want to write about and what our audience will like. I pull out my phone and start writing.

Ruben appears from down the hall. Looking at him, it's easy to know why this song came to me easily.

"You're not going to believe this," he says.

"What?"

"Geoff requested a call with us," he says, and the excitement in his voice is unmissable. "He wants to, quote unquote, 'work things out.'"

"Really?"

"Uh-huh. But there's more. Monarch Management wants to meet with us. Apparently they know about our situation, but were so moved by our story they are interested in a meeting."

Right. Spending time with Ruben must be rubbing off on me; I don't buy that for a second. From his raised eyebrow, I get the impression he doesn't, either. This isn't for charity—they'll take the loss now to make more money in the future. And apparently, with us charting like we've never done before, this is an attractive enough deal for them that they think it'll pay off in the long run.

Even for us, with all our success . . . never in a million years did I expect a management team to take us on for free. For two albums.

But here is one, offering us a meeting.

If this works out . . . it could get us away from Chorus. For good.

And this time, we wouldn't be naive sixteen year olds, signing a long-term contract with no grasp of what we were agreeing to.

We'd have our own lawyers. And we'd know exactly what we were signing. "Holy shit," I say. "When do they want to meet us?"

"Geoff wants to talk this afternoon, Monarch want to meet the second we're available."

"That's fast," says Mom, who leans back on the sofa. "I say you tell Geoff where he can stick it and just meet Monarch. You guys decide what you do now, not him."

I laugh. "What do you think?"

Ruben scratches his chin. "I think we should hear everyone out. Worst-case scenario and we don't like what they suggest, we walk."

"Agreed."

"This calls for a celebration," says Mom. "How do you two feel about waffles?"

Ruben and I smile at each other.

"I'm sorry," says Geoff.

Ruben and I are seated side by side, on a Zoom call with

Geoff and the rest of Saturday. Angel is wearing a black tank with SAVE SATURDAY on it in neon pink, and Jon is wearing a crisp navy-blue button-down. He's got light stubble for the first time that I've seen. It accentuates his jawline and makes it clear just how handsome he is.

"I acted rashly," continues Geoff. "Emotions were high, and I said things I don't mean. Truly, boys, I'm sorry."

I want to laugh in his face.

I do believe that he is sorry, but not because he has realized he's out of line. He's sorry because he underestimated just how powerful our fan base is.

He also underestimated us.

"Now that you're done fake-apologizing," says Angel. "What do you want?"

Geoff grimaces. "Fine, let's cut to it. We at Chorus would like to start working with Saturday again. Galactic has plans to launch 'End of Everything' as an official single, and we could set up a marketing blitz, along with a big-budget music video. We believe, with the right push, focusing on the angle of Ruben and Zach's relationship, we could get it to number one. That would make Saturday the American boy band with the most number ones in history. But timing is critical, and we'd need to move fast. If we reach an agreement, we'd like to start filming at the start of next week."

Nobody says anything.

Mentally, I start putting the pieces together. This seems like a great thing, and could be enormous for young queer kids out there, like that boy in the crowd I saw when we came out. But I've worked with Geoff long enough to know that he doesn't do anything out of sheer goodwill. This is to restore his public image, that's all. He's being ripped apart online, and if they take us back, it'll quiet down, and make them look less like villains than they currently seem.

This isn't to be nice. It's to save himself.

"So, boys?" he says. "What do you say?"

Angel clears his throat. "We'll need to get back to you."

"*What?*"

I'm not sure he's ever heard that before.

"We will consider your offer," says Ruben, his voice clear. "However, you *did* effectively sever your relationship with us."

"I—"

"So," I say, cutting him off. "We will be exploring our options. When we're ready, our lawyers will be in touch."

"Jon . . ."

"I'm sorry, Dad, it's just business. Goodbye."

Jon's window goes black. Ruben takes that as our signal, and he ends our call as well.

Everything has gone according to plan.

Ruben is flushed, and is smiling really big.

"That felt good," he says.

And it's only going to get better from here.

Our driver is a fan of Saturday.

She's been talking nonstop this entire drive, asking us questions about what's been happening with the band and our management. Given we're in the middle of contract negotiations, we haven't been able to answer a lot of her questions, but the fact that she's so curious is incredibly sweet.

She's driving us to the main office of Monarch Management, so I think she knows what we're going to do.

I'm hoping, sometime very soon, we'll be able to tell our listeners everything. Going forward, that's what I want. No more secrets, no more pretending to be people we aren't.

We'll be Saturday, but our actual selves this time. Seeing

how well "End of Everything" and our back catalogue are performing, our lawyers are confident Monarch will want to work with us, and we'll be able to make some amendments to our contract, to make sure what happened on tour this year never happens again.

I'm sharing the car with the rest of the band. We thought it was a good idea to arrive at the same time, to show what we are now: a united front.

"So, boys," says Angel. "I was doing a bit of research the other day."

"Now that's a scary thought," says Jon.

Angel crosses his arms. "I'm not telling anymore."

"Fine, sorry, what is it?"

"Well, I had a quick look, you know, and I've found that there is this really nice four-bedroom penthouse currently up for grabs in Marina del Rey. It's got city and mountain views, and a separate theater room. Plus you can have pets! You know I've always wanted a French bulldog, right?"

Somehow, I'm not surprised that even after knowing Angel for this long, I'm still learning stuff about him.

"What do you say?" he asks. "Shall I book a viewing?"

Ruben glances at me. "It can't hurt to take a look, right?"

"Yeah," says Jon. "What's the harm?"

"Book it," I say.

"Already done," says Angel, grinning. "It's next Tuesday."

The car goes around a corner, and I see the Monarch Management building. Out front is a crowd of about a hundred or so people. Given how widespread the news of our battle with Chorus has been, I'm not surprised they're here. What does surprise me is seeing how many of them are holding rainbow flags or are wearing rainbow shirts. They see the car, and start cheering for us.

Not screaming. Cheering.

It thrills me more than I think a stadium ever has.

The car pulls to a stop, and Angel climbs out, waving like he's royalty.

Jon is next, stepping out and adjusting his top button, before flashing a dazzling smile and making his way up to the fans, his posture perfect. If I could have anyone in the world leading us into what comes next, I'd pick him.

Ruben gets out, and turns back, to offer his hand to me. I grab it, and step out into the sunshine, holding his hand.

The cheering gets even louder.

I squeeze Ruben's hand, and he squeezes back. As we walk up to the fans, I'm hit with a surefire thought: this is going to work out.

It's not going to be okay, or good.

It's going to be great.

ACKNOWLEDGMENTS

When Cale approached Sophie to write a book together back in 2019, there was no way to predict how this would go. Neither of us had ever co-written a book before, and we wrote fairly different stories for our solo works. What we did have going for us were three important things: a friendship that started on Twitter in 2014 as we both began to pursue our dream of publication, a love of writing queer stories, and a passion for this story concept. It was Cale who initially proposed the premise of two members of a boy band who fall for each other, but it was together that these characters took form.

It didn't take long for Sophie's character, Ruben, and Cale's character, Zach, along with Angel and Jon, to become real to us. If reading can be described as sharing a vivid hallucination with a writer, co-writing is something else altogether. The way we immediately agreed on the primary character traits and story arcs was uncanny, the suspicions we held about characters' inner lives were shared before we even discussed them out loud, and the consistency of the characters between the chapters we'd email each other was incredible from the very start. In many ways, it felt as though these characters were real, existing on another plane, and in co-writing this book we got joint, simultaneous access to their lives.

If there's anything we hope our readers take from this book (other than thorough enjoyment, naturally!), it's a greater awareness of the pressures placed on artists—particularly queer and/or otherwise marginalized artists—within the entertainment industry. While our characters are entirely fictional, the depictions of exhausting working conditions, invasion of privacy by the media, and abuse of power were unfortunately inspired by endless public accounts given by artists—especially those who rose to fame at a young age—describing their experiences. Closeting, whether blatant or insidious, is a well-documented occurrence, with multiple celebrities over the years openly discussing the pressures they felt to appear straight in order to preserve their careers. *If This Gets Out* explores how you can start to lose your sense of self when you're forced into a role you never chose, and the many ways a person can be trapped by those who abuse their power over them.

But it's also a story of hope, and of pushing back against those bindings. We hope to see a world in our lifetimes when the systems that strip power and agency from individuals working within the entertainment industry are restructured, with these bindings done away with altogether.

To Moe Ferrara and the team at Bookends, and Molly Ker Hawn and the team at the Bent Agency: thank you so much for supporting us and believing in us and this book, and working tirelessly to make it the best it could be! We couldn't have done it without you.

Thank you to Sylvan Creekmore, editor extraordinaire, who will always jump on a video chat at odd times to hash out a particularly tricky plot tangle with us, and for letting us take the story where we hoped to.

Thank you so much to the team at Wednesday Books, for believing in this book, and for making it such a special experience. Special thanks to Rivka Holler, DJ DeSmyter, Alexis Neuville, Dana Aprigliano, Jessica Preeg, Sarah Schoof, Sara Goodman, Eileen Rothschild, and NaNá V. Stoelzle!

Thank you to Olga Grlic for the amazing jacket design, and for supporting Sophie so very patiently during her first scary foray into jacket illustration!

To the UK and Commonwealth team at Hachette, with special thanks to our editor, Tig Wallace: thank you for your close support from the beginning, and for bringing this book to our home country.

To our early readers and those who provided advance praise, Julia Lynn Rubin, Phil Stamper, Adam Sass, Shaun David Hutchinson, Lev Rosen, Mackenzi Lee, Caleb Roehrig, Robbie Couch, and Jacob Demlow: thank you so much for your kind words, and for helping us with American terms and cultural differences (it's harder than it sounds!).

To Becky Albertalli, who generously offered us her time and platform to get the word out about this book early: we adore you!

Sophie would like to give special thanks to Julia, Becky, Claire, Jenn, Diana, Alexa, Jacob, Ash, Samantha, Ashley, and Emma, for being the best writer/reader friends anyone could ask for! I would also like to send my love to Steph, Ryan, Jono, Paige, Laura, and Brendan, for learning the ins and outs of an unfamiliar industry to effectively participate in my challenges and successes; and to Sarah, Mum, and Dad, for bringing excitement and listening ears. To Kathryn and Mark, thank you for letting me stay with you—much of this book was created in your house, and I'm so grateful for that! To Cameron, you've been there from the first novel I ever got published, through to number four right now! The patience, excitement, and care you've shown for me throughout the whole journey means more to me than I could ever say. Thank you so much for doing life with me.

Cale would like to give special shout-outs to Caleb Roehrig, Adam Sass, Adib Khorram, Julian Winters, Tom Ryan, Lev Rosen, and Alex London for the group-chat shenanigans; Tricia Levenseller for being the best writer-twin and CP ever; and Callum McDonald for editing expertise and help! To friends Shaun David Hutchinson, Christy Jane, Rogier, Allaricia, Kimberly Ito, David Slayton, Jaymen, Raf, Mitch, Sarah, Dylan, Asha, Lauren, Maddy, Dan, Ryan, Ross, Brandyn, and Kyle, thank you for being amazing! SHAYE! You're the freaking best, and I'm so happy to be your older brother. You're as good as *Scooby Doo 2: Monsters Unleashed*, which you know is the ultimate praise! And finally to Mum, Dad, Kia, and Jayden for being total rock stars in so many ways—I love you all so much.

Melbourne Actors Headshots

Shaye Beth

SOPHIE GONZALES is a young adult contemporary author. She graduated from the University of Adelaide and lives in Adelaide, Australia, where she can be found ice skating, painting, and practicing the piano. She is also the author of *The Law of Inertia*, *Only Mostly Devastated*, *Perfect on Paper*, and *Never Ever Getting Back Together*.

CALE DIETRICH is a YA devotee, lifelong gamer, and tragic pop punk enthusiast. He lives in Brisbane, Australia. His debut novel, *The Love Interest*, was named a 2018 Rainbow List Selection. He is also the author of *The Friend Scheme*.